BLOOD ENTANGLED

AMBER BELLDENE

OMNIFIC PUBLISHING

DALLAS

Omnific Publishing
10000 North Central Expressway, Dallas, TX 75231
www.omnificpublishing.com

First Omnific eBook edition, July 2013
First Omnific trade paperback edition, July 2013

The characters and events in this book are fictitious.
Any similarity to real persons, living or dead,
is coincidental and not intended by the author.

Library of Congress Cataloguing-in-Publication Data

Belldene, Amber.
  Blood Entangled / Amber Belldene – 1st ed.
  ISBN: 978-1-623420-43-7
  1. Romance — Fiction. 2. Paranormal — Romance.
  3. Vampires — Romance. 4. Vampire Hunter — Romance. I. Title

10 9 8 7 6 5 4 3 2 1

Cover Design by Micha Stone and Amy Brokaw
Interior Book Design by Coreen Montagna

Printed in the United States of America

To my children:
My longing for you inspired this book,
and being your mother has taught me more
about what it means to love
than I ever thought possible.

CHAPTER 1

Sunlight filtered through the coastal fog, falling soft and gray onto Lena's page. She closed her book and curled up on the sofa, which sat beneath a picture window facing the churning ocean. With her eyes shut, she pondered the poem, mentally rotating the possible meanings of phrases until they fit together like pieces of a puzzle. She hadn't even known she liked poetry. Browsing through Kos's library in luxurious solitude, she was in heaven, the couch her fluffy cloud. She never had to go back to the Kaštel Estate, never again had to face Andre's rejection.

He'd never really wanted her, and she'd been a fool to hang on to hope for so long. Shame burned across her cheeks, but it didn't matter. In fact, maybe she should thank him for kicking her out. It was the wake-up call she'd needed. She would find a new vampire to work for, begin a new life, and finally find what she was looking for.

In the meantime, she would enjoy Kos's house, and his books. She snuggled deeper into the sofa, sighing with contentment.

A knock on the door roused her.

Kos would have called before returning, and his house was hidden far from the highway. She shivered, and fear rolled over her in a slow wave. No one lived nearby, and the once-luxurious solitude suddenly turned creepy.

She peered through the eyehole. A man in a Highway Patrol uniform stood at the door.

He pounded on the door again. "Hello! I can hear someone in there. I'm Officer Nash from the Highway Patrol. Please open the door."

No patrol car was visible in the drive, and sunglasses hid his eyes. Would they be the golden color of a Hunter's?

Maybe she was over-reacting, Hunters were only human, after all. But they were ruthless when it came to women like her. Blood servants were the Hunters' favorite playthings. She hurried to the phone and dialed 9-1-1 anyway. It was better to play it safe. The loud drum of her heart made it difficult to hear the ringing on the line. She peered out the windows for signs of danger. The deck off the back of the house overhung the cliff—no one could reach it from the yard. But outside the kitchen window she spied another man in a police uniform lurking in the tall shrubs.

"9-1-1," droned the dispatcher, her voice official and nasal. "What's your emergency?"

"Two men in Highway Patrol uniforms are at my house, but they look suspicious and I don't see their patrol car. Can you please confirm their identity with their dispatcher before I open the door?"

"That's unusual. Let me check."

The man on the side of the house poured clear liquid from a red plastic gas can. At the front door, the other banged louder, demanding to be let in.

Her heart boomed in her chest, as much with anger at the dispatcher as with fear. "One of them is pouring gasoline around the house. He is not an officer. Send the real police. *Now.*"

The dispatcher paused for only a second. "Ma'am, what is your address?"

"I'm on Highway One, five miles north of Jenner. West side of the highway." Frantically, she searched Kos's desk for a piece of mail with an actual street number on it, and when she found it, she read it to the woman on the line.

"There's a sheriff's deputy about ten minutes away, ma'am. Stay on the line."

"Okay." Lena nodded, even though the dispatcher couldn't see her.

The Hunter shouted at the closed door. "Come out, lady. Or we'll burn the house down with you inside."

Anger overrode her instructions to stay on the line. She slammed the phone down and jogged to the door. "Hey asshole, the real cops are coming. They won't take kindly to you borrowing their uniforms!" Lena hurried back to the desk and picked up the phone. "I'm back."

The dispatcher sighed with relief. "Have they ignited the gasoline, ma'am?"

"It's not catching. The wind keeps blowing their lighters out." Lena could barely breathe; she stood frozen at the window.

"Good." The dispatcher's word rang hollow and hopeless.

Time slowed down as the man's lighter blew out over and over again. If he only bent down, he could catch the gasoline covered grasses instantly. But, to her astonishment, he didn't. She waited, chewing her cheek until she tasted blood. Finally, the other Hunter—surely that was who they were—shouted for him to give up, and they fled into the trees.

Sirens heralded the arrival of the deputy. Lena opened the door to him before collapsing onto the couch.

She recounted what had happened, and the young officer leaned his hip against the dining room table, scratching his chin. "Ma'am, the sheriff's department isn't equipped to patrol out here regularly. We just happened to be nearby. You shouldn't stay here alone. Is there somewhere we can take you?"

Emptiness carved out a pit in her stomach. She had nowhere to go, shy of the two-hour drive to San Francisco. She could hardly impose on the deputy for such a long trip. And, since moving to Andre's, she'd grown apart from her friends in the city. There was only one person to call—the one who had already shown her great kindness by rescuing her from Andre and sheltering her in his home—Kos.

"Let me call a friend. He'll come pick me up."

Kos pulled his car into the driveway of his house too fast, and the tires kicked up gravel into his wheel wells. A Sonoma County Sheriff's Department patrol car was parked near the door. He leaned close to the car and sniffed—real cops, not Hunters. Lucky for them. But the elemental scent of Hunter lingered. They hadn't been gone long.

White against the darkening sky, the fog hovered close to the roof of the house, muffling the sound of waves crashing against the cliffs below. The scene was so peaceful it was hard to believe they'd tried to burn his house down with Lena inside only an hour ago.

When one of the uniformed officers opened the door, Kos plastered on his I-know-how-to-deal-with-cops smile.

"You her friend?" The cop's efficient gaze traveled over Kos.

"Yes, officer." Kos extended his hand. "Kosjenic Maras. This is my house. Thank you for keeping her safe. Is she all right?"

The deputy had a good, firm handshake. "She's fine. The dispatcher thought the call was a crank, or a nut job, when Lena..." He flipped open a notepad. "Ms. Isaakson said two men in Highway Patrol Uniforms were trying to light the house on fire. But Lena insisted rather forcefully, and the dispatcher sent us over."

Kos spun to survey the tree line. "Any sign of the men?"

"Afraid not." The young man tapped his notepad on his thigh. "They pulled away in front of us, and we stopped to check on the victim. No other patrol units out here, so they got away."

Probably for the best. Kos wouldn't have been able to question a Hunter in a human jail anyway. Taking two off the streets didn't matter. There were always hundreds more of them than you ever saw, like cockroaches.

Her safety had come first to the patrolman, and that warmed Kos up to the young man. Still, he stood in the doorway, keeping Kos from Lena. "Is there anything else we can do for you, officer?"

The boyish cop scratched his high-and-tight brown hair. He surveyed the yard and then frowned at the doorframe he was blocking. His frown turned sheepish and he stepped out of the way to let Kos in. "Sorry, sir. No, sir."

Inside the house, the air was much warmer, and smelled like wood smoke and Lena.

She called out the moment she saw him. "I'm not going." His father's cook—no, *former* cook—sat on Kos's sofa looking fierce and lovely.

"Hello to you, too."

She seemed fine—no scent of fear, pulse slow and steady—surprisingly calm and composed. For the first time since she'd called, he took a full breath, because she was safe and unafraid. She drew her long legs up underneath her on the couch. That was good—he found them immensely distracting. She crossed her arms over those awe-inspiring breasts, which was also helpful.

"Come on, we've got to go." He pointed his thumb at the door.

She pouted. "I said no."

When had she grown so stubborn? Dropping into a squat with his elbows on the coffee table, he peered into her eyes, the same dark blue as the ocean outside. "You're not safe."

"I feel better than I have in years. Away from Andre, I'm my old self. I won't go back. I have friends I can stay with in San Francisco. Take me to Santa Rosa and I'll get a bus."

Krist i svi sveci—by Christ and all the Croatian saints, she was difficult.

"Good chance the Hunters know your name," Kos said, "which means they can find you anywhere. It's possible they'll even tail us from here."

"I won't go." She shook her head and crossed her arms more tightly.

If her resistance weren't so infuriating, it would have been cute. Kos set his jaw and put on his most determined expression. "You will."

Her mouth opened in surprise, but she still said, "No."

Damn, she had a way of making him tense. He rolled his shoulders. Reason wasn't working, neither was coercion. He had one more option.

"Lena, do it for me. I'd never forgive myself if something happened to you." It wasn't strictly manipulation if it was true.

"What do you mean?"

He leaned over the coffee table. "In Croatia we lost four members of our household. I promised I'd never let that happen again. Please don't endanger yourself and put me through that a second time."

She inched toward him, still hugging herself tightly.

"Please?"

At last, she dropped her arms to her sides. "Okay. I'll go if I can borrow one of your books."

"I have loads of books at Kaštel too. You're welcome to any of them."

"But I like this one." She touched the cover of *A New Selected Poems* by Galway Kinnell where it lay on the coffee table.

"You do?"

"I like the one about the footsteps." She blushed, her eyes aimed at the book.

A lump formed in Kos's throat—the poem was a favorite, about how Kinnell's young son appeared every time his parents finished making love, to climb between them in the bed where he was conceived. The last time he'd read it, it had stirred longings for impossible things, so he'd abandoned Kinnell entirely.

Lena thumbed the pages of the book where it lay on the table. She still didn't look at him. "It got me thinking I might not want to do the whole blood servant thing anymore. Maybe it's time for me to leave household service and have a normal life."

"I understand that feeling, but the decision will have to wait. I'll help you find a job, with humans *or* vampires, but first we need to keep you safe."

Her head tilted, but she finally nodded and grabbed her overnight bag.

As they approached his father's winery, she rummaged in her purse, closely examined her fingernails, bounced her foot rapidly. Poor Lena. His shoulders bunched again and he clenched the steering wheel. Damn Andre. He had done this to her — made her so unhappy, neglected her. She was a flesh and blood woman in need of kindness and affection, not to mention sex.

How had Andre resisted her charms? She was easily the most desirable female Kos had ever met, and Andre had treated her like a gadfly.

Kos turned off the highway into the estate's winding drive and his skin went cold. Something was wrong. The rank smell of Hunter wafted out of the air conditioner vent. There was a loud burst, and the steering wheel jerked.

Krist! A tire had been shot — they were under attack.

Her eyes were huge with fear, welling up from wherever she'd hidden it earlier.

"Lena." She didn't respond, so he shook her shoulder gently. "Listen to me. Hunters are shooting at us. When I say go, get out of the car and run to the front. I will carry you from there to the house."

"I don't want to weigh you down. I'll run myself."

"Lena, your weight is nothing to me and I'm ten times faster than you. I will pull you across the seat and out my own damn door, unless you do what I say. Okay?"

She stifled a whimper, bobbing her head in obedience.

"Now."

She opened her door and scurried out. Two Hunters were waiting for her, their eyes burning golden in the darkness.

Krist, he'd let his guard down—hadn't seen them. He froze in place as two of them pulled her backward off the drive toward the bushes. Just humans, but the gun pointed at her head made them dangerous and forced him to stop and think. They would want her alive, to enjoy in all the sick ways Hunters used household women. But they would kill her too, if it was expedient.

His heart pounded and rage boiled up inside him. They dared to threaten her. Twice in one day, they'd invaded his domain, coming after a woman under his protection.

No time to get possessive. Think.

Six yards to one Hunter, eight to the one with Lena. He could break both their necks and have her safe before they could shoot. Another shot rang out and a bullet grazed his side.

Lena cried out. She paled, her fair hair a halo in the moonlight. He had to save her. Power surged through him, gushing through his veins and contracting his muscles tight around his bones. Toes twitching in his shoes, he gave himself a countdown. Three…two…one.

He was on the ground behind the Hunters before he realized he hadn't sprinted, but flown. He'd flown—for the first time in his life.

Laughter burst from his mouth, and on its heels a string of triumphant Croatian expletives. Both Hunters turned. He went for the bigger one first, gripping his head and shoulder to snap his neck. The other one yanked Lena and tried to hold her in front of him. She fought him, throwing an elbow to his gut and a heavy stomp to his foot. He pushed her down and she landed hard.

"Lena?"

Kos froze, and the sharp shooter had time to aim. A bullet tore through his shoulder, burning through flesh and bone before exiting the other side.

It didn't matter.

Was she hurt? Her slender rib cage rose and fell rapidly where she lay on the grassy edge of the drive. The Hunter stood over her, his frightened eyes glued to Kos. In one fast step, Kos closed the distance between them and twisted the man's head until his spine severed with a pop.

Hunters approached on all sides. A line of blood trickled from Lena's hairline. Banding his arm around her ribs, he said, "Hold on."

She laced her arms around his neck and his shredded shoulder burned like hell, but it was already knitting back together, causing his skin to itch and tingle. He launched them into the air, fueled by the need to protect her.

"Oh my God," Lena whispered. "You're flying. Kos, you're flying!"

He landed at the front door more gracefully than he expected.

His brother Bel promptly opened the door. "Son of a bitch. You flew!" He dragged Lena inside. "Shit, Kos, you're soaked in blood. How bad are you hurt?"

"Fine. Healed already. Shield holding?"

"Seems to be," Bel replied.

Good. They were safe from any firepower the Hunters might try. Kos shooed him away and focused on Lena. She trembled, but otherwise held herself together.

"Kos, you're bleeding." She touched his shirt and her hand came away red.

She would worry until he proved he was fine.

"Not anymore. Look." He undid two buttons on his ruined shirt and showed her his bare chest.

"Oh, wow." Dazed, she looked from her hand to his chest and back.

"Where are you hurt?"

"I'm fine."

"You have a head wound. Anything else?"

She touched her head where she was bleeding. "My wrist."

The swelling worried him. He manipulated her hand and she flinched, but her range of motion was good. "Doesn't appear broken. Just a sprain. But let's get some ice on it."

In the kitchen, he sat her down on a stool next to the counter and made an ice pack. While she held it to her wrist, Kos cleaned the blood off her head.

He'd never been so close to her, aside from their quick flight to the front door. Her blonde curls were feather soft under his fingers.

"Lena, this is already bruising. How hard did you hit the ground?"

"I don't remember." Her forehead creased with the effort.

"That's not a good sign."

"I guess not." She wiped her brow with the back of her hand.

"Are you feeling tired?"

"Very. Do you think I have a concussion? I didn't think I hit that hard."

"You said you don't remember."

Her crooked smile seemed to be an admission of some sort.

He filled a glass of water at the sink and slid it across the counter. "Listen, I want you to stay in my room so I can watch for any signs of a concussion. I'll wake you up every few hours."

"There's no need for that. I'll sleep in my room. I can set an alarm and wake myself up." She took a tentative sip, then swallowed the rest of the glass in one gulp.

"Sleep wherever you're most comfortable. But I'll keep watch either way."

Her mouth parted. "Really?"

"Yes."

She closed her mouth, pressing it into an unreadable expression. "Fine. Then I'd prefer your room. Mine will bring back all the unhappy memories of living here."

About that they were in perfect agreement. Two whole years of self-denial and unmet expectations weren't good company for her at the moment.

"No problem. Let's get you settled."

He took her to his room and went to hers to gather some essentials. Only, what were essentials for a woman like her? A bra hung on the door to her bathroom, and he shied away from it as if he'd snuck a glance at her bare breasts. His gaze landed on a large dresser. If he brought it upstairs, she would have whatever she needed. Soon she would leave Kaštel, and it would be someone else's job to take care of her. But he would do it right until then.

He stopped midway down the hall and shifted his load. The weight of her dresser was insubstantial, but he just couldn't find a way to grip the awkward thing. He dragged it the last few yards into his room.

Behind the bathroom door, water splashed in the sink. Her toothbrush scrubbed and then the sounds of whatever else women do to get ready for bed came through the door. When she emerged, she had on over-sized flannel pajamas. They were turquoise with a dark-blue unicorn print, making her eyes an even deeper blue. His hands ached to touch her, his palms breaking out in a layer of sweat at the force it took to resist. With her clean face and her hair brushed out into waves, she was the picture of girlish sweetness.

If he weren't two-hundred percent certain she wanted Andre, and not him, he would have kissed her.

"Everything okay?" he asked instead. Idiot. It was only the millionth time he'd voiced the question already. With all the books in the room, with all the brilliant words from renowned authors in his mind, he should be able to speak more eloquently.

"Kos, really, I'm fine." She looked around the room. "But, I feel bad taking your bed."

"You know I don't sleep. Never use it." Mostly true—since he didn't actually need sleep. Beds were purely recreational, and he preferred not to recreate at his father's house. He folded himself into his favorite chair and kicked his feet up on the ottoman. "The sheets are clean and the bed is comfortable. I'll just sit here and read. I'll wake you every now and then to be sure you're not having complications from the head trauma."

"You make it sound so…traumatic. Really I'm fine."

"I'm sure you are. But, this way I won't worry."

"Right, that's good. I don't want you to worry." She pulled the sheets down and sat, swinging her legs up and under the covers. Settled into the bed, she let out a contented sigh.

"Comfortable?"

"Yes, and suddenly I'm very tired."

He turned off the lights and picked up a book, but he didn't open it. Instead, he studied Lena, curling on her side under the quilt. He'd wanted her from the moment she'd arrived at Kaštel, and he'd had the good sense to stay away from her for those two years. It had been easy, because she wanted Andre. And that was good, because if she ever wanted him—

"Kos?"

"Yes."

"Would you read to me?" She propped her head on the back of her hand and looked toward where he sat with eyes unfocused by darkness.

"What do you want me to read?"

"Something you like. Anything. It doesn't matter."

He opened up *War and Peace* and once his eyes adjusted to the nearly black room, he began to read it aloud. Long after her breaths evened out into the rhythm of sleep, he read to her. Her steady inhalations soothed him, melting the tension from his shoulders. There was no denying her effect on him, and deep in his heart lodged the certainty he'd made a terrible mistake.

CHAPTER 2

Lena awoke slowly. Foggy tendrils of a dream curled away from her, receding deeper into her mind. It was the same one she'd been dreaming her whole life — she carried a tow-headed child in her arms. Only, for the first time in twenty-six years of dreaming, she recognized his eyes.

Then his image dissolved, and she was warm and cozy in a soft bed. She'd slept there every day for more than a week, but it still felt strange.

Through her half-open eyes, she saw Kos watching her. He sat in his ratty leather armchair near the foot of the ornately carved bed, his book open in his lap. She thought so — that baby boy from her dream had Kos's light gray-blue eyes. How strange. Had she always dreamed them that color, or had her subconscious given Kos's best trait to the dream baby? Probably so, after how much she'd been thinking about him in the last week.

His dark blond hair, too short to comb, was tousled. The collar of his blue shirt hung open several buttons and revealed the top of his broad, fair chest. Pale coloring of his skin was so different from the olive complexion of his father. At first, she'd found Andre more handsome, but now she wondered why. Kos's high cheekbones and full mouth were enticing. She'd imagined kissing them way too often since he rescued her. The scarlet bedspread nearly matched his lips. She pulled it up to her chin, stretched her arms overhead and arched her back.

"Good morning," she said, smiling under his intense gaze.

"Good morning."

There was an especially warm sound to his voice, like she'd said something funny. Was her hair sticking up?

"What?" She patted her head. "Why are you laughing?"

"I'm not." Quickly, he looked down at his book and buttoned up his shirt.

"How far did you get?" she asked.

"About half way."

He read her *War and Peace* each night until she fell asleep. But, since he didn't sleep, he'd finished it himself in just two and a half nights. Now, after she dozed off, he put it aside to read *The Brothers Karamazov*.

"No offense, but I'm finding *War and Peace* pretty boring," she said.

"It is slow. I remembered it as more entertaining when it was first published."

Ooh, goody—what she did not find boring was Kos. "Were you still in Dalmatia?"

"No, Hunters had driven us out. We were already here on the estate." Kos examined the spine of the ancient leather-bound book. "I missed Dalmatia terribly when we first arrived, so I read a lot to practice my English, and later for fun. California was the Wild West back then, and the only entertainment was go to a saloon—gambling and fighting, mostly. Got boring fast."

She'd seen enough Westerns to know the word missing from his list was whoring. It was nice of him to leave it off. He'd had lots of girlfriends since she'd known him. Several at a time, usually, but he always spoke about them with respect.

She tried to get back to the thread of the conversation. Whores, saloons, Wild West. Oh, right. She wished she had something intelligent to say. Kos was really smart and had read about ten thousand more books than she had. But all she could think was to ask, "Did you wear leather chaps and ride a horse?"

He grinned and she didn't feel stupid after all.

"I've worn just about everything fashion demanded of me since I was born. Things change a great deal in two hundred years."

She would really like to have seen those chaps, but she wasn't dumb enough to say so. "If you're bored with *War and Peace*, we can read something else. A mystery or a thriller."

"Dull works for me. I just need something to occupy my mind, since Andre's no longer free to play cards. But, would you prefer a more exciting book?"

"Boring is perfect, puts me right to sleep."

"Maybe it's my company." He winked, offering up his sexy smile, complete with uneven dimples.

"That's not it," she said, mimicking his grin. If she didn't know better, she'd have thought he was flirting.

He was so funny and kind. In his bed, while he read to her from the armchair, she could almost forget how badly she wanted to leave the Kaštel Estate. *Almost.* Then she remembered the life she really wanted, felt the ache of all the years she had wasted chasing Andre Maras.

"Still no response to the advertisement?" she asked. It was *so* past time for her to leave Andre's house, if only someone else would hire her. She was a complete failure as a blood servant.

"Nothing yet, but don't worry. Something will come up soon."

With every drop of blood in her veins—blood intended for a vampire who actually wanted her—she hoped Kos was right. In the meantime, she kept on cooking, because she liked it, and the household needed her...

A hungry household, which was probably ready for breakfast by now. It was time to get up and go to work.

She threw off the covers and slid out of bed. September had brought a late summer wave of warmth, and she only wore a pair of shorts and a tank top. Not exactly Victoria's Secret, but Kos's eyes darted to her legs.

He cleared his throat and stood up. "I'll give you some privacy."

Shame heated her skin from head to toe. Did he think she was coming onto him?

"Kos, you don't have to go." She grabbed her robe and threw it around her shoulders.

"No, no, it's fine." He fast-forwarded to the door. "Take a shower, take your time. Zoey should be ready to work by now. I've got to arrange for the bottles, and the labels, and the laborers, and..."

He was rambling. Obviously she'd worn out her welcome and made him uncomfortable.

"I'll move back to my room today, get out of your way."

He turned to face her, hanging his thumbs from his waistband. It was a strangely casual gesture, given the dressy cut of his tailored slacks and expensive shirt. She wanted to ruffle his perfectly smooth hair and try to draw him out every time she glimpsed that easy-going side of him.

"If it's all the same to you, I'd rather have you here. Even a sleeping friend is better than no friend." His lips pressed into a sad smile and then he closed the door.

She stared at the closed slab of oak. Friend — that was the problem. She was feeling way more than friendly. And it was a lost cause. She'd thrown herself at Andre recklessly for years. And then she'd made the unforgivable mistake — stripping to her underwear and offering herself up to him out of desperation. That stupid move plus his rejection was a humiliation beyond repair, and the week that followed was the longest of her life.

It would be so easy for her to mistake Kos's kindness for something else, but he treated every woman like a queen. For one thing, he would never want his father's castoff.

From her dresser, Lena selected a purple knit skirt that would keep her cool in the hot kitchen. She held it up to her waist and noticed her knobby knees. Leaning in, she scrutinized herself in the mirror. Two years of Andre's rejections had left her uncertain about her appeal. Sometimes the woman staring back at her in the mirror seemed pretty enough, with pleasant features and a shapely figure. Other times all she saw was a convention of flaws — hips too wide, nose too pointy, hair dull. Everything about Andre Maras and life in his house made her hate herself.

She needed to get the hell out of the Kaštel Estate with her dignity, or what remained of it, intact.

Zoey curled her lips into a smile against the soft skin of Susan's neck. Andre's toes tapped a nervous beat, his jealousy a tense knot in Zoey's belly, pulsing in time with his foot. She could sense his frustration through their blood bond, but she didn't mind. His possessiveness was cute.

Susan *was* aroused. The scent was unmistakable, although the smell of Zoey and Andre's sex hung in the air, too. It always did in the morning. Becoming a vampire had made her intimately familiar with the smells of her own body and those of others. At first the odors overwhelmed her, but now she reveled in the scents of her world—the sweetness of ripe grapes blowing off the vineyard at night, or Andre's dark spice mixed with her own after a night of making love.

She savored another swallow of Susan's warm, tasty blood and then traced her tongue over the puncture wounds in the other woman's neck to stop the bleeding. Squeezing Susan's arm, she said, "Thank you. I'm grateful, as always."

"You know I'm happy to oblige," Susan said, winking at Andre. She gave Zoey's hand a reciprocal pat, which she let linger, probably just to piss him off.

He growled at her, and followed her to the door, glowering, before he slammed it behind her. "She likes it too much."

"So what? She just goes back to her room and gets busy with Ally, like she did when you fed from her all those years."

Before Zoey had bonded to Andre and become a vampire, she hadn't anticipated what an inconvenience it would be for them to feed from others, their bites arousing their prey like a raw oyster dinner with a Viagra chaser. She didn't like seeing Susan or Ally squirm and cross their legs when Andre fed either, so she didn't watch. He, on the other hand, insisted on chaperoning her meals.

"That was different. She does not like men."

"Andre, relax. I don't want her, and she doesn't want me." Zoey rubbed the pads of her fingers in a circle over her heart. "Baby, I know you can feel that you have nothing to be jealous of."

"I do not like it." He pouted, even as he touched his own chest, able to sense the wave of unfettered love she'd called up in her own heart. "I am hiring ugly, straight women for this household right away. Or, as soon as..."

In the silence of his unspoken words, every uncertainty of their life came into Zoey's mind. As soon as the eternal war with Hunters was over. Or, as soon as they were forced to flee the estate and settle in a new household, he without the wine that had cured his wasting disease, and she in a new exile, to begin her own downward slide into the devastating condition.

She'd known it all when she said yes to him, and she wasn't sorry. But that didn't mean she wasn't afraid. He stared out the window, scanning the horizon in search of his enemies. Suddenly, she needed the comfort of his big body again, as if she hadn't had it all night long. In two steps, she crossed the hardwood floor to him, encircled his waist with her arms, and pressed against his back.

"Baby, make me feel safe."

He turned and lifted her, nuzzling his face into her neck as she wrapped her legs around him. Into her ear, he whispered, "That much I can do, love."

CHAPTER 3

In the narrow, oak paneled hallway, Kos leaned against the wall outside of his room and banged his head. Hard. From behind drawn curtains, the light of dawn seeped into the hallway. He should encourage Lena to go back to her own bedroom, but she seemed so sad whenever she mentioned the memories waiting for her there.

Still, it was excruciating to have her so close.

Every night that he watched over her sleeping form, his urge to protect and take care of her grew. And those weren't the only urges. When she'd throw back the blanket and bare her long legs, it was all he could do not to kneel at her feet, kiss her slim ankles, and slip his hands up her smooth thighs.

He'd known better than to get so close, known she was the one woman to tempt him. As much as she made him wish it weren't true, love was something to be feared. Love meant an addiction to her blood worse than any human street drug. Love would be a noose around his neck, or worse, a razor blade in her bathtub. And he wanted both his neck and Lena's delicate wrists safe from its seductive destruction.

A suffocating pressure at his throat made him realize he'd been squeezing off his airway. *Krist.* He needed a distraction, and there were plenty waiting for him in his office.

The house was quiet, its rooms filled with every Croatian antique his father could acquire—rustic tables, ornately carved chairs, oil paintings and watercolors of their homeland. Croatian humans weren't sentimental about old junk. But vampires were different. Nature made them nostalgic in their very blood. Amidst the historical objects, Kos could almost believe he was back in their family home on Šolta. Not a bad fantasy, since an escape into the past would rid him of the troublingly gorgeous blonde in his bed.

Papers were piled on his desk in the same neat rows and precise angles as everything in his office. He sat down and straightened their already straight edges, mentally listing his priorities for the day. Rhythmic noises from the master bedroom overhead told him all too clearly why Zoey wasn't in the office yet. He didn't begrudge the new couple their happiness — they should enjoy it while it lasted.

Because it wouldn't last forever. Andre's marriage to Kos's mother had proven that. Theirs had been a passionate, love-at-first-sight kind of match. Although Kos was only five when they met, he remembered the way Andre had gazed at Mila, or touched her. But that love had soured quickly, their misery a shroud over Kos's childhood — until Mila's suicide, which had nearly killed Andre.

He shuddered. Kos had learned the lesson well. Love could not withstand the eternal demands of a blood bond, and when it failed it tore everyone apart. He could not stand to be the destruction of a woman, especially not Lena.

The sounds of Andre and Zoey's *happiness* thudded overhead — just one of the many ways his vampire-sharp hearing was a nuisance. He queued up some classical music on his computer. Booming symphonies and dramatic violin sonatas were perfect for dampening the sounds of their love.

He powered up his computer and found the email he was looking for — a shipping notice from the bottle supplier. The shipment had left Santa Rosa already. Getting Blood Vine bottled immediately was his number one priority. Beneath the house, in the wine cellar, barrels and barrels waited. And all around America, vampires waited too, slowly wasting away. Only last week, Kos had been aged and weak. But the Blood Vine had cured him, had even made him strong enough to fly. And he'd played the hero, taking Lena in his arms —

The door to his office swung open, startling him. Andre stood there, freshly showered and radiant with health.

Kos turned off his music. "Good morning."

"Yes, good morning." Andre's smile spread the width of his face.

It was very much worth noisy mornings to see his father happy. "What's in the box?"

"The wine labels have arrived already." Andre set the small cardboard box on Kos's desk and ripped it open. "Zoey did a fine job on these."

Kos examined the roll of labels, branded with the efforts of Zoey's marketing campaign for Blood Vine. Metallic red letters spelled the wine's name, overlying the looping Glagolitic letters of the Croatian text on ivory paper. The words sent a shiver of nostalgia up Kos's spine. Just letters and words, and yet, somehow, they took him home to Šolta. Surely the labels would speak to the other Croatian refugees too, no matter where the vampires had hidden themselves after fleeing the homeland, driven out by Hunters so long ago.

"The bottles will be here any minute," Kos said.

Reaching across the desk, Andre grazed his knuckles across Kos's arm in a playful, fatherly assault. "Soon, all our old friends will be cured."

Since Andre had begun drinking Blood Vine, the lines around his green eyes had vanished and his sweater had pulled tight across his chest, thick with new muscle. Somehow, the wine restored their strength, as if they'd returned to the land of their making and been cured of the wasting disease caused by their forced exile.

Andre wove around Kos's desk. At the window, he shielded his eyes from the bright sun and peered out. It was the same gesture Kos repeated a thousand times a day, and he went to Andre's side. The low hills in front of the estate were golden with the dry grasses of late summer. On the opposite side of the highway, the boulder on the peak of the tallest hill was vacant. No Hunter lookout there for more than a week.

"Every time I hear a door slam, I'm convinced they're back with their rocket launcher," Kos said.

"I'm rather jumpy myself. I would feel better if I could see the damn shield. Every five minutes I look out the window and wonder if it is still functioning."

"It's hard to believe that skinny Trys has to eat thousands of calories to fuel her magical energy for the shield. She likes some fancy chocolate from London, but she's settled for ice cream — gallons and gallons of it."

"Bel told me as much. I understand absolutely nothing of her witchcraft, but chocolate seems an absurd fuel. I never tasted the stuff," Andre said. "Smells decent, though."

"It is. Better than decent, if I recall." Kos wet the roof of his mouth with his memory of the delectable food, a memory more than a century old.

A barely audible scuff alerted him to Zoey's entrance. Freshly showered and put together, she entered the room on newly light feet. She'd adjusted with ease to becoming a vampire, and already moved with supernatural grace — silent and fast.

She held up her phone, her posture unusually rigid and her knuckles white where her fingers curled around the edges. "RSVPs are coming in for the Blood Vine launch party. All the Sonoma County locals are coming, and a few of my contacts in San Francisco. Even some folks from the national wine magazines."

"Really?" Kos asked. "That's great."

Andre watched her with the most idiotic look on his face, like she deserved the Nobel Peace Prize for throwing a damn party.

"Thanks," she said. "But there's something else." Fangs retracted, she bit her lower lip, as she had so often as a human.

"What is it?" Andre asked, no doubt already clued into her anxiety through their blood bond.

"I got an email from a person named Dana through the website."

Andre's eyes lit up. "Dana Zulim?"

"That's right." She handed him her phone. "She says her husband Teodor died last month of the wasting disease."

The phone trembled in Andre's hand. "Just one month too late."

"She heard about Blood Vine because her American son owns a wine store. She didn't say where, obviously. That's the good news — the PR is working." Zoey's voice was thin, forcing the point.

Kos poured them three glasses of Blood Vine from a decanter on his file cabinet.

"To Teodor." He raised his glass.

"To the homeland," Andre said and took a sip.

Zoey lifted her glass in silence. She took a sip and then said, "Tell me what happens, what *actually* happens, when someone dies of the wasting disease."

"To a human, it would look like normal aging." Andre set down his glass and moved his hands as he spoke, as if to illustrate his words. "A thin, frail vampire, wrinkled and desiccated because he cannot take enough nourishment from the blood he drinks." His hands came to rest on his hips. "The vampire experiences the wasting as a constantly cold, aching hunger and fatigue. Blood satisfies for only a short time."

"This is what you felt, before Blood Vine?" she asked, looking first at Kos, then Andre.

Kos nodded in time with his father.

"Was Teodor your friend?"

"Yes," Andre replied. He picked up his glass and stared into it, twirling the stem in between his palms. "Teo was quiet. Rather retiring for a vampire. But a good neighbor, reliable."

"He made piss-poor wine, though," Kos said.

Andre laughed at their old joke from the good old days. The sound heartened Kos. It was his job to keep his family laughing in hard times. Hunters may prevent them from returning to the homeland, but they had not forgotten their home.

Zoey finished her glass in one swallow and slammed it on Kos's desk. "I don't want anyone else to die. We will do our damnedest to get Blood Vine into the hands of all the refugees."

"Yes, we will." Kos tipped back his glass.

Blood Vine was his priority—bottled, delivered, shipped far and wide, with marketing targeted at all the Croatian vampires. Perhaps they could distribute it to all displaced vampires, if they had enough time. But the Hunters would be back any day, attempting to drive them away from Kaštel, and the cure, once and for all. They must do everything they could to save their old friends first.

"Back to work, then." Zoey slid her phone into her pocket before heading to the door.

When she was gone, Andre asked, "Any luck finding Lena a job?"

"None." Kos sat on the edge of his desk and rolled his shoulders.

"What's the hold up?"

"I don't know. The ad's been online for five days with no response."

"Online." Andre snorted. "In the old days we did these things by word of mouth."

"Well, since all the vampires are in hiding, word of mouth doesn't work anymore. Don't worry. It's the same thing, and I used the same old code words."

He brought the ad up on his computer and read it aloud. "Female, twenty-six, seeking live-in position as cook in an established household. Trained at the California Culinary Institute. Willing and able to work all hours. Excellent references. Experience with special diets." That part made him chuckle every time. Special diets was part of the vampire code, but today's unknowing reader would assume it meant vegan, or gluten-free, or one of those other trends.

"No wonder no one is interested."

"What do you mean?"

"Vampires do not care if she is an excellent cook. You have left out the most important part — she is beautiful."

Of course he was right. Sex and feeding went hand in hand; prospective employers would want to know just how delicious Lena was. "You think I should mention she's gorgeous?" It made Kos feel like a pimp to advertise her beauty, even though Lena wanted to leave Kaštel above all else.

"Yes. That should help. Why not say so in the first place?"

"She helped me write the ad. She's modest."

"She did not look very modest stripped down to her panties in my room last week."

Kos raised his voice, surprising himself with a near shout. "Andre, you drove her crazy for years. She came here expecting to serve you in every way. And then Zoey showed up and you were clearly falling for her. She was desperate."

"I never promised her anything."

"That's how households work."

"That is how they used to work. This is the twenty-first century. She is a professional, she is paid to cook and give me her blood. She is not entitled to get fucked." Andre wiped his hands down his face then pinched the bridge of his nose. "That is all she needs — a good fuck. You should give it to her, make her happy." Before he finished his sentence, Andre turned toward the door sniffing the air. "Someone is coming."

"Someone's already here," Lena said, pushing the door open. Her mouth was pinched, her eyes narrowed. *Krist,* she was light on her feet; it was damn near impossible to sneak up on a vampire.

Andre's face twisted, his lips pressing into a thin grimace. He could be insensitive, but he wasn't intentionally cruel. "Lena—"

"Save it. I'm leaving, so there's no need to pretend we like each other." Her dark eyes shimmered with unshed emotions, but she

stood tall and spoke with confidence, once again proving tougher than Kos expected.

He wanted to fold her in his arms, but he settled for apologizing on Andre's behalf. "Lena, please. He didn't—"

"It doesn't matter Kos. Just find me a job and get me out of here as fast as you can."

When she'd closed the door behind her, Kos shook his head. "She has every reason to think you're an asshole."

Andre shrugged. "Let us hope your ad works, then. She will be happier away from me. And we have far greater concerns."

Kos went to his computer where the ad for Lena was still displayed. To the existing text he added, *Exquisitely beautiful. Contact current employer for more information.* With the click of a button, he re-listed the ad.

With the windows rolled down and an early morning breeze blowing through the cab of his pick-up, Leo Caroli waited outside California Bottle and Container for the delivery truck. Man-sized fennel weeds grew in the cracks of the sidewalks, making the morning smell just like his grandma's homemade sweet Italian sausage. Of all the Hunter clans, the Italians ate the best.

In the sprawling outskirts of Santa Rosa, the streets were nearly silent before seven a.m. when the trucks went out for delivery. Crickets chirped, and the highway droned in the distance. Inside the warehouse, a forklift groaned and wheezed, and men shouted instructions about which pallets went where.

His pistol was loaded, but he hoped he wouldn't have to use it. After all, a delivery truck full of empty wine bottles wasn't exactly an armored car. It was just full of something the vampires wanted, and so Leo wanted to prevent them from getting it. When the eighteen-wheeler pulled away from the dock, Leo's pick-up crawled out of its parking place.

Between the warehouse and the highway, he'd scouted several ideal spots for a hijacking. He got lucky. In the very first stretch of straight and narrow, there wasn't a car to be seen. He gunned the Toyota's reluctant engine and passed the big rig. Then he came to a complete, road-blocking stop in the middle of the lanes. He vaulted out and opened the hood of the truck, hunching over the engine.

The eighteen-wheeler screeched, grunted and finally ground to a halt. "What the hell was that?" the truck driver shouted from his window. "Cut me off and then stall out in the middle of the road!"

"I know, man. Sorry. It was a lousy move. Give me a hand steering, and I'll push it onto the shoulder, out of your way."

Suspicious, the driver hesitated. Leo had dressed his unintimidating five-foot-eight self in boring wrinkle-free khakis and a polo shirt. He didn't look like a carjacker. And, the driver's cargo was inexpensive, if important enough for Marasović to order on rush. Just as Leo had calculated he would, the driver climbed out of the rig and hurried toward the driver's door of the pick-up, ready to be on his way. Leo slammed the hood closed. When the driver sat down and put his hands on the wheel, Leo pulled out his handgun. His palm sweat around the grip, and he reminded himself that he was a good shot, thanks to endless target practice with the other Hunter initiates last month. Turned out, he'd learned one thing of use in that bunk operation against Andre Marasović.

Ethan Bennett was stupid to call off the Hunt. Leo wasn't going to sit on his hands while Bennett jerked off over some ancient artifacts. Maybe he was little, and was no expert in weapons or torture, but Leo did have an area of expertise. He could make the Internet do anything he wanted. He'd hacked into all the email at the Kaštel winery, where he'd seen confirmation about the shipment of bottles. He hadn't found his way through that shield or anything, but he could be a major nuisance, and make damn sure Marasović could not accomplish anything.

"Slide over," Leo said to the truck driver, remembering to turn off the safety before he brandished it.

The man's eyes grew wide and watery. He began to shake. "Hey. Just take the truck, kid. Leave me alone."

"Can't. And I'm not a kid." Leo waved his gun, motioning for the driver to move over. He felt sorry for the guy, but he couldn't drive a manual transmission, and he sure as hell didn't know how to handle all the gears on a big rig.

"Please. I've got a wife, and a baby." The driver scrambled across the bench to get away from Leo.

"Listen. I'm not going to hurt you. I just need the bottles." Or, more precisely, needed Marasović not to have them.

With his gun aimed at the driver, Leo drove the Toyota into the tall grass alongside the road. Then he forced the driver back into the cab of his eighteen-wheeler, and gave him directions to the empty garage waiting for them.

Ten minutes later, he locked the driver into the trailer with water, some power bars, and a bucket. Now Leo had two hundred cases of empty wine bottles, a hostage, and a lot of time on his hands.

He opened up his laptop to see what else he could learn about the Kaštel Estate. The email that popped up on his screen was interesting. An advertisement for a cook seeking employment. Marasović's cook was the blonde that the initiates had called a swimsuit model. If another vampire hired her, Leo might just learn the location of another household.

CHAPTER 4

Ethan Bennett emerged from the subway in Morningside Heights to search for a cup of coffee. A glance at his watch showed ten minutes to spare before his appointment with Professor Gwen Evans at Columbia University. He found a café that pressed him a shot of espresso with perfect *crema* on top, and he had just enough time to savor it, watching the last of the morning's commuters bustle past. Ethan loved Manhattan, the whole East Coast really.

Once he exterminated the Marasović vampires and their household, he would return home to lead the Hunters from Boston, with Zoey Porter at his side. His stomach flopped, pushing espresso back up his throat. He didn't mind the burn in his esophagus. In fact, he marveled at Zoey's ability to elicit feelings in him—an anxious excitement he'd never experienced before.

He didn't care that she was being fed upon and fucked by his enemy. It would have repulsed him, if he were a normal Hunter. But to him, only two things mattered. He wanted to control the ragtag army of Hunters around the world, and he wanted Zoey—his beautiful, broken, ice-cold Zoey—the only woman who stirred his abyss of a heart.

Ethan set down the demitasse. It was time to find this Gwen Evans, expert on ancient Britain's culture and language. She was the only academic who knew about his book to remain alive. He'd shot one, poisoned the other, and he would eventually kill Evans too. But first he would find out if she had discovered anything of value in the book, or codex, as the ivory tower types called it.

He found her in what she'd aptly described as her shoebox of an office. She was a cute little Welsh fairy—petite, with an upturned nose dusted with freckles. Just what someone named Gwen Evans should look like.

"Hello, Mr. Lovac?" Her lilting Welsh accent completed the profile.

"Hello, Doctor Evans."

"Gwen is fine," she said, offering her hand.

"All right. I'm Edwin." He gripped her thin fingers carefully, but firmly.

"Well, Edwin, I must say that your codex keeps blowing my mind."

"What do you mean?"

She waved for Ethan to take the seat across from her as she sat down. "How much did Doctor Oliver tell you before…before he was murdered by that deranged graduate student?"

Her eyes shimmered with tears. Quite a display of emotion over the death of her colleague. She was cute, but definitely not his type. Too emotional. He preferred Zoey—a wise and aloof Pallas Athena.

"He told me it was the only written text he'd ever seen in that language—British?"

"Brittonic. That's true. Until I saw this text, I believed it had never been written down, only spoken."

Her Welsh lilt had become hard-edged and didactic. He liked it better that way. "So it's really a rare artifact?"

"The most unusual I've seen. It's completely uncharacteristic of the Celtic mind."

"What do you mean?"

"The Celts saw the world as a place of natural harmony and balance." She tapped her finger on a book, its cover depicting a branching tree. "They didn't see forces of good and evil in an eternal battle. But your text is about a battle between the worshippers of the sun god and those of the god of the night, who happen to have very long fangs."

"Yes. The teeth are curious. What about the translation? Were you able to complete the portions that stumped Oliver?"

"I did, yes."

"May I see it?" he asked.

She squinted at him across the desk. She was no pushover, even if she grieved the death of Oliver. "Edwin, how did you come by this text?"

"It's been in my family forever."

"I find that hard to believe. It's been expertly preserved. Why has no one brought it forward for study before now?"

"My family is extremely private." He looked her in the eye and spoke firmly, as if that should answer all her questions.

She was not appeased. "Are there other artifacts?"

"Excuse me?"

"You seem rather nonchalant about possessing the codex, which leads me to believe there may be other artifacts. Perhaps they are of family interest to you, Mr. Lovac. But to me they are invaluable objects, keys that may unlock the mysteries I obsess over. They may be of great historical importance. So I ask you again—are there other objects?"

Ethan considered lying to her. He was a master at deception, his whole personality a lie. But something told him he couldn't easily fool her. He leaned forward and put his elbows on his knees. "Yes, Gwen. There are other artifacts."

She leaned in too, shortening the distance between them. "Where are they?"

"My family home in Boston."

"Books?"

"No. Tapestries, weapons, household objects."

"From the same period as the book?"

"And older."

"Damn." She leaned back in her chair and twirled a ring on her index finger—a band of gold Celtic knot work. Her hands were dainty, manicured but with unpolished nails.

Her eyes focused on the space immediately in front of her nose. At last, she looked at his face but waited another beat before she said, "You already know what I'm going to propose. That's why you told me about the other objects."

"I believe so, yes."

"*Quid pro quo.* My full translation for access to the objects."

"You may study them in my home, but they will not leave the premises."

She nodded.

"When do you want to start?" he asked.

"Today. Do you have a car?"

"No."

"I'll rent one," she said. "We leave this afternoon, before rush hour."

"I'll read the translation in the car."

"No. You'll have it when I see what else you've got. I'll pick you up at your hotel at two thirty."

He told her where he was staying and went back for a second espresso. Sitting in the café, he replayed his interaction with Gwen. Underneath her perky façade was a surprisingly firm backbone. This was working out even better than he had hoped. In addition to translating the book, she might provide him with information about the other artifacts.

Whistling a happy tune, he reached into his pocket and took out his little green soldier. He'd brought it on a whim, to mock his father's bumbling attempts to lead the Hunters' operation against Marasović. But now Stephen Bennett was dead, and the plastic toy had become Ethan's talisman, symbolizing the army he would command—a tribe of Hunters, zealous, full of hate, and at his disposal. The more he knew about the Hunters' past, the better. Those ancient secrets might very well be enough to incite a war, and he would be the Hunters' commander in chief.

That left him with only one problem—how to get Zoey back.

CHAPTER 5

After serving breakfast to the human members of the household, Lena canned tomatoes. Yesterday it was corn, the day before, green beans. Since the Hunters attacked, she'd added to her pantry every day, making certain the household could survive a lengthy siege.

Hands in thick kitchen gloves, she carried the heavy rack of steaming-hot mason jars to the pantry to cool. Her muscles burned from their weight. She grunted as she set the rack down and leaned against the wall to take stock. The shelves spanned all the way to the twelve-foot ceiling, lined with orderly rows of jars — jam, peaches, all sorts of vegetables.

Canning was hard work. When she'd begun to stock the pantries at Kaštel two years earlier, she took great pride in the emergency supply of local fruits and vegetables, and she sure as heck planned to be at Kaštel if they were needed. Now she resented the daily effort. She was ensuring the future of a household where she was unwelcome, because Andre was a big mean jerk. But they would need the supplies if the Hunters returned, so she may as well keep at it. She had nothing else to do but feel sorry for herself.

She returned to a splattering mess of tomato juice and skins in the kitchen. She went to work, taking out her anger on every stain and fingerprint that marred the kitchen's surfaces. Finally, black granite countertops gleamed in the morning light of the kitchen. Lena hated the damn things; they were impossible to keep clean because they showed every water spot and smudge. Though, when they were spick and span, the kitchen *was* nice—roomy, with modern, industrial appliances and honeyed oak cabinets.

Now, it was perfectly clean, just in time to prepare lunch.

But first she would sit down and enjoy a cup of tea in her momentarily spotless haven. With a mug of Earl Grey two bags strong, she perched on a kitchen stool. What to dish up for the midday meal? Trys would only eat ice cream, but the rest of the food-eating types preferred protein. She listed ingredients for a chicken salad with bright red peppers from the garden. Yum. Her stomach growled. She'd forgotten her own breakfast again.

A nasty puddle of dried dishwater caught her eye. How had it escaped her sponge on the first go round? Armed with a freshly rinsed sponge, she went to work on it, and all her frustration returned with a vengeance. In her mind, she heard Andre's words again. "All she needs is a good fuck."

She dropped onto the kitchen stool so hard it skittered several inches across the tile floor. He was right, of course, but it was his fault she hadn't had one. She'd certainly tried. The shameful memory took hold of her, all at once, transporting her to the kitchen a week earlier.

She'd been up late baking scones and fretting over the spark between Zoey and Andre. She stirred her ingredients like a woman scorned, flinging flour out of the bowl. After all the years of offering herself to him, of him taking her blood while refusing her sex, he wanted someone else. He'd made her crazy-desperate, and it was her last chance to win him.

She had overheard them part ways and spied Zoey on the stairs. From Zoey's strained expression, it was obvious that they weren't planning a rendezvous. So Lena snuck into his room and shed her clothes. She was down to her plain old cotton bra and panties when he entered, sporting an impressive erection that he freed from his pants in a hurry.

Seeing it stung—in all the times he'd fed from her, she'd never felt any evidence of desire. Still, she was determined to make the best of her opportunity. Trying to sound sultry, she said, "Let me help you with that."

Startled, he jumped back. "*Davo.* Lena, not now."

"Andre, please. I want you." But it was no use. Watching his erection deflate, she accepted her failure. "You asshole. What's wrong with me?" She hurled herself at him and pounded on his chest with her fists. "I came to your household to serve you with my body. I'm dying for you to give me that pleasure, but you only tease me. Please!" She burst into tears.

He gripped her wrists, holding her at arm's length as he turned his head away. The muscles of his jaw bulged from grinding his teeth.

She couldn't stop herself. If he wouldn't accept her, all her years of serving him were in vain. "Andre, please, it's my destiny. I can't move on with my life until you've given this to me." Then she dissolved in sobs. When the tears stopped, she felt like a zombie—numb over the foolishness of her actions.

Kos had taken her to stay in his cabin on the coast. Kos—always the gentleman. No wonder she'd gotten attached to him. That was what happened when someone showed kindness to a stray dog. She'd never wanted to show her face at Kaštel again.

Yet, here she was. God, it was time to go.

Wasn't there anyone out there who would want her?

Once the chicken salad was assembled, she ate a piece of toast and used Post-it notes to mark Croatian recipes for the Blood Vine launch party.

Except, no recipes struck her as appealing. Her fingers didn't want to turn the pages. They wanted to scribble angry doodles on her notepad. Zigzags, crosshatches, a large man with a pig nose, horns and a devil tail. Then her naughty fingers reached for a green marker in the pen jar. Two beady green eyes made the drawing perfect.

The door swung open, and Zoey strode in wearing a broad smile. "Hey."

Startled, Lena flipped the notepad face down.

Zoey didn't seem to notice. Her big eyes shone, and the corners of her mouth lifted further. She had an expressive face, probably couldn't fake an emotion to save her life. When she first came to Kaštel, her smile had never reached her brown eyes, but now they were always bright.

The corners of Lena's mouth curled automatically. She was glad to see her new friend so content, even if it was with Andre. "You look like you had a good night."

Zoey's grin faltered. "Oh Lena, I'm sorry—"

"Don't apologize. I'm glad you're happy. Although you're too good for him."

"Uh oh." Zoey crossed her arms. "What did he do now?"

"Nothing."

Nothing new, at least. Zoey didn't need to hear about Andre being a jerk.

But she clearly wasn't convinced. She marched over to Lena and flipped the notepad over. "Nothing, huh?" She chuckled. "Nice drawing."

"It's not hi—"

"Right, it's the other green-eyed devil pig that lives in this house."

Zoey's eyes danced with humor, assuring Lena she wasn't angry.

Still embarrassed, Lena ripped out the page and balled it up. She tapped the cookbook. "Should we plan the menu now?"

"No. I've got a lot of work waiting for me. I just came by to say hi. Any job offers yet?"

"Nope." Lena tried to keep her worry off her face, but the constant ache of rejection turned sharp.

Zoey wore a tailored blouse and crisp slacks like the business-woman she was, her shiny dark hair falling heavy on her shoulders. Lena tugged at the casual knit skirt hanging off her hips. She was a plain Jane compared to Zoey's dark beauty.

"You could stay," Zoey said.

"Andre and I agree that is a bad idea."

"Who cares what Andre thinks? What about Kos?"

What about him? Lena stood and straightened items on the countertop, her back to Zoey. "He's been very helpful."

Zoey stepped up to the counter, well into Lena's personal space. "Helpful—that's nice. But does he want you to go?"

Lena pivoted to face Zoey and shrugged. "He says he wants me to be happy."

"He would. He's that kind of guy." Zoey sounded wistful. "Have you thought more about taking a regular job?"

"I've thought about it."

And an adorable baby boy with Kos's eyes. If that baby looked like anyone else, she might follow her heart right into a human life. But he resembled a very sexy vampire who by definition could never father a baby, and the resemblance stoked impossible hopes.

"If I left blood service, I feel like I'd be letting my grandma down. I just don't know what I'm supposed to do anymore."

Zoey waited, quiet. She seemed to know when Lena needed silence. It was something she especially liked about Zoey.

"Can I ask you a personal question?" Lena asked.

Zoey's eyebrows drew together. "You know you can."

"Is the whole bitey sex thing as good as they say?"

Zoey's lower lip jutted. Lena knew that look—it was pity, and Kos wore it all too often when he looked at her.

"To be honest, it's spectacular. But honey, it's nothing to hang your life on."

Tears stung Lena's eyes before she could stop them. That was exactly what she'd been doing. When Andre hired her, she thought all her dreams had come true. But the sex, the mysterious pleasure—none of it materialized. Maybe it was time to give up on the whole destiny thing.

Zoey hugged her close. "It's going to work out. You're beautiful, and kind, and from what I remember, a damn good cook. Who wouldn't want you?"

Lena's spine went rigid. Zoey meant it as a kindness, but it didn't feel like one, because the answer to her question thundered in Lena's head. Andre didn't want her, the one who had chosen Zoey instead.

"Thanks." Lena pulled away. "Hey. If you don't mind, I kinda want to be alone right now."

"Sure, okay."

The pity lip was back under worried eyes, but Zoey left without another word.

Lena sunk onto the floor in blessed solitude, letting the tears run down her face. Though the air in the kitchen was warm, the tile floor was cold, and she shivered. How had she ended up so miserable, an object of pity in a vampire household?

She closed her eyes and inhaled the scent of lemony kitchen cleaner. Tracing her fingers along the lines and corners of grout, the smell and sensations dragged her into a memory. When she opened her eyes, she was in another time and place, tracing the same angles in harvest gold tiles. It was the kitchen of her childhood home in Juneau. The windows were bright, but her Alaskan internal clock told her it was late, possibly eight or nine in the evening. Her legs stretched out in front of her, skinny and covered in golden fuzz. She was just a girl, hadn't even started shaving them yet. That meant—

"Lazy *lille*. What are you doing down there? Taking a nap? I need the mixing bowl."

Nona was alive!

Lena hopped up to hug her. "Sorry. Here it is." She handed her grandmother the large metal bowl she favored. "How can I help?"

"Measure out the currants."

Nona never slept. She said it was because of her days in a vampire household, feeding humans her home cooking and vampires her blood. Whenever Lena's father was off in the wilderness leading tourist treks, Nona let Lena stay up late for marathon cooking sessions, and her recipe for cream scones with currants was etched in Lena's heart.

Standing alongside her sturdy Nona, she inhaled the woman's scent—flour, rose perfume, and cigarettes. Nona was thick-waisted, and only as tall as twelve-year-old Lena, which made it funny that she called her *lille*, little one, in Norwegian. She whistled along to the Hank Williams tune on the radio, her hands moving like a younger woman's to measure out salt and baking soda. The stocky bundle of energy seemed invincible, but those cigarettes would do her in pretty soon, if Lena was dating the memory right.

She measured currants, flour and sugar, while Nona poured cream into a glass pitcher.

"*Lille*, it is a fine summer night, a good night for us women to talk about woman things."

Yes. Lena was right about the memory. The birds, bees, and vampires talk.

"Okay, Nona, I'm listening."

"Don't just listen, *lille*, ask. You must ask every question." Nona set the metal bowl of dry ingredients on the counter, and it rang out like a bell, echoing in the small kitchen—such a familiar, homey sound.

"Yes, Nona, I promise."

"You already know about vampires. That they are mostly good and kind, just like regular people."

"Are some bad, Nona? Like some people are bad?"

"Yes. Some are bad, but most are good. When I served a vampire, he was very good to me, and to others. If there were women in the village who lost their husband or father, he brought them to the household. He took care of everyone who needed help."

"But, did he drink their blood?"

"Only if they wanted him to, *lille*."

Lena rubbed her neck. "Why would they want him to?"

"This is a very good question." Nona turned to Lena. Her eyes were blue like a cornflower—sharp, and clear, but also warm. "Because his bite gave them pleasure."

"Pleasure?"

"Pleasure like a man and woman feel when they make a baby."

"Oh." Nona had told her about that kind of pleasure last summer, on another long Alaskan day when her father had been away. And Lena had gone back to her room for the brief hours of darkness and touched the secret place Nona had told her about. She still touched it sometimes in the dark.

She looked at her hands, but Nona's floured fingers took hold of her chin and tilted it up.

"Yes, *lille,* that kind of pleasure."

Her face burned. Did Nona know?

Nona smiled, her tanned face wrinkled and her teeth yellow from tobacco. She stroked Lena's hair gently. Lena leaned into the touch of the only mother she'd ever known.

"*Lille*, Lena, my granddaughter. You are destined for this pleasure. You are from a long line of household women, generations and generations, destined for the honor and pleasure of serving vampires. I will teach you everything you will need to know, and when you are a woman, I will find a household for you, with a kind and handsome master. And he will honor you, and please you."

She had a destiny, and it was wonderful, every girl's dream. Like Sleeping Beauty, awoken from a deep sleep by a charming vampire, Lena would have her very own fairy tale.

Alongside Nona in the kitchen, Lena had absorbed everything she could—about cooking for a household, about Hunters, about blood, and bites and sex, and what happened when they went together. She could hardly wait to grow up, so that Nona would help her find her prince.

Cancer had stolen Nona instead, and Lena had to find her prince on her own. Except, she'd found Andre...

Fingernails scraped against grout, sending a shudder up her back. Andre's kitchen. Andre's house. Her tears fell again. Maybe Nona had been wrong, and she didn't have a destiny at all.

With a whoosh and a squeak, the kitchen door swung open. From where she sat on the floor, she couldn't see who it was.

"Lena?"

Crap. Kos. He was the last one she wanted to see her tear streaked face. He would look at her with the same pity Zoey had, only worse, because he had the power to make her feel better, and he wouldn't.

He rounded the corner of the counter and strode to the coffee pot without looking at her. Liquid swished into his cup. Normally, it was cute the way he liked to sniff it and carry around a warm mug cupped in his palms. But at the moment she cursed his un-vampirely habit. He lifted the mug and turned to look at her, pity already on his face. Clearly, he'd known she was there all along and had probably smelled her tears. She wanted to shout, *I hate pity*, but she clenched her teeth and swallowed the words instead.

"Le—"

"Kos, I'm fine." She stood up and brushed off her hands.

His lopsided dimples appeared when he frowned, just like when he smiled. "What happened?"

"I was just telling Zoey how much I want to leave."

He set the mug down. His frowny, pouty, pity look became hazier, and his eyes turned gray. "I'm doing my best."

"I know. I'm grateful. It's just…hard."

Without warning, he pulled her into his arms, and pressed her face into his hard chest. In spite of herself, she relaxed into him and let his warmth soothe her aching heart. He stroked her hair.

Some of the tension melted from her shoulders and she stepped back and leaned against the counter. He picked up his mug, and looked at her, patiently waiting for an explanation.

God he was handsome. She wanted to trace his brows, slightly darker than his blond hair, and those red, kissable lips. Without thinking, she leaned toward him, then jerked back.

He tilted his head, pulling his eyebrows together.

She felt her face warm with a blush and turned to fiddle with the sponge in the kitchen sink. Long fingers wrapped around her shoulder, spinning her to face him. Then, those red lips were on hers without warning—soft, firm, sparking desire down her spine.

She parted her lips for more.

He did not.

Oh God. Pity kiss. She pulled away.

He reached for her. "Don't—"

"Kos, I'm sorry." She evaded him, spinning to face the counter. "I don't know what came over me. Clearly, I'm extra emotional today. I'm really embarrassed."

With her back to him, she sensed him watching and waiting. Finally, he gave up, with a sigh. He crossed to the door in a blink. "Zoey asked me to plan the menu for the party with you."

Lena's jumbled thoughts refused to straighten out. Shame heated her cheeks and made her brain pound. She shook her head, trying to follow what he'd said. "She did? I thought she wanted to do it?"

He hadn't had a meal other than blood since Andre turned him into a vampire in the nineteenth century. Zoey had eaten a grilled cheese sandwich last week.

"She said she misses food and it will make her sad to plan a delicious menu she can't enjoy."

That didn't make any sense. She'd just told Lena she didn't miss food at all.

"Okay. When do you want to do it?"

"Would later this afternoon work?"

"I'll be finished prepping for dinner around four."

"I'll meet you back here then." He pushed the door. "Oh. I wanted to tell you that I'm going out on patrol with Bel's crew tonight. So you'll have the room to yourself. I need to get out. It's making me antsy that we haven't seen any sign of the Hunters."

He wouldn't meet her eye, and she didn't believe him for a second. Clearly, he just wanted to get away from her.

She swallowed and forced herself to sound chipper. "That's a good idea. I'm sure they'll be glad for the help, if there's any trouble."

Then he was gone.

She touched her lips where he'd kissed her, and clenched her teeth behind her closed mouth. Damn Andre and Kos both, for treating her like an unwanted child. She would leave Kaštel and give her destiny one more chance. She owed it to herself, and to Nona.

CHAPTER 6

Pedro was hungry. He'd gone a whole week without blood, which was unheard of—a young vampire was supposed to be crazed with bloodlust. It began with an aching cold in his bones. His gut churned and growled around the gnawing hollow. He wouldn't be able to stand it much longer.

If the wasting disease Andre and Kos had suffered felt anything like this, they were *mas macho* than he gave them credit for. He felt like *mierdo*, and he wasn't wasting at all. He was just goddamn hungry.

A single bunch of purple-black grapes lay on the stainless steel countertop. Sweet and sharp, their fragrance made his mouth water—strange, since he could no longer eat them. It had been a good year for grapes: heavy rain in the winter and spring followed by a cool summer that spiked hot right at the end of the season. From the smell, he guessed this batch of Blood Vine would be excellent.

Andre strode into the workroom and came to stand next to him. Pedro squeezed one grape to see if the seeds would separate from the fruit's flesh. Nope.

"Not ripe yet. I predict another week or two until harvest," Andre said.

"Yeah, and the good news is, they're ripening evenly." For the fifteen years Pedro had worked with Andre, this was their constant challenge—Zinfandel grapes on a bunch tended to ripen at different times. "It will save us a lot of time if we don't have to harvest by—"

A cramp in Pedro's gut stole his breath. He'd hoped work would distract him from his hunger. No luck. His skin felt dry and tightly stretched over his body like too-small clothes. He spread the fingers on his hand to test the pulling sensation.

Andre shook his head. "You need to feed."

"I'll have more wine."

"You have had enough wine. You need more blood. Newly turned vampires must feed once a day. I cannot believe you have made it this long."

"I wasn't hungry at first," Pedro said.

"But you are now. You *must* feed."

Problem was, his body only wanted blood from Lucas Bennett. Pedro had a legion of reasons to stay away from Lucas. Damn good reasons like betrayal, torture, a gratitude he resented, and oh yeah—lust. He was staying in the south wing, and Pedro hadn't seen him in days. But every time the ex-Hunter's scent hit him, he shuddered with desire, like an addict.

"I can't feed," he said.

"Of course you can."

"I'm not hungry for anyone but Bennett. I can smell him everywhere in the house—he's all I can think about."

"I can smell him too and it puts me on edge, like a Hunter is waiting behind every corner." Andre ground his teeth so loudly Pedro wanted to cover his ears. He would rather listen to nails on a chalkboard.

"You're not hearing me, man. I can't feed from anyone else."

Andre dropped the bunch of grapes. "Have you tried?"

"Yeah. I tried with all the household women. Didn't work. Kos is pretty sure it's not a gay thing. But just in case, he took me to a bar in Guerneville last night—met two willing dudes. Still nothing. I was hungry and I could smell their blood, but my fangs wouldn't come out to play."

"I have never heard of this before."

"Great, as if being a vampire didn't make me enough of a freak, I'm a freaky vampire."

Andre threw a grape at him. "So, Bennett then. He is your only option."

"I don't want to get that close to him."

"Believe me, I understand. Feeding was salt in my wounds every time until Zoey came. Still, you must eat."

Maybe Pedro was being a wimp. After all, Andre had survived the death of his first wife and the broken blood bond it caused. In some way that no one could fully explain to Pedro, Mila had been a living part of Andre and her death had torn him in half, body and soul, and caused him decades of torment. Surely, by comparison, Pedro could handle feeding from Lucas, no matter how awkward it was.

Pedro allowed himself to imagine drawing near to Lucas—his body, his neck, his blood. Pedro's muscles coiled under a wave of anger, his skin heated with shame, and blood pounded in his ears. He was a fucking wreck, emotions firing off one after another. The room spun, and he shuffled to a nearby stool.

"What will happen if I only drink Blood Vine?"

"You will not grow strong. It is not a good idea. You are on the soil where you were turned. This is where you will become powerful. If the Hunters come back and we are forced to flee, your exile will cause the wasting disease, just like Kos and me. And if we flee, we will not have Blood Vine to counteract it."

"*Mierda.*"

"Tell me, son. What are you afraid of?"

"That I'll lose control. That I'll fuck him. Or kill him. Or both."

"*Davo,*" Andre said.

Pedro winced. Andre always saved that curse for his worst moods. Apparently, it was some ancient half-Slavic, half-Latin accusation against the devil that two-thousand year old Andre, alone among living creatures, still said. With the harsh word, Andre had reassured Pedro he understood how royally screwed the new vampire was. Pedro would willingly accept that small comfort.

"Exactly."

"Well, as your sire, I tell you it is unwise to kill your blood supply. Especially if he is the only one you can feed from."

Pedro opened his mouth to point out the absurdity of advice so obvious, but caught the glint in Andre's eye and swallowed the retort. They held each other's gaze for a moment. In his cold, empty belly, Pedro felt a flare of heat—fatherly affection he'd known rarely from his human father. If he had to be a vampire, at least Andre was his father.

Andre clapped him on the shoulder and the moment was gone.

"News from Bel?" Pedro asked.

"He arrived in Los Angeles and will begin the research today. I hope for your sake he finds results fast. If he learns the secrets of Hunter blood, maybe he can cure your addiction to Lucas Bennett."

"You think so?"

"I do not know. But if anyone can, it is Bel."

CHAPTER 7

With time to kill and a laptop, Leo did what every other twenty-year-old guy would do—chats, email, porn, more of the same. Not just his email, but Kosjenic Marasović's, which proved far more interesting than the half-ass flirtations he had going with girls at school.

Some vampire had responded to the ad for the cook—a blood-sucker named Mason Kearney wanted to hire her. And Leo wasn't sure what to do about it. Even if he could find this Kearney's address, he could hardly show up on a vampire's doorstep solo.

He knocked on the truck trailer. "Okay in there?"

"Please let me go. My wife and my—"

"Chill out, man. I'm not going to hurt you."

He wasn't. He just hadn't figured out how to get rid of the guy without having him come back with the cops. Next time he carjacked somebody, he'd think that part through better.

The abandoned garage was hot, but he couldn't risk opening a door. There was a toilet which didn't flush, making for a hell of a ripe stink. His mind bounced from idea to idea at the same speed he opened and closed windows on his computer, unable to focus on a game, an email, or a video for long. Unable to think straight at all, really, like he'd had a bunch of those super caffeinated sodas. Only, he hadn't had one of those things.

A doubt whispered in his ear that he might be in over his head.

He forwarded the email to Ethan Bennett with a note explaining he'd hacked Marasović's email. His finger hovered over the send button, and then he recalled Bennett's words to the Hunters when Stephen Bennett had been killed. Ethan had been all fake-sad about his dad dying, and he promised to find all the deep, dark Hunter secrets before he took down Marasović himself.

Dude thought he was Jesus H. Christ for Hunters. Hey, maybe that's what the "H" stood for. He'd always wondered. Leo opened another window to Google it, and his email to Bennett got buried on the screen.

Ethan leaned his hip against the doorframe, interested in observing Gwen's reaction to the basement of his family home.

She scanned the room, rubbing her elfin chin. "Who are you?"

He had expected the question. Years ago, his father had the lower level equipped to preserve Hunter artifacts in museum-like conditions with temperature and humidity controls, as well as airtight cases for the objects that required them. Low filtered lights prevented damage to the ancient heirlooms.

"What do you mean?" Ethan plastered a show of puzzlement on his face. Very few people had private facilities like this, and especially not beneath an unassuming house in the Boston suburbs.

"Give me a break, Edwin." Her accent added a certain charm to the colloquialism.

His real name formed on his lips, but he swallowed it. That kind of slip could ruin the best-laid plans.

Still, the more of the truth he told her, the more useful she would be. He rolled up his cuffs, settling in for a night of research. "My family is part of a Welsh tribe that has preserved its traditions and artifacts for centuries. I believe we originated somewhere in Central Asia and migrated across Europe."

"Your name isn't Welsh."

"I'm descended from the Welsh community, and one in Eastern Europe."

She flitted around the basement, looking inside each display case. Her focus was so intense that each time she bent over a glass cabinet, he longed to see inside it too. But watching her petite frame bend over the cases was also interesting. The climate control fan hummed in the otherwise silent room. She didn't speak for ten minutes, and he was startled when her voice sounded over the droning air conditioner.

"Let me see this." She pointed at a bronze brooch.

He held a ring of small keys, each one opening a different case. It had been his father's idea of security. Ethan had pointed out that if all the keys were on the same ring, it wasn't secure, just inconvenient. Yes, well—there was a reason his father was dead and he wasn't. He would call the locksmith in the morning.

He opened the rear panel of the case. Tissue in hand, she reached inside to grasp the object. She held the brooch on her open palm and they bent their heads together to peer at it. For the life of him, he could not figure out why she had selected it from all the other objects. It was round and bronze, with a bull's-eye pattern surrounded by a silver circlet, braided in a style similar to her ring.

"What is it?" he asked.

"A brooch."

He ignored her sarcasm. "I've always believed this piece to be unremarkable."

"Logical, but mistaken. You think your tribe migrated to the British Isles from Central Asia. When do you think this migration occurred?"

"Early Iron age. The third or fourth century before Christ."

"There are many improbable things about that hypothesis, but the codex makes me curious and this brooch supports your theory. It's a *nazar*."

He rifled through his mind until he located the definition. "A charm for warding off the evil eye? Don't those have blue irises?"

"Yes, except in your codex, there are people with golden eyes. This is a golden-eyed *nazar*. I'd place its origin farther west, in Turkey."

"Are you certain?"

"No." She didn't elaborate, but continued to examine the artifact. Then she set it on top of the case and resumed her walk around the room. Minutes passed before she spoke again. "I am going to tell you something about the codex, in exchange for your honest answer to the following question. Do we have a deal?"

So this was how it would be between them—*quid pro quo,* all the way. Of course, there were other means to get information from her. He was skilled in them, and ever since Pedro had escaped, he had itched for another chance to use the sharp objects in his little black bag. But he could not extract information she did not yet have, which meant he would have to wait for her to study his Hunter relics and feed her the history she wanted.

"Obviously, I can't agree until I know the question."

"Fair enough." She trailed her hand along the cases, sauntering toward him. Much too close for his comfort, she stopped and tilted her face up. "What color are your eyes?"

He relaxed his cheeks and mouth to block an expression of surprise. "What a strange question. You can see for yourself that they are brown."

How the hell had she guessed? He routinely hid his yellow eyes behind contact lenses. Disguised as Lovac, his were brown and he wore glasses.

He aimed for a casual tone. In order to convey emotion, he always had to determine the sentiment before he spoke. "What does my eye color have to do with anything?"

"Your codex is called, *The Book of the Day*."

That got his attention. A title. "Tell me more."

"That's all you get."

"Our agreement was that you would share your translation when you saw my artifacts."

"I've changed my mind. There's something you're not telling me, and the translation is my leverage. Don't bother looking for it, by the way. It's not on my computer or written down anywhere in my belongings." She tapped her temple with her index finger.

"I wouldn't dream of intruding on your privacy."

Damn, she was either incredibly suspicious or she saw right through him. Being seen was a curious prospect—highly unlikely, but strangely appealing.

"Of course you wouldn't intrude. I'm simply taking every precaution. Will you show me to where I'll be staying?"

"Certainly. Are you hungry? I can order in dinner."

"Please. Chinese?"

"Fine. I know a decent place. What dishes do you like?"

"Oh, I'll eat anything. The spicier the better." She prattled off the names of her favorite dishes and he struggled to understand them with her lilting accent.

Charming that she could switch from shrewd to chatty on a dime. She was more and more intriguing. Only Zoey had been more of an enigma.

"I just need to phone my brother, then I'll place the order."

Lucas Bennett awoke with a heart-pounding jolt. Where was he?

His arms slid across soft sheets, good cotton with a four-figure thread count. Bare ivory walls begged for adornment behind an antique desk with a Tiffany lamp. The bed's rustic and clunky frame was right out of the Restoration Hardware catalog, if they had a Croatian edition.

Right. After almost a week staying at the Kaštel Estate Winery, it was still a shock to wake up there. Although he wasn't technically a prisoner, the charming place had become his holding cell. The vampires didn't trust him, and he didn't know what to do with himself since he'd disavowed the Hunters. Only those same damn Hunters knew what to do with him—they wanted him dead.

A tangle of feelings about Pedro sat heavy in his gut, making him queasy and lethargic. Sympathy, guilt, sorrow, bone deep attraction—he could pick at the knot all day long and fail to unravel one thread. He hadn't even seen the guy for a week—seven days spent failing to cool his heels. It was a shitty existence, living out of a duffel bag, and only leaving his room to eat. But it wasn't like he had anything else to do, or any place else to be. Not unless he had a death wish.

Maras's household treated him with surprising kindness. Rescuing Pedro had made his Hunter origins forgivable. Thing was, a week in a vampire household had been a course in desensitization therapy. With all the mundane details, the humanity of everyone at Kaštel, both human and vampire, he'd found he had no hate left for the creatures. In fact, he missed Pedro something wicked…Pedro, who surely hated him…

His absence was proof.

The muffled ring of his phone sounded, and he followed it to a pair of pants, vibrating where they hung over the desk chair. An unctuous feeling slithered over his skin even before he looked at the screen. The name on the phone confirmed his intuition — Ethan. He hadn't spoken to his brother since he knocked him unconscious to rescue Pedro from Ethan's fun-with-tools torture session. Well, this should be interesting.

He answered the call.

"Lucas," Ethan said.

"Don't worry. I know the consequences for what I did. We have nothing to talk about."

"Is he alive?"

"What?"

"Your friend, Pedro — is he alive?"

Lucas hesitated.

"I'll take your silence as a yes. Marasović turned him, then?"

"No he didn't. He's here recovering. The gunshot wound wasn't bad. His feet are worse."

"You've never been able to deceive me. Has he fed from you?"

This time, Lucas was ready with the lie. "Hell no. I wouldn't let that happen."

"Good. It would be very, very bad if you did."

They were silent while Lucas considered his next move. It was worth the risk to get any modicum of information from Ethan. "You think our blood does something to them?"

"Why would you say that?" Ethan asked.

Barely there beneath his indifferent tone, Lucas heard Ethan's desire for the answer.

"Well, I know you stole Stephen's book."

"It is hardly stealing to make use of Father's belongings. I am simply curious about our past."

At Ethan's nonchalance, irrational rage threatened to boil up inside of Lucas, but he tamped it down. Besting Ethan would require cool reason. "Yeah, right. Curious. Well, now that I'm here at Kaštel, I'm curious too. I find myself wondering about all those vampires in the book, the ones walking in the daylight. Then you go and insist I shouldn't feed Pedro…"

Ethan remained silent, so Lucas pushed once more with his best guess.

"Makes me think our blood gives them special powers. Sun tolerance, maybe?"

"Don't be ridiculous." The pitch of Ethan's rose minutely, but Lucas heard it.

It wasn't easy to provoke his brother, but Lucas had honed the skill. You couldn't go straight at him, or his wall of ice would descend fast. You had to circle, make him come after you instead. "Okay, whatever you say."

A thud came through the line as if Ethan had punched a wall. "God dammit, Lucas. If you so much as hint at this to Marasović or your little friend, you could unleash a nightmare. Not just for Hunters, for all humans. Do you understand?"

"If you think I would tell them, you don't know me well."

"Lucas…" Ethan sighed like a long-suffering brother. "I know you better than you know yourself."

Lucas's chest constricted around his aching heart. Did his brother miss him, or was he doing his pretend-I-have-feelings thing?

The back of Lucas's neck prickled, and, rubbing it, he turned to see Pedro in the doorway.

"Well, Ethan, after your demonstration on Pedro in the shed, I can finally say I know you too — I saw the monster you've been hiding all these years."

"Hmm. Is that what you thought you saw?"

Lucas's mind blanked, and everything he'd been sure of vanished. He missed the sense of belonging Ethan had always provided.

"Make no mistake, Lucas. You chose Pedro over your fellow Hunters. I'm coming for you and you will pay for your betrayal. I'm coming for everyone in that house and no one will survive. Would you kindly relay that message to your host?"

Lucas's doubt vaporized. "I don't think so Ethan. Let him know yourself."

His brother's chilling laughter cut into Lucas's bones before his phone went silent. He turned it off to guarantee there would be no more friendly calls from his brother.

CHAPTER 8

The door hung open. Pedro approached cautiously and stood just outside. Lucas sat on the edge of the bed, speaking into his cell phone.

The sight of his long, lean body stole Pedro's breath. Lucas's dark hair, falling over his yellow-gold eyes, made Pedro's fingers curl, wanting to touch.

Madre de Dios, he would give anything to go back in time to that day in the tasting room when they first met, when they were just two guys who might hook up. But there was no way to erase the trauma of Lucas sauntering into the shed where Hunters held him captive, mouthing an apology and then beating the shit out of him. Or that he'd begged Lucas to kill him while Ethan pulled out his toenails and peeled the skin from his ankles. And somehow the most infuriating part—Lucas's mercy—he'd betrayed his family to rescue Pedro from certain death.

Lucas spoke the name Ethan into his phone, and it brought Pedro's memories to life. Ice crawled from his nail-less toes up his bones and into his heart. The chill reached his brain, and, dizzy, he gripped the doorframe.

Ending the call, Lucas turned to look at him. His yellow eyes pinned Pedro in place then narrowed above tightly pressed lips. Their stare stretched out further and further.

"Back to dominate me?" Lucas broke the silence, his words like a whip slicing through the air, a reminder of Pedro's recent threat to do whatever he wanted to Lucas. And, again, Lucas showed no signs of fear.

Anger burned the back of Pedro's throat. "Was that who I think it was?" Could Lucas be spying, even after Ethan had tried to kill him? Inconceivable.

Lucas's hands trembled, and sweat formed on his upper lip. "Yes."

Pedro gulped back his anger. Man, Ethan had Lucas all shook up. Being that asshole's brother couldn't be easy.

"Did he call you?"

"Yes. To taunt me, I think. And…" He grew suddenly fascinated by the carpet.

"And?"

"And to ask about you."

"What about me?" Pedro stepped closer, and the proximity forced Lucas to look up.

"He guessed that Andre turned you."

"Damn." It was not good for Ethan to know there were more vampires at Kaštel—it might accelerate the Hunters' return. "And you just told him he was right?"

"No, I lied. But I'm a shit liar, at least to Ethan. I'm sorry." Lucas's fine lips pinched tighter.

"Does he know about Zoey?"

"No." Lucas's lips relaxed, approached a smile, even. "I'd like to be the one to tell him she's a vampire now, just to see the look on his face. For one thing, she can probably kick his ass."

"That I would like to see. A dude who gets off on power taken out by a girl." Surprising laughter bubbled from Pedro's own chest. He dropped onto the bed next to Lucas, and for a moment, they were friends.

The moment lasted too long.

"You look like shit," Lucas said.

"I need to feed."

"No kidding. Your skin is pulled tight like a bad face lift."

Was it that bad? He hadn't looked in a mirror. Ever since he'd fed from Lucas moments after becoming a vampire, he hated to see the way his formerly blue eyes now mirrored Lucas's golden ones, and Ethan's.

"I need to feed from you. I can't…with anyone else."

"What do you mean?"

"My fangs don't work. Apparently, whatever's in your blood has spoiled me for the regular stuff."

Lucas's eyes flashed amber with fear. A fair reaction to the reality Pedro had been avoiding for a week—they were stuck together.

Lucas stood, inching away from Pedro. "You tried?"

"Yeah, from Ally and Susan, then a couple hotties we found at a gay bar in Guerneville. No tooth action."

Lucas backed up even further. "Shit."

Pedro rose and puffed up his chest, wishing he were taller than the Hunter. "I don't like it either, asshole. It seems to me like you get the better end of the deal. At least you get off on it."

Lucas's sharp gaze narrowed in on Pedro. "Technically, I don't get off, I just get turned on." His tone was even, and it melted away some of Pedro's defenses. Lucas frowned. "This is a problem. I can't provide enough blood for you by myself."

"Maybe you can. I've gone more than a week without feeding because there's something strange about your blood."

Lucas chose that moment to study the carpet. Again. "Strange?"

"Its effects are long-lived. Maybe it's a Hunter thing. Seems like I only need to feed about once a week. Not too much of a demand on you."

With long fingers, Lucas pushed his hair off his forehead. "Of course you have my blood. I just assumed you were feeding from others. I didn't rescue you to see you starve."

Did he have a secret list of all the things Pedro didn't want to hear? Like, don't ever forget I'm your motherfucking savior. "Yeah, well, when I decide I give a shit about being alive, you can tell me why you bothered. In the meantime, lay down and give me your goddamn vein."

Not entirely true—last week he'd had a death wish, but he was over it. Even with all his problems, Pedro preferred to be alive. Although he wasn't going to go thanking Lucas for keeping him that way.

Lucas climbed onto the bed, following Pedro's orders without the slightest whiff of obedience. Nice trick—pretty much the same way Pedro responded to Andre's gruffness. Andre would give Pedro instructions to do precisely what he was already doing, so Pedro would just go about his business, subtly reminding Andre he was his own man all the while.

Message received—don't be a jerk—Lucas wanted to help. Pedro chuckled, shaking his head. But still, he couldn't find his footing, couldn't decide whether Lucas was his friend or enemy.

Lucas lay down, the slight angle of his head a clear invitation. Pedro knelt next to him. He would be a goner if he lay down alongside the other man. Up close, Lucas's scent hit him differently. His smell had cloyed and taunted, lingering in rooms where Lucas had been. But now it was the real, male smell of skin and soap, sweat and breath. And his distinctive Hunter scent was so much more delicious for all the ways it blended with Lucas's own human essence.

By pressing Lucas's shoulder lower, he exposed more of his succulent neck. The skin stretched across tendons, and his pulse fluttered. A pulse under skin was such a delicate thing, like the wings of a hummingbird. Pedro couldn't help it, he groaned. His fangs—reticent at the necks of several other humans—were out in a flash. His mouth watered and he tongued the pulse point under Lucas's jaw. At the contact, Lucas let out his own throaty sigh.

Damn, it was intense, and they were just getting started.

He slid his teeth into Lucas's neck and took a long pull of the blood he'd been jonesing for. Almost instantly, his skin softened and loosened, but the cold ache in his bones and the cramp in his gut held fast. He lost all sense of time. There was only Lucas's warm metallic blood filling his stomach, swallow by swallow. There was only the smell, the taste, of Lucas in his mouth.

Finally, Pedro grew warm.

Tingling energy spread from his belly outward, into his hands, his feet, and yes, his cock. Kneeling was good—it meant Lucas couldn't feel his hard-on.

Nearly sated, he became aware of Lucas's shallow breaths. Lucas arched up, creating as much contact as possible; they were almost chest to chest. He dug his fingers into Pedro's shoulder and gasped.

Oh yeah, Lucas was definitely rolling.

Pedro slowed down his swallows on his neck, but he wasn't ready to break the connection. Maybe it was the other lingering craving, deeper and lower in his belly. He wanted power over Lucas, to show him he wasn't weak, he was a man—no, more than a man. He was a super-strong badass vampire.

He pulled blood from the open vein and ran his tongue along the tendon his teeth had latched onto. Lucas shivered. Without warning, he lifted Pedro's hand, and shoved it against his rigid cock, wrapping Pedro's hand around him and thrusting.

Pedro gripped him and took another pull of blood.

Lucas raised his head and bit onto Pedro's shoulder. He must want something in his mouth. Pedro had seen that oral arousal when Andre fed—the household women bit their lower lip, or sucked their fingers.

I could give him something better to—

No. Time to stop.

He licked Lucas's neck, sealing the punctures. The flesh wriggled, knitting back together under his tongue. Man, that was cool.

Lucas thrust again. He threw back his head, his neck straining as he pumped his hips.

Pedro wanted him to beg. "Tell me what you want." He worked Lucas through his jeans, demanding an answer.

Lucas's golden eyes were huge and wild with lust. "Skin. Against skin. You. In my mouth."

It was exactly what Pedro wanted to hear, and his own cock jumped in agreement. But wouldn't it be even better to leave Lucas hard up, to walk away and show his control? Only, damn if he didn't have a vampire-grade hard-on. Apparently his ears and nose weren't the only things that worked better now.

"Pedro, please."

Madre de Dios. Lucas's hungry rasp made him tingle all over, the begging better than any orgasm, vampire-grade or not.

He flung his leg over Lucas, straddling his chest. If he sprung his cock from his pants, Lucas could wrap his lips around it in no time. He kept his left hand on Lucas's hard length and moved the other to his own fly. With one hand on each of Pedro's thighs, Lucas looked up and licked his lips. Seeing that red tongue almost changed Pedro's mind. He bit down on his own, slung his other leg over Lucas, and hopped off the bed.

Shocked, Lucas looked like a kid whose lollypop had been taken away. But he recovered quickly, and his eyes went sharp in his flushed face. "Feels good to have power over me?"

Pedro looked away from him and tucked his erection into his jeans.

"I think you're making a mistake," Lucas said.

"Really? Are you that good at sucking cock?"

"Good enough. But, from what I've heard around the kitchen table, you're stuck with that hard-on, while I can finish myself off with a few quick strokes."

Oh shit. Forgot about that. It was lesson number two for the baby vampire—Sorry, But Now You are Unable to Masturbate. It came right after the first lesson, which Andre called The Things that Kill Us.

Yes, his epic erection might be an epic problem. But Lucas's desperate plea made it worth it. *Right?* "Don't worry about me. Knowing you'll be thinking of me when you finish is satisfaction enough."

Pedro left, hoping his words were true. He walked into Kos's office to find him talking into the air. Must be on speakerphone. Andre and Zoey stood around the desk.

When she glanced at him, he mouthed, "Bel?"

She nodded.

"Bel, Pedro's just joined us, and he's looking much plumper. Did you finally feed?" Kos asked.

Pedro reached into his pocket to pull out his wallet. "Yeah. I fed. Bel, I'm laying a crisp one hundred dollar bill in Kos's hand for safekeeping. It's yours. I lost a bet."

"We didn't make a bet," Bel said.

"When you told me the worst part of being a vampire was not being able to…uh, you know. I thought, 'I'd bet him a million bucks there are worse things.' Turns out, I was wrong."

Kos exploded in laughter.

Zoey's mouth gaped and she stared at Pedro's bulge, until Andre covered her eyes. "No ogling," he said.

Bel coughed. "Keep your money, dude. I didn't bet you anything."

"It's also not a million dollars. Just take the money and let me eat crow."

"Fine. Let's finish this up so I can get back to the lab." Bel's voice crackled over the speaker.

"Can you start over from the beginning for Pedro's sake?" Andre asked.

"Just admit you need him to explain it again," Zoey said.

He glowered at her until she wrapped her arms around his waist and kissed his cheek. Pedro bit his lip to hide a smile. Poor Andre.

He had a house full of smartasses on his hands. It was quite a coincidence. Maybe he actually liked it.

Bel cleared his throat, making the line crackle. "Okay, here's the simple version. For some reason, there is gold in Blood Vine, and in Hunter blood. I've managed to isolate the molecule containing the gold, and now I'm trying to determine what the hell it is."

Zoey nodded impatiently. "But, what does it do?"

"No clue, and it could take years of research to find out."

She pouted. "I guess we'll have to keep Lucas around as a guinea pig."

If she meant it to be funny, no one laughed.

"We need him to feed Pedro regardless." The stark neutrality of Andre's tone betrayed his worry.

Pedro's mouth went dry. Shit. His little blue-balls stunt with Lucas foreshadowed every meal he would ever have. What the hell had he been thinking? Andre had warned him not to kill his food. But apparently he needed to be told not to taunt or otherwise torment Lucas either. They were stuck together until they found a solution. Pedro could either play nice, or force Lucas. Lucas whom he hated, Lucas who had saved his life—

Over the speaker, Bel's tinny voice sounded. "Still no luck with other blood, then?"

Pedro peeled his tongue from the roof of his mouth and croaked. "*Nada.*"

Three worried faces turned toward him, no doubt hearing his fear.

"That's the best reason I can think of to get back to work, friend." With a click on Bel's end, the line went dead.

Pedro glanced from face to face. "There's something else I need to tell you all. When I went to feed from Lucas earlier, he was on the phone with Ethan."

"*Davo.*" Andre slammed his fist into Kos's desk, making the stapler bounce. "Did he call him?"

"No, absolutely not. He was freaked—actually shaking when he hung up."

"Shaking? What do you make of that?" Andre straightened the papers he'd disturbed on Kos's desk.

"Hell, I don't know. I didn't ask him to lie down on a couch and tell me about his feelings."

"But what did you overhear?" Ever patient, Kos's gentle tone soothed Pedro.

"Basically, Lucas said his brother is a sadistic sociopath."

An unnaturally high laugh came from Zoey.

Andre pulled her closer. "Your words?"

"Yes," Pedro said, "but Lucas wouldn't hesitate to use them. He was so not on board with what they did to me. Even before he rescued me, I could see his fear, and revulsion. I don't know how the dude faked it with them for so long."

He shivered. The icy fear triggered by Ethan's voice jolted through him, freezing him from remembered wounds to brittle brain. He sank into a chair and squeezed his eyes closed.

He was safe. He was whole. He was a badass vampire.

Slowly, he thawed, and regained control. He opened his eyes to find everyone watching him. Kos handed him a full glass of Blood Vine. At four in the afternoon? Why not? Vampires had no five-o'clock rule.

Andre opened his mouth, but Pedro cut him off. "Ethan said he knows Lucas better than Lucas knows himself." He tightened every muscle to keep from shivering again. A sip of the wine sent heat down his esophagus. "Creep could mean anything with a statement like that. It's sort of like his torture technique—get into your head, use your own fear and doubt against you."

"So he's trying to psych Lucas out over something?" Kos dropped into his chair and stroked his chin, looking professorial.

Pedro's fingers curled with fury at Ethan, and he wished he possessed Kos's characteristic calm. In the chair across the desk from Kos, Pedro sat on his hands. "Exactly."

"But you trust that Lucas isn't spying for him?" Andre took the third chair, and pulled Zoey onto his lap.

True, Lucas had seemed too interested in the carpet when they talked about his blood, but Pedro was certain about one thing. "I do. He's hiding something from us, but he isn't trying to help the Hunters."

Andre shook his head. "I'm not convinced. I want to question him."

Question? The ice prickled through Pedro's veins again. Oh hell no. He owed Lucas. Andre was no sadist, but he was ruthless when it came to Hunters. Pedro would not let him *question* Lucas the way Ethan had questioned Pedro. Slowly, he leaned forward in his chair.

"No. Fucking. Way."

Andre ground his teeth in reply.

Kos leaned forward, straightening the stapler, the phone, the stacks of papers on his desk. "Will he talk to you?"

"What do you mean?"

"I mean, can we use you as a carrot, since you don't want Andre to be the stick?"

"Unfortunately, I was being a stick earlier." Pedro looked at his still bulging erection.

Kos snickered, and Pedro glared at him.

Under the hostile gaze, his vampire-brother turned sympathetic. "So that's how you ended up with the hard-on from hell? I don't envy you, but it sounds like you better make nice and figure out what he's hiding."

"I hate making nice." Pedro finished off his glass of wine in one swallow.

Kos frowned with his sensitive therapist expression that got him all the chicks. "Are you angry with him?"

Pedro spun the stem of his glass between his palms, watching the remaining drops of wine slosh and swirl. Could he do it so vampire-fast that he made a whirlpool?

Andre coughed, an annoying ploy for Pedro's attention.

Pedro took a deep breath. "I'm furious, I pity him, and I resent my debt to him. But I won't let any harm come to him while he's here. And right now, I could really use a distraction. Where the hell are the wine bottles?"

Kos looked at his watch. "I don't know. I've got to go meet Lena, but I'm sure they'll be here any minute."

"I'm going to call, just to be certain." Andre removed his phone from his pocket.

A knock sounded on Lucas's door and Ally appeared.

"This is all I could find in the office."

She handed him a pile of blank copy paper and a box of colored pencils. Nothing fancy—the kind he'd had in his school supplies as a kid.

"Thanks, this is great."

"No problem, I imagine you're getting a little stir crazy. You know you're welcome to hang out in the living room. There's a television, and help yourself to the bar."

"That's kind of you, but I'm not really a TV person."

"If you prefer to read, Kos has practically every book ever written in his room. I can ask him for something, if you want."

He bounced, dying to get started. But he pushed his hair out of his eyes, smiled, and tried to be polite. "Oh yeah? I may take you up on that."

"Good. See you at dinner? Lena's making her homemade lasagna."

"Yeah, later." He closed the door behind her and set the paper and pencils on the desk.

In his fantasy life—the one where he wasn't raised a Hunter—he lived with a hot guy who looked a lot like Pedro, a Golden Retriever, and a daughter adopted from China. And he was an architect.

As a kid, he could sit with paper and pencil and draft for hours. He had a nearly perfect visual memory—if he paid enough attention, he was able to recall it in exact detail. And, he could get the memory on paper pretty nicely too. He wasn't an artist; he was a copyist. He could walk through a house for a few minutes without taking any measurements, then go back to his desk and draft an accurate picture of the house to scale.

Could he remember the book, though? He hadn't seen it in twenty years. But when Pedro's eyes had gone yellow, its ancient, gory images came back to Lucas.

Vampires, in the sun.

If his blood did that to Pedro, he needed to know. He hunched over the desk and began to draw.

CHAPTER 9

K os made his way to the kitchen. The sound of leaves rustling outside drew him to the window to investigate. In the back garden, Lena perched on a stool, picking green figs from a tree. Reaching high, she bared her belly above a low-slung purple skirt. Her taut, fair skin was hidden again when she placed the fruit in a bucket dangling from her other arm.

She was an angel, and they'd brought her only grief.

Over and over, the rhythmic reaching and picking bared her belly and lifted her full breasts. Her movements mesmerized him, casting a hypnotic spell. With her every stretch, he inhaled, and then exhaled as she placed a fig into her basket. His cock stirred, and suddenly he felt like a creep. Voyeurism was acutely unsatisfying, given his vampire limitations.

He tapped on the window. She waved and then stepped down from the stool. It wobbled, and fear flashed across her face. His heart lurched before she righted herself. She hadn't been in any danger, yet her momentary panic swept through him like it was his own. Palm pressed to the window, he took a moment to calm himself.

In the kitchen, she rinsed the figs in a colander.

"Sorry to keep you waiting." She spoke to the fruit.

"Don't worry. You didn't."

Her shoulders slumped over the sink. He'd done this, stirred up all her shame with one kiss. He wanted to shake her and say,

Wake up, I want you like crazy! He didn't even care anymore that she wanted Andre. His pride could be damned. He ached to rescue her from all that hurt.

But how could he, when it already took every ounce of his will to stay away from her?

"I've got some recipes marked over there." She pointed to the kitchen table where one well-worn cookbook lay.

An array of sticky-paper flags poked out of its pages. He loved those things, had a whole drawer full in his desk. When he first discovered them, he'd used so many to mark his favorite passages in books they had become unreadable. Lena's lined up in perfect rows, just as orderly as her well-stocked pantry.

Of course, fate *would* send a planner to tempt him. Her penchant for being prepared was possibly as sexy as her long legs, or her full… his eyes dropped to the assets in question. No. Those were, in fact, far sexier than her sticky notes.

Swiping his tongue over his lips, he forced himself to turn away and sit down at the table.

"Coffee? I just made a pot."

"Thanks."

"So tell me what kind of food you're thinking about." She carried two mugs over and sat across from him.

"Kind of food?" What did she mean? Back when he ate food, there was only one kind.

"I mean, California cuisine, or traditional Croatian fare…that sort of thing."

He had no idea. Did Zoey realize how poorly suited he was to plan the menu? Lena waited for his answer, peeling off a sticky note and aligning it with the edge of a photo inside the cookbook.

Idiot—Zoey knew precisely what she was doing, and damn she was good. She'd fooled him completely with her thinking-about-food-makes-me-sad story.

"To tell you the truth, I haven't thought much about it. Do you have any ideas?"

"I thought it would be fun to do a combination. Blood Vine is this ancient wine coming to life in a new place. So what if I did some California takes on the traditional foods?"

She passed him the faded book of Croatian recipes and stretched over the table to find the marked page. Her shirt rode up, and she twisted awkwardly, kneeling in her chair. They really couldn't look at the book together when she was so far away. She glanced at the seat next to him.

"Lena, please, come sit here."

Her head bowed. Then, without looking up, she obeyed. She smelled like figs, both the sweet fruit and the green leaves she'd brushed against. He hadn't especially liked figs when he was human, but he pictured her biting into a ripe one, and licking her lips. *Krist*, it was hot in the kitchen. He tugged at his collar.

Focus.

The cookbook looked fifty years old, at least. "Where in the world did you get this?"

"I ordered it online when I first took the job. Thought it might come in handy."

Of course she did. The faded black and white pictures showed food Kos couldn't even imagine was appetizing, but he vaguely remembered eating it. He waved his hand over the book.

"What did you have in mind?"

For the first time, she met his eyes. "Well, grilled sardines. I can get fresh ones from a guy I know at the farmers' market."

"We ate those all the time when I was young. The fishermen pulled them out of the Adriatic and filled cart after cart."

She almost smiled, and he wished he could go back in time to that morning, when they'd talked easily about his past.

"I was also thinking about stuffed peppers. They're still in season."

"Yes, those are very traditional — good idea."

"Okay, and this is the special one." She sat straighter, her voice growing more confident. "What about wild truffles and pasta? A friend in town just brought me a sack full, and he promises more next week. The season's just started up north."

"Truffles? Those mushrooms they hunt with pigs?"

"Yeah. The ones growing here are different from the European variety, but I think they're just as good."

The dish sounded familiar. He squinted at the antiquated cookbook photo and tried to place it — a steaming earthenware bowl of noodles, the rich, meaty smell of the mushrooms, his mother smiling. Nostalgia gripped him, and he fell backward into the vision.

"My mother used to make that. I loved it." His words caught in his throat.

Lena watched him, the corners of her deep blue eyes creasing. Always kind, her compassion had swallowed up her awkwardness. She inched her hand toward him, but stopped just short of his arm. "Were you remembering her?"

"Yes, an unexpectedly happy memory amidst the tragic ones."

"Oh." Lena closed the cookbook, leaning forward. "Your mother wasn't a vampire, was she?"

"No. She didn't want to turn."

"And Andre adopted you?" She studied him with an intense focus he'd never seen from her before.

"Yes." Where was she going with these questions?

Her bottomless eyes held his. "But what about Bel?"

Bel? *Krist.* She wanted to have babies. And, she wanted to serve a vampire. Of course she wondered about Bel. He looked exactly like Andre, was clearly his biological son. Kos clung to the seat of his chair, the wood denting under the tips of his fingers.

If only life were the fairy tale where he could give her everything she wanted.

"Bel is a mystery, Lena. He's the only one of his kind. Even Andre doesn't know how he was conceived."

"So there's no way…" Averting her gaze, she tucked a strand of her silken hair behind her ear, and he wanted to pull it out and run it through his fingers.

"There's no way to have a baby with a vampire, Lena. If you want to be a mother, you must leave household service and choose a human life. Is that what you want?"

She folded her hands on the table, an almost peaceful gesture. But her fingertips turned white with a pressure rivaling his grip on the chair.

"I'm not ready to decide."

"I understand. Then, I will continue to advertise your services, unless you tell me otherwise. All right?"

Her eyes glittered, and she stared toward his mouth. He wiped his lips—could they be stained by a drop of blood? He hadn't fed all day. Maybe it was wine.

"Yes, that's all right." She squeezed his hand. "Thank you."

"It's my duty, and my pleasure, to help you, Lena." He pulled his hand away, unable to stand the longing her touch stirred. He tapped the cookbook to refocus her attention. "Now, did you have any other dishes in mind?"

"I thought I would make baklava. I know it's not really Croatian, but I have tons of pistachios."

He laughed. A memory came to mind, of Bel pouting and pointing at him.

"What?"

"Our cook made it often and I loved it. I would steal it from the kitchen and get in trouble. I would always blame Bel and then get caught licking my sticky fingers." He doubled over with laughter, his eyes tearing up. Who knew that discussing food could bring on floods of emotion and fits of nostalgia?

She wore the first real smile he'd seen all afternoon. "Baklava it is, then. I have a whole case of honey I bought at the farmers market. I wonder if I can find it? Somewhere high in the pantry, I think."

The fear on her face when she'd teetered under the fig tree flashed in his mind. "Let me help you get it down."

Lena's neck flushed with Kos behind her. Was he looking at her, or was she just imagining he was? More importantly, had he noticed her staring at his mouth? He must think she was a total freak. Some kind of succubus who'd turned her attention to him since she'd failed to seduce his father.

She swung open the door to the pantry and flipped on the lights. A folding step stool hung from a hook on the wall, and she placed it on the floor in front of the shelf. Kos's gaze left a trail of embarrassed heat down her body. Maybe she just wanted him to be looking at her, while in reality he was reading the labels on her obsessively organized shelves.

"The case of honey is on the top." She pointed. "I can't see it from here. It must have been pushed behind something." The distant top shelf spanned the room about nine feet off the ground.

"Why did you put it all the way up there?"

"Pedro did it months ago. I took one jar out and he put the box on the shelf."

Kos climbed the ladder and looked down at her over his shoulder. "What does it look like?"

"It's just a regular cardboard box, maybe a foot square."

"Labeled?" he asked, winking.

She smiled, feeling a little more like herself. "Oh, I don't know. Probably not."

"I still don't see it. I'm going to have to stand on the top of the ladder. Would you mind keeping it steady?"

"Of course."

Her view of the shelf was blocked by his very nicely shaped butt. She bit the inside of her cheek. It was seriously a tragedy that he was so beautifully built, and she would never get to touch him the way she wanted. Her fingers twitched. Good thing her job was to keep the stool steady or her hands would be all over him.

Above her, boxes scraped against the wooden shelves. "Any luck?"

"No, nothing that matches that description."

"Darn. I guess I better look."

He stepped down. She put her foot on the first rung then faltered.

He braced the stool. "Don't worry. I'll hold you steady and catch you if you fall."

She rubbed at her chest where his words made her ache. But he only meant fall off the ladder, and it was true, he'd saved her from worse. She kicked off her kitchen clogs, climbed up to the very top of the ladder and started reading the labels on boxes anywhere close to the right size.

"Do you see it?"

She could feel his hot breath on her hip. He had the same view of her that she'd just enjoyed of him.

"No. I don't see it." She stood on her toes to peer around another box.

"Lena, that's not safe." He grabbed her ankles.

Her body betrayed her—moisture pooled between her legs. Oh no! He would smell her. How many times had he known from her scent she was turned on by Andre's bite? *Succubus, succubus, succubus.*

"Damn." Still gripping her ankles, he whispered so quietly she barely heard.

She had to crane her neck to look at him. "Kos?"

He gazed at the stool between her feet. "I can smell you. So sweet." After a moment, he looked up. "Really?"

There was no lie that would spare her from the humiliating truth. "Yes."

"Damn." He turned and walked out the door.

Lena climbed off the stool and plopped onto the floor. Through her moist panties, the tile was cool on the hot flesh between her legs. She should lay her cheek on the floor to cool the even hotter flush of embarrassment.

She hated Kaštel. She was sick of being humiliated, sick of men who didn't want her, who made her wonder what was wrong with her. She had to go.

Kos still smelled Lena from the other side of the pantry door, sweet like the honey they'd been searching for. He would like to lick *her* off his fingers. Inside, with the scent of her filling the room, he'd had no control. He needed oxygen to think straight.

He puffed up like a prize rooster. She wanted him, not Andre. His heart somersaulted, like it was the best news of his life, when, in fact, things were suddenly, infinitely more complicated.

He could worship her and make sure she never doubted her desirability again. But, if he let himself get close to her, would he be able to send her away to a new household when it was time?

The iron-sharp smell of his mother's blood, spilled in her own bath and never forgotten, cut through the scent of Lena's arousal. Yes. He would send Lena away, because he could not destroy her. But for a little while, before he found her a job, he could be a doting lover.

Ready to make his proposal, he opened the pantry door.

She'd curled up on the floor, cheek pressed to the tile and face beet-red. She cried with her fist in her mouth so he wouldn't hear her sobs. As he entered, she turned her face away.

Krist. She thought he'd rejected her.

"Lena." He knelt, touching her chin to turn her tear-stained face. Her eyes were red and her nose ran, and still she was achingly beautiful.

He lifted her off the ground and cradled her to his chest for a moment, then set her down on the top of the stepladder. "Lena—"

She wiped her nose with the back of her hand. "Leave me alone."

He pulled his handkerchief from his pocket and handed it to her, glad to actually use it for once. She ran her thumb across his embroidered initials before dabbing the thing against her face. When she finished, he shoved the damp cloth into his pocket and gripped the back of her head to kiss her. She opened her mouth with surprise and he seized the opportunity. No teasing, no coaxing. His tongue was in her mouth, searching out hers. She gasped when he found it and began to stroke her.

She went limp, all the tension in her body escaping as she surrendered to his kiss. Wrapping her arms around his neck, she matched his enthusiasm.

Their tongues met clumsily until they found a rhythm—stroking and teasing each other. Their teeth collided, and Lena pulled back, laughing. All the awkwardness of the day vanished, and the easy comfort between them returned.

He dove for her mouth. Her soft lips sent sparks skittering over his skin. His heart pounded at double time. If only he had more hands, more mouths, so he could consume all of her. He'd wanted her for so long, but she'd been off limits, beyond reach. He never once imagined what it would be like between them. *Krist.* It was electric. He'd never felt anything like it.

A warning whispered in his mind: It would be that much harder to send her away.

He silenced the thought, already itching to get inside her, his tongue, or his fingers, or his cock. After all these years of wanting, he would gladly accept whatever access to her body she gave him. He just wanted *in*.

Kos backed her against the wall and lifted her up, cradling her ass in his hands. Her skirt bunched around her waist as he pressed between her thighs. Her heat seeped through his pants where he pushed his erection into her, and she rocked her hips in response.

He nuzzled her neck. "Aren't you impatient?"

"I'm afraid you're going to change your mind."

Krist. Look what they'd done to her. "Lena, the truth is I've wanted you since the moment you walked in my father's door. But you wanted Andre, so I left you alone."

"Kos, don't tease me."

He pinned her with his gaze. "I swear it. For years."

Tears spilled out of her eyes. "God, I was so stupid. Ever since you saved me, I realized I've been blind. Why did I want him when you were here all along?"

"He is kind of a jerk."

She laughed.

"Let me show you how much I've wanted you."

Her eyes went wide then heavy lidded in a matter of seconds. "Promise?"

"Cross my heart."

"Because apparently all I really need is a good fuck."

If only that were true. Still, he smiled because she meant for him to. There were countless things she needed that he couldn't give her, but all thought of them vanished when she took hold of him through his pants.

"I want this inside me five minutes ago."

Possibly the hottest thing she could have said. He thrust into her hand and rested his forehead against the smooth wall next to her head. "Me too, sweetheart, but let's make this last a little longer."

She didn't respond.

He pulled back to look at her. "Okay?"

She exhaled, her lips forming a little pout. Cute. Hot.

"I want you thoroughly loved, completely satisfied. No room to doubt my feelings."

Her pulse sped up, letting him know she found him persuasive. He bit her jutting lower lip gently. "Okay?"

She nodded.

He lowered her feet to the ground and dropped down in front of her. His fingers grazed her supple legs as he slipped her panties down to her ankles. Taking a moment to get himself under control, he folded them and set them next to her feet.

She gripped her skirt in both her fists so that she was almost entirely bared to him below her waist, but her legs were only slightly parted — like she wasn't expecting his mouth on her.

Under a tiny triangle of golden curls, her silky skin was lovely. But he wanted to see more, wanted to see her folds, wanted to see right inside her. He could have gazed all day, as if he'd never seen a woman's sex before. Her skin was softer, her scent sweeter, everything about her was different from other women.

She wriggled under his gaze and he looked up at her. Her brow crinkled with worry. It was so cute.

"Kos, what are you doing?"

She had to know he was going to taste her. It had been ages since he was with a woman who feigned innocence. The nineteen seventies seemed to put an end to that nonsense. He didn't want an inexperienced woman. It was a huge burden—one wanted to make things special for them. Too much work.

Lena obviously wasn't an innocent, but she also wasn't pretending. Maybe years of unmet needs and shame had made her forget this pleasure. He would remind her, lavish her with attention, make her scream and beg.

When he ran his tongue along her seam, she gasped. "Oh my God."

Her knees bent and he placed her thigh over his shoulder. Finally, she was open to him. He was too close for a proper view, but still he noticed the rosiness, the slickness of her most private skin. Then he licked her everywhere, inside and out. He wished his tongue were longer so he could lick her womb. Yes, that's where he wanted to be—all the way inside her. He needed more. He began to tease her open with his fingers.

"No!" Her pulse was too fast, her fists clenched.

"What's the matter?"

"Not yet. Don't put your fingers—"

"Sweetheart, I just want to make sure you're ready."

"Kos, I want all of you. Don't get me ready."

Okay. So, she liked it hard and fast. Not what he would have chosen for her first time in years, but she should have what she wanted.

More pleasure would help. He already knew where she liked his tongue—he delivered long, slow strokes and then fast, short ones. Her mewls, her breath, the blood pounding in her veins—everything told him how much pressure she liked. Her thighs tensed on either side of his head; she was getting close. He sucked her into his mouth, and just like that, she was coming on his tongue. He held her as her trembles slowly subsided.

"Wow." Her voice was husky.

With a wriggle, she pulled away. He held her hips, lapping at her. "You taste just like honey."

All flushed and disheveled, she was gorgeous. And she was still skeptical, like she thought he was sweet-talking her. He stood up to kiss her, knowing she would taste her salt on his lips, but probably not the honey that was already tempting him back between her legs.

"I am going to carry you upstairs and make love to you."

She wrung her hands, looking down at the floor. What could be wrong now?

"Kos. I really want that. But not yet." She reached for his erection and met his eye. "I want to see you. I want to know what you taste like, too."

Well okay. Upstairs could wait.

She let go of him, untucked his shirt and began to unfasten it. With every button, she delivered a chaste kiss to his newly bared chest. Each peck sent a shock down his spine. When she reached his abdomen, she knelt down and tongued his skin, making it burn. She sat back on her heels and unzipped his pants, taking his cock out carefully.

Her touch was tentative. "This is big."

There was no dignified response a man could make to a statement like that. He kept his mouth shut and concentrated on sensation. Fingertips feathered up his length, teasing and sparking his desire to greater heights.

"And hard, but soft, too."

Krist, her touch felt good. He would play doctor with her anytime.

His cell phone beeped in his pocket with a new message. "Ignore that."

She frowned, and he took her chin between his fingers.

"I'm all yours."

"Good." Her tongue darted out to circle his tip.

Need coursed through him, and he groaned. She kept her eyes locked on his and put the entire head in her mouth, teasing the underside with her tongue. The warmth of her mouth closed in on him, sparking incredible sensations, even though she seemed unpracticed—like she understood the technique, but had never done it before. She couldn't possibly be as innocent as she acted. But he let himself pretend he was her first. It made him even harder. His breath came faster.

His cell phone rang.

"God dammit!" He threw the phone against the tile floor. "Lena, you're killing me. Please don't stop."

She sucked on him and teased him. The scent of her arousal only intensified, and she moaned around his cock. She wrapped one hand around his base, taking him as far into her throat as she could, not that deep, but good enough.

So good.

She moved her mouth up and down. He flew higher and higher, pleasure and need blurring together with an intensity that made it like his first time. He dug his fingers into his thighs, trying to hold on as long as possible.

"Sweetheart, I'm going to come." He tried to pull free of her, but she gripped his hips. She wanted to taste him? He didn't fight her. His balls tightened and he grew even harder in her mouth. "Lena!" He exploded, his body stiffening and his mind blanking.

Palms flat on the wall, he tried to catch his breath. She stood, and he pulled her into a kiss. It was his turn to taste himself in her mouth, and it made him hard all over again. Thank God for vampire erections. He would be ready to go again as soon as he got her upstairs.

"You're incredible. That was the best."

She blinked. "Really?"

He stroked her cheek with his thumb, loving her modesty.

"I enjoyed it too, more than I…" She stopped herself.

More than what?

She bent for her panties, but before she could pull them on someone knocked on the door.

"Are you two finished in there yet?"

It was Zoey.

"*Krist.*"

"I heard that," she said, her scolding tone clearly meant only to mock.

He gave Lena a chance to finish dressing and then opened the door. Zoey peered at them, sniffing. "Clearly you had a very successful meeting. Did you talk about the food at all?"

He ignored her question. "Did you want something?"

"Andre finally got someone on the phone at the bottle wholesaler."

"Finally? And...?"

"The driver's been missing all day."

Kos's shoulders bunched. "Hunters?"

"Andre thinks so. He tried to call you." Zoey bit her lip.

"Why didn't you come get me sooner?"

"I, uh...knew what you were doing."

Lena's already sex-flushed face turned pinker. The blush was lovely, and he took her hand.

"And it's still daylight," Zoey said. "We sent Vania and Arden out."

The humans were more than competent. They'd helped Bel rescue Pedro and Lucas from Hunters. Still, something had to be done if a human hostage was in danger.

Lena watched him deliberate, but the look on her face said she already knew he would go. He tucked her angel-soft hair behind her ear. "Can I find you later?"

"Yes. You'd better."

He bent down and kissed her. It started as a gentle peck, and she leaned in. He deepened the kiss, slipping his tongue into her mouth.

Zoey cleared her throat. "Andre's in his office with Pedro now."

It required all of Kos's will to leave Lena, closing the door behind him. As Kos rushed through the house toward the cellar, he noted the sun setting behind the hills — fifteen minutes or so before they could go out.

Pedro fired words at Kos the moment he walked through the door. "Damn man, do you think it's macho to walk around smelling like that, 'cause I think you need a shower."

"Fuck off."

"I want my hundred bucks back. Now I know the worst thing about being a vampire is smelling Le — "

"Really? Because from here it looks like you're going to burst the fly on your jeans."

Pedro reached down and adjusted himself gingerly.

Andre blew out a breath. "Son, you do smell like...Lena."

"Yeah. And I'd like to get back to her. So let's save this human, find the bottles, and I can get back to business."

It was his duty to get the wine bottled and on the shelves for the other vampires, and an innocent human who'd been pulled into a war with Hunters needed their help. But it felt far more important to heal some of the hurts Lena had suffered at Kaštel. As soon as he got back, he would lick her wounds, head to toe, as many times as it took until she knew just how lovable she was.

Through the dense branches of the lemon tree outside the kitchen window, Kos kept his eyes trained on the sky. Slowly, dusk turned to dark, and he swung open the back door, springing into the air. With a gentle scuff of earth, Andre ascended a moment later.

Exhilaration swept through Kos, stealing his breath. When he'd flown before, rescuing Lena from the Hunters, he hadn't had time to think. He'd pushed off the ground with so much force he'd launched himself, and once airborne, it was simply a matter of direction.

In all the years he'd longed to fly, he'd pictured false starts and failed attempts, like a hatchling. Flying would have been worth it, but it was so much better that the skill came naturally. Feeling like a baby bird wouldn't have been good for his ego, and he couldn't have tolerated lessons from Andre.

They flew directly to the warehouse district and worked outward. Kos swept down and inspected any building that looked large enough to hold an eighteen-wheeler. Occasionally he heard the whoosh of Andre cutting through the air overhead. Kos peered through the broken window of an empty industrial building—only sloppy stacks of wooden pallets inside.

Andre whistled.

Kos bounded off the sidewalk into the air and followed the high pitched sound several blocks.

"I smell Hunter." His father crouched under a window.

Kos landed next to a looming garage—the perfect place to hide a delivery truck.

Kos sniffed. The odor was faint, but distinct, even over the smell of human waste. "How many?"

"I only hear one inside. If the human is still alive, he is bound, or asleep."

Kos peeled open the aluminum garage door. With a nerve grating squeak, the metal sheet came off its tracks. The missing truck sat inside, bright yellow with a telltale wine bottle logo. A scrawny kid perched at a card table with his laptop open.

"Oh, shit." Shooting to his feet, he toppled his chair and knocked the computer. It slid off the teetering surface, but he caught the silver rectangle before it crashed to the ground.

"Initiate," Andre said.

The boy was silent. A full circle of white ringed his golden irises, and the tart smell of his fear pumped into the air. He was scared to death.

Kos scanned the room. "Where's the driver?"

Not a peep from the Hunter, but something thudded inside the truck.

Andre opened its rolling door. "He is in here. Alive."

"Who are you guys? Cops?" Cowering further into the shipping container, the driver rubbed his bloodshot eyes.

"No. Not cops." Andre untied him. "But you are safe."

Kos tossed the man a mobile phone. "Step outside and call home. They're searching for you."

Prowling like a jungle cat, Andre circled the boy. "Where are the others, Hunter?"

Sullen, the kid crossed his arms. "They all went home."

Kos leaned in, examining the kid. "You planned this alone?"

The boy's eyes flicked toward his laptop. *Krist.* Some teenage hacker had thrown a wrench in Kos's plans.

"Did you get into my email?"

A sly smile appeared on the kid's face. "Trying to whore out your hot blonde cook?"

Kos tackled the kid. Pinning him, he wrapped his hands around his throat, but Andre pulled him off before he did any serious damage.

"You will not get any information from him like that. Back off and let me do it right."

That scared the kid. Kos could hear the Hunter's heart race faster, even over the sounds of his own pulse hammering.

If Hunters got hold of Lena, they'd rape her, torture her and kill her—and not necessarily in that order. Their cruelty to humans in household service was sickening, and he couldn't let it happen to her. He threw the laptop to the ground and crushed it under his shoe.

"Hmmm." Andre scratched his head. "I do not know much about these things, but that seems hasty. Might there have been information on there?"

"Fuck." Kos spat.

"We'll just have to get it out of him another way." Andre kicked the kid's leg just below the hipbone, not hard, or it would have cracked. Andre did crack his knuckles, and formed two meaty fists. "Talk."

Even Kos thought his father was scary at that moment—this kid would shit his pants. "I'll ask you again. Where are the other Hunters?"

The boy sat up, aiming his chin at the distant ceiling. "Like I said, they went home after Ethan Bennett called off the Hunt. We were pissed we wouldn't earn our daggers. But he promised to call us all back together once he was fin—"

The boy slammed his mouth shut, and actually covered it with both hands.

Kos rolled his eyes—they were dealing with a real professional. "Finished with what?"

"I don't know." The baby-Hunter sniped. Insolent brat. He didn't seem to understand he was being questioned by his mortal enemies, not his parents.

Andre uncurled and flexed his hands, cracking his knuckles a second time.

"I'm serious. I don't know. He said he was trying to figure out why you could still fly, after being exiled so long."

Kos wasn't trained in interrogation, but even he could tell the kid was holding back.

Andre toed the kid's calf muscle. "I will break your leg if you do not tell me everything."

"Break it. You're going to kill me anyway."

"Kill you?" Surprised laughter burst from Andre. "I will not—you are just a boy. Unlike your kind, I do not kill women and children."

"I'm not a—" Again, he clamped his mouth shut.

Kos shook his head. The kid wasn't one for thinking before he spoke, but at least he had enough sense not to argue himself out of the protected status.

The Hunter's eyebrows shot up and he uncovered his mouth. "You can't feed from me! I won't let you."

Now Kos laughed. "Boy, neither of us would bother. You're not our type."

Andre pointed into the kid's face. "However, I am not opposed to hurting you. So tell me, what is Ethan Bennett trying to finish?"

"I don't know." Indignation thinly veiled the boy's fear.

Kos took a more gentle tone. "Tell us what he said, then."

"He said—" the kid puffed up his chest and lowered his voice "'—I have uncovered clues about the origin of our tribe.'"

"Pompous prick, is he?" Andre asked with a grin, as if enjoying the news that Zoey's ex-lover was an asshole.

"Pretty much." The kid looked at the floor.

"That's all? Clues about the origin of the Hunters?" Kos dropped to a knee, looking the boy in the eye.

"Yeah. And everybody was jazzed." The kid raised his hands palm-up in the air, his head bouncing with emotion. "I was pissed I wasn't going to earn my dagger 'cause he called off the Hunt, and they were all like oooooh, aaaaah."

Kos exchanged glances with Andre and they chuckled. Funny kid. "I guess you didn't drink the Kool-Aid."

"What Kool-Aid?"

"Never mind." Kos peered into the truck, scanning to make certain the cases were upright and intact. "What are we going to do with him?"

"We will take him prisoner, keep him in the storage closet."

"Ah, yes. You always said we might need a holding cell." Kos pulled down the door of the tractor-trailer, closing it with a loud clang.

Sprawled on the ground, the kid's ankles bounced, revealing his fear.

"Are you going to carry him back?" Kos asked.

"*Davo*, no. He stinks. You do it."

"Sure thing, Andre. You drive the big-rig, then."

Andre clenched his teeth, his jaw muscles twitching. "Fine, we will all ride in the truck."

Half an hour later, Kos backed the truck into the loading dock in the workroom. Pinching the kid's ear, Andre dragged him off the truck, and the household gathered to see the prisoner.

"What are you going to do with him?" Zoey stepped forward to examine the Hunter, a wistful look taking over her face.

"He knows nothing." Andre took his place beside her. "He is useless as a captive. Simply put, we keep him so we do not have to kill him."

Lena drew closer to the Hunter. "He's just a kid. How bad can he be?"

"You must be that hot cook." The boy thrust his pelvis at Lena.

Rage curled Kos's fists and he lunged, but Andre's hand was on his collar fast, holding him back. Lena's head pivoted toward Kos and her tawny eyebrows pulled together.

From behind the onlookers, Lucas spoke up. "He can be bad, Lena, very bad. He's been brainwashed to hate you all for his entire life. He may seem harmless, but he cannot be trusted."

"Traitor." The kid shouted back at Lucas. "I'll kill you with my bare hands."

Lucas rolled his eyes and walked away.

The boy shouted after him. "They're coming for you! They'll never stop coming."

A chill crept over Kos, and his gut sank halfway to the floor. The Hunter's words weren't just for Lucas, but all of them, and they were all too true. Worse—the hateful humans knew about Lena. He needed to get her that job, get her to safety, and soon.

CHAPTER 10

On Ethan's computer, virtual yellow pins marked Hunter communities on a map of California. The tribe was concentrated around Sacramento, Mendocino, Bakersfield, and Watsonville. He'd updated the elders of each community that his research was proceeding rapidly. Within two weeks, he'd promised, they could resume their assault on Marasović.

An email from Derek Nichols reported he'd been hired by Marasović's wine distributor, which would give the Hunters data about who exactly purchased wine from the Kaštel Estate. Data that might one day prove useful.

Ethan fingered the toy soldier in his pocket. Only a full translation of *The Book of the Day*, or Zoey on her knees before him, could make the day more perfect.

"Be bold in your new endeavor," Gwen said.

"What?" Ethan looked up from his desk.

She sat at a table nearby, the codex open in front of her alongside a notebook full of illegible scrawl. Her fingers gripped a tiny slip of paper—a fortune from the cookie she had eaten after their dinner.

"On the advice of this cookie, I am going to ask you to tell me the truth."

He straightened his spine. "Everything I've told you is true."

"That's irrelevant, since there's clearly a great deal you've withheld." She smoothed the slip of Chinese proverb onto the desktop with her thumb.

"That goes without saying. For example, I haven't told you what I ate for breakfast on Monday before we met."

Ever so slowly, she looked up, meeting his gaze with a piercing stare. "Don't be an asshole, *Ethan*."

So she had discovered his name. He tried not to show his surprise. Finding it wouldn't have been difficult, but she had to go snooping for it. "What would you like to know?"

"Are you some kind of vampire slayer?"

Laughter rose up in him and he opted to let it out. The images and cryptic messages of *The Book of the Day* clearly depicted vampires, but he never expected her to take them for reality.

She slammed her notebook closed. "Here's what I think. Your tribe believes you have a sacred duty to exterminate vampires. This has been your mythology for at least three thousand years. There was a mysterious historical incident that brought about this mandate, perhaps taking place in the tribe's native Turkey. You want to know what it was." Twice she tapped her manicured nails on the desktop, her lips pursed. "How am I doing?"

His instincts told him to deny everything, but her knowledge was invaluable to him. He may as well tell her the truth since it would make her even more useful—he'd already planned to kill her, anyway.

Gwen blew a strand of hair out of her face, tucking it behind her ear before she crossed her arms. "Am I hot or cold?"

"You've guessed correctly, and with astonishing accuracy. Although whether you actually believe it remains to be seen."

"Not a guess, a theory, and a well founded one." She looked him up and down. "You kill vampires?" Something like admiration glinted in her eye.

"Yes."

"That explains your...physique."

Not really, considering all the pudgy Hunters he knew. He swam daily and trained in martial arts to maintain his fitness. Interesting that she had noticed.

"So you just accept all this as real? Vampires exist and these artifacts are the evidence of a tribe of vampire slayers?"

She shrugged. "I study the history of the British Isles. I'd be very closed-minded if I assumed all the traditional beliefs and practices of my ancestors were bogus." She slid her notebook into her briefcase.

"May I see your full translation now?"

"Nice try. As I told you yesterday, it's not written down. Based on what I'm learning from your artifacts, I'm revisiting several tricky sentences."

Clamping his teeth shut, he bit back his impatience.

"I think it's time we call it a night," she added.

"Fine. Sleep well."

"I said we."

Spinning his chair to face her, he let his gaze linger as she approached. He did like the sway of her hips, and taking her to bed would help him figure out what made her tick.

That was how he had learned the depth of Zoey's cold detachment—she fucked like she was on fire, trying to thaw out her frozen heart. He had matched her frenzy while maintaining an emotional distance that kept her desperate for warmth. It was why she couldn't quit him until Marasović got his fangs into her.

Ethan did not want Zoey thawed. When he went back for her, he would kill the vampires and all Marasović's household in front of her. Her husband's suicide had wounded her deeply, but Ethan needed to make sure the wound never healed. Only when Zoey was completely dead on the inside would she know she belonged to him.

In the meantime, there was Gwen. She held the keys to unlocking the mysteries inside Kaštel Estate. Why were the vampires still able to fly? What would happen if his pathetic brother did, in fact, let Pedro feed from him? The answers were coded in the artifacts surrounding them, and Gwen was the cypher.

She gingerly placed herself on his lap, straddling him with those mesmerizing hips and brushing her little round breasts against him.

"Thank you for telling me more of the truth," she whispered.

It wasn't really gratitude, but a declaration that she knew he was still holding back information.

And that was something Gwen had on Zoey—she saw the shadow surrounding him, the one he so easily hid from everyone else. Perched on his lap, her pupils were big and her pretty mouth tense. She was afraid of him. But rather than scare her off, the fear lured her.

He rolled his shoulders with a rush of power. For the first time in his life, he tasted being seen and wanted in all his dark glory. It was intoxicating, tugging at his dick in an intense surge of arousal. She wanted that side of him? He would gladly give it to her, so hard and so many times she wouldn't be able to walk tomorrow. Without a word, he cupped her ass and picked her up, carrying her to his bedroom with her legs wrapped around his waist.

In his pocket, his phone buzzed with an incoming email. It could wait until morning.

A few loose ends required Kos's attention, and then Lena would be all his. He called Bel to tell him about the prisoner. Bel had no advice, but he confirmed Lucas's warning that the kid wasn't harmless, no matter how naïve he appeared.

Then Kos left a message with his buddy at California Containers, asking to borrow their truck for a day or two to deliver the wine to the distributor, once it was bottled. Small favor, but it saved him the hassle of arranging another delivery that could get hijacked.

In the process of shutting down his computer, the bold-faced type of a new email message drew his attention.

> Subject: Exquisitely Beautiful? I'll take her.
> From: Mason Kearney, Jr.

A spasm of tension gripped his body and he shuddered. *Krist.* He had to read it. How could he go upstairs and make love to her, pretending the message wasn't there?

> Kos, old buddy, I'm in desperate need of a cook, or at least one hot dish. Sounds like you've got what I need. On your recommendation, I'll take her, sight unseen. Shall I pick her up, or will you deliver? Call me.

He could practically hear his old friend as he read. Mason was all right, a stand up guy. A native of San Francisco, from an old and wealthy family. Lena would find him good looking, too.

He used to go out on the town with Mason in the nineteen fifties and sixties. Back then, Mason had a thing for stewardesses, so they'd frequented a hotel bar where the Pan Am girls stayed. They'd loved him — sometimes he would hit it off with the entire crew from a 707. Once, he'd left the bar in a train of women wearing matching gray suits and pillbox hats. Inside the elevator two of the women tipped their hats to Kos. At that same moment, Mason whispered so that only vampire ears could hear, "I'm bringing them in for a landing."

Kos had different tastes. He was on the lookout for that Midwestern housewife attending a conference with her husband. There was usually at least one in the hotel bar. She was always seated in a corner drinking a cocktail and pretending to read a novel while her husband was off doing manly things. Kos knew something Mason didn't—stewardesses partied in every port, but housewives were still waiting for the party.

He enjoyed relieving the missuses of their inhibitions. They peeled them off easily, just like their nylons. He was pretty certain one newly liberated housewife could blow your *mind* better than a dozen party girls. And he always hoped they left those inhibitions behind in San Francisco so that things were more exciting in their marriage beds. Kos never shared his housewife secret with Mason. His buddy wouldn't have believed him anyway.

He laughed, remembering their good times. Lena might like Mason—he was charming and fun. But Kos hadn't considered the unsettling possibility she would serve someone he knew. A nameless, faceless employer hadn't troubled him, but Mister fuck-fifteen-flight-attendants in one night? Lena was special, and she deserved to be treated that way.

On the other hand, Mason was a known quantity. Better she work for someone Kos knew and trusted than a stranger. Lena was a grown-up. She knew what it meant to work in a household, knew she wouldn't be somebody's one and only. But she deserved so much more, and he wanted to spare her added hurt. The idea of Mason's hands and fangs on her made him cringe.

As if there was even a choice. No strangers had replied to the advertisement and the longer she was at Kaštel, the more danger she was in—it had to be Mason.

There. It was decided. And it left him feeling empty.

The movie was one of Lena's favorites, a teen romance from the eighties rerun on cable. John Cusack was so young and cute, chasing after a girl way out of his league. Lena could relate. She tried to watch it—kept waiting for that amazing scene when he held his boom box overhead and played that one song—but she couldn't focus. Her mind only wanted to replay every stroke of Kos's tongue between her legs, or the rapture on his face when he'd come in her mouth.

She lay on his bed, fingering her neck and imagining his bite. After years, she would share sex *and* blood. And then, maybe she would know for certain her destiny—blood service or a normal human life?

The loose brass doorknob jiggled, and the door creaked open. Kos didn't open it wide, just slipped in sideways. His stiff, upright posture gave him away. Something had changed. But what? She squinted to find a clue on his face in the dark, his high cheekbones illuminated only by the flickering blue light of the television.

His eyes flicked to the television. "*Say Anything*?"

What? Oh, the movie. "Yeah. You know it?" That would be a surprise, since he had distinctly classical taste in music and literature.

He leaned against the wall next to the door, exposing his muscular white neck as he rested his head. Rubbing his eyes, he replied, "I'm a Peter Gabriel fan. He's a genius and he wrote the song—"

"Kos, what happened?"

He opened his eyes, and they were solid gray. The handsome planes of his face flattened, dimples invisible. Oh well, at least she'd known what it was like to be wanted for a while. She drew up her knees, suddenly nauseous.

He turned on the lights, and reached for the remote control, powering off the television. "I'm sorry it took me so long to come back."

"Don't apologize. You saved the driver. You captured that Hun—"

"You mean that kid." He shook his head, crossing his arms.

She stared over her kneecaps, her eyes drawn to his full lips, which had kissed her so sweetly, kissed her everywhere. She wanted them again, but something told her that wasn't going to happen now.

Impatient, she asked again, "What is it?"

His chest rose and fell with a deep breath, and he cleared his throat. "It's good news. I found you a job."

No! No! No! Not now, not when she was so close to what she wanted, so close to Kos. "Oh, thank you."

"An old friend, Mason Kearney. He lives in San Francisco. He needs a cook."

"He's your friend?"

"Yes, we were close for a time, but we've been out of touch." Kos sat next to her and folded her hand into his. "I like him, Lena. And you will too. He's very amusing. He's handsome—women love him."

An ocean of distance spread between them at the promise that she'd like another vampire. In the end, she was merely a blood source. "Well that's good for me, I guess."

He flinched. If she sounded bitter, she hadn't meant to.

"Lena, I think it *is* good. I trust him, and you'll be close by. I can check on you, make sure you're happy, and…satisfied."

A piece of lint on Kos's shoulder captured her focus. He took her chin between his thumb and forefinger, gently turning her face to meet his gaze.

"Everything I said before is true, Lena. I'm crazy about you. I want you constantly."

He kissed her. Gentle. Slow. Oh God, his lips were so slow and sweet. She wanted to surrender to the kiss, to him. But every time she tried to fall backward into sensation, her mind yanked her out.

She pushed him away. "Why?"

"Because everything about you is sweet." He put his hand over her heart. "You're kind, and—"

"No. I mean, why should I go? I could stay with you." She looked him in the eye—cloud gray and sky blue swirled, fighting for dominance.

"Sweetheart, it's for the best. You'll be safe away from the Hunters. You'll have what you've always wanted—a place in a normal household. I can assure you Mason will have none of Andre's compunctions."

Everything he said made sense. Surely she was imagining his sadness, just like earlier she'd imagined his eyes on her when they walked to the pantry. Only that time, she'd been right, hadn't she?

She rose up on her knees, eye to eye with him. "But I want you." She hated saying it. It was too close to the way she'd begged Andre.

"And I want you. But I can't…I just don't do commitment."

He was a rock. He was the most reliable man she'd ever met. What was he saying?

"You can have me. I'll be your household. We can live in your house at the coast."

He flinched, drawing back and frowning. She sounded so pathetic. God, she was making him hate her.

"Lena, I'm just not the type to settle down. I don't want a household."

Finally she understood. He wanted her, but not for keeps. She could feel his desire sparking in the air, in the heat of his hand and the desperation in his eyes. But he didn't want the burden of her in the future.

The realization squeezed her heart, stealing her breath. It was Andre all over again, only worse. Kos had thrown this stray dog a bone, then taken it right back.

"When does he want me to start?" The question trembled across her quivering lips.

"I'll call him tomorrow to work out the details." His words rasped, barely more than a whisper.

"Okay."

"I'm going to miss you so much." He pulled her against his chest, stroking her back. His erection pressed into her hip, his fingers sliding around her sides to her breast.

How could he not feel her tension? She was taut as a bow.

"Yeah, right."

He tensed too. "*Krist.* This is the last thing I wanted to do to you—make you feel this way again." His arms still held her firmly. "I should have stayed away from you, let you go back to your room and get on with things."

No. It wasn't Andre again. Kos gave a damn. He was sorry.

"I don't wish that." She flattened her palm on his chest. "We would never have become friends. We would never have—"

Then he was kissing her again and not gently. His tongue was in her mouth demanding she accept his affection. She tried to relax, to enjoy his kiss. Probably the last one...

He withdrew, kissing the side of her mouth and up her jaw. He circled her ear with his tongue. "Let me make love to you, show you how special you are to me."

His breath was hot on her wet skin, igniting her desire.

If she said yes, he could give her what she was longing for all those years with Andre—sex, and blood, and pleasure beyond belief. She could surrender to him now, let him show her his version of love—warm, and generous, and freely given to any woman he cared about.

She could admire that about him, if she weren't flat out in love with him.

He nuzzled her neck and her body responded. She had to act fast, or it would be too late.

"Kos."

"Hmmm?"

"I can't do this."

He stopped instantly and looked at her. He was that kind of male — no means no.

"I'm sorry. It's not enough, anymore."

He blinked his sad gray eyes and nodded. It was impressive to see the way he reeled himself back in, his heat, his embrace, slowly coiling up inside him with immense self-control. She was burning for him, electric blue on the inside, and he was made of steel — they obviously were not meant to be.

CHAPTER 11

Slouched over the sturdy old desk, Lucas divided the piece of office-supply paper into four squares because that was how many illustrations he remembered. His memory stopped there. He creased the folds in the stark white paper again, but no images from the damn book came to mind.

Damn it. He knew what he would have to do, and he wasn't looking forward to it. In order to access the images, he must descend deep into the past, back to when he saw the Hunter relic for the first and only time as a teenager. Most of the time, his childhood hadn't been a terrifying nightmare inside the very normal two-story house with wood siding and dormer windows. The Hunter stuff—the hate and violence—was well hidden under placid domesticity, not infrequently interrupted by his father Stephen's rages. But that just made them like every other family on the block.

Lucas lay on the bed and let his mind wander back to how he had found the book. As a kid, he'd had the habit of skulking around the house, always preferring to remain invisible. Coming down the stairs of their suburban Boston home, he'd overheard Ethan and Stephen talking about a special book locked away in the basement.

"Where did you get it?" Ethan asked.

"It's always been in our family, like the tapestries, and the weapons." Stephen's gravelly voice made Lucas cringe, even from where he lurked on the stairwell.

"What language is it written in?"

"I don't know. No one can translate it. But the pictures are self explanatory, don't you think?"

Smiling to himself, Lucas had begun to plan how to get his hands on the book. He was dying to see it simply because his father had hidden it from him. It was one more teenage rebellion in his singularly subtle style. He didn't join the punk scene, or go downtown and let older men suck him off. Instead, he messed with Stephen's mind—broke into all the locked cabinets in the basement and shuffled artifacts, forged checks to move Stephen's money between accounts, even impersonated his father on the telephone. Every trick he played was harmless, causing just enough confusion to disorient his asshole of a father and make him paranoid.

Late one afternoon, Lucas had the house to himself. He rummaged through a wall of cabinets in the basement. Before Stephen had remodeled the basement to preserve artifacts better than the Louvre, his security had been a joke. In the bottom drawer, the objects were shallower, closer to the rim, hinting that something had been stored underneath. Below them, he discovered a case with a far more sophisticated lock than the ones on the cabinets.

He started to pick it, but grew anxious. Would he run out of time? Tense, he listened for the sound of a car in the driveway, sweating with concentration until he felt the lock give. With his tools stowed in his back pocket, he perched himself on the edge of Stephen's desk chair, which smelled of his father's aftershave—not cheap, but not nice either.

The ancient book was wrapped in a cracked, mottled leather cover, and it smelled of vellum. The binding was intact but looked fragile and would require careful handling. If he damaged it, Stephen would discover his snooping. Lucas wielded his picks again, using one to turn each page. He looked quickly, fearful he would be interrupted, and then started over from the beginning.

Stiff with anticipation, he lay on the bed at Kaštel, watching the first illustration come into focus before his adolescent eyes. Most of his mind was still in nineteen eighty-seven, in the cool basement, but he was aware of his goal—to capture the images so that he could draw them accurately. He didn't rush or try to alter the memory, letting it unfold at its own pace while four, no, five illustrations were revealed.

Finally his past self glanced at his watch. It was time to put the book away and return to his bedroom before his father returned.

He broke from the memory and crossed to the desk in a foggy haze to stare at the blank paper. With relief, he discovered that the images still occupied his mental vision. He sketched quickly, capturing as much as he could of all the illustrations. Later would be the time to enlarge the drawings, filling in color and detail. Now, he could only draw, unable to interpret the significance of the images. That would come later too.

Hours passed before he finished the last sketch and collapsed backward in his chair, his head lolling against the high seatback. Since he broke up with his cell phone, he had no way to tell time. But he seriously needed a drink. It was dark out, so it couldn't be too obscenely early for booze. Not that he cared. Ally had mentioned a bar in the living room. He put the drawings in the drawer beneath a phone book. No one used those things anymore, so surely no one would bother to look under it either.

He found the bar very well stocked and, more importantly, it had an icemaker. Room temperature vodka and tonic was disgusting. A large television covered half the wall. He rarely watched TV, but why not start? He wasn't Lucas Bennett Vampire Hunter anymore. He could drink in the morning and watch soap operas if he damn well wanted to.

It took a minute to figure out the remote with all its buttons and then scroll through some sort of menu. Since when had television become so complicated? He flipped through a documentary about lions — too bloody. Women's basketball — yuck. Something that purported to be news but wasn't. It was as bad as he thought. He couldn't even find a stupid soap opera.

"I thought I'd learn something about you from what you chose to watch, but you're a compulsive channel surfer."

Lucas froze with his hand raised, remote pointing at the idiot box. He angled his head to find Pedro studying him from the doorway. Butterflies jittered through Lucas's gut. And, damn it, he was glad to see the vampire.

"Surfer? Not really. I'm a compulsive avoider of the television. Everything on here is awful. Join me?"

"Awful TV. How can I say no?" Pedro plopped onto the couch like he owned it, kicking his feet onto the coffee table. "What kind of show do you like?"

"A good mystery or drama, I guess." Lucas wasn't about to admit that if he was going to watch TV, he really liked a trashy soap.

His skin now supple and smooth, Pedro looked a thousand times better than he had earlier, when he was starving. Boyish and playful—that's how Lucas would have described Pedro when they first met. His eyes had sparkled, there was a bounce in his step. Facing Lucas on the couch now, Pedro's features were grave instead.

Lucas glanced away, powering off the television. "To what do I owe this honor?"

"I came to apologize..." Pedro combed his fingers through impossibly thick chestnut hair.

Lucas waited, shifting to face him on the couch.

"For earlier, for..." Pedro's eyes were downcast.

The chuckle seized Lucas before any sound came out, but eventually his laughter grew audible.

Pedro frowned, and shadows clouded his golden eyes. "What?"

"Just curious how you were going to finish that sentence."

Pedro shrugged. "I have no fucking idea how to finish it."

His lighthearted admission melted Lucas. "Hey, man, I get it. Although I wish you'd stayed so we could finish what we'd started."

"This situation is totally fucked." Pedro threw his head back against the cushion, looking up. "I want to be angry with you, but I can't."

"Fine by me. If you're going to need my blood, I'd prefer you less angry. I'm still getting over my vampire phobia."

"It's not that easy to stay—"

"I know." Carefully, Lucas inched his hand toward Pedro's jittering knee. "Just do your best to keep cool when my blood is flowing and things are getting sexy. Neither one of us can handle all that anger and lust at once."

"It's not so easy to keep it on lock down." Pedro thumbed his chest.

Lucas exhaled in a rush—the vulnerable revelation was a relief after all the crap that had happened between them. "So we take it slow, nice and easy. See if that makes it easier."

Pedro faced him, and without a word or a sign, they met in the center of the couch. When they'd kissed before, in the winery's tasting room a million years ago, Pedro had given a come-hither look, and Lucas had pounced. This time, Pedro did not wait. Their lips met, tongues and teeth collided. Pedro pushed Lucas down and climbed on top, his erection an iron shaft between them.

Lucas pressed into the cushions, away from the obscenely hard length. "Ouch, no relief since this morning? I thought for sure it would ease up a little."

"It did, some." Pedro hovered over Lucas, still and steady like a plank. "Had to sit around in my briefs for a while until I could get my jeans on. I kept thinking about you in the shower taking care of yourself, and I'd be back where I started."

Sucker that he was, Lucas couldn't help but be flattered. His lips pulled into a gratified grin. "Maybe we should go back to my shower, make sure your fantasy was accurate."

"Is that a good idea?" Pedro's expression remained serious.

"I'm pretty sure it's not. And I'm also sure your cock is going to burst like an over cooked sausage. I'm offering to help."

Finally, Pedro returned the smile. His Spanish accent thickened. "It would be ungracious of me to turn down an offer of help."

Grasping Pedro's muscular forearm, Lucas led him back to his room and turned on the shower in the shiny modern bathroom. He took off the vampire's shirt and then slid his jeans to his ankles. Pedro wore a pair of black boxer briefs underneath, and his erection peeked out of the fly.

"Have I ever told you that you are exactly my type?" Lucas took in his muscular torso — a flat stomach and large pecs dusted with dark hair.

Pedro's abs rippled as if Lucas had touched him. "Tell me another day, and get your fucking clothes off."

Lucas pulled his shirt over his head and dropped his jeans and boxers. He was at half-mast, but seeing Pedro naked and aroused got his blood moving.

Pedro kissed him again. The hunger in his lips revealed just how desperately Pedro needed a release, but he kept the kiss gentle and his demons locked up tight.

Lucas wrapped his hands around Pedro's erection and the vampire whimpered. "Okay?"

Pedro sucked in a breath. "Sensitive."

No kidding. Lucas had never seen anything like it. Not just that Pedro was thick, but he was so hard the skin on his cock was pulled too tight.

Cold granite reared up and hit Lucas square in the chest, pushing the breath from his lungs. No, the countertop hadn't moved—Pedro had bent him over the bathroom sink.

Fuck. This was a problem. Their eyes met in the mirror over the vanity. This was backward, he was the one who—

Pedro's eyes were begging. He already knew. "I want you like this."

Lucas's chest constricted; his pulse hammered. On display for the volatile vampire, he was too vulnerable.

Shit, his new fuck buddy wanted to fuck *him* and not the other way around. He could feel Pedro's erection against his ass. Pedro, who could be playful and sweet…and who got off on his power over Lucas.

"Pedro, I don't do this." He tried to keep the fear out of his voice, in case it turned Pedro on.

"You'll like it. I'll make it good for you."

Pedro was way past reason. What could Lucas do? "Pedro, no."

Pedro prodded him gently, and all the muscles in Lucas's body tensed.

"Haven't you ever?"

"No." Lucas spoke firmly, as if he were talking to a child, or an animal.

Pedro just blinked; obviously he wasn't surprised. They'd never discussed this because they didn't need to, had sent each other cues from the start. A few things had changed since that moment, but one thing had not—

"I never have, and I don't want to."

With his new strength, Pedro could do anything he wanted to Lucas. He gripped a hip hard and pressed Lucas's shoulder into the countertop. But then he stepped back.

Lucas's chest filled with air against the cold granite. Thank God. Only, Pedro still looked miserable, with no relief in sight. *Well, here goes nothing.* Lucas dropped to his knees and took the swollen cock into his mouth.

"Fuck yeah," Pedro whispered on a breath.

Lucas didn't go down on a guy often, but for Pedro…carefully and gently he suckled the engorged cock, which grew even harder with every pull. It didn't take Pedro long to come, ejaculating for an eternity.

Lucas stood up and examined the vampire, whose shoulders sloped, loose. Pedro hopped up to sit on the counter and pulled Lucas into his arms.

For what felt like a long while, Lucas let Pedro hold him. Then his stomach growled, echoing in the small room. "What time is it?"

"It was about eight when I found you watching the television." Pedro feathered a kiss on Lucas's temple. "You missed dinner and cocktails don't count. Lena tried out a special recipe with truffles—smelled like stinky feet, but the humans raved."

Lucas chuckled, shaking his head with amusement.

Pedro nuzzled his neck. "You have to eat, if I am going to take your blood."

The self-preservation masked an expression of care, so Lucas conceded. "I'll get something soon. Lena keeps late plates labeled in the fridge."

"I forgot about that. How did I forget so fast?" Pedro spoke into his hair, the breath making it stir.

"Because it doesn't matter anymore. I'm your late plate now." Lucas closed his eyes, his face pressed against his vampire lover's chest.

Pedro took a deep breath and held it. "So, how is this going to work between us? I'm not the same anymore. I can't let you fuck me. It feels…submissive."

That was exactly how Lucas had felt bent over the sink. "Are you saying it didn't feel that way before?"

"Yeah, pretty much. It was just about getting off. I could switch back and forth. But now…"

Lucas ran a gentle hand up and down Pedro's spine. "I guess there's a lot of blow jobs in our future. Foreplay forever."

"That sucks."

For the first time he could remember, Lucas laughed from his gut and it felt good. "Yep. It sure does."

CHAPTER 12

Kos insisted Lena stay the night in his room and then retreated before she could mount a counter argument.

Neither his fear of love, nor her grief, were enough to wipe away his desire. His erection throbbed, a dull ache growing sharper. For the very first time since Andre turned him into a vampire, he sympathized with Pedro about the cruel limitation of their species. Who cared about the sun? He needed relief by his own hand, but he could try all night long, and none would come. In an empty guest room, he stepped into a shower and twisted only the cold-water tap.

What if he kept her? The question whispered through his mind—the serpent tempting Eve in the garden couldn't have been half as seductive.

No woman had ever caused him to doubt his conviction. Could Lena be the exception? Could the love sparking between them last when his mother and Andre's had failed?

Frigid water ran over his head, raising up goose bumps and stinging his skin. He closed his eyes and tried to imagine a future with her, but he couldn't picture it. All that came to mind were images from the day of his mother's suicide.

Piercing screams had shattered the windows of their house on Šolta. Kos had followed the cries to where Andre knelt next to Mila's lifeless body, still lying in cold bathwater, pink with blood. The metallic smell was pungent even to his human nose. Face to face with her corpse, he wasn't surprised. Her misery had shrouded their home, a palpable suffering...

Had Kos secretly expected her to take her life? The thought made his gut sink with remorse.

In the days that followed, as Kos overheard the servants chatting, or shared dinner with Bel, or watched Andre in the vineyards, he noticed the lightness. The atmosphere of the household shifted, free of the oppressive weight of the unhappy marriage. It shamed him to be relieved by his mother's death, but the freedom was undeniable. And it taught him an invaluable lesson—there was a flaw in the fabric of the universe—love simply could not survive the demands of a vampire's eternal bond.

More than a century later, his skin burned under the cold water pouring over his painful gooseflesh in the shower at Kaštel. He wiped a soapy hand over his flaccid cock. The long-buried memory had done the trick. He turned off the tap and reached for a towel. Once he was dry, he wrapped it around his waist and met his own gray eyes in the bathroom mirror.

He'd made a vow, dripped his own human blood onto Mila's grave and promised never to do to a woman what Andre had done to Mila. Not that he blamed Andre. His father had been undyingly solicitous to her, which proved love could not last. Ever. The icy water's chill had seeped into his bones, and he shivered.

Showered, changed, and newly re-committed to vampire bachelorhood, Kos needed someplace to spend the night. Going out on patrol with Bel's crew of mercenary vampires no longer appealed. He needed sympathetic company. It was a long shot, but he went down to the cellar hoping to find his father in his office. The two had played cards there nearly every night for decades before Zoey had arrived.

Halfway through the cellar, the sound of Andre and Zoey bickering reached him. They argued over how much Susan enjoyed her bite. A little tension about whom Zoey fed from? Hopefully it wasn't already the beginning of their inevitable end.

Kos was about to scuff his feet against the stone floor to warn them he approached when Andre called out. "Just come in already."

Inside his dark office, Andre leaned against his desk, holding Zoey snugly by the waist and staking his claim that she belonged to him and not the sexy lesbians of his household.

Kos swallowed a surge of irrational jealousy. "Did you question the kid?"

"You mean the Hunter." Andre's jaw muscles bulged.

"Yeah. The Hunter kid."

"His name's Leo." Zoey extricated herself from Andre's grip and dropped into a chair.

Were they conspiring to annoy Kos with this argumentative nonsense? He sucked in a calming breath. "Because of his yellow eyes?"

She shrugged. "Because it's his name."

Andre took the seat next to Zoey. "From our interview, I ascertained the boy Hunter knows absolutely nothing. I did not have to get aggressive. He is rather frightened."

Relief washed over Kos, taking with it some of his sadness. "So that's it? We just keep him locked up?"

Andre nodded. "For now."

Good. Kos could broach the real reason he'd come to find them. "You two up for Uno?"

"What about Lena?" Zoey sat up straight in her chair. "I thought you had...plans."

Kos could also speak in euphemisms, and carefully too, so that the emptiness he felt stayed out his voice. "Our plans fell through."

Two sets of eyes scrutinized him for too long.

Finally, Zoey spoke. "We could play Uno. Or, if you'd like to see me hand your father his own ass, we could play poker."

Nice. If she could deliver on that promise, his night would get a lot better.

"Five card draw?" He began to shuffle the always-ready deck of cards.

"Texas hold'em," Zoey replied, clearing space off the coffee table.

It was Andre's worst game—it was the only version of poker at which he couldn't dominate. Although against Kos, he still won.

Andre poured them wine. "Woman, if it were possible, you would be the death of me."

"Come on—Kos needs company." She flashed Andre a smile.

His father's heart sped up, pounding out a loud and fast rhythm in Kos's ear.

Another wave of jealousy rolled over Kos, and he reminded himself their happiness would come to an end. In the wave's aftermath, mild irritation lingered. Kos picked up his cards and chided them. "Cut out the flirting and focus on the game. You offered to keep me company. There will be no sneaking upstairs between hands."

CHAPTER 13

Ethan jerked awake, his phone blaring from the nightstand. The clock read three a.m. Grasping the phone, he slipped on pajama bottoms and sprinted into the kitchen so Gwen wouldn't hear the conversation.

"What the fuck are you thinking calling me at this hour?" he hissed at Rob Caroli.

"Marasović has my son."

Frustration gripped Ethan so hard he shuddered. "What?"

"Looks like Leo planned a little operation on his own. Hijacked a truck of wine bottles, but got himself captured." Caroli had the deeply resonant voice of a radio announcer, although it could not cover his innate gruffness.

"Leo?" That twit could not be older than seventeen, the puniest of all the Hunter initiates who had come on the Marasović operation to earn their Sun daggers.

"I want to attack the estate again. I've got everyone on alert."

"No."

Caroli coughed into the phone — the sound of someone choking back an insult. Excellent. Ethan had their respect, or at least their obedience.

"There's something else," Caroli rumbled.

"What?" Ethan barked.

"I just spoke to Derek. Apparently, Marasović is throwing a party for a new wine."

"Wine?" That detail tickled something in Ethan's brain, where a theory had taken root. They had hired Zoey for the purpose of launching a wine…

"They're calling it Blood Vine." A lilt in Caroli's baritone hinted he thought the name significant.

"Blood Vine is it?"

"And that name got me thinking, Bennett. And I remember crystal clear when we tossed our rockets and Molotov cocktails at Kaštel, that shield wrapped the house real snug. But not the vines."

"Yes, I recall the same thing." He rapped his knuckles on the countertop twice. Could it be so easy? "I'll be on the first flight. Don't start without me." Ethan pulled his thumb back from the phone's screen just before ending the call. "Caroli?"

"Yeah?"

"You realize we're not going to save your son?"

The phone line crackled in the brief pause before Caroli replied, "The little shit got what he asked for."

Ethan analyzed the other Hunter's tone. The man's fury seemed to far outweigh his grief. That zealous dedication was precisely what Ethan loved about his tribe. Lord, how he wanted it under his control.

"But we can't let the vampires get away with harming him." Caroli's words vibrated with vehemence straight into Ethan's bones — an oddly pleasurable sensation.

"Fair enough. Have you given any thought how to destroy an entire vineyard?"

"Napalm."

A surprised laugh erupted from Ethan before he could contain it. "Seriously?"

"Yeah, I'll round some up tomorrow. I know a guy."

"Well, Caroli, I admit I am impressed." Ethan ended the call and rolled his shoulders, suddenly full of anticipatory energy for the coming events. At the bottom of his telephone screen, a red circle caught his eye. A new email, from Leo Caroli. Was he still alive? Could this be a message from Marasović?

Ethan rushed to open the message. The email said nothing about being captured, but it nonetheless contained very interesting information. Ethan scribbled the name Mason Kearney on a piece of paper. He needed the address of this vampire. He would put his assistant Justine on it in the morning. That woman could find out anything about anyone.

Upstairs, Gwen was still sprawled in his bed. She'd been quite a surprise. She fucked like a hellcat. In the throes of doing her from behind, as hard as she'd begged him, he'd let his mask of normalcy slip. He'd slapped her haunches like she was not a hellcat but some domesticated animal to be ridden. She went crazy — thrashing, growing wetter, begging. Yes, her begging had driven him wild.

He had spanked her so hard welts formed on her buttocks and thighs. It was the sight of those red marks that took him over the edge, and right before he came, he pulled out to ejaculate on her raw flesh. She whimpered until his hot spurts hit her and she cried out her own climax.

She'd collapsed on her belly, and after attempting a roll, winced and left her abused backside pointing in the air. Knowing he had caused her pain brought him even more pleasure. And then she had looked over her shoulder at him and said, "More."

At the top of the stairs, he slid quietly into the room. The visceral memories of the night tumbled through his mind, shooting blood into his dick once again. She stirred, and rolled onto her back, silently spreading her legs. He strode to the bed, dropped his pants and penetrated her without ceremony. At the force of his entrance, her grunt turned into a groan of pleasure. He pinched both her nipples as hard as he could. She writhed under him, and he loved it. Tomorrow he would look for some clamps in the garage. Tomorrow…

He stopped mid-thrust.

What would he do with her?

She whimpered, squeezing her hands over his, pleading for more of what he had to give.

Grabbing her hips, he resumed pounding into her small, hungry body. A black leather bag came to mind, full of blades, pliers, clamps — his tool kit, containing all the instruments he had used to torture his brother's fag Pedro. It was safely locked away in his apartment in San Francisco. Gwen might like it. Or it might cross even her line. Beneath him, she was pinching her own nipples now, arching up to meet his thrusts.

A fantasy of her pretty face truly afraid brought on his orgasm, his body tingling with strange pleasure. His chest heaved as he struggled to catch his breath. When he could speak again he announced his decision.

"Tomorrow we're going to San Francisco."

Her eyebrows drew together. In the dark room, there was just enough light to show that tears striped her red face. Strands of her chestnut hair were matted to her forehead and she wiped them off with the back of her hand. There was something so broken in her stare—broken like Zoey. His over-used dick miraculously twitched again.

She sniffed and then nodded.

A heavy wave of satisfaction crashed over him. He collapsed and the next thing he knew, the room had filled with the gray light of dawn. He showered, and when he stepped out of the bathroom, Gwen was no longer in the bed. A page torn from her notebook lay in her place.

Finally.

She'd scribbled a portion of her translation, annotated with her notes. On the top it read, *I think you earned this.* He felt rather triumphant about his performance himself, but was too curious about the translation to dwell on it.

> The Day Walkers lived according to the ways of Dela-Malkh.
> (This is one name for the sun deity of the ancient Caucuses.)
> Their eyes shone with Dela-Malkh's light. (Look in the mirror.)
> When the Night Walkers came, they drank death. (Blood?)
> Dela-Malkh hated the Night Walkers. They drank the death
> of Dela-Malkh's people. They were unclean. (Death was
> considered unclean by many ancient cultures.)

> Dela-Malkh punished them with his flames and banished them
> to the darkness. But at Night they came to the Children
> of the Day. They brought shame on the Children with their
> teeth (fangs?) and their bodies. The Children of the Day were
> enslaved to the power of Night Walkers. The Day Walkers
> warned their children: Dela-Malkh will punish you.

> But the Night Walkers drank death and stole Dela-Malkh's
> light. The blood of the Children of the Day made them strong.
> Dela-Malkh lost his power over the Night Walkers. They could
> walk in the Day and the Night. (Do you suppose your blood
> has this power?)

The answer hardly mattered. The mere possibility would be Ethan's greatest weapon. First Marasović, then the whole world. Blood pumped oxygen into Ethan's brain so fast he became dizzy, could barely contain his excite—

A shrill scream rang out from downstairs. Gwen.

Was there an intruder? He rushed toward the sound of her wail.

In the far corner of the kitchen, she sat with her head folded over her splayed legs, sobbing onto the tile floor. She gripped the piece of paper where he'd scrawled a name—Mason Kearney.

He shook her, but she wouldn't speak. He slapped her. Still, she only gasped and returned to the hysterical keening. Like a sharp blade slicing through the chaos came the instinct to hit her, not out of anger, but because she needed it. He punched her, full on the mouth. She went rigid, and her eyes focused on him even as her hand pressed to her bleeding lip.

"Tell me," he demanded.

She held his gaze for a long second. "If we're getting on a plane, best not to batter my face."

In that moment, he understood her submission was not a weakness. It would be very difficult to bully the information from her. An interesting challenge. He took the paper with the vampire's name from her, folding it carefully and placing it next to his keys.

She was practically catatonic as they prepared for the trip and drove the rental car to the airport. In no time, they were airborne. Under the plane, a patchwork quilt of Midwestern states passed by, each one home to countless Hunters in search of vampires. Soon, those throngs of hateful humans would be Ethan's very own golden-eyed army, his to command.

Ethan grazed his thumb over Gwen's puffy lip, a split down its center freshly scabbed over. "You have a very pretty mouth."

She met his eye silently, her expression guarded. Who the hell was this Mason Kearney?

Her reaction did explain why she'd so easily accepted the existence of vampires—apparently, she knew one.

The flight attendant set complimentary champagne on their trays. Gwen flinched when she took a sip. The bubbles probably stung when they hit that sliver of raw flesh.

With the length of his finger, he caressed the back of her hand. "I will get this secret out of you. I'm very good at getting information."

"I have no doubt you are." She leaned closer to him, even though her tone was chilly.

He pretended to sip his champagne, hoping to encourage her to do the same. It might loosen her tongue.

"Do you know where he lives?"

Justine hadn't been able to turn up the slightest evidence of a Mason Kearney in legal records besides one who had died in an automobile accident in 1928. Probably the vampire—they were good at faking these things. But, still, Justine had found no address.

Inching even closer, Gwen whispered. "Are you going to kill him?"

"Eventually. First, I will get any information from him I can. He has a connection to my primary target."

Although there was no champagne in Gwen's intriguing little mouth, she swallowed. "How many of them are there?"

Them? Ah, she meant vampires. Ethan closed his eyes and estimated. "Thousands. Possibly millions, all over the world."

"Are they all like him?"

"I don't know, Gwen. You refuse to tell me anything about him." He dropped his voice so he could not be overheard. "But they are all evil parasites who enslave humans."

Her hand trembled, nearly spilling the wine. She steadied it, clasping the plastic cup with both hands. She gulped down the rest of the champagne, and her pink tongue came out to wipe at her cut.

His dick hardened instantly. What was it about her?

She looked into her empty cup. "He has a house in Pacific Heights."

"Can you find it?"

Her delicate white throat clenched again. "Yes."

"Are you willing to help me?"

That question earned him a direct look, the first one in hours. "Yes."

A plan took shape in his mind. "I'm going to station you outside his house, on a stakeout, of sorts. Anyone who comes or goes, I will need you to take note of them, and photos, if possible."

"All right."

She was finally being a good little girl. He surprised himself by bringing her hand to his mouth and kissing it. Her thin fingers squeezed around his and he felt almost protective. This Mason

Kearney had hurt her, perhaps had even given her a taste for being hurt. For that, Ethan was grateful. But anger pulsed somewhere deep inside him, in a place others referred to as their hearts — she was his to hurt, and his alone.

When they deplaned at San Francisco International Airport, Ethan's phone chimed with a text message.

Napalm in hand. We're gathering at HQ.

CHAPTER 14

Kos reclined in his chair, shaking his head at the way Zoey scraped the last of his poker chips into her lap and licked her lips like a cheetah finishing off a zebra carcass.

His phone rang, and Mason's name appeared on the screen. It was two thirty in the morning, but between vampires there was no such thing as too early or too late.

"What is up, man?" Mason drawled, the contemporary phrasing slightly at odds with his old-fashioned enunciation.

Mason would find the truth amusing, so Kos winked at Zoey and said, "Just lost my shirt in a game of poker."

"Strip poker?"

"No, just my metaphorical shirt." The image of Andre and Kos buck-naked and Zoey fully clothed came too easily to mind. No, he would never be foolish enough to accept that challenge. "Can I call you back from my office in a few minutes?"

"Sure."

As Kos ended the call, Andre took hold of Zoey's hand. He'd accepted her victory over him so gracefully, as if her ferocious sense of competition was so adorable that Andre himself no longer cared to win.

Kos scratched his chin. Did love change you like that? He stood and offered Zoey his hand. "Thanks for the company."

Andre rose too, and clasped Kos's palm firmly between both his hands. "Yes. We should get back in the routine. Cards clear my head like nothing else. Better even than—"

"How about tonight?" Zoey asked.

Suddenly modest, was she? No, her smirk suggested she was protecting Kos's propriety more than her own. Meanwhile, Andre glowered. Apparently he didn't mean to resume their old card playing routine quite so soon after bonding with her.

She leaned into his side and jutted her hip into him. "Don't pout. We can spend the afternoon together."

Her offer of another night of cards was generous and good-natured. All night, she'd perched in an armchair, legs folded underneath her. With her wide smile and heavy lidded eyes, she was a picture of contentment even as she talked smack about their poker games. Better yet, she'd been still and easy during their extended silences, a particular intimacy between Kos and Andre.

Kos liked her, and his father was as happy as he'd ever been, which made Kos's insides freeze up with cold dread. Perhaps when things went bad between Andre and Zoey, it would not be the kind of mutually assured destruction Mila had initiated. For all their sakes, Kos could hope.

Pretending to notice something on Andre's desk, Kos turned from the happy couple and straightened a stack of papers. "Let's play it by ear. I may go out on patrol with Bel's crew."

"Sounds good." Zoey nodded.

Passing through the musty cellar further dampened his mood. He was in a full-blown melancholy by the time he reached his office. At his desk, he kicked off his shoes and put his feet up.

Mason answered the call on the first ring. "Kos, buddy, good to hear your voice."

Kos feigned lightheartedness. "Same here. How've you been?"

"Great, just great. You?"

With a whistle, Kos let out a long breath. "To tell the truth, it's been a rough summer. Hunters found us."

"Seriously? Why haven't you fled?"

"It's a long story, but the gist is, we need to stay if possible. We had some help from my brother Bel to fend them off. They retreated, but we know they'll be back any day."

"I don't know what to say." Mason's voice pitched slightly higher. "It's terrible news."

"Yeah. But, I'm pleased about getting Lena out of here to safety."

"Good. Good. Are you holding up okay to the wasting disease?"

"Remarkably well." No sense getting into details about the wine that was keeping them healthy and tied to Kaštel. Mason was a San Francisco native; he wasn't wasting, so Blood Vine wouldn't help him anyway.

"So tell me about this Lena of yours, or is she Andre's?"

"Andre's." *Technically.* "She's amazing. The household loves her food. She's a knockout. An eleven, if you know what I mean."

"Big, little, fair, dark?"

"Blond, tall and lean, but with curves." Huge eyes, too clever and too blue to be doe-like, the sweetest smile, thoughtful. These attributes were probably not important to Mason, so Kos catalogued them silently.

"Why does she want to leave?"

The simplest explanation was best. "My dad's bonded now. He doesn't have sex with the householders. She wants the whole package."

"Sounds perfect. I'm happy to oblige."

Kos was certain about that, but he really didn't want to think about it. His heart lurched. Yeah, he really, really didn't. "I can bring her to your place. Are you still in Pacific Heights?"

"Same as always. Can you come on Friday?"

So soon. His heart stopped altogether. Yes. The sooner the better. He pounded on his chest to start the damn thing up again. "I'll check with her, but I think that should work."

"Kos, are Hunters watching you? No offense, but I don't want them to follow you here."

"Don't worry, I've thought of that. I'll have someone from Bel's crew follow us and check for a tail. If there's any sign we were followed, we'll leave Lena in a public place and you can pick her up once we're sure she's lost the tail."

Mason fell silent, and Kos could appreciate his caution.

Eventually the other vampire said, "That will work. But hopefully it won't come to plan B. It would be great to see you. We can reminisce about the good old days."

"Yeah, I'm looking forward to it. See you soon." Kos ended the call, fixating on the blank screen of his phone and remembering. For him, those good old days weren't any better than these days. Hearing Mason's voice brought back memories, but all the women and all the blood blurred together.

Then one unexpected memory leaped out. He'd gone into the living room of Mason's house one night to find a naked girl, pale as the moon and unconscious on the couch.

Kos had gone to her immediately. "What happened?"

Mason looked up from his newspaper. "I may have taken too much blood. Should I get her some orange juice?"

"She looks past juice." Kos noticed faint bruises on her wrists. Vampire saliva could heal an open wound, but not an internal bleed like a bruise. "Did you restrain her?"

"Relax, buddy. She's into that. She pretends she's afraid, I pretend I'm Dracula. That kind of shit."

Sure, some girls liked to role-play. But Kos could never get into scaring women—he'd sent more than one fetishist Mason's way. Damn it if San Francisco wasn't attracting a kinkier sort every day. He'd covered the girl with his coat and patted her cheek to rouse her. After a few seconds, her eyes fluttered open. The fear in them was unmistakable, though it passed quickly.

"Hey sweetheart," Mason called out. "Want some orange juice?"

"Yeah, with vodka, please." She set Kos's coat aside. Her voice was nothing like what he expected—sharper and older sounding that her frailness suggested. "Where are my clothes, anyway?"

Mason shouted to her from the kitchen. "On the stairs."

She padded into the hallway and bent over to pick up her blouse from the bottom stair, showing Kos the only part of her he hadn't yet seen. Her casual display burned a blush up his cheeks and over his scalp, and it persuaded him she was not in need of his protection.

And from whom, anyway? Mason wouldn't hurt her.

Shortly after that, he'd bought his cabin at the coast and given up his jaunts in San Francisco for a more settled existence.

Kos did look forward to seeing his old friend, but he wouldn't mind skipping the reminiscing. He opened his drawer of sticky notes and memo pads, quickly penning a message to Lena.

Does it suit you to leave Friday after sunset for your new position? In the meantime, please make yourself comfortable in my room. -Kos

He slid it under his door, and stood for a moment to listen to her sleep-steady breaths. Nothing on earth appealed more than slipping into his bed, curling around her, and holding her while she slept. His cock stirred, sending him a message—there was *one* thing even more appealing.

The thought of another cold shower made his skin sting. He would get some work done in the office and then spend the day bottling Blood Vine with Andre and Pedro. He could use the distraction.

Hours later, he had to admit that bottling wine was even better than playing cards. He didn't have to place bets, had nothing to lose. His consciousness could recede, and his mind could unravel itself, processing the things human brains did while sleeping. He rolled one bottle at a time through the manual labeler, a task more blessedly mindless than a game of Uno.

Bottling didn't seem to work so well for Pedro.

His job required him to shoot each bottle full of nitrogen gas and place it on the turret, which rotated bottles toward Andre as they filled with wine. Once they were full, Andre placed them under the corker.

"Turn the speed up, or this will take all day," Pedro said, shifting his weight from one foot to the other.

"If it goes faster, the bottles will not be full when they reach me," Andre replied.

"Let me see." Pedro cranked the dial without waiting for Andre's agreement.

The bottles circled the turret more quickly.

"*Davo*, Pedro. Look. Now you have disrupted the rhythm. These bottles are only three-quarters full. We have to start over."

"Andre, we can do this so much faster, just push the corks in with your thumb."

"The equipment is made for humans. We must be patient. Relax."

Pedro blew out an exasperated breath. "Kos, can I borrow a book to read over here while grandpa takes his time filling the bottles?"

From the sidelines, Kos chuckled. "Turn on some music."

"Already tried that. Andre hates music."

"Do not be absurd." Andre flipped the switch and the turret came to a stop. "No one hates music. I just hate that garbage you call music. Kos, you tell him."

Although Kos didn't care much for Pedro's electronic dance music, he wasn't going to take Andre's side. "It's nothing personal. The only music Andre finds acceptable is Balkan choral music."

"Fine. Turn that on. Anything is better than the squeal of this machine and having to listen to you two."

"Exactly what has crawled up your ass, son?" Andre asked.

"More like, 'whose ass didn't I get to crawl up,'" Pedro muttered, taking an iPod from Kos's outstretched hand.

Kos and Andre exchanged a silent glance. Andre's lips were pressed into a tight smile, trying not to let Pedro on to his amusement. Kos plastered his palm over his own mouth to reinforce Andre's efforts.

A woman's bright soprano suddenly filled the workspace, followed by two alto voices carrying the haunting Balkan harmonies. Kos didn't trouble himself with the words: he simply let the music carry him home to Šolta.

The complex rhythm of the music paced everyone's efforts, and Kos's heart beat in time. He placed a full bottle of Blood Vine in a labeling machine and cranked the handle, rolling Zoey's painfully nostalgic label into place. His limbs felt heavy with the gravity of the job. It was humbling to think of what they'd lost when they left home, and what they'd gained with Blood Vine. The deadening ache in his heart over Lena was minor in comparison to the need of all those vampires still wasting away. He tried to ignore it, and take his responsibilities seriously.

He held each bottle reverently, sending up a silent prayer that it would reach their friends safely and bring them health.

When he'd turned the labels onto another dozen bottles and placed them into a case, he carried them into the loading bay. Tomorrow night, they would deliver a thousand cases of Blood Vine to their distributor, and within a week, it would be on the shelves of wine shops and high-end grocers all over the country.

"To the homeland, my friends, and to your health," he whispered as he set another case into the truck.

His chest still ached. His heart was not getting the message that other things were more important than his crush on a human. But it would, eventually.

CHAPTER 15

Lena squeezed her eyes closed. She wasn't ready to open them. Unlike yesterday, Kos wouldn't be watching her wake. She'd dreamed about the little blond boy again. What was her subconscious trying to tell her, anyway? That all her longings could never come true? No kidding. Vampire babies were pretty much like flying pigs.

But this morning of all mornings, the dream was a sharp betrayal by her own mind, reminding her she could not have the thing she wanted most—Kos.

Even worse, her head hurt, probably from the three fingers of brandy she'd drunk to get to sleep. Thanks to Zoey, she'd discovered its medicinal benefits. It worked well, inducing two minutes of pain free, crystal clear thinking, followed by a sleep so deep she had drool in her ear.

She wiped at her damp lobe, rubbed her eyes, and managed to open them onto the sunny room. Kos's chair was empty, the two fat Russian novels in his place. She sympathized with the vacant piece of furniture—she was empty too.

The best cure for heartache was hard work. It had gotten her through years at Kaštel and it would see her steady to the end. She headed for the bathroom until she saw a note that had been slid under the door.

Leaving Friday.

The party was scheduled for Saturday, which left three full days to prepare. If Susan or Zoey could warm food and do the finishing touches, then yes, she could have everything ready in time to leave on Friday. Except the truffles—no way to do that dish ahead of time. She would nix those and cancel her order first thing.

Good. Friday was soon. The sooner she left Kaštel, the sooner she could get over Kos.

Under the hot water of the shower, she made mental lists of what to do and the fog of her sadness lifted. It was almost seven when she got to the kitchen. She laid out breakfast in the dining room, and then closed off her domain with signs that said, "Keep out." Maybe she should add a happy face to each sign? *Nope.* She didn't give a flip if she sounded rude; she wanted zero distractions, and she really did not want to see Kos.

She cooked all morning, forgetting to eat or drink until her headache started up, demanding a full meal and caffeine, pronto.

Out of habit, her hand slid to open the knick-knack drawer. Inside was *New and Selected Poems.* She didn't need to take it out to remember the poem by heart. Every time she pictured the little boy pattering across a hardwood floor to his parents' bed, it was the boy from her dream—the one who had Kos's eyes.

Palm on the cover of the book, she whispered a prayer to whomever was out there listening. *Please lead me to my destiny, whatever it is.*

As evening approached, she cleaned the kitchen. She opened the dishwasher and grabbed two plates. Turning toward the cabinet, she jumped to find Zoey perched on one of the stools at the high counter.

"How long have you been there?"

"Not long."

Lena's heart raced. Inhaling, she placed her palm on her chest and waited for her pulse to slow. "It freaks me out that you move like them, all fast and silent."

"I know. I love it." Zoey shrugged, not even a shred of guilt on her content face.

Lena laughed for the first time all day.

"Kos said if it's okay with you, he'll take you to San Francisco on Friday."

Tension squeezed Lena's spine. With her stiff back to Zoey, she laid the plates on their shelf. "That's fine. But please tell him for me. I'd rather not see him."

"Are you angry?" Zoey's tone was perfectly neutral, which meant she was using her supernatural strength to suppress her nosiness, or at least keep it out of her voice.

Lena faced her, leaning a hip into the countertop and tucking a loose lock of hair behind her ear. "How can I be angry? He's been kind, and respectful, and honest."

Zoey turned up her palms, betraying her frustration. "Then what's the problem? Why don't you just—"

"Because, I don't want to." The emptiness came back, making her feel queasy. She shelved some coffee mugs, nesting their handles carefully so they'd all fit in the cabinet.

"Has he told you much about Mason?"

Mugs clanged together, jarring Lena. She unclenched her teeth to say, "He told me a little. I guess he's handsome, women like him. Kos says it's a good match."

Water had pooled in the mug's pedestal, and she dried it with a dishtowel.

"So you've been waiting your whole life to do the blood-sex thing and you're going to give it up to a stranger?"

"Yeah, if he wants me. Nobody around here does." She showed no mercy to the water spots on the mug, her damp towel squeaking against the glass.

"Kos wants you, Lena."

"But not for keeps." She sucked her lower lip into her mouth, embarrassed to pout in front of Zoey.

"Which do you want? Keeps, or blood and sex?"

Urgh! Okay, so maybe Lena was a little angry. She wanted to hurl the mug onto the tile floor and watch it shatter. Maybe it would crack the tile too, and she would know she'd left her mark somewhere at Kaštel. Instead, she clenched it tightly with both hands to resist the urge.

"Zoey, if I knew the answer to that question, I could decide between a vampire life or human life. But it wouldn't do shit to help my broken heart."

"Heart?" Zoey's mouth fell open, making her look like Lena had just stripped off her clothes and danced a naked Irish jig in the middle of the kitchen.

For no clear reason, she found Zoey's surprise satisfying. "Yeah. Heart."

Lena set the mug onto the countertop with extreme care, proud it was still whole, unbroken. If only she could get out of Kaštel equally intact. She walked out of the kitchen without saying goodbye to her friend.

Exhausted from her work in the kitchen, Lena pressed her forehead against the window in Kos's room and admired the view. The sinking sun washed the sky pink over the brilliant green vineyards. She wouldn't miss Kaštel, but she might miss the breathtaking hillsides, the sunny weather, her friends, Zoey, Kos...

No, she wouldn't miss Kaštel at all.

She wiped at a smoky smudge on the window. It didn't come off. It wasn't a smudge. A thin line of smoke snaked upward off a nearby hillside.

Oh God. A fire.

The coil of smoke grew thicker from the heart of the vineyard.

Trys first, or Kos? Trys could extend the shield. "Trys! Kos! Fire! Fire!" She dashed from the room yelling louder than she thought possible.

She was at the top of the cellar steps in search of Kos when Trys called from the dining room's doorway. "Where?"

"The vines are on fire! Look out the window."

Trys pivoted to face the flames. "Shit."

The doorknob in Lena's hand jerked suddenly, and she scurried back to get clear as Kos and Andre barreled through.

"Where's the fire?" Andre barked. Raw, wild emotion played on his face.

Lena's voice came out a strained whisper. "It's the vines."

"Trys!" Andre bellowed.

"On it," the witch called out. "Feed me."

"I'll get the ice cream," Lena exclaimed, glad to have a job.

Andre and Kos pushed passed her toward the dining room.

In the kitchen, she tucked a scoop and a spoon into her back pockets, hefted the five-gallon container of Deep Dark Chocolate

Secret onto her hip, and balanced a bowl on top. She hurried into the dining room, where Andre, Zoey, Kos and Pedro stood in a line, their faces plastered to the windows. The sky faded from pink to gray. Lena scooped the ice cream and set a bowl in front of Trys, who had gone pale with effort. Eyes closed tight and hands fisted, the witch sat ramrod straight at the table. Lena set the bowl in front of her.

Trys's eyes popped open. "Feed it to me."

Lena scraped a mouthful of ice cream and held it up to the witch's tense mouth. "Is the shield...?"

"Up," Trys replied in between swallows. "Vania and Arden are out there with fire extinguishers."

Lena stole glances out the window, trying to see how much of the vineyard had burned, all the while continuing to spoon calories into the witch's mouth.

The vampires remained speechless.

Trys licked her lips. "Lena, the shield is ten times bigger than it was. That means—"

"Ten times the ice cream. Got it."

"I'll need more than ice cream." She opened her mouth for another spoonful and swallowed it in a quick gulp. "High-protein, high-calorie foods. Peanut butter, eggs, those shakes old folks drink. Non-stop. Understand? My mouth must be full all the time."

"I'll take care of it," Lena said. It was one more thing she could do before she left, and it might just save them all. For a while, at least.

Minutes passed in pregnant silence interrupted only by the spoon scraping the ceramic bowl.

A door slammed downstairs. Moments later, a soot-smudged and sweaty Vania walked in. "Fire's out."

"Tell me," Andre demanded.

"Coulda been worse."

He nodded. "I want to see."

Only then did Zoey turn away from the window. "I'm going with you." Andre pulled her to his side tightly, and Lena's stomach sank. She wanted someone to hold her like that, to reassure her.

The muscles of Andre's jaw rippled when he unclenched them to speak again. "Vania, if the fire department arrives, please deal with them."

"One of my specialties," she agreed.

The sky had darkened to near dusk. A few more minutes yet before it would be safe for him to go out.

The windows lit up with a flash of light and everyone jumped.

"Damn it. They've got those damn Molotov cocktails again. And flame throwers this time too. But they weren't expecting the shield." Vania hopped onto the table, and ruffled the witch's hair short brown hair. "Amazing, Trys! Your biggest by far."

Haggard and wan, her face appeared ten years older than when Lena told her about the fire only minutes earlier. She barely acknowledged the compliment.

Zoey pressed both her palms against the window. "Why aren't they retreating?"

"They've got all their guns and nothing to do with them, I suspect." Vania ran her finger along the inside of the ice cream bowl and licked it. Lena envied her ability to remain casual.

The last hint of pink turned to twilight in the sky.

Kos moved to the door in a flash. "Let's go."

"I'm going too." Lena handed Trys's spoon to Vania.

"Like hell." Instantly, Kos hovered over her like he'd been there all along.

He was just being overprotective.

"Back off," she whispered and followed the vampires outside. The smoky smell of burning wood and gasoline hung heavy in the air. They moved quickly in the narrow aisles between two trellised grapevines. Lena jogged to keep up, holding her hands in front of her so the stray tendrils of vine didn't lash her face. After a few minutes, they reached a charred swath of earth the size of a basketball court. The fire had left nothing but black sticks straining to reach the trellises.

Lena bent to examine a burnt stub of vine. Movement in the corner of her eye grabbed her attention. Zoey raised her arm, pointing up the hill at a group of Hunters, who stood within throwing distance on the other side of the invisible shield. A crouched man aimed something that looked like a skinny cannon right at the group, and Lena found herself wrapped in Kos's arms without knowing who had gone to whom. She buried her face in his chest as a grenade launched from the weapon and exploded against the shield above them, flashing like lightning and shaking the ground.

Pedro sprinted toward the men, but before he took three steps Andre had both his shoulders in what looked like a painful grip. Lena barely heard his growl.

"On the other side of that shield, a flamethrower is as good as the sun to you."

Pedro acquiesced, dropping into a crouch.

Zoey crossed her arms and called out. "Hello, Ethan."

"Zoey. And my old friend Pedro." Ethan offered a mocking salute. "Marasović, how nice to meet you face to face. And I assume this is your son. Who is his lovely friend?"

"Ethan, why don't you give up this and go home?" Zoey's voice did not waver, but exhaustion deepened its pitch. "No one's getting hurt in this household, and no one is here against their will."

The Hunter squared his lean hips at Zoey. Lena had to admit he was handsome, and powerfully built, for a human.

But he spoke like a real blowhard. "That is not an option. It is our solemn duty to exterminate the vampires and their household. However, Zoey, my men know you are special to me. They know you are an innocent victim of Marasović. We will offer you safety and protection from him, should you decide to leave."

Andre snorted, and in that moment, Lena almost liked him and his cocky assurance that Zoey had chosen him over the human.

She crossed her arms over her chest. "This is my home now, and the shield isn't coming down."

"I do miss your willfulness." Ethan's cruelly playful tone turned Lena's spine to ice. Men shouldn't talk that way to women. Ever.

Kos must have felt her shudder; he pulled her closer.

"Fuck off, Ethan." Zoey spun, striding toward the house, and the Maras household followed her.

Even though they were once again under siege, energy prickled from her nape to her shoulders, where she imagined the gaze of the Hunters. Turning her back on her enemies was a new kind of power, far better than waving her middle fingers at the creeps would have been. Her lips curved into a private smile.

The last of the group, she shuffled into the kitchen next to Kos. He took hold of her arm and raised his voice, calling everyone to attention. "We owe Lena our thanks. She spotted the fire and acted fast. Your quick thinking saved the vineyards."

"Kos is right." Andre stepped toward her and extended his hand. "Thank you. Just as with your pantry, you have proven yourself invaluable to our safety and wellbeing."

The praise glanced off her. It was too little too late. But the proud shine in Kos's eyes — that she could accept. She bowed her head at him. His face reddened and he looked away.

"Speaking of which," Lena said. "I need to make arrangements for Trys. I'll prepare food for her, but given what she told me about her energy needs, you may need to get her an IV. I don't think it's possible for a human to eat as much as she says she needs." She glanced between Zoey and Kos, unsure which of them would become responsible for these things that Andre couldn't be bothered with. Both of them nodded, so she continued. "And take care of her. The shield is a huge strain."

One by one, they filed out of the kitchen. Lena cooked until she could barely stand on her feet. By the time she crawled into bed, she had no trouble falling asleep and no need of brandy.

Lena tried to cling to the diaphanous threads of her dream, knowing that, when they slipped through her fingers, the soft, warm, sweet smelling baby would also be gone. She loved him as deeply as she imagined a mother loved her child. And then he was gone, his round face vanishing in the gray morning light.

The sharp ache in her breast turned the pleasant fantasy into a nightmare.

She shook it off. *Keep busy. Only one more day. Prepare for the party. Don't stop to think!*

She poured her energy into work stuffing peppers, cleaning sardines and dressing them with olive oil, laying flat breads on the countertop to cool.

Finally, she surveyed the food, ready to declare victory. She'd accomplished the work of two chefs. But her head swam. She'd forgotten to eat, so she tried some of the dishes she had made. Everything was good and the peppers were sweet and savory and absolutely delicious.

Last on her to do list — desert.

It was the baklava that did it.

How could she not imagine Kos as a boy, licking his fingers? When she drizzled the sweet-smelling liquid all over the flaky, still-hot pastry, his words came back to her. *You taste just like honey.* Her blood heated and rushed between her legs, where she began to throb.

Tomorrow she was going to give herself to a stranger.

Maybe Kos *should* be her first instead. At least she could have him once. He would give her what she'd been waiting for all these years, if she could put aside her sense of rejection long enough to enjoy him for one night.

Afterwards, leaving would be more painful.

But moisture had already pooled in her panties and there was no sense arguing with her body. If he would still have her, then she would give herself to him before she left. The work was done. She would spend her last night at Kaštel with Kos.

She was a wreck—work jeans covered in flour, a dish towel tucked into her back pocket, smelly clogs made for standing all day, a tank top splattered with tomato sauce. It was probably in her hair too.

A shower first, and then she would find him. She opened the kitchen door and took down the *Keep Out* sign. When she turned around, he was there. Her hand flew to her hair and she frowned. She'd wanted to be dressed for seduction.

He mirrored her expression, concerned. "What's wrong?"

Stepping close, she wrapped her arms around his neck and brushed his lips with hers. He stiffened, so she let her tongue slip along his closed mouth. He groaned.

"Lena…"

Oh God. What if he said no?

She deepened the kiss to head off a rejection. He grew hard against her belly—a good sign.

Then he pulled back. "Sweetheart, I love kissing you, but you said you didn't want this."

"I changed my mind."

He looked at her expectantly. Darn. She would have to say more, even if she couldn't tell him everything. Hoping for some privacy, she pulled him into the kitchen.

"I want it to be you."

"What?"

"My first time sharing sex and blood."

"Lena, Mason will—"

"I want it to be you."

He smoothed hair off her forehead and then cupped her cheek in his palm. "Won't that make it harder for you? *Krist*, Lena, it will make it harder for me."

His eyes were sad and gray, his mouth stretched into a tight grimace. She hadn't expected him to be conflicted.

"Yes, it will make it harder for me. But, it also means I'm giving myself to you for the first time, not a stranger."

His eyes dilated and he pulled her closer. She'd hit the right note. He was nothing if not protective.

He whispered in her ear. "How can I argue with that?"

Unadulterated joy barreled through her, followed by a wave of grief. But when the bliss passed, she held the smile on her face. He mirrored it, like he had her frown. He was radiantly beautiful, eyes crinkling at the edges, full lips stretching wide, and sexy dimples deepening. To have him look at her like that, even for just a little while, was worth almost anything.

"Let me go upstairs and clean up. Give me fifteen minutes?"

"I'm not letting you out of my sight. I'll clean you up."

She should have been embarrassed, but his offer sent tingles up her legs.

He picked her up and cradled her to him, carrying her to his room. Inside the door, he pressed the lock and slid into the bathroom. Moments later, the shower pounded water into the tub. She flipped on a lamp beside the bed and its warm light glowed like a flame on the crimson quilt. Back at her side in no time, he pulled her tank top over her head and lowered his eyes to her chest. She wore a functional pink bra, and under his electric blue gaze her nipples hardened.

He stroked the side of her breast. "You are too beautiful for words. If I undress you and bathe you, this will be over in the bathtub in two minutes flat." He licked his lips. "You deserve better."

Her skin heated with a blush. This was why she loved him—with Kos, she could believe she was special.

He handed her the fluffy pink bathrobe she'd left on the bed. "I'll wait out here."

She tiptoed into the bathroom and undressed. Her hair wasn't too bad, so she swept it into a twist—taking time with the blow dryer would probably kill them both. Under the hot water, she rinsed off the kitchen grime. Beginning with her feet, she lathered herself and imagined what was coming. Would he bite her first? Could she take him in her mouth again? That had been an unexpected pleasure. But, for this to work the way she wanted it to, she would have to time everything just right.

She soaped between her legs and remembered his mouth on her. And like that she was ready for him. Her soapy hands raced across the rest of her body. She rinsed and dried off in a flurry of motion, into the bathrobe and out of the bathroom in seconds. She was breathless when she came to stand in front of him.

He was in the armchair. *The Brothers Karamazov* was open and face down on his knee. If her time in the shower had increased her urgency, he'd used it to get his under control. His stare was not exactly predatory, but it left no doubt he intended to devour her. Desire flooded her body.

His nostrils flared. "I can smell you."

"I know." And knowing made her even wetter.

"Come here."

She took a step toward him, and he untied the sash of her robe. It fell open and slid off her shoulders, then dropped to the floor.

Pulse racing, she asked, "Aren't you—" Her throat hitched, and she had to swallow twice to moisten it. "Aren't you going to take your clothes off?"

"Soon. I just want to look at you."

And he did. After long minutes, he stood up and walked behind her. She wanted to turn around so that she could keep him in her sight, but when she shifted her weight, he said, "Stay where you are, beautiful. I want to see all of you."

Occasionally, the sole of his shoe quietly rubbed on the hardwood floor, signaling his movement. In that stretch of time under his gaze, she realized most men would have asked her to turn around, but he circled her like she was a fine sculpture to be admired.

The sound of rustling fabric hinted he was undressing. She swallowed and clenched her fists, summoning a hefty dose of will power to keep from turning around. He stepped against her, and all at once, his hands were lightly gripping her shoulders, his erection bumped against the small of her back, and he ran his lips along the nape of her neck. In her haste, she'd left her hair up, and now she was glad.

With one arm around her waist, he pulled her flush against him and whispered. "I promise to savor you slowly, even if it takes every ounce of self control I possess. I'll do this right."

Kos was going bite her, and make love to her. It was really happening—after all those years of longing.

She turned and laced her arms around his neck, pressing her body into him. He sucked in his breath and she seized the moment to kiss him, trying to communicate her gratitude and her desire.

Then the urge to see him won and she broke the kiss, stepping back. He grunted at the separation. The sound gave her goose bumps. To be wanted—even if only for a little while—meant everything.

Smiling, she straightened her spine. "I'm going to look at you now."

He clasped his hands behind his back and flashed her a wicked smile.

Her gaze moved down his body quickly. His erect penis jumped like it could feel her gaze and she laughed. She'd never seen anything like that. More slowly, she took in his appearance from the bottom up. Muscular calves and thighs, dusted with dark gold hair. That impressive erection centered between lean hips. His abdomen was a feast of rippling muscle and without thinking she reached out to feather her fingers along his stomach.

"You look like you do sit-ups all night instead of reading."

He turned his palms up. "It's the Blood Vine. It's turning me into a beefcake."

"You weren't exactly chopped liver before," she scolded.

"I'm lucky that being a vampire makes it easy for bookworms to maintain our muscle tone."

"Uh huh, and the work you do in the vineyards has nothing to do with it?"

He shrugged, clearly uncomfortable with the praise.

What could a woman say to admire a man as beautiful as him? She would have to show him instead. Her fingers itched to touch, so she placed her palms open on his chest and drew her hips against him. She kissed his collarbone and when she darted her tongue out to trail it along his skin, his cock leaped again where it was pressed between them.

It demanded attention, and she giggled, reaching for it. When she took him in her hand, she tilted her face to find him watching her with a curious expression. "What?"

"Sweetheart, you know how to make a man feel special."

"What do you mean?"

He hooked a finger under her chin. "It's hard to describe...but there's something innocent about you. You make me feel like it's my first time."

From her cheeks to the tips of her breasts, she heated, blushing at the compliment. But it was a little too close to home. She had to act quickly. "Kos, will you bite me?"

Kos's fangs responded to her request, dropping rapidly. Damn, she was killing him with her wide eyes and giggles.

Some animal voice inside him said, *Oh yeah, give her what she wants.*

Her vulnerability spoke directly to that hungry animal, and the way she'd put herself in his hands stirred his primal instincts. He wanted to growl out a promise to protect her and please her.

Under the fair skin of her neck, a blue vein pulsed. Saliva filled his mouth and he imagined biting her. Her first time sharing her blood during sex — he felt like he was claiming her, marking her as his. Of course, he wasn't and he couldn't. But his fangs were ready to go.

Oh fuck. His fangs.

Was he hungry for her? He knew the smell of her blood, if not the taste. Was this desire intense enough to bind her to him? He ran his tongue over his long canines, smelling the salt of her blood and the honey of her arousal.

It was a heady scent, but it wasn't making him hungry for her blood so much as her body. At least he didn't think so. He wanted to be certain, so he bought himself some time.

"No biting yet, sweetheart. I'm just getting started."

He lowered his head to her chest. When her robe fell open, he knew that he'd never seen a more beautiful pair of breasts in all one hundred and eighty years of his life, but to say so would have been…well, she wouldn't have believed him. He determined to show her instead. Lightly, he licked every inch of her, tasting the shape of her curves.

She shivered. "Kos, stop, that tickles."

Then he suckled at her breasts, drawing hard on them like a hungry baby. She moaned and pushed her hips toward him.

"Like that, do you?"

She whimpered. "More."

He'd never heard a sweeter word, and a laugh welled up in his gut. "Gladly." First he picked her up and laid her down on the bed. Stretching himself alongside her, he returned his attention to her other breast, mouth open wide, his fangs grazing her nipple. No urge to bite—good, he wouldn't bond to her.

He slipped his open palm down her belly and her legs fell open at the barest hint of a caress. He ignored the hint and, teasing her, stroked up from her knee. Her thighs were slick with arousal and she squirmed, trying to find more contact. What had he done to deserve her desire? She was more than any male could ask for. He ran his fingers through her slick folds.

"Remember, no fingers inside me. I want all of you at once."

Krist. She was wanton and wide-eyed at the same time—one of a kind. "Then let me bite you, get you good and ready."

What position would she like best? He could kneel over her, spoon behind her. But he was nervous to push into her without testing the waters. Usually, his lovers appreciated his efforts to get them open and ready. Since she didn't want that, he would give her all the control.

"Lena, climb on top of me." He rolled onto his back and pulled one of her legs over him. "Like this."

She followed his instructions, straddling his torso, her core hot and wet against his belly. He closed his eyes, savoring the contact, then gazed at her. She'd been watching him with a sad look, but smiled when he caught her.

"Hey. What's the matter?"

"I was just thinking this is our goodbye."

The words reached right into his lungs and stole his breath. Without thinking, he said, "I'll miss you."

Tears shimmered in her eyes.

Why couldn't he keep his mouth shut? He didn't want her asking to stay again. Not now, when he might just decide to keep her.

But she didn't. She simply smiled at him with a heartbreaking mixture of affection and longing. He should have known; she'd done her begging already. She wouldn't humiliate herself again. Especially not now.

"Lena, I want you on top of me like this. So when you're ready, you can control things — how fast, how hard, how deep."

She nodded, cupping his face with her palm. The tenderness pierced him, and he had to look away.

He ran his hands up her arms and pulled her shoulders close to him so they were nearly chest to chest. On the side of her neck, he found that small blue vein under her skin. To drag things out for her pleasure, he didn't need a main line but a low flow he could sip from for hours. He licked and then sucked her skin into his mouth, drawing the vein closer to the surface and finding its exact location with his tongue. Carefully, his aim true, he slid his fangs through her flesh into the narrow vein.

He took a pull of her blood. Warm, metallic, salty, and underneath all that, the sweet honey taste that was just her. He groaned.

She released the breath she'd been holding and arched her back up. Then she inhaled deeply and rubbed her whole body against him. He thought of a kitten burrowing for warmth. She braced her arms alongside his head, supporting her weight as she leaned forward to give him access to her neck. The weight of her breasts, the silk of her skin — she surrounded him, flooding his senses. If only it could last forever. He reined in that emotion before he reached to find her wet center, making circles around her opening with his fingertips.

Her throaty whisper tickled his ear. "Give me your fingers to suck." She bit down gently and ran her tongue along the tips over and over again. "This is so different than with Andre," she murmured breathily.

He didn't break his suction on her vein, but his chest vibrated with a silent laugh.

"Skin against skin, and the way you're…" she panted "…touching me. I feel everything a thousand times more…"

He took it as an invitation, remembering exactly where she was most sensitive. After another draw of her blood, he found the bud with his fingers and gently circled.

It was her turn to groan. "Oh my God."

Somehow he knew if he could see her face her eyes would not be closed, but wide with pleasure. She lifted her hips and trapped his cock between them, slipping and sliding along his length, torturing them both.

The feeling of her, so soft and slick, up and down his length—it was too much. He broke the suction and licked her wounds closed. He whispered against her neck. "Are you ready, sweetheart?"

She raised herself to look at him. "I'm ready."

His cock pointed straight up, desperate for her. Very slowly, she lowered herself onto him. Amazing. The softest, tightest thing he had ever felt. Did she know she felt so good?

She studied his face intently. For what?

And then everything happened too fast. He bumped against the unexpected barrier. She slammed herself down, forcing him through it. Lena let out a cry and her muscles clenched, trying to push him out.

Slow motion. His body frozen, his mind racing. Everything suddenly made sense, and nothing made sense at all. Her innocence wasn't an act—

She had given herself to him without any expectations.

What a gift. If she had offered, he would have refused. But this was right—better him than Mason.

He shook his head, coming back to the moment. Above him was an angel desperately in need of his love.

Her tears, which had only just shimmered, now spilled. "I'm sorry I didn't tell you." Her voice was a reedy sob and he knew she was in pain.

"Shh, shh." He wiped her tears. "How bad are you hurting?"

"Not too bad."

"If I bite you again, it will help you relax, help you feel good again."

"I don't think I need that. It's getting better already."

He looked down at where they were joined, the lips of her sex spread around him, a rusty hint of blood ringing the base of his cock. His primal need to possess and please was awakened again. She'd made herself his.

Of the thousands of women he had taken to bed, none had ever mattered as much as her.

"Let me touch you." He reached again for the sensitive spot above where they were joined and stroked her, watching her face and gauging the tension of the muscles wrapped around him. At first she was very still, then she wriggled, little by little. Slowly, the vise around him eased. He almost missed the tightness, but it would return when he built her up again for a climax.

As he caressed her, Lena began to rock, finding the spots inside herself that pleased her. He gazed at her face as the new sensations played through her body. Too beautiful. It almost hurt to look at her.

Then she let out a frustrated sigh.

"All right, sweetheart?"

Eyes squeezed shut, she put her hand on his, trying to show him how she wanted him to stroke her.

He could admit it. "Lena, sweetheart, you can do it better yourself."

Her eyes flew open and flashed dark with desire — he'd shocked her. He gritted his teeth to keep his control.

"Let me watch you," he growled.

Obeying, she found a rhythm to her grind. She bloomed around him, opening, moistening, slipping down his cock further until he was all the way inside her. Her walls pulsed around him and she opened her eyes in a question.

"Yes, now you're ready."

He rolled her so fast the bed creaked. She pressed her palm to her forehead, disoriented, her eyes heavy lidded. She kept getting more and more beautiful. Finally, she smiled. "Are you going to make love to me now?"

"What did you think I was doing before?"

Her grin widened. "I was doing all the work."

"So you were. Yes, it's my turn now."

He slid into her easily, though she was still tight and new and so fucking soft. She found the angle she wanted and matched his thrusts. Her pure, raw passion…he'd never experienced anything like it, like being inside her as she learned her own pleasure, never seen anything as beautiful as the wonder that played over her face again and again. Finally, it all got to him — the taste of her blood on his tongue, the feel of her untouched body around him.

"Lena, you feel too good, I can't hold back anymore. I know you're not finished. I promise we'll keep going."

She opened her eyes and gave him a look of unbridled love. *Krist.* No one had ever looked at him like that. *Ever.* He exploded inside her.

"Oh my God," she said and wrapped her legs around his hips, drawing him even closer. Then she spasmed around him, ready after all.

Her breaths were staccato, and he continued to move rhythmically as she came, slamming her against the mattress over and over again. She remained quiet as her orgasm unfolded, the powerful contractions milking his last drops of pleasure. He hoped she was satisfied when, with her hands on his shoulders, she stilled him. And then she laughed, a deep, musical laugh he'd never heard from her before.

The sound of her contentment. He could listen to it all night.

Seconds or hours later, she spoke. "Kos, how can I ever thank you?"

Balanced on his elbows, he looked down at her. "I'm the one who will do the thanking."

She placed her palm flat over his heart. "I'm sorry I didn't tell you. I hated being sneaky."

"Shh. No apologies. Let me hold you." Within minutes she was asleep in his arms.

CHAPTER 16

The pleasure that had rocked Lucas when Pedro's fangs had first slipped into his neck—it had been a shock, an earth-quaking, life altering shock. A week later, he still hadn't quite made sense of it. Hunters didn't know about the ecstasy of a vampire's bite, and they didn't understand why humans submitted to it so greedily.

Pedro's bite was officially better than a blowjob, but a bite-plus-blowjob was the very best. Naked on his bed, Lucas lay back against the headboard and stared at a blank stretch of wall. Pedro cupped his balls and ran his thumb up the underside of his cock as he drew blood from an artery in Lucas's thigh.

Lucas sucked on a piece of sour lemon candy because the vampire bite made him desperate for something in his mouth to lick and taste, like the old days when he'd enjoyed taking Ecstasy. Earlier, Pedro had looked at him under heavy lids, sheepishly placing the offering of the candy in his palm. Now its sweet tartness was an ecstasy in and of itself. Lucas's skin was on fire and the ceiling fan blew cool air all over him like a cute cabana boy with a palm frond.

Pedro took a deep pull of blood and Lucas's skin tingled along its path. All the way from his fingers and toes, the tingle headed toward his cock, which twitched. Pedro sucked again, probably trying to get the same reaction. He did. With his tongue, Lucas flattened the candy to the roof of his mouth and smiled at the ceiling. The vampire groaned into his thigh—a deep, sexy sound. Then Pedro's tongue circled the puncture wounds and swept over them to seal them.

Fucking vampire super speed—before he knew it, Pedro had taken his cock deep into his throat, sucking it up and down with the same powerful draw he had used to swallow the blood.

Damn. If there could be no fucking, a hoover job like this was an excellent consolation prize. Pedro found a sensitive spot behind his cock and pressed it rhythmically. The tension built and built—it was in his balls, and higher, deeper, more intense. Pedro kept up the sucking and the pressing.

"Oh, fuck yes," Lucas said, and then he came, shuddering. Pedro drew every last drop from him. His mind blurred until all thoughts disappeared, and there was only the sound of rapid breaths—his or Pedro's, he wasn't sure.

After some timeless stretch, Pedro released Lucas's cock and wiped his mouth with the back of his hand.

Suddenly, Lucas worried for him. "It's not blood. Will it make you sick?"

"Don't know." Pedro pushed his hair out of his face and grimaced. "I'll find out soon enough. Besides, I'm not about to ask the Maras boys."

"Oh they have to know. In their long lives, surely some lady vamp has…swallowed." Lucas took Pedro's hand. "God knows I'd do either one of them."

Pedro laughed. "All three you mean. Yeah, they are very doable, but don't let Kos hear you talk like that. He gets squirrelly at the thought of a dude admiring his ass."

Lucas looked down at Pedro's cock, firm and proud, but not frighteningly tumescent the way it had been. It was a nice cock and he wanted to suck it again. He reached for Pedro and kissed him, tasting himself in the other man's mouth. He had always loved that—but the dark taste of both blood and cum was somehow even more erotic.

"Your turn." He wrapped his hand around Pedro's erection and shifted lower to face his groin.

"How about a hand job, instead?"

Lucas withdrew quickly. "Really?"

"Yeah, tell me a dirty story while you touch me. Tell me about the first time you fucked a guy."

Lucas laughed, but Pedro was serious. "Why?"

"I don't know. I want to see your face. I want to know more about you."

Lucas's heart thudded. *Crap.*

It was really, really not good to get all sentimental with his vampire almost-fuck-buddy. Sex and friendship were the most he could afford, and probably not even those. Pedro placed his hand on Lucas's chest, must have heard the flutter there. His yellow gaze locked onto Lucas.

It never stopped being weird to see his own eyes staring back at him.

Pedro took his hand. "Why do Hunters hate vampires?"

Where did that question come from?

"We always have."

"But why? Don't you have some history, some reason? Otherwise, there is no explaining why someone would think your father and Ethan are good guys and Andre and Kos are bad."

"That's naïve . Think about homophobia, or ethnic hatred. It's always us versus them, even if the others like us are assholes."

Pedro pressed his lips together. He obviously knew it was true, just didn't like it.

"I'm sorry. I know you're not naïve. And I like that you see people that way—as reasonable, and…good. Plenty of people are like that. I just happen to know a lot who aren't." He interlaced their fingers and squeezed Pedro's hand.

"Did they come after me to hurt you?"

"Yes. And to test my loyalty."

His thick, handsome eyebrows pulled together. "You chose me over them?"

"I chose doing the right thing for once, and the fact I was hot for you made it an easier decision. I've been a coward for a long time."

"Were they cruel to you?"

"To my face, Ethan was kind. But I suspected for a long time he was hiding that sadistic side. My father was a mean bastard ever since he guessed I was gay. At my initiation, he set me up to kill the gay lover of a vampire."

"How did you get out of it?"

His gut knotted to remember the man's blood pooling on linoleum. But if they were going to do this star-crossed lovers thing, they needed to get all the cards on the table.

"I didn't get out of it."

Pedro was quiet for a long time. What was he thinking? Their hands were still entwined, and Lucas's wrist was twisted at an awkward angle, but he forced himself to remain still.

Finally, Pedro spoke. "So, tell me the truth. Why do Hunters hate vampires?"

Lucas wasn't ready to confess his suspicions. He needed more time to finish the drawings and double-check his theories. What could he say to put Pedro off?

"Vampires feed off human beings. It scares them. They think you are parasites."

Pedro withdrew his hand, stiffening. "You don't seem to mind."

"Yeah, you wouldn't either. I wish I could make you feel the way you do me."

"Do you?"

Lucas had said it without thinking, but it was the truth. "Yes."

"But I still can't fuck you?" Pedro gave him a dopey grin —

Phew. Not a serious question.

Lucas chuckled and leaned in to kiss him lightly. "No, but I will give you that hand job and tell you about the best fuck I ever had. The first one isn't worth mentioning."

"That's a deal. But first I have to ask. Do you know what Ethan's planning with all his research?"

Lucas had to wrench the lie from his chest. "No. I have no idea."

The words turned bitter in his mouth as he drifted off to sleep next to his almost-lover.

Hours later, he woke alone, slowly drifting into consciousness.

Absolutely still, he observed his body and mind from some third space outside both. It was rare for him to be so mellow. He felt that post-coital — make that post-super-hot-coital — kind of laziness. The off-limits fuck remained tempting, but the bite plus blowjob plus boyfriend feeling of his time with Pedro was pretty damn good. It was hard to get his ass off the bed and start drawing again.

Why do Hunters hate vampires?

Pedro's question rang in his ear like an alarm bell. He had to get up and get to work.

Keeping secrets from the vampire sucked, especially when things were so cozy. But, with Lucas's potentially magic blood, the idea of becoming a vampire commodity sucked even more, no pun intended. He needed to know for certain before he decided what to do.

He sketched with graphite and only used the colored pencils sparingly, nearly completing the first drawing. If only he could rush, leaving out unimportant details, so that he could piece the story together faster. But his memory didn't work that way. Instead, he got lost in the image, line by line, and could only emerge from it when he had precisely completed a segment. Besides, he didn't really know which details he could afford to leave out.

At least the illustrations were simple. They were two-dimensional line drawings similar to religious icons.

First came a couple—a male vampire and a female Hunter. His fangs dripped blood, and his obscenely large penis jutted across the image. The caricature of a predator, he feasted on the Huntress, who did not seem to mind being the prey. With her golden eyes rolled back in her lolling head, and her legs splayed around the vampire, she appeared equally lascivious. It was not a leap to infer the illustrator disapproved of such relationships.

Lucas shaded the blue-black night sky behind the pair, and then focused on the second drawing. It was nearly identical to the first, except that the vampire and the Huntress embraced one another in broad daylight.

Just as he'd remembered—it must have been her blood that allowed him to stand in the sun.

At a desk piled high with textbooks, Pedro was lost in thought. Lucas had dozed off, all loose-limbed and fine, spread out on white sheets, so Pedro had returned to his room and cracked open a painfully dull encyclopedia—ideal for relaxing his gray matter.

The sound of knuckles rapping on his doorframe made him jump. In the back of his mind he'd been aware of footsteps, but didn't guess Andre was actually coming to see him, since Zoey kept him pretty busy most nights. Pedro had considered hanging with a snoozing Lucas on the other wing of the house just to hear less of their busy.

"What's all this?" Andre asked.

"I'm studying."

Andre used his finger to mark Pedro's page and closed the book to read its cover. "*Una Historia de Vino y la Cultivacion de Uvas*. I am certain that is fascinating. What is the expression—a page-turner?"

"Maybe not, but it's the definitive resource."

"I am an excellent resource myself. What are you looking for?"

"Hard to believe, but, I'm looking for information even older than you, O Ancient One." Pedro tucked a scrap of paper into the book and slid it to a remote corner of his desk.

"Impossible." The corners of Andre's mouth turned up ever so slightly. He always could laugh at himself, something Pedro had long admired.

"Bel's research is so focused on the blood. Don't you want to know why the wine works? It can't just be a coincidence."

Andre sat on the end of Pedro's bed, his small smile becoming a frown. "I see your point."

"So, I want to know where your grapes originated. Were they native to Šolta, or did they come from somewhere else?"

"I acquired the vines from other growers on Šolta."

"Right, so did they domesticate a wild species, or bring the grapes from somewhere else?"

"Good question. That was centuries before even I was born."

"This book says grapes were grown for wine in the Caucasus six thousand years before Christ."

"Truly?"

Surprising Andre with a wine fact was something to be proud of. Pedro grinned. "For real. So here's my question. Where do Hunters come from?"

"Everywhere, they are everywhere."

"But they didn't start out everywhere. They spread out from some place, and I want to know where."

"Have you asked Lucas?"

"No. But I did ask him why Hunters hate vampires."

"What did he say?"

"Nothing really. He thought it should be obvious, because of our need for blood."

Andre shrugged. "That is to be expected. If you are raised with those beliefs, you take the reasons for granted. I take it you managed to make nice?"

Pedro's making nice had left him *feeling* nice about Lucas. "Yeah, we're better."

Andre glanced at his groin.

"Eyes up here, man. Yeah. We hooked up."

Relief and concern crossed Andre's face, one after the other.

"Have you forgiven him?" he asked.

Pedro's feelings were constantly shifting. His attraction to Lucas remained strong, and he liked the guy. He'd thought growing up a gay kid in the Spanish countryside had been hard, but the Hunters had really put Lucas through the wringer. He'd done some fucked up things for them, but now he wanted to make them right.

Still, he'd stood by while Ethan—

Icy stabs of pain shot up Pedro's legs and he shut down the memory. He curled his toes in his shoes and willed warmth into them. Next came the fury—

Lucas had brought that torture down on Pedro, let it happen—

The dime flipped, and fury surged through him. *Madre de Dios*, he was a regular Jekyl and Hyde. "No. I haven't forgiven him. But for the time being, friendly works better."

"Good, on both counts. Do not let your guard down. You must hold onto the memories of what happened to you, and his part in it."

"Like I have a choice. Every moment I'm alone, I'm back in that shed." Pedro snorted, and reached to stroke the book with mock affection. "So I'm curled up with *Una Historia* instead."

"With time, you will forget. But for now, it is good to remember. Otherwise, fucking and biting is a heady combination. You will grow attached, and start feeling responsible for him, even without a bond."

Pedro wasn't about to tell Andre they weren't fucking. Too complicated to explain. But a bond?

"A bond like you share with Zoey? Could that happen?"

Andre scratched the black stubble on his jaw. "I have known several homosexual vampires in my life. Only one pair was bonded." Andre smacked his lips together, as if he suddenly had a bad taste in his mouth. "*Davo*, it was like Caligula all the time at their place."

"Caligula? That old porno?"

"I was thinking of the real Emperor Caligula, but I imagine it is much the same."

It was a nasty comparison. "Fuck, Andre, you sound like Kos."

"What?" Andre's eyes brows pulled together in sad perplexity. Then his lips parted. "You mean that I am implying all homosexuals are perverts? You know me better. Those two in particular were sick bastards, and they happened to be bonded. The other gay vampires I knew were perfectly wholesome. The kind of males you would want to bond with your sister, if only."

Pedro chuckled at the choice of words, and instantly cooled off.

Andre stood and placed a firm hand on Pedro's shoulder. "You must be careful. Even with the complexity of your relationship with Lucas, it could happen. You will know you are in danger of bon—"

"Danger? You still think of it that way, even with Zoey?"

Andre's mouth formed into a secretive smile. "Old habits die hard. And Zoey is dangerous in her own way."

Best not to think about whatever that meant. It gave Pedro the heebie-jeebies, like he'd walked in on his parents having sex.

"And it *would* be dangerous for you to bond with him." Andre patted Pedro's shoulder. "You will know you are at risk if you hunger for him, and him alone, even when you have no appetite for blood. This hunger signifies a deep attachment."

"Um. That's a problem."

"What do you mean?"

"I *already* feel that way about his blood. Because of the Hunter mojo, or whatever."

"*Davo*." Andre dropped back onto the bed and crossed his arms.

"What will I do if I end up bonded to him? How will I even know?"

"You will know. A part of him will be inside you, you'll feel him all the time."

That sounded good, hot, even, to Dr. Jekyll. To Mr. Hyde, it sounded like a death sentence. He clenched his fists, feeling his nails dig into his palms.

"As to what you'll do if it happens, we'll cross that road…" Andre chose his word carefully. "*If* we get there."

Great, it was more than just possible. It was too goddamn likely.

"Andre, let me get back to my book. Maybe I'll learn something helpful."

He wasn't really hopeful. Even in the monster book, he'd never find anything that would satisfy his hunger for Lucas.

"Of course," Andre said. His mouth remained open to speak, making him look like he wanted to say something else.

Pedro leaned forward, suddenly aching for a word of reassurance.

None came. After a moment, Andre closed his mouth and walked out.

CHAPTER 17

Kos had let Lena fall asleep in his arms, and, hours later, he still wasn't sure if he was sorry. On the upside, the most amazing woman he'd ever met was wrapped around him and occasionally purred like a kitten. The downside was that, while she slept soundly, he was a beehive of anxiety, forced to remain perfectly still.

Had he really seen love burning in her eyes?

Maybe it was his imagination.

No. It was love, and it had connected his cock and his heart with a live wire, jolting through him in an orgasm of body and soul. Which was exactly what he was afraid of.

He'd fallen in love, and so had she. And he would never have sex like that again. Every relationship, every kiss, every climax, would pale. With time, he would forget. Though it would be a very, very long time.

Krist— Pedro might forget all the horrors he suffered at the hand of Ethan Bennett before Kos could let go of Lena.

Love. It only made him more determined to send her away. Surely this was exactly how Andre had felt about Mila, how he cared for Zoey now. And it was only a matter of time before love failed. Love was for humans, because it only had to last their trivial lifetime. Perhaps at best it could last centuries, but eventually it would implode, destroying Lena, and him, in its collapse.

He stared at the ceiling, cocooned in her scent and her soft embrace, barely containing his panic.

Someone drove up to the house just before dawn. The front door slammed shut and Bel's voice drifted upstairs. Kos grew restless.

Lena squeezed him tighter. "Hmm."

"Sweetheart, Bel is here. I need to talk to him. Okay?"

She rubbed her eyes. "Sure. Kiss me first."

He brushed his lips over hers, then again. His tongue was in her mouth before he knew it. Then he caught himself. "Okay. I'm going. Please don't move. Don't shower, don't brush your hair. It will break my heart if you aren't in the exact same place when I get back."

She giggled.

"Lena, I'm serious. I'm keeping you in bed all day. We have lots to do before you go." He hoped his intent look pinned her there.

At least she stopped laughing, her lips parted in surprise. "I should go make breakfast."

"Let them fend for themselves."

Before he reached the door, she said, "Toss me *War and Peace*. I know how you are with Bel, you could be gone all morning. And bring me coffee when you come back. It sounds like I'll need the energy."

"Yes, ma'am." He handed her the tome with a little bow then slipped from the room.

Bel was in the workroom with Andre, trying to explain his research. Andre was piddling with the bottling machine, spraying lubricant on its many parts for when they resumed the bottling, after the party.

"Fascinating, Bel," Andre said absently, without taking his eyes off the machine. He probably hadn't heard a word of the explanation. He turned to face Kos and spoke in the same distracted tone. "Who did you deflower?"

Bel coughed.

Kos froze. "What?"

Andre's mouth fell open, as if he'd just realized what he had said. "*Davo*. Lena? A virgin? I never would have guessed."

"How in the world can you smell that?" Kos asked.

"Very distinct. Virgins were a hobby for a while when I was first turned."

Bel shook his head. "Christ, Andre, that's sick."

"Do not be so self-righteous. They were all quite willing, and not only after I bit them. I can be very charming when I bother."

Bel hopped onto the work table, his arms crossed over his chest. "Are you sure? It's not like riding a bike. You *can* forget how to charm."

Andre glared at him. Great, another father-son fistfight. Kos rose up on his toes, ready to intervene. But Andre didn't take the bait after all. Impressive resistance. Maybe they were on the road to reconciliation.

He wiped his hands on a rag. "So, did she traipse around naked, pop her cherry on you, and then insist you keep her?"

Kos hit him. Neither of them expected it. His fist came so fast that he caught Andre off guard and actually landed a good hook to his jaw.

"Ow! Damn it, Kos!" He rubbed from his ear to his chin.

Perched on the table, Bel swung his dangling legs. "Pop her cherry? Where did you pick up that charming euphemism?"

"Zoey, of course." Andre laughed. "Good for you, Kos. I do not think you have ever hit me before."

Bel snorted. "That's not what you say when I hit you."

"That became tedious long ago, son."

Kos stared at the bruise on Andre's face, which purpled and then faded just as quickly. "Don't talk that way about her. She wouldn't do that."

"Did she ask you to keep her?"

"No. Not that it's any of your business. We just had a friendly good-bye, which I plan to continue for the rest of the day."

They stared at him.

"What?"

"Friendly good bye? The rest of the day? You've got it bad, bro."

"Perhaps I do, but she's leaving, so there's no reason to worry."

Andre cocked his head. "She truly did not beg and plead?"

"No, Andre. You managed to steal every shred of hope from her. She didn't ask twice." And a good thing too, because he didn't know if he was strong enough to say what had to be said.

No, I cannot risk loving you, for your own sake and for mine.

"Do you love her?" Andre asked.

Kos lifted his chin toward his father. "Don't be ridiculous."

Bel turned to Andre with his dark brows raised.

"What?" Kos asked.

Andre shrugged and then put his hands in his pockets, tight lipped.

"I'll walk with you," Bel said. Several steps into the damp, musty cellar, he spoke again. "It's all over your face. I've never seen that look before. Why don't you keep her?"

"You know damn well why."

"Uh, no, I don't."

"Because of Mother. Because of the vow we took."

"Vow?"

"Bel. You must remember. We bled on her grave. We promised never to marry, never to bond."

"Kos, I was, like, eleven."

"Of course I wouldn't hold you to it. And I always did like Lexi—"

"But you were only nineteen. You weren't even a vampire yet. You can't hold yourself to a vow you made then. You had no idea how long forever was."

"You're right. I didn't. But I do now, and I know for damn sure it is way too long for any love to last. Vow or not, I cannot keep her."

"She looks a little like Mom, doesn't she?"

One of Kos's shoes stuck to the stone floor as if it had been glued there. The other slid out from under him like it had been greased.

Bel caught him before he toppled over.

As soon as he was on his feet, he said, "No. She really doesn't, Bel, besides her hair. She's taller and thinner. Her face is fuller, her nose narrower."

"I suppose you're right. I hardly remember what Mom looked like, and Andre destroyed all the pictures. You're my only memento." Bel opened the door into the foyer and held it for Kos. "You and Lena suit each other nicely."

"You're not helping."

"Oh, sorry. Kick her to the curb, bro, like the needy blood slave she is. Hos and bitches all of them."

In spite of himself, Kos laughed. They'd reached the kitchen, and he was grateful to find a full pot of coffee. He poured a cup for Lena. "Bel. About Lexi. Did you want—?"

"More than you can possibly imagine."

"Really? Even after everything with Mother and Andre?"

"Yep. Even then. I always held them personally responsible for the mess they made. Doesn't mean everyone in the world is destined to cock-up their forever."

For the first time in his life, Kos really wished he could believe that.

"Goooaaal!" shouted the announcer.

"Piss off," Bel shouted back at the television, waving a nearly empty beer bottle at the TV.

Pedro didn't care a lick who won the game, but football was the sport of his youth, so it was still fun to watch. He kicked his feet onto the coffee table, and curled his finger around open air, wishing he could drink his own cold *cerveza*.

With the mouth of a beer bottle between his lips, Bel shut up for once.

Pedro seized the moment. "So, you've found the mysterious magic ingredient in Hunter blood and Blood Vine, but you're no closer to learning why it's there."

Bel's eyes turned to slits over the beer bottle. He looked closely at the bottle, then began to peel the label off. "The more I think about it, the more it becomes clear that the only explanation is vampires evolved to need Hunter blood, with Andre's wine as an inferior substitute."

Pedro took the bottle from Bel, forcing the other man to look at him. "But vampires don't need Hunter blood if they live in their homeland, only if Hunters drive them out. So, which one is the chicken and which the egg?"

"Right. That's the million dollar question. But no bets on this one, buddy." Bel's eyes flicked to Pedro's groin and back, and he winked.

"Yeah, yeah." Pedro cleared his throat, unsure if he was ready to share his theory. Damn, he'd like a swig of that cold, malty beer to moisten his dry mouth. "I have an idea. But I'm not willing to put a million bucks on it."

Bel lifted his beer. "Shoot."

"At some time in the past we were all together, and vampires exploited the Hunters for their blood, enslaved them, and that's why they hate us."

"Nope. Doesn't work. Vampires didn't need their blood unless they were exiled. Why bother exploiting them?"

"Well, that's the thing. I've never tasted any blood but Hunter blood, but I think it's different. I've seen Andre and Kos feed from humans all the time. For the humans, it's hot, but for vampires, it's nothing special—like a peanut butter and jelly sandwich. Feeding from Lucas is…" Hunger and lust surged through his veins, and he took a breath. "It's every good feeling at once. It's like your favorite home cooked meal and waking up on Christmas morning and a hug from your mom, and the best sex of your life, all rolled into one, which I realizes sounds creepy, but *Madre de Dios*, it feels really damn good."

Bel's dark eyebrows pulled together and he scratched his head. "I didn't know that."

He sipped his beer and looked at the ceiling for a long time. Pedro waited, hoping Mr. Vampire Wizard would have some kind of whopping brilliant epiphany and cure Pedro of his Lucas addiction. Not that he wanted rid of Lucas, exactly. He just didn't want to need him so damn much. Need his firm lips, his long arms and legs wrapped—

"Normally, things that feel good have an evolutionary benefit," Bel said. "For humans, eating and sex support the survival of the species. For vampires, feeding from people who get blissed out from a bite serves the vampires well, helps them survive."

"You're saying that maybe vampires didn't just feed from them for the, uh, vampire crack effect?"

"Exactly. Maybe the blood doesn't just feel good, but does something else to you."

"I need to feed less often than Andre and Kos."

"Right. That could be it." Bel didn't sound convinced at all. "Maybe Lucas knows."

The idea of Lucas keeping something like that from him made Pedro queasy.

"You should ask him."

"Yeah, right."

But Pedro wouldn't. He couldn't stand another betrayal.

CHAPTER 18

Lena arched her back and stretched, reaching her hands over her head. Kos's fingers were lodged inside her for an anatomy lesson, and she'd decided to play dumb.

"Sex Ed class is a lot more fun with you than with my health teacher, Mrs. Humphries."

"That's good to hear." He breathed the words into her ear, his hot breath heightening her sensitivity. "But you're sure this doesn't hurt?" He wiggled his fingers slightly. "I can't believe you're not sore."

The pain lingered, a dull ache that kept all her core muscles on alert, but she didn't want him to stop touching her.

"I'm surprised too. I promise that when you do that, what I feel is the exact opposite of pain."

Half true. She wanted the pain because it reminded her this was their one and only chance to be together. She didn't want to take for granted any sensation.

She groaned.

He grinned at her, all satisfied male. "That's your g-spot."

She'd known that the moment the broad head of his penis had hit it and her insides had melted.

"Oh. I've heard about that." Then she pushed herself further onto his fingers. "More please."

Later, she knelt between his legs and asked him to tell her about how he liked to be touched. She was a student of sex, after all, and she should use him as a live model to learn how to please her new employer. Though, really, she wanted to learn *his* body and his alone.

"In the pantry, was it the first time you—" He rubbed a finger across her kneecap.

When he didn't finish the sentence, she asked, "Gave a blowjob?"

He blushed red. "Yeah."

"It was. I've read just about every magazine article titled *Men Reveal Twelve Secret Turn-Ons.* And, I watched a lot of porn." She ran her fingers from his base to his tip.

"Really?"

"I was studying up to join a household. But porn's not a good way to learn. It's all the same, really. Just put it in a hole as far as it will go. There's not much technique to observe."

She stroked him up and down with her fingertips, until an awful thought occurred to her. She froze. "Did I do a bad job?"

"Honestly, I thought your innocence was an incredibly sexy act. Turns out you're inexperienced, but not really innocent. The idea that you were studying and waiting and you chose me is…" He took both her hands in his. "It's an honor I'll never forget."

"I'm glad you said yes."

A curtain of gray closed over all the blue in his eyes. "It was something special, and I'm sorry to say it's not always like that—so intimate, so intense."

That was a relief. She could have sex with this Mason Kearney, but she didn't want to be intense and intimate with him. It would be a long time before she was ready for that again.

"I still have to pack. But will you make love to me one more time?"

"I hope it's okay, but I asked Susan to pack your things so I could have you to myself all afternoon."

She pictured her suitcase. Who cared if it was a mess? "No, I don't mind. I'd rather be with you."

"But I will only make love to you again if you promise me you're not in pain."

"Not in the least." White lie. He stood up and circled behind her on the bed. "Where are you going?"

In answer, he guided her from a kneeling position onto her belly, with a pillow under her hips. "I want you like this." He spread her thighs just enough to fit one leg between them.

She arched her back to present herself to him, feeling like an animal—in a good way.

He groaned, wiping away every fear she had about knobby knees and dull hair. And he didn't treat her like an animal—he entered her slowly and rode her gently, kissing her neck and shoulders, running his hand down her side and back. This time, he reached to find her clit, swollen and sensitive, and he stroked her with gentle circles that matched his thrusts.

His touch was too slow, it wasn't right or how she would do it herself, but she wanted him to do it. And finally, after so much longer than it would have taken if she were in charge, her muscles began to tighten around Kos of their own accord. By surrendering to him, she'd drawn out both their pleasure. Pressure and need coiled inside her, building and building until a powerful orgasm rocked through her womb, shaking her thighs and curling her toes. He pressed her into the bed, covering her and breathing hard. Every inch of her skin tingled, and his body called to her, and through the veil of hair falling over her eyes, the whole world was brighter and more alive.

Oh God. Kos had done this to her, given this to her. And, soon, she was leaving. Her tears spilled into the mattress.

She was a blubbering idiot, and she couldn't let him see. Tears were desperate and she would not beg or bargain.

"Lena, sweetheart?"

She sniffed. "I'm fine. But, I thought you said it wasn't always like that."

He rolled and lay down beside her, quiet. When he spoke, there was something like awe in his voice. "It's *not*."

Good. She wanted him to miss her, to hurt over saying goodbye as much as she would—badly, and for a long, long time.

The ugly thought felt wrong, and right. Anger bubbled up in her. It was his choice to send her away, to deny them both this pleasure, this love. She hugged her arms over her chest tight, and corralled all her emotions up tight inside.

When she spoke, she heard the strain in her own voice. "I'm going to take a shower."

"Can I join you?"

She wiped her hand across her forehead, pushing back stray strands of hair. "Kos, we can't do this forever. I need to get ready to go."

She'd never taken a sharp tone with him before, and surprise took hold of his face. It wasn't fleeting—he was stunned and frozen that way. She ached to comfort him, to thaw him and reassure him of her affection. But no, it was time to move on—a new home, a new vampire, and a chance to decide once and for all whether she was destined to be a householder or a mother.

Kos stood in the foyer with Vania, discussing the route to San Francisco.

"If they follow you, you drop her at the mall downtown. I'll keep my eye on her, and we'll catch a cab to Kearney's."

Kos's shoulders were knotted liked someone had winched his trapezius muscles up to his ears. He rolled them, but it didn't help.

Vania put her hand on his arm. "Maybe it's out of line for me to say this—"

Her head was slightly angled, and the soft set of her mouth was unusual. Her black eyes were almost tender, very unlike the hardened warrior he'd had an affair with years ago. *Krist*, she was about to give him relationship advice, advice that he really did not want.

"Vania—"

"Kos, shut up and listen."

"Spit it out, and then we go." He swallowed and tried to roll his shoulders again. His muscles were immovable.

"You're different with her. I think she's your one. You shouldn't let her go."

"Vania, I don't have a one. Get your ass in the van."

She didn't flinch at his tone, just gave his arm a squeeze and spun toward the door.

Lena came down the stairs, and he dropped his car keys. She wore a pair of jeans that showed off every curve of her flawless legs. It was so much worse because he knew what they looked like wrapped around him. He could even make out the sexy shape of her kneecaps.

Kneecaps? *I'm lost to her.*

Another minute at Kaštel, and he would profess his love. But he couldn't tear his eyes from her. She had on a loose blouse that draped temptingly over her delicious breasts, and she held a sweater in her hands. Fashionable boots covered her calves. He'd never seen her dressed so stylishly.

"Boots?"

She swung her purse onto her shoulder and angled herself away. "The ocean makes it colder in the city."

"Right." Another shrug. Still, his muscles wouldn't budge. "Susan put your suitcases in the car."

"Has the sun set?"

Enough light came through the windows that it was still unclear whether the sun had passed the horizon. He looked at his watch. "Yes. It will be safe for us to leave in another five minutes. Vania is waiting to follow us — she'll make sure we aren't tailed by Hunters."

"Okay." She sat down in a straight-backed wooden chair near the door. The heavy antique dwarfed her, its rustic lines at odds with her modern style. In her fashionable clothes, she looked out of place. She was. She didn't belong at Kaštel, and she didn't belong with him.

She fiddled with something in her purse — already gone.

His heart fell into his stomach. She'd put up a wall and it wouldn't come down again, not for him. There would be no passionate goodbye kiss, no heartfelt confessions of a love that could not be. Grief pounded into his chest like a punch, stealing his breath. It was over already.

This was my choice.

He'd made the decision that was right for everyone. If he tried to keep her, he would hurt her worse than this. If they lost themselves to the passion between them, it would be even more devastating when it came to an end.

Andre appeared in Kos's mind, three stones too light and starving after Mila's death. How had his father withstood it? If Lena belonged to Kos, she would be his everything, his reason for living. If she killed herself like Mila had, breaking their bond, Kos would walk right into the sun.

Lena combed her fingers through her hair, shielding her face. *O Krist* — she knew he was watching her, and she was avoiding his gaze. He made it easy by looking away.

"Is it time?" she asked.

He checked. "Yes. Let's go."

He crossed the drive to Andre's sporty Mercedes coupe because Kos's more practical four-door model had been parked in by the vans for Bel's crew.

In the car, the silence was sharp. She had a plethora of reasons to be angry with him, and they cut through his mind, although there was nothing he could do to make them right.

"Music?" he asked, to deflect the quiet's sharpness.

"Yeah, maybe some of your classical music. But not that dissonant Russian stuff. It makes my head hurt, especially right…I don't feel like it."

Maybe Franz Liszt's "Years of Pilgrimage." The piano pieces had the perfect amount of melancholy for the occasion. He hadn't realized she'd paid any attention to his musical taste. Aside from Andre and Bel, she might know him better than anyone. He plugged in his iPod, preparing to scroll for the album, but the last track he'd been listening to blared — Peter Gabriel's "In Your Eyes."

Fuck.

She let out one surprised sob before she covered her mouth. No way to deny it — he was caught being a sentimental, self-pitying fool. His face heated with anger for only himself. Finally, he found the Liszt, and forced his mind to the music, letting each note fill him, so he didn't think about her scent, the softness of her skin, the blaze of love in her sated eyes, the horrible pain they'd brought her at Kaštel. Yes, he was a master of self-control. Thanks to Liszt, he only thought of her a hundred times a second.

"Did you study music?" There was an uncharacteristic coolness in her voice, but at least she was talking.

"No. I didn't have any talent for it. My Aunt Uta was an incredible musician." Words poured out of him, and he was grateful for another distraction. "She's better than any professional soprano I've heard and plays the violin beautifully — she's best with the old Croatian folk songs. When she was at our house, it was full of music. I suppose I learned to appreciate it because of her."

"Was or is?" Ever so slightly, her shoulders tilted toward him.

"What?"

"You said she *was* a musician, but *is* a great singer."

He kept his eyes glued to the road, afraid even to glance her for fear she would shut down. "Uta's a vampire. She fled Croatia with us, but like all the refugees, she's in hiding and we don't know how to find her."

"Is she your mother's sister?"

In spite of the tension in his body and the air, he chuckled. "Uta? No."

"She can't be Andre's sister."

"No, she's not really our aunt. She's Bel's godmother." Of their own accord, his fingers curled around the steering wheel. "She was close to my mother and very close to Bel. But when mother killed herself, Uta abandoned Bel. It was terribly cruel. I can't forgive her for it, and I know Bel hasn't either."

"Are you sure she's still alive? Could the wasting disease have killed her?"

"No, she's even older than Andre, which makes her the strongest vampire I know."

The chatter carried them across the Golden Gate Bridge. They drove into San Francisco just as Kos's phone rang. Vania.

"All clear?" he asked.

"Yes. You weren't followed. You're safe to proceed to Kearney's house."

"Thanks. I'll see you back at Kaštel."

Vania blurted a final warning. "You're a fool to let her go."

He hung up. So what if his heart was breaking. If he tried to keep her, hearts, bodies and lives would break one day too, and it would be worse. Much worse. At a stoplight, he turned to look at Lena, straight and motionless, taught as the skin on a ripe grape. The force she was exerting to hold in her emotions was impressive. Surprising she didn't tremble with it.

Mason lived near the bridge in Pacific Heights. Pulling up to his house, Kos felt nostalgic, or maybe sentimental. No, neither of those were the right words. He just remembered. All the years he'd spent—visiting Mason, chasing women, wasting time—they flashed before his eyes, making him feel empty.

"Nice house," she said quietly. Indeed, on a block of nice houses, his was the biggest and best maintained, as always.

Ethan parked his car on Union Street and answered his phone. "Bennett."

"It's Derek. I've got news."

"What's that?"

"Marasović's distributor is expecting a shipment of their Blood Vine any day now. Let's be sure it arrives."

"Indeed, it could be a trail of bread crumbs, leading us right to the other vampires."

"Exactly."

"Good work, Derek." Ethan hung up.

He grabbed a paper sack and walked a block up Lyon Street, where he slid into the passenger seat of the car he'd rented for Gwen. Handing her a sandwich, he said, "Best deli in the city. It's not New York, but it's not bad. Extra peppers for you."

A crease formed between her eyebrows, and she glanced away, reaching into the bag. "Thank you."

When he'd ordered the sandwich, he'd heard her lilt. "The spicier the better." He had no idea if Zoey liked spicy food. Gwen had invaded his mind little by little, but that was how tectonic plates shifted, slowly moving entire continents, building up enough pressure to fuel volcanic eruptions and earthquakes.

"Seen Kearney?"

She held her sandwich aloft, pausing before she took her first bite. "No. Just a middle-aged man. Pudgy. Short. Definitely not Mason."

Ah. Mason, was it? She knew him well then, and apparently he was not short or pudgy. No surprise there. Vampires were fit by nature, and attractive by selection.

At the sight of the unassuming Pac Heights mansion, deeply bred instincts rose up in Ethan. He reached for his phone to call in the Hunters. They could storm the house and take down Kearney so easily—but, no. He patted his phone where it remained in his pocket, feeling the rough lump of the toy soldier alongside it. Mastery of his instincts set him apart from the Hunters, and qualified him to lead them. They could point and shoot, but he could orchestrate a war of strategy. Mason Kearney was his newest pawn.

"How did the assault go?" Gwen asked.

"Poorly. They have an invisible shield around the estate. It's like nothing I've ever seen. And as soon as someone in the house saw smoke, they extended the damn thing to the boundary of the property. If I didn't know better, I'd think it was magic."

"You believe in vampires, but not magic?"

"I've seen vampires."

"Sounds like you've seen magic as well." She scolded him like the professor she was.

It was a taunt, a challenge, and it gave him an erection. When her stakeout was over, he would take her back to his apartment and remind her who was boss. The backseat was too risky. Although, he could keep an eye peeled if she leaned over and—

A Mercedes pulled up and Kosjenic Marasović and his girlfriend stepped out. The vampire tilted his nose up to the air. Could he smell Ethan? The foggy wind was nearly a gale, and the Presidio's eucalyptus trees were pungent. He'd thought he was safe. Then Marasović was all eyes for the woman, and Ethan knew he was in the clear.

"That's my target's son and the blood slave."

In the vineyard, the blonde had clung to the vampire like a lifeline, and he had grasped her protectively in turn. Ethan was surprised he was pawning her off on this Kearney, though the vampire's bunched shoulders made him look less than pleased about it. Did he know what kind of punishments Kearney could deal out? Of course, that was still only a suspicion.

Kearny burst from the front door, well dressed and slick. Gwen shuddered, shaking the car and confirming Ethan's suspicion. The vampire had severely traumatized her. Ethan both hated him for it, and was rather grateful. Kearney had turned her into Ethan's perfect match.

Zoey had looked lovely, stalking through the blackened and ashy vineyard like it was just another conference room for her to command. And, as always, she'd willfully challenged him. Once he had thought he liked her assertiveness, but thanks to Gwen he knew what he really wanted was to break Zoey. Maybe he could learn from this Kearney just how to go about turning a brilliant woman into his masochistic pet.

For now, he had Gwen, already satisfyingly submissive.

"What do we do?" she whispered.

"We watch. We wait. Soon, we will get the girl. She is clearly that vampire's Achilles' heel."

"I want to rescue her from Mason."

He patted her knee. "Of course we will."

CHAPTER 19

Kos's chest squeezed so tight he could barely breathe. Lena stepped out of the car. Leaving. Forever.

He stood and reached his hand over the top of the car. "Lena, wait."

She spun, looking from his hand to his face.

"No, Kos. It's time."

Mason exploded from the front door, looking the same as ever—an exquisitely cut, exquisitely expensive suit, hair a little messier than the clean cut of their carousing days, as current style demanded. His face held that blinding smile.

"Hello, beautiful."

Lena smiled at him, lowering her eyelids, clearly pleased by the compliment. Hadn't Kos praised her beauty enough already?

"Hi, old buddy." Mason offered his hand.

Kos returned the grasp. "Good to see you, Mason."

"Please, come inside."

Mason interrogated Kos about what he'd been doing lately, Kos answered absently, watching Lena take in the house from the corner of his eye. Mason's home was stylish, always up to date, which made it a stark contrast to the stodgy Kaštel Estate. Another reason this was a good place for her—after all, Kos was only slightly less aloof to fashion than Andre.

On a dime, Mason's face went blank, revealing he'd lost interest in Kos's news. He'd always grown bored easily.

"Where is the lovely Lena?" He turned, looking for her.

She occupied the doorway of a sitting room, peering in, but too polite to enter without an invitation.

"Please lovely, let's go in and have a seat."

Lovely? How slimy, a nickname already.

She sat down on a sofa, and Mason sat next to her and leaned in. Lena stilled, understanding he was sniffing her. Andre had probably done the same thing to her when they first met.

Mason looked up, narrowing his eyes at Kos. "I thought you said she was Andre's. Your scent is all over her."

Krist. He'd forgotten about that part. Lena jerked her head to stare at Kos, eyes brimming with tears. Shit. She did not need this. What would spare her dignity?

"Mason, Lena works for Andre, but we've become friends. She is very dear to me, as are you. I'm pleased she will be working for someone I trust. I apologize if our intimate goodbye offends your sense of propriety, but she wasn't yours yet."

Mason leaned back into the cushion, pressing his palms together and steepling his fingers. "Of course. Who wouldn't want to say a thorough farewell to a women as stunning as Lena?"

Cold sweat broke out on Kos's hands.

Lena had wiped her tears quickly, before Mason noticed, but she was trembling, poor thing, her emotions finally shaking her composure. He could relate. But she was stronger than him, had risked her heart on him, even after Andre had crushed it once. A weaker woman would have trained herself to feel less.

And suddenly, he knew — life in a household would never work for her.

Mason continued to speak to her, but Kos couldn't hear them. Why hadn't he seen it before? She was too passionate, too sensitive to be used that way. Blood service would always be exploitation for her.

He interrupted their chitchat. "Lena, I just thought of something. Can I speak to you?"

Again, Mason glared. Kos ignored him.

She pressed her lips together and shook her head. "I'm just getting to know Mason. Can you tell me another time?"

"No, it really can't wait. I forgot until now."

"Lena, let me make sure your room is ready." Mason settled the matter by blurring out of the room.

"What is it?" she snapped.

He didn't care if Mason could hear, the words just poured out: "Lena, you can't stay here. I see now, it's all wrong. You're not cut out for this life. Let's go back to Kaštel and start from scratch. You need a real, human life."

"No."

"Listen to me. This isn't going to make you happy. It's going to kill all your passion and generosity."

"You have no right to tell me what will make me happy. There is only one thing you can say that will make me leave with you, and if it's not on offer, then I'll find my destiny with someone else."

Her ocean blue eyes blazed with the same raw look he'd seen when they'd made love. It was a challenge—admit he felt the same way, or deny it.

She deserved the truth.

He rubbed the back of his neck, rolled his shoulders, tried to work up his nerve. "I love you, Lena. I've never felt this way about anyone. But we can't be together. It never lasts. And then we would end up like my mother and father, broken, if not dead. I can't do that to you."

"You love me?" The tears spilled down her face.

"Yes. Which is why I can't keep you."

Her thumb came up to her mouth and she bit the nail as the tears flowed. She wiped them away with the back of her hand and sniffed, shifting her feet and standing straighter.

"I don't know whether you're a liar or a coward, but I want you to leave. Don't come back."

And then Mason was back with smug smile that showed he'd heard the whole thing.

Kos didn't say another word; he turned and left. How many barrels of Blood Vine would it take to drown this feeling? He drove back to Kaštel as quickly as possible, determined to find out.

Lena faced Mason, and her knees went weak. She locked them, reaching for the back of a chair. God she was tired. Could probably sleep for a week. "I'm sorry about all that. We should have had our words in the car, but I stonewalled him. It's not his fault."

"I understand, he's remarkably sensitive. Always has been."

"Yes, he is." She rubbed her eyes with her fists.

"You're tired. It seems Kos's goodbyes have worn you out."

Charmed in spite of herself, her lips pulled into a tight smile. "That's true."

"What do you say to an early night? We can get better acquainted tomorrow."

Tomorrow? No, damn it. She wanted to get this over with, needed to move on, find her destiny.

"Mason, if it's all right with you, I would like to get acquainted tonight."

His eyes moved up and down her body. Her skin grew hot under his gaze, but goose bumps sprung on her arms and legs. He didn't answer. Oh, God. Maybe he didn't like her.

"I mean if you want to…"

He strode to her in two longs steps and wrapped a lock of her hair around his finger, tugging it gently. "Ah. It's like that, is it? They didn't want you."

She bit her lip, and nodded, trying to hold back another round of stinging tears.

"They're fools, then. Let me show you to your room. You can get settled, and then find me when you're ready."

He didn't have to spell out what she would be ready for.

Her room was unbelievably luxurious, decorated in cream, and gray, and slate blue. Her muscles eased, and a little energy returned to her bones.

"It's lovely, thank you."

Through the bathroom door, her eyes lighted on a Jacuzzi tub. Nothing sounded better than a long soak.

His hand grazed her shoulder and traced a line down her arm. "I'm glad you like it. Would you like to take a bath, and then meet me in my room at the end of the hall?"

Her throat closed up, but she forced it open with a swallow. "Yes. That sounds great."

"I'm so glad you're here." He brushed his lips on her cheek. They were as cool as the colors in the room. They sent no electric sparks through her, and that was soothing too.

"Thank you," she said. "I hope I'll be a satisfactory addition to your household."

"Lena, you couldn't possibly be more to my liking."

How could he know that already?

He sped from the room in that stealthy vampire way, and she turned on the hot water tap. She found bubble bath scented with wild angelica, which invaded her yard back home in Alaska every spring. The body aches she had acquired over eighteen hours in bed with Kos melted away in the water. The heartaches, not so much.

She lost track of time, but the water cooled eventually, and she dried off. A white shirt box with a white satin ribbon lay at the foot of the bed. How had he come in without her hearing? Sneaky vampire.

Inside the box was an elegant cream silk negligee that would fall just past her knees. It wasn't frilly or garish like most lingerie. Its simple, clean lines were trimmed in blue lace, which matched her eyes perfectly. How on earth had he managed that? And because San Francisco was always too cold for sexy nightwear, there was a matching cashmere robe — to die for.

Not exactly a ball gown, but she felt a little like a princess, which somehow seemed like a betrayal of Kos. Only, she didn't owe him anything.

Underneath the robe was a note card. "Why bother dressing? Just come in something more comfortable."

She floated down the hall on a raft of expectations. Her feet hardly touched the bamboo floors. She knocked, and Mason opened the door, wearing white silk pajama bottoms that matched her nightie and no shirt to hide his muscular frame. He was all bulky muscle — that explained why he'd looked so good in his suit. His body was sexy, if very different from Kos's lean, sculpted one.

He stood still, knowing she was appraising him, and his eyes glinted. "I hope I'm to your liking."

She blew air from between her lips. "You're handsome and I think you know it." It took all her nerve to keep cool as she spoke, but he bared his teeth in a hungry smile. She'd earned herself some respect.

His bedroom looked out over the street, past the houses across the way and onto San Francisco Bay. Thousands of shining lights from Alcatraz, from boats on the water, and on the hillside across the bay glinted in a large bay window. A chaise lounge faced the window, and Mason dropped himself onto it.

"Come sit with me." He flung his legs up, and gestured that he wanted her between them.

She tried to be graceful as she climbed across one of his legs and positioned herself there. He sat upright and pulled her by the hips close enough to lean against his hard chest. So far, that was the only part of him that felt hard, which was just fine. She preferred to take things slow.

He ran his hands up the outside of her arms, the pleasant gesture not at all sexual. "Kos said you come from a family of householders?"

"Yes, on my paternal grandmother's side. She raised me for service."

"And you decided to follow in her footsteps?" His voice was soft and low, vibrating against her back in a soothing bass tone.

"Yes. It's what I've always wanted."

"Lucky for me."

It was so nice to have someone take pains to flatter her. "It's kind of you to say so."

"Tell me what you like about serving a vampire."

"At Andre's, I enjoyed being part of a big household and cooking for all the women. I love being bitten; Andre seems to think I find it especially potent."

"Does he? How delightful."

Regret squeezed her heart. "He didn't think so."

"We've already agreed he is a fool."

She giggled, and some of the pressure unwound. "And I want the pleasure of a bite while making love."

A loud burst of laughter erupted from Mason, surprising her.

"Ah, Lena, you sound like Kos. You should know, I have no intention of making love to you." He pulled her robe down off her shoulders and ran his fingers up and down her neck, like he was prospecting veins and arteries to find the juiciest one.

His touch sped up her pulse, made her skin tingle. She sighed, collapsing into him. "That's good, I couldn't take any more of it. I want a professional arrangement."

"Perfect. Are you ready?"

"Yes."

With his tongue and his lips, he tasted and teased the sensitive skin on her throat in a way neither Andre nor Kos ever had. Then, he struck without warning, piercing her flesh. She tensed, and fear flooded her veins until his bite relaxed her, helping her to remember that she was submitting willingly.

Her skin prickled with extra sensitivity. The sultry silk brushed her thighs, the cashmere on her arms was divine. Mason reached around to cup her breasts and tease her nipples. She arched her back into him.

Huh—there was no hard bulge against her tailbone. Kos had been hard every time she touched him. But there was nothing wrong with being slow on the trigger.

The oral urges would come soon. She would want to kiss, to suck on something. She'd usually chosen her thumb when Andre fed from her. Although she liked it better when Kos had offered her his own fingers to satisfy the craving. She raised her knuckle to her mouth, but Mason beat her there, and popped the most exquisite chocolate truffle between her lips. As it melted into her taste buds, she let out a groan.

His fingers dropped between her legs. He broke his suction on her open vein to say, "It should be illegal for a woman to eat fine chocolate without having someone stroke her cunt."

Maybe the word should have shocked her, but it was thrilling. He lapped up the blood that trickled down her neck and resealed his lips to her neck, taking a deep draw of blood. It burned in her veins from her fingertips to her core. She was on fire, all over her body, and the hottest flames danced between her legs where his fingers moved.

The final wave of pleasure hit her. It was her favorite part—the deepest relaxation—like floating in a hot spring. The muscles that supported her organs and wrapped around her bones went limp. If an orgasm was a little death, this was much bigger, pulling her out of herself and anchoring her inside her flesh at the same time. Impossibly heavy, her body sank into Mason.

A loud crack rang out, as if someone had bit into a cracker. What was that?

Around her sternum, her muscles went liquid. Oh shit—it was her—she'd cracked. Mason had melted away all the control damming up her feelings. A sob crawled its way up from her gut. Once it was out, they kept coming, wracking her body, and squeezing her heart. Andre, Kos, destiny, dream babies. It was all too much.

Mason broke the seal on her neck another time to say, "That's it, Lena, let it out. Let me taste your anguish." His voice was a rasp. He didn't stop sucking, and continued to stroke her between her legs. His now-firm shaft pointed straight up into her back.

A demanding force built in her belly, burning and hungry. She wanted him to stop, wanted to surrender to her misery, to feel no pleasure. But with his teeth in her neck, she needed to come so bad she could barely stand it. She needed to feel better, she needed Kos, she needed to come. She sobbed harder, rocking her pelvis into his hand.

Finally, he applied just the right amount of pressure to her clitoris, and she exploded in a blubbering catharsis of an orgasm—one big wave of emotion and pleasure crashed her back into Mason's chest, and the room went black.

Kos drained his glass of Blood Vine.

"Tell me what happened," Andre insisted.

He should just shut up and play cards, not make Kos talk about Lena.

"S'none of your bishness," Kos slurred.

"It is my business, because you have severely dented my supply of Blood Vine. If you anticipate keeping up this bender, I am going to hire intoxicated humans to feed you. We cannot waste our cure so that you can try to forget her."

"Won't work anyway." Zoey spoke from behind her hand of cards, fanned out like a peacock's tail.

"Always works for me." Bel flashed his more-charming-than-Andre smile at his new stepmother. "Lay off. He doesn't need therapy. He needs to get shit faced. Then he'll get over her, and we'll have our ladies' man back."

Good ol' Bel, coming to his defense. But ladies' man—really?

"Won't work." Zoey shook her head.

Kos's own head swam, but he liked everything Bel said. That's what he needed. Why was Zoey being such a downer? Of course it would work. Bel said so.

He affirmed the mantra aloud. "Ofkorz il ork. Be sz."

"What?" Andre and Bel chimed.

"I'm sorry honey, but it won't." She sounded uncharacteristically maternal.

Bel leaned forward. "With all due respect, Zoey, what the fuck do you know about it? You've known him for all of three weeks."

Andre growled at Bel.

"Shush," Zoey said.

They were so cute together. Cute, cute! Who would have thought his father could be cute? But Zoey was talking, and he needed to pay attention.

"Andre, he's right, I'm new. But I think Kos has it bad."

"S'true. She's perfect. Allah want."

"Allah?" Andre asked.

"She's all he wants." Zoey translated. Bel and Andre looked at Kos, who nodded to confirm she understood.

Bel leaned over the table and canted his head to look directly at Kos. "It will go away. You're probably just infatuated."

"Hopesho."

"Kos," Andre shouted.

"Not deaf, drunk!" Kos shouted back.

"Do you love her?"

He rolled his neck; his shoulders were getting tighter and tighter. Why couldn't they just play cards? Suddenly Andre was standing over him, pulling him out of the chair.

Kos swatted his hands away. "'ack off."

"Look at me and answer the question. Do you love her?"

"Yesh."

Bel smirked. The ass had known all along.

"*Davo.* Why on earth did you let her go? Perhaps she's the one for you."

Andre an apologist for love? — *Krist,* things changed fast.

"Can't be the one. S'no such thing," Kos said, closing his eyes and shaking his head. His voice sounded clearer in his own ears. His thoughts were clearer too. *Must be sobering up.*

"What do you mean?" Andre asked.

"True love's bogus. Can't last forever, and everybody winds up broken, or dead, like Mother."

The room fell silent. Maybe it was the eye of the storm, but Kos took a deep breath and enjoyed it.

"Kos, your mother…do not make generalizations from that marriage. There are things you do not understand."

"I understand perfectly. When you're bonded, there's no end besides the one Mother chose."

It was like shattering a mirror—all of their smug expressions collapsed. Now they were being honest.

"And what about Zoey?" Andre asked. "I found my one after all."

"It's only been a few weeks," Kos said. "Can't last."

Oops. My head's not clear enough, or I wouldn't have said that.

A rumble came from Andre's chest. Damn-it, would they come to blows again?

Instead, Zoey laughed. "Well, at least now we know how you really feel."

Kos shuffled toward the door. "Yeah, well, sorry." He shrugged. "I'm going to take a shower and then finalize some arrangements for the launch party tonight. Is the bottling finished?"

"Almost," Andre replied. "If there's time, I'll deliver the bottles tonight after the party."

Kos's fingers closed around the cool brass doorknob and his nose filled with the cellar's must. Before he walked into that dark hall, he owed them something more. He craned his neck.

"Zoey, I'm glad you're bonded to my father. I wish you an eternity of happiness together, if such a thing is possible. I just don't think it is."

CHAPTER 20

Lena awoke without the fantasy Kos would be there watching. There weren't even traces of her recurring dream, only panic that she'd left his copy of Galway Kinnell's *A New Selected Poems* in the miscellany drawer at Kaštel. Losing it might have broken her heart, but there wasn't anything left to break. Maybe today she could walk to one of the bookshops on Union Street and see if they had a copy. It wouldn't be the same — his fingers wouldn't have touched the pages, the fingers that had also touched her everywhere…

Still, she needed that book.

She dressed in clothes as stylish as the ones she'd worn last night. Style seemed important to Mason. Then she went searching for him. He lounged at the kitchen table reading a newspaper.

"Good morning, lovely."

He had a rakish smile, like the bad-boy heroes in one of those novels where women drank brandy as medicine. It wasn't a smile a girl fell in love with, like Kos's lopsided, dimpled grin. No, not like his. But Mason's had appeal. She couldn't help but smile back.

"Good morning."

He didn't glance up from the paper. "I made coffee. All humans drink it, right?"

She couldn't tell if he was joking or being naïve, but it amused her. On a laugh, she replied, "Perhaps not all, but most. And I do, so thank you." She poured herself a cup. For a moment, she faltered, remembering Kos's habit of carrying around a half-full mug just to smell. Mason cleared his throat and she came back to her senses, scanning the counter for cream. When she didn't see any, she perched on the chair across from him. "How many people will I be cooking for in your household?"

"It's just you, and my man Nicholas — he's my driver, housekeeper, all that stuff."

"So two, including me? You hardly need me."

"Lena." With her name, he captured her gaze and held it.

Oh, right. Now she was the one being naïve, he needed her for the other household duties. But no cooking? She was getting paid for...

A blush seared her cheeks. Paid to be his whore, his blood whore — but then, she'd known that all along. Wasn't that her destiny? She sipped the coffee. Black and bitter, not how she liked it at all.

"Just me in your household? Surely you need more blood than that."

"I do, you're right. But I mostly eat out." He winked.

She swallowed another caustic mouthful, determined to learn to like it. "Oh. You pick up women in bars and things like that?"

"Yes, and things like that."

Lena composed herself, aiming for nonchalant and sophisticated as her imagination scrolled through all the ways Mason might hook up with his food.

He shook the newspaper then folded in half. "Please, make yourself at home." He pressed the crease of the paper into a crisp line. "There's a gym, and an entertainment center, a garden. *Mi casa es su casa.*"

"So should I go out to get some groceries for myself?"

"Out? No, no, don't worry about that. Nicholas is shopping right now and if there's something else you want, just tell him." He came around the table and crouched so that they were eye to eye. "I very much hope you will come to want me as much as you want Kos."

Before she could argue, he kissed her artfully, as if he had practiced kissing the way Michelangelo practiced sculpting. It was beautiful, and absolutely without sentiment. She tuned out her heart's protests and enjoyed his lips and his tongue. Her skin heated, and her pulse quickened.

"Later, lovely." He pulled back, grinning with satisfaction at her response even as he turned toward the door.

"Mason, I left a book at Kaštel. I think I might walk over to Union Street to look for it in a bookshop."

He froze with his hand on the doorframe. "Nonsense, Nicholas will get the book for you. What's it called?"

"*New and Selected Poems*, by Galway Kinnell."

"Never heard of it. One of Kos's?"

She nodded, reaching for her mug as an excuse to look down and hide her second blush. He'd probably seen it anyway, but she hoped he assumed it was arousal, and not embarrassment.

After working for a while to organize the sparse pantry, she grew restless. It was about two miles to the Golden Gate Bridge where she could walk along the bayshore. She dressed in layers and left a note in the kitchen explaining her plan.

The front door was locked.

The knob turned, but the door didn't budge. She searched for a bolt somewhere. Nothing. No key pad either. Obviously, she was missing something. There had to be a way to open the door in case of an emergency. What an idiot—why couldn't she find it? She examined the same stretch of the door and wall over and over again. After the umpteenth time, her hands clenched, and she pounded on the door.

"Mason. Are you here?"

No answer. Her heart pounded. She slid to the floor, panicked.

Don't be silly. You're not a prisoner.

She shook with nerves. Of course she was overreacting. But she couldn't make it stop. The best thing would be to wear herself out. In the small gym in Mason's basement, she found a treadmill. She climbed on and set the pace to a fast jog. Her breathing fell into a rhythm with the exertion, and sweat rolled down her spine.

She ran hard and fast for a solid hour, until she'd flushed the last trace of adrenaline from her system. Unsteady legs carried her up the stairs, and she collapsed on the bed, falling asleep in her sweaty clothes.

A soft rap on her door woke her up, but no one was in the hall, only a parcel wrapped in brown paper. Inside was a spotless copy of *A New Selected Poems*, and underneath it a bit of folded silken fabric. She shook it out, to see a quintessential little black dress. It was silk, with a draping halter neck, and not too short. Sexy, but tasteful, and of course, the perfect size. From it fell a notecard that said *Dinner at eight. Wear this.*

The third time her phone rang, showing Kos's number, she turned the damn thing off. She drew another bath and punished herself with the pristine copy of Kinnell while soaking in the floral scented bubbles.

A different poem at the back of the book captured her imagination. It was an ode to the secret rapture of Kinnell's marriage bed, a poem of content domestic intimacy. It squeezed her heart so hard the vital organ was at risk of turning to coal, then brilliant diamond. Kinnell had painted a picture of what a life with Kos would be, if he weren't a lying coward.

Glancing through the bathroom door, she saw the red numbers on the display of the clock radio. Four p.m. She had hours until dinner. Why not continue to wallow?

She read the poem over and over, like hitting her head against a wall, until her tears fell onto the pages. At the sight of wet streaks slicing through the lines of verse, fury seized her. Shaking, she gripped the book and hurled it into the mirror.

She sunk into the tub, submerging her head and holding her breath, until the shakes finally stopped. Tilting her head back, she came up and stared at the ceiling as water sluiced off her face.

A skyscape of fluffy gray and white clouds against cornflower blue adorned the ceiling. The clouds were so real, she could almost see them move. She hadn't seen clouds like that since she used to go hiking with her father.

Her memory took her back to the last time, the summer before she'd left for San Francisco. They'd flown in his two-propeller airplane to his favorite lake and hiked all morning, then sat on a Black Watch plaid blanket and shared a picnic lunch. The red and white plane bobbed gently on its pontoons, floating in the lake. It caused her a jolt of longing; he'd died when it crashed two summers later.

That same wild angelica grew along the creeks, perfuming the air. She gazed up at enormous clouds and enjoyed the sun warming her face.

"Sweetheart," he used to call her, just like Kos did. "I wish you would stick around and go to college here."

She bristled, hands fisting. They'd had the discussion so many times. Why did he have to bring it up again? "This is what I want, it's what I've always dreamed of."

"But you could do anything, Lena. You're as pretty as you are smart. Why spend your life serving one of them?"

She huffed. "It's what I want."

Oh how she wished she could take back that stubborn whine, now that he was gone.

Still, he'd scratched his head, the picture of fatherly patience. "Don't you think it's possible your grandmother idealized her life with those vampires? To an old widow, it probably looked rosier than it really was."

"Sure, a little. But Dad, I have to try." In the silence that followed, Lena passed him a bag of dried fruit and nuts. "It's not like I'm going to work at a strip club or something. I'm going to culinary school."

"I know, I sent the tuition check." He jabbed her hiking boot with the toe of his shoe. "Believe me, it's the only part of your plans I feel good about."

"So maybe I'll never meet a vampire, and I'll become a celebrity chef with my own show on the Food Network."

"I love it! Let's send them those head shots from when you were modeling."

"Dad." She poked him with her elbow. He'd always insisted she was pretty enough to model, and she'd always thought he was blinded by fatherly love.

"I know you think this is about me being uptight about sex. But it's not. You're an adult and I trust you can make responsible decisions."

"Uh huh," she said, not believing him. Adolescent Lena hadn't, but adult Lena kind of did.

"The thing is, Lena, you're a good girl. And you're signing up for the type of life that doesn't make good girls happy."

She blinked, and the ceiling of Mason's house came back into focus.

The kind of life that makes good girls happy, the Galway Kinnell life of motherhood and domestic contentment? She tried to picture meeting some nice human guy and settling down. Her stomach twisted. He wouldn't be Kos. He would never make her feel the way Kos did, in bed or out.

If she didn't get to have Kos, it had to be the household life.

She picked up *New and Selected* from the floor. It was damp from tears and bathtub steam. She shredded it, one page at a time, into the toilet.

Sorry, Dad. You were wrong. Nona was right. I have a destiny to live.

Kos surveyed the dining room. "Zoey, the house looks festive and inviting. Don't be disappointed."

She'd dreamed the launch party would be in the back yard with twinkling lights. But, with the risk of Hunters throwing Molotov cocktails at the shield, they'd decided to move the event inside. Andre and Bel agreed the Hunters would stay away from such a public event, but no one wanted to tempt them.

"You're right. It's just hard to put on my party face."

"It will be a great night. The Hunters won't be back today. They ran off with their tails between their legs."

Zoey's lips stretched wide, but they didn't quite make a smile. He must not be very reassuring. No surprise there. His black mood left him unqualified to cheer anybody.

He'd called Lena all day, sent her message after message. At first he apologized, wanting to make things right. Then he didn't care if she was mad, as long as she called to say she was happy, or even just okay. Every time, he would wait for her to call back while trying not to think about it. He knew waiting for a phone call was like watching a pot boil. If he could turn his attention elsewhere, surely she would call. So he kept busy, taking orders from Zoey, but the urge to try again would rise up in him with irresistible force. He would call. She would not answer. Another message.

Zoey witnessed the cycle without comment, until late in the afternoon when she collapsed into a straight-backed chair, looking exhausted. "She's stronger than you think. If you let her go, she'll find her own way to being happy. But if you cling, she'll never move on."

"I know. I'm just afraid she'll be miserable in household service. She deserves to be happy." Across the table, Kos gripped the crossbar on another dining room chair.

Zoey's eyes flicked to his white knuckles, so he moved his hands into his pockets.

She kicked her feet up into a nearby chair. "If Lena's not happy with Mason, she'll leave. I think she really wants a husband, and a family."

Kos suspected the same thing, yet Zoey's words hollowed out one more chamber in his heart. "One more reason we're not meant to be."

"You could give her a family."

"Oh, hell. Please tell me Andre explained to you vampires can't make babies."

"Yeah. But there's Bel."

"Andre has sworn on everything that matters to either one of them that he doesn't know how Mila conceived Bel. He only knows his part, or so he says."

Zoey swung her legs off the chair and leaned over the table to whisper. "Do you know what his part was?"

Kos couldn't help but lean forward and match her hushed tone. "No. Do you?"

"No. But, he said he knows who to ask, someone who knows how Mila managed it."

There was only one person that could be—Uta, his mother's closest friend. "Those were his exact words?"

Zoey thought about it for only a nanosecond. Her human brain had been fast, but as a vampire her brain worked lickity-split. No wonder she kicked their ass at poker. "Close enough."

"Zoey, do you realize Bel might kill Andre over this?" Although, if Kos's suspicions were right about who held the secret, he finally understood why Andre had kept it for so long.

"I'm not telling Bel, I'm telling you. If you could get over your chicken shit fear that every relationship ends badly, you could give her everything she wants—you, and a child."

It wasn't a chicken shit fear. It was the truth.

"You're right. She's better off without me. No more phone calls."

Zoey bolted out of her chair, poised to argue, but she collapsed back down, suddenly pale and wan.

Kos sped to her side. "Are you alright?"

"Hungry." She clutched her belly.

"When did you last eat?"

She extended one finger at a time, counting. "Tuesday."

"*Krist*, Zoey. That's too long. You're only two weeks old. You should feed every day."

"It makes Andre crazy." She squeezed her eyes and crossed her arms over her gut.

"What does?"

"Watching me feed. He gets jealous."

"Off Susan and Ally?"

"I know, it's ridiculous. Is it a vampire thing?"

"No. It's an Andre thing. I'm calling Susan now. And my father." Even in a hurry, the blank screen of his phone registered as he dialed. Lena hadn't called.

His father and Susan arrived in the dining room at the same time. Andre positioned himself against the wall like a chaperone.

Kos yanked his elbow. "Talk to me in the hall."

Andre tugged his arm away, but Kos set his jaw, adopting Andre's own intimidation tactics. It worked, and his father followed him outside.

"Andre, she's faint from hunger. She's putting off feeding because you're jealous."

As Kos expected, regret flashed across Andre's face. "*Davo.*"

"Damn it, Andre. You're the one that wants me to believe it's possible for love to last forever, and you're screwing yours up in two weeks? Get yourself under control. You trust Susan, you trust Zoey. Let her feed on her own terms."

Andre's teeth ground like porcelain plates rubbing together, and his jaw muscles bulged. He rubbed his knuckles over his sternum. "You're right. I'll get over it."

After one deep breath, the tension melted from his face and he padded into the dining room, slumping penitently.

His words poured out into the hallway where Kos stood frozen to the narrow Turkish carpet runner.

"Zoey. Susan. I am sorry. I have been a fool. Please arrange feedings at your convenience. I trust you both without limit."

Moments later, he walked out of the dining room with a well-fed Zoey tucked under his arm, and a wide smile on his face.

Love — 1, Kos — 0.

He slammed his gaping mouth closed. Could he be wrong?

If it were possible, Hunter Headquarters was even filthier than it had been two weeks ago. Ethan tried not to touch anything.

Derek Nichols and Rob Caroli waited on the back porch, presumably because not a glimmer of daylight got into the boarded up house. There were no more initiates camped out on the living room floor, only a few full-fledged Hunters doing target practice in the back yard.

In his pocket, Ethan fingered the little toy soldier. Soon he would control all the Hunters worldwide, and do with them whatever he pleased. Pillage, plunder, terrorize. He hadn't decided yet. Because, just like with Gwen, the how was more important than the what. He would control them with absolute domination.

Caroli squared off his hips and spoke in that deep and impersonal radio voice. "What do you make of the shield?"

Gwen's words came back to him — *sounds like you've seen magic.*

Ethan tested the porch's crumbling railing with his palm before leaning a hip on it. He slid his fingers into his pockets. "It defies explanation, as far as I can see."

Caroli grunted an affirmation. "Tonight is a big party at the estate, celebrating that Blood Vine stuff. We could go after the guests on their way out."

Before Ethan could refute the suggestion, Derek said, "Too risky. Lot of high profile guests. We'll get the attention of law enforcement. Media too."

Smart Hunter. It was worthwhile to avoid unwanted attention at all cost.

"Yes. And, following its distribution could lead us right to the other Croatian vampires. But if we're right, and the vines are what's keeping Marasović and the son so strong, then they must be destroyed."

It would be a significant, if only symbolic victory, garnering him prestige, and the right to command.

Caroli tilted his face toward the low gray clouds. "But how, with that shield up? That's the question."

Ethan turned to face the sky as well, wrapping his fingers around the decrepit railing and leaning on it until it creaked. "I want the men to remain on the ready. Prepared to go back to Kaštel with their napalm and flamethrowers. I have a strategy for taking down the shield, a secret weapon of sorts."

"What's that?" Derek's voice rose with curiosity.

"Who, actually. But let me worry about that." Ethan's lips pulled into a smile. The strategy was a very pretty blonde, for whom Kosjenic Marasović would move mountains, or even dismantle magical shields. Once they'd delivered Blood Vine to the distributors, all Ethan had to do was get to Mason Kearney, and he'd have his hands on the precious Lena.

Gwen sent him a text message:

Ordering Chinese. Finished translation. Home soon?

Ethan wasn't sure what sounded better, the translation or Gwen herself. He could tie her to his bed, and rub her most sensitive flesh with Chinese hot peppers until she was on fire. Even the aphrodisiac of controlling each and every Hunter around the world was less arousing than Gwen's pain.

CHAPTER 21

Thirty minutes before the party was scheduled to start, Kos descended the stairs. Everything looked gray without Lena, the walls, the furniture, people, like a thick fog had rolled into his life making it hard to see. His body was strung tight, and his suit jacket fit all wrong. How on earth would he manage to schmooze, given his foul mood?

He walked into the parlor and Andre poured wine for three. For Zoey's sake, he bit out a polite phrase. "Congratulations on this party."

"To Zoey, and to the homeland," Andre said, adding the traditional blessing of all vampires in exile.

Zoey clinked her glass against each of theirs, and they sipped the wine — currant and pepper, tart and sweet, and underneath all that, the taste of home. The fog receded, and Kos remembered their purpose. The shambles of his love life were small potatoes compared to the fate of his kind, the other vampires wasting away, weak and starving.

Zoey bit her lower lip and drummed her fingers against her thighs. She hadn't forgotten their purpose for a second. Andre touched the small of her back, and she seemed to relax.

Kos crossed to the stereo. Although it might grate on Andre's nerves, Kos turned on Ella Fitzgerald's cover of "Our Love is Here to Stay." It was a peace offering. He did truly wish them an eternity of such contentment.

After Andre and Zoey had bonded, Kos and Lena had thrown them an informal celebration. Lena said the happy couple needed a song and suggested the Gershwin piece. She'd arranged the whole thing behind the scenes for her new friend, and she'd been so alive at the celebration, her laughter drifting above the party sounds as she floated among people chatting. And when she'd thrown back her head to laugh, exposing the curve of her throat, she was the most beautiful thing he'd ever seen.

Now he knew how soft her skin was there, under her jaw. And he knew the taste of her blood pulsing underneath it too. The honeyed flavor still lingered in his mouth, the last blood he'd swallowed. He should feed from someone else and stop teasing himself with it, but he couldn't bring himself to wash it away.

The doorbell rang, and he hoped the guests were arriving to distract him. He opened the front door as Andre and Zoey emerged from the parlor. A delivery person stood outside holding an enormous flower arrangement.

Andre turned to Zoey. "Did you order those?"

"No."

His father strode to the door. "They're Dalmatian Irises. They only grow in Croatia."

The delivery woman confirmed. "That's right, we had them flown in this morning."

Who on earth could have sent such an extravagant bouquet?

Zoey signed for the flowers as Andre opened the envelope. Kos hovered behind and read over his shoulder. There was a card inside and a folded piece of paper. Andre read the greeting aloud.

Congratulations on Blood Vine. Very good news for all of us. It's time for us to talk. I'll be there soon. —Uta

P.S. Say hello to the halfling for me.

"Who's Uta?" Zoey's eyebrows scrunched together.

"An old friend," Andre croaked, his voice thick with the dread Kos felt.

Shit. She was coming? Here? Not good, especially given what Zoey had told him about Mila's secret. Kos tried to hide his concern with a joke. "I believe the modern term is frenemy, father."

Bel and Pedro slid into the room together. Kos hoped he hadn't heard the message from his estranged aunt. With any luck, Bel would be back in Los Angeles before she arrived. Perhaps he could avoid dredging up the past—

"Did you say Uta?" Bel barked. "What does she want?"

Damn it, Kos had no luck whatsoever.

"Who's the halfling?" Zoey asked, all unknowing curiosity.

"Did she call me that? Bitch!" Bel snatched the card out of Andre's hand.

Kos held the paper Uta had enfolded in the card. Opening it, he was stunned by what he saw and took a moment to speak. "*Krist*," he finally rasped, before passing the paper to Andre, whose eyes widened.

"What is it?" Pedro and Zoey asked at the same time.

Kos ran his palm over his scalp, searching for the words. "It's a color photo of an ancient Greek text, with illustrations."

"Saying?" Zoey didn't keep the irritation from her voice.

"I don't know, my Greek is rusty. It's the illustration that's got my attention."

Andre flipped the paper to show them the odd, vibrant image of a battle scene. Warriors fought with heavy swords, and both armies of soldiers had yellow-gold eyes. Half also had fangs, exaggerated in length by the rudimentary style of artwork. It was a battle between Hunters and vampires, both with golden eyes. Pedro, Zoey and Bel huddled around the sheet of copy paper, trying to get a good look.

When it was clear they couldn't all see at once, Pedro gave up his spot to step next to Andre. "This gets us closer to learning why they hate us."

"Not really. All it tells us is hostility erupted in a battle long ago."

Pedro frowned. "Not quite. It also tells us I'm not the first vampire with Hunter eyes."

"*Davo*. I didn't catch that. Double *Davo*." Andre looked from Pedro's eyes to the paper.

"You're all missing the most important thing." Zoey annunciated each word as if speaking to school children.

Kos hadn't missed it — he just didn't know what the hell to say.

She let go of the paper so Bel could have it to himself and continued to explain. "They're in the sunlight, all of them. The battle takes place in the middle of the day."

Bel still hadn't peeled his eyes off the paper, but he was the first one to pipe up with a theory. "Pedro, my man, maybe you can tolerate the sun."

Kos had thought the same thing the moment he saw the illustration. And if he fed from Lucas, or perhaps a prettier Hunter, maybe he could walk under the sun too. He didn't even know he craved daylight until the possibility occurred to him. In a place inside him already full of longing for another radiant body, his desire for the sun also bloomed.

Everyone was silent. A grandfather clock ticked in the dining room.

"How on earth could you test that?" Zoey finally asked.

Bel dropped into the high-backed chair by the door. "Maybe a tiny laser beam of light with the same radiation composition as sunlight—some ultraviolet and infrared in addition to the visible light. But even that much of the solar spectrum might turn a vampire into bacon."

"Don't you mean Vacon?" Pedro's laugh sounded forced.

Bel cringed. "Dude. You wouldn't laugh if you'd ever smelled it. Not good."

He was right, a vampire turned to ash was a nasty, smelly, horrible thing. Kos was not about to volunteer to be a guinea pig in that experiment.

He rose his voice to steer them back. "I'd like to keep thinking about sunlight, but there are more important questions. Where is this picture from? Why does Auntie Uta have it? And how did she know to send it to us?"

"She sent it because of the Blood Vine," Andre said, his tone certain. "She must know there is a connection between the wine and Hunter blood. She knows something of the history and the little witch did not share it with me for the two thousand years we were neighbors."

"No surprise she never told you," Bel said. "She's a selfish bitch."

"Ah," Zoey said. "I'm getting the frenemy thing now."

Andre folded up the paper. "Pedro," he commanded, "go to your Lucas and see if he knows anything."

Pedro paled. "How could he possibly know anything?"

"Relax," Kos whispered. "Just go ask."

Pedro put his hands in pockets and strode from the room.

Just as the young vampire cleared the door, Bel spoke up. "May I be dismissed? I couldn't stop thinking about Hunters even before this picture arrived."

Andre nodded, and Bel followed Pedro.

His father pressed the paper into Kos's palm. "Put this somewhere safe and we'll deal with it after the party."

Kos unfolded it and smoothed out the creases before carrying the photocopy to his office as if it were the ancient page itself. Only a game changer of this magnitude could distract him from Lena enough to move on. He almost felt grateful to his Aunt Uta. Almost.

When Ethan stepped into his apartment, Gwen called out. "Dinner?"

"I want to see the translation." He strode to the desk where she had been working.

"I'm not ready to show it to you."

His head jerked back to her, and her eyes gleamed in hungry defiance. She was looking for a fight.

He dragged her to his room and tied her to the bed. Her eyes shone even brighter with anticipation. But once she was secured, he gagged her and went to look for her notebook. The sound of her frustrated grunts faded as he walked down the hall. The translation wasn't on the desk, or in any of the drawers. He searched her bags, pried open her locked briefcase — nothing.

On the bed, Gwen's wrists and ankles were red from straining against the ropes.

"Where is it?" He kept her gagged and searched her eyes for an answer. They still showed defiance. He hit her hard with the back of his hand. "Where?"

She grunted from the impact of his slap, then attempted to speak behind the gag. He untied it.

"Fuck me."

He hit her face again, and her grunt was louder without the gag.

"You must be confused, Gwen. I fuck you when I want to, on my terms."

Her chest heaved, and her skin flushed — her game had worked. Astonished, he realized he'd given her exactly what she wanted. No harm in that — it was what he wanted too. The translation could wait. He raised his hand again to strike.

"Not my face."

She'd said the same thing before they'd boarded their plane. And it was a good point. If they were going to approach Kearney, it wouldn't do for her to be black and blue.

Or would it?

"Let's show Mason Kearney that you belong to me now." The first punch landed on her jaw. The second would leave a nice black eye.

Then he punched her in the rib cage, under her left breast. She didn't make a sound. No protest, no begging. But her eyes gleamed with the most intoxicating blend of fear and submission.

He wanted her naked, but didn't want to untie her, so he rushed to the kitchen to find a pair of shears.

Later, when he collapsed on top of her, she said, "My notebook is under the mattress."

He actually laughed, aloud, deep from his belly. She'd played him like a fiddle, anticipating his every move. Not that he liked the idea of being predictable. He would be certain to surprise her later, with a punishment to match her manipulation. His cock was already stirring again at the notion. Her submission was becoming addictive. She saw into him and craved precisely what he wanted to give her. A match made in…well, somewhere unholy for certain.

He unbound her, and found her notebook under the mattress, remembering the way teen-aged Lucas used to hide pages he'd torn from the Sears Catalog men's underwear section in the same place.

Gwen sat cross-legged, with the sheet pulled over her breasts, annotating her translation. "Here it says: *The Night Walkers had the Sun in their eyes. Dela-Malkh did not know who was of the Day and who was of the Night.* Accompanied by the picture, I'd assume that means the vampires' eyes turned golden when they fed from the Hunters."

"Or were they Hunters who had been turned into vampires?"

"Oh. I see. I don't know. Here, it says: *Many Children loved the Night instead of the Day. Dela-Malkh was angry. The Day Walkers were angry. No Children loved the Sun anymore.* It sounds like some sort of generational conflict, the younger children abandoned devotion to the sun god, and began to worship the night god, or perhaps the vampire way of life."

"Yes. That makes sense. The younger generation was possibly seduced by the vampires."

"It's always something. Sex, drugs, rock and roll. Vampires." Her playful lilt made him chuckle, but then her tone grew serious. "Except this doesn't always happen: *Dela-Malkh told the Day Walkers to kill everyone of the Night. Dela-Malkh commanded the Day Walkers to kill their Children."* Her head swiveled to face him. "Ethan, they killed their children."

He gripped her chin, and forced her to look at them. "Do you think they were wrong to do it?"

She shrunk back, but he held her face tight. Her eyes widened for a flash of a second. "I…I don't know. I was seduced too."

Ah. One day, he would ask her about that.

"Gwen, I don't blame you."

"Would the other Hunters, though?"

She was a perceptive little thing — smart — and attuned to power, and its uses.

"You belong to me. Not Mason Kearny, and not them. No one will hurt you." As an afterthought, he added, "Besides me."

She shivered and leaned her face into his palm like a puppy. "Ethan, what will happen to the girl when you rescue her from Kearney?"

"I will use her as bait to get to Marasović."

"But will you give her to the vampires?"

"No, I won't."

His men would demand the woman's death, on account of her being a vampire slave. And probably not before they'd had their own fun with her. But there was no cause to tell Gwen that. She seemed the type to fret over the ethics of the situation. As far as he was concerned, there were none besides his victory. But, to her, he was the good guy — a sadistic good guy to be sure — and one she trusted.

Gwen sighed, and choked once on her words before they flowed freely. "I worry for her. I was different before, and I don't want her to end up —"

"Yes. Of course you worry. But we cannot rescue her yet. A few more dominoes need to fall into place."

The last illustration Lucas had unearthed from his memory was a battle, and he was almost finished tinting it. Golden-eyed vampires fought golden-eyed Hunters to the death under a bright yellow sun. Corpses of each were piled on both sides of the drawing, like tallies. The dead vampires lay headless, and the outcome of the battle was unclear. Lucas suspected the vampires had retreated. Did they take their Hunter mates?

The drawings answered some of his questions, but didn't illuminate a path ahead. Should he show them to Pedro or escape before every vampire in the house wanted to sink their teeth into him?

He'd earned a modicum of trust at Kaštel, but he wasn't invited to join the launch party. He would put the drawings away, make a vodka tonic, watch television and ponder his dilemma. He'd found some very melodramatic soaps over the last week, and he could enjoy the eye candy while he decided his next steps.

His door opened tentatively, but without a knock. Pedro loomed in the shadowy frame, somehow filling it despite his average height. Behind him stood Lobel Marasović.

So much for his plans; the decision had been made for him. It was too late to hide the drawings. He needed to explain fast—

"What the fuck, Lucas?" Pedro asked, instantly at Lucas's side and looming over the desk.

Bel was there a second later. "It's the same damn picture. Practically identical. Seriously, what the fuck?"

The same picture? What were they talking about?

"Lucas?" Pedro mouth hung open, his eyes pools of molten gold. He was beyond stunned—he looked like he was back on that table, at Ethan's mercy.

Fuck. Lucas hadn't expected that.

"What the hell are these drawings?" Pedro shouted, desperation creeping into his usually confident voice.

Great. Tonight I'll get to live my very own soap opera. At least the men are just as beautiful.

Bel looked back and forth between them, scratching his head. He must not have known they were lovers, or almost, anyway.

Lucas stood up, pressing his fingers to his mouth. "I was going to show them to you later." It was possibly true, and that mattered. Lying to Pedro had been a torment, even when it meant saving his own ass.

"I don't understand." Pedro's gaze volleyed between Lucas and Bel, lost. He gripped the chair, as if trying not to sink into the trauma that was dragging him under.

God, Lucas wanted to grab him and hold him tight. He'd probably get his throat ripped out if he tried.

"I drew them, from memory."

"What were you remembering?" Bel asked, a voice of reason in the unfolding drama.

"A book, an ancient book of my father's. I haven't seen it since I was a kid...but I have a...a good memory."

Bel flipped through the drawings. "Better than good, I'd say. Perfect recall?"

Lucas folded up a corner on one of the pages. "Yeah. For images."

"So let me get this right." A steel edge sharpened Bel's voice. "An ancient book of your father's, that you saw as a kid?"

Lucas's heart sank, and he nodded.

"Fuck, you've been lying to us from the beginning," Bel said.

Finally, Pedro spoke. "You've known the entire time? Known your blood would do something weird to me?"

"I didn't know for sure." Lucas shrugged. "I just suspected."

Pedro seized his throat in an instant, pinning him against the wall with one strong hand under his chin. He stood on his toes to meet Lucas's eye, but he didn't teeter—he was graceful, poised, lethal.

With one secret, Lucas had unleashed all the rage Pedro had barely controlled.

"Pedro, heel," Bel said.

The vampire growled. When had he started doing that? He was a fucking animal. The hair on the back of Lucas's neck stood up, but, so did his cock. Jesus, did he really have it this bad for the guy?

"We need to know." Bel said. "What exactly did you suspect?"

What could they deduce from the drawings? He paused too long, obviously considering how to best preserve himself. Pedro squeezed his throat.

"Answer." Bel was cool and commanding next to Pedro's fiery fury.

"That my blood might give you special powers. Might allow you to tolerate the sun."

"No shit?" Bel said. "What else?"

May as well come clean now. "Maybe these drawings are the story of where Hunters came from."

"Fuck you, Lucas." Pedro spat. "After everything, I still trusted you again. I'm a fucking fool."

Pedro glared at him, golden eyes burning with hate. Lucas wanted to flinch at the sight of his own eyes hating him like that, but he didn't look away.

Maybe Pedro felt foolish, but really, Lucas was the fool — not to have realized how the vampire would react to a secret like this. "I was afraid if you all knew what I suspected, I'd be bled dry. Everyone would want a taste."

Bel snorted. "That's what Hunters would do, not us."

"Maybe he's right." Pedro's voice changed, suddenly distant, detached. "Maybe that's what the vampires did to cause that battle — enslaved the Hunters for their mojo." He still looked in Lucas's eyes, but he was talking to Bel.

Enslaved? That's not what Lucas was getting from the drawings. He was getting frisky fuck buddies of the prehistoric variety. A willing partnership between some Hunters and the vampires. But, if the whole enslavement idea lent Pedro some sympathy for him, he wouldn't argue.

Bel placed a large tanned hand on Pedro's shoulder. "What are we going to do with him?"

White-hot fireworks went off in the vampire's eyes, and Lucas's stomach did a somersault.

"I still need him to feed. Let's put him with the other Hunter in the cell." Pedro locked his right arm around Lucas's elbow. "Now, I'm going to walk you to the cellar. If you see any party guests, you will smile like you're my fucking prom date and couldn't be happier about it."

He marched Lucas through the wine cellar over to the big warehouse space where Pedro and Andre made wine. Silently, Pedro opened the door to a closet and shoved him inside.

Little Leo Caroli sat on floor looking miserable and pissed off. He sneered at Lucas. "Fight with your boyfriend?"

The comment wasn't a surprise. His father would have denigrated Lucas in every way possible to distance himself from his son's treachery.

Lucas took a play from Pedro's book. "Kid, do not fuck with me right now," he growled.

CHAPTER 22

A maître d' held out Lena's chair, which was covered in nubby tan ostrich leather. She'd never been to the restaurant before. It was well regarded, and she couldn't afford it when she lived in the city. Damn it if she was going to think about the party at Kaštel, about all the food she'd lovingly made, and all the fun they would have without her. Not while she was out some place so special.

A waiter set a glass of champagne in front of her, and opened her menu before stepping away.

She dug her nails into her palms and skimmed the offerings before glancing up at Mason. "I'm so excited to try the lamb. They're famous for it."

"Delightful, lovely. But pick two dishes for every course. It would look rather odd if only you appear to be eating. And you can try some of everything."

He smiled his rakish grin and the event at Kaštel receded into the back of her mind. After she ordered for them both, he asked about her childhood in Alaska, and her time in San Francisco. He proved his impeccable manners by not once mentioning Kos, or Andre. It was her best first date ever.

As she drank coffee and tasted both a plum tart and a chocolate mousse, he leaned forward. "I'm looking forward to my dinner too."

"Just no more truffles. I'm stuffed." She patted her belly and smiled. Yes. It would do her good to have sex with him. Together, they could wipe away her memories of Kos.

He winked. "No more truffles. I have something else in mind."

She shivered, anticipation creeping up her spine.

On the street, he clasped her elbow, pressing firmly with the pads of his fingers and watching her face. Her pulse stuttered, then found a faster rhythm. He ran his tongue over his teeth, then locked his elbow around hers, leading her back toward his house. He told her about San Francisco during Prohibition, and the walk flew by as her mind swirled with images from the past.

Outside his house, he turned her toward him and kissed her with his artful lips and practiced tongue. She allowed her body to relax into the pleasant sensations — just bodies, no emotions.

He broke the kiss. "There's a surprise for you upstairs in my room."

"Another one? This dress is gorgeous."

"I'm glad you think so. That bodes well for the surprise."

Could it be more clothing?

He took her arm again, leading her upstairs. In his bedroom was a slender woman wearing an identical dress. "Lena, this is Alyssa."

Lena's stomach felt funny. "Hello." She tried to lift the corners of her mouth.

"Mason, she's as pretty as you said."

"Of course she is." Mason's smile had gone from rake to wolf since they climbed the stairs.

Alyssa was very pretty herself — of Vietnamese or maybe Thai descent — slim and shorter than Lena, with apple-sized breasts compared to Lena's grapefruits.

"Lena, Alyssa is joining us for my dinner."

"All right," Lena whispered.

"Lena, honey," the other woman said, "why don't you sit here in this chair. Mason would like to watch us get to know each other."

Mason gave a nod to confirm her request.

Lena sat, and Alyssa stood in front of her. "Relax, this will be fun. You know, with Mason and his fangs, it has to be."

Lena took a deep breath. The other woman lifted the hem of her dress, and straddled Lena.

She kissed her cheek and whispered in her ear. "Just pretend sweetie. He'll make it good for you."

Did she not know Mason could hear her? Over Alyssa's shoulder, Mason stared at Lena with no expression.

Then Alyssa slipped her tongue in between Lena's lips and began a slow kiss. It wasn't unpleasant. The woman's tongue was small and slender compared to the male tongues she'd had in her mouth. Her lips were somehow more gentle. But it wasn't arousing either. She'd wondered if being with a woman would turn her on — that would be a no.

They kissed for a while and Alyssa purred and wiggled, rubbing her breasts against Lena. Was she faking it, or really into this?

Mason cleared his throat. "Alyssa, let's get you out of that dress."

She stood up and slipped it off, revealing a sweet little body, completely bare between her legs. Lena kept a narrow patch of her golden curls — it seemed more wholesome somehow — and now she knew why.

"Lena, Alyssa would like it if you kissed her breasts. Enthusiastically."

In other words, fake it, and that's an order.

Lena leaned forward to lick one nipple, which perked to attention under her tongue. Again, she didn't find the experience arousing, but she was a little curious to see how the other woman responded. Alyssa's hips began to rock on Lena's lap and she reached to cup her breasts through the dress. Mason watched them for a long time, although Lena didn't look directly at him again. Looking somehow made it worse.

"You're doing a good job turning her on, Lena. But I'm not sure she's ready to get fucked. You tell me."

Alyssa looked her in the eye, a subtle nod of agreement. Lena ran her hand down the other woman's hip and across her thigh to where she was spread open in Lena's lap. The woman's body felt different from her own. Lena must have grazed her clit because Alyssa sucked in a breath.

Then her finger found its way into the other woman's core. "She's very wet, Mason. You must be able to smell her."

Alyssa's eyebrows shot up. Clearly, she didn't know anything about vampires. Lena shrugged.

"What else is she like, Lena. What does she feel like to you?"

She feels interesting, like I'm feeling my body from the other side.

"She's tight, pulsing. She's ready for you."

"She's going to have to wait. First, I'll feed from you."

Lena froze, couldn't draw in a breath. If he bit her, she wouldn't be able resist them. They could do whatever they wanted to her, and she might even like it.

"Take off your dress and come to me."

Warily, Lena stood. What would happen if she said no? She would have to leave. She would be unemployed and out on the street looking for a restaurant job somewhere. It was impossible to live on those wages in the city—she'd already tried. She could go back to Kaštel until she found another job, ask for Kos's help again—

No way. She'd rather have sex with Alyssa than go back to him, begging.

Come to think of it, didn't he send her into this mess in the first place? Did he know Mason was like this?

"Let me help you with the zipper," Mason said, forcing her decision.

His eyes dared her to say no. He reached around her, unzipping her dress, and she stood in her underwear until he unhooked her bra, and Alyssa slid her panties down.

Fully clothed, Mason sat on the chaise and waited for her to sit between his legs.

The same ritual as last night followed—he searched with fingers and tongue for where to bite her, covering her neck with his saliva so that she would heal no matter where he chose to sink his fangs. Again, he gave her no warning before he struck.

Once he was drawing on her blood, Alyssa climbed onto the chaise between Lena's legs.

Oh God, that's what they intended. She tried to close her knees, but Alyssa was already between them, and the other woman stroked her bite-sensitized skin—thighs and breasts and belly. And now, because of his bite, her touch was delicious. She kissed her mouth when the oral urges hit. And then, when Lena sunk into the deep, relaxing bliss, she felt the other woman's lips on her now-wet core.

Alyssa's little tongue felt so different from Kos's. She worked Lena into a frenzy, and Mason matched it with the pace of his suction. Then, to her surprise, Alyssa slipped her fingers inside Lena and touched that secret place only Kos knew, and she was climaxing and sobbing just like last time. At least she didn't pass out again.

Mason sealed up her wounds with a lick. "Good girl. You come so beautifully."

After a moment, she stood up on wobbly knees, and Alyssa crawled up Mason and took his erection from his pants. She deep-throated him like a professional, which she probably was. But then, Lena had no room to judge. That was what she was now, too.

She hugged her arms across her breasts and tried not to move. Mason watched her with the same expressionless intensity as Alyssa bobbed up and down his length. But then he closed his cold, cold eyes, and she was dismissed…for the time being.

CHAPTER 23

The chandelier in the foyer glittered. The guests' faces shone too, with the enjoyment of a party. Bodies packed into the dining room, the parlor, and into the central entryway, scenting the air with the blood and soap and perfume and sweat of nearly one hundred humans. Kos's stomach rumbled. There were even a few friends who'd be happy to feed him flitting around the party, somewhere, but he had no real appetite.

In contrast, the guests seemed ravenous. They devoured the food Lena had prepared. Occasionally remarks about how unusual and delicious it was floated to him amidst the loud buzz of the conversations. Non-stop laughter and the clinking of glasses rang out over the chatter. By nearly every standard, the party was a success.

Wedged into a dark corner of the foyer, he sipped a glass of Blood Vine and kept his eyes trained on his father. With Zoey at his side, shaking hands and talking about his wine, Andre might have been at his own wedding. He stood straight, lips pulled into his truest smile. Perhaps at that moment he was able to forget what Kos could not—Hunters, that damn note from Uta, Lena.

Zoey broke from a gathering of smartly dressed journalists and wine critics to mount a handful of stairs. Andre climbed to stand behind her, and they faced the crowd. Under some invisible force of her charisma or their infectious joy, the room hushed.

She raised her hand to quiet everyone, but they'd already grown silent. Her mouth was rather wide to be beautiful, but it made her smile all the more dazzling. "We are so grateful that you've come tonight to celebrate the launch of Blood Vine. I agreed to work with Andre because I was intrigued by his vision for this wine. I had no idea I would come to believe in it, or him, so completely." Hardly exquisite rhetoric, and yet, the room hung on her words, or on the passion that undergirded them, making her voice quiver. "And so I ask a personal favor of you, to help us spread the word far and wide about this very special wine, and this very special place."

A smattering of applause bounced in the room, but Andre cut it off by clearing his throat. "Zoey speaks correctly of my gratitude for your help. If you have known me any length of time, you might wonder at her presumption in doing so." He wrapped his arm around her shoulder and drew her close. She beamed at him. "She possesses every right, because she has agreed to be my wife and my partner in this endeavor. *Forever.*" His last word was spoken so quietly few humans would have heard. It sent a chill across Kos's scalp all the way to his haunches. If only…

But the crowd clapped in earnest, and even a few bawdy whistles sang out from among the winemakers. They'd bonded, but now they would unite in a human ceremony, making their relationship public and official—a mistake Kos could not help but envy. As the couple descended the stairs, guests queued up to shake their hands and say good night. Kos used his thumb and forefinger to shape his face into a smile and carved his way through the crowd to make his own farewells.

A brief hour later, the partygoers had all drifted out and the house had undergone a cursory cleaning. He leaned into the doorframe of Andre's office, pushing his full weight into the muscles along his neck and shoulder, attempting to massage out the golf-ball-sized knots that were bunching them.

Zoey and Andre reclined in the brown leather armchairs, sipping Blood Vine and chatting, with their feet propped on the coffee table. Their hands were clasped between the chairs, and Zoey's quiet laughter made her appear more relaxed than she'd been in days.

Kos couldn't stop thinking about the picture Uta had sent. Hell, he couldn't stop thinking about the sun, about standing beneath Lena while she plucked figs from the tree, his fingers splayed across her belly and the sun warming his head and his shoulders, which relaxed slightly at the image, then scrunched up again at its impossibility. He might actually walk in the sun, but he'd never touch her again.

Bel and Pedro came through the cellar, and Kos stepped aside so they could enter. In the dim light of Andre's office, both their mouths formed hard lines. Kos braced himself against the doorframe, ready for another blow.

"Bad news," Bel said, unnecessarily.

Andre closed his eyes. "What now?"

"Lucas knew," Pedro spat.

Andre flew to his feet and crossed to Pedro in a flash. "Knew what?"

Bel extended a roll of papers toward Andre.

He untied them and viewed the top sheet, his eyes widening.

"Lucas drew them from memory. They're from an ancient Hunter book his father owned." Bel droned in his matter-of-fact, I-kill-Hunters-all-the-time voice. "Practically identical to the one Uta sent. He's suspected all along his blood might allow Pedro to tolerate the sun."

"*Davo.*"

"He lied to me," Pedro said, his voice reedy.

Zoey crossed to him and stroked the back of his head, offering the kind of comfort only women could give—women like Lena. Saliva pooled in Kos's mouth; he could still taste her, smell her, feel her skin.

"Snap out of it, Kos," Andre said. "I need you here, not up Lena's skirt."

"Sorry." Kos joined the circle forming around Andre's desk. How had Andre known his thoughts?

Then Andre did it again, his tone almost kind. "A set of drawings that explains the mysteries of the universe is in front of you and you're navel gazing. Only one navel you find that distracting."

Andre cleared the table and spread the papers out in the order of the stack.

"*Krist.* Five pictures?" Kos said, his mind clearing. This was way more information than what Uta had sent.

The sketches were in graphite and colored pencil. Lucas was good. With basic supplies, he'd captured the quality of light and line that gave the feel of an ancient illustrated manuscript.

"We examined them upstairs during the party. I have some ideas, but take a look first." Bel rearranged the papers in some sort of order.

Kos reached for one, but it was so like a genuine artifact that he stopped short to prevent himself from touching it. "It's a wedding. He's wearing the red band for the blood bond ceremony."

"You didn't wear that," Zoey said to Andre.

"As you keep reminding me, lover, we are not married. I will wear that when you make an honest vampire out of me."

Andre turned to kiss Zoey with an open mouth, and Kos regretted seeing his father's tongue slip between her lips. How could he tease and kiss at a time like this? It was lewd. Or did it only seem that way because Kos was jealous?

Bel ignored the make out session. "You're right, a wedding. Then, in the next picture, the happy couple is standing in the daylight."

Andre broke the kiss to look.

Stunned silence stretched out. Twice in one night, Kos had seen drawings indicating that, with Hunter blood, he might be able to go into the sun, after almost two centuries in the night. He didn't pine over daylight—why bother? That would be as useless as wishing you could breathe underwater. Andre was a hundred times older than him, and Kos could only imagine how the idea of walking in the day messed with his sense of reality.

"This next one's a kicker too. At least, Bel thought so." Pedro tapped his index finger on the margin of one drawing.

Bel's lips were pinched tight, and a tingle went down Kos's spine—it wasn't going to be good. But somehow he worked up the nerve to look at the third illustration. Sure enough—the happy vampire family had a baby. Again, no one said a thing.

Zoey broke the silence, pointing at the fourth drawing. "Looks like a little Electra complex going on here." The female Hunter was eviscerating her parents.

"Electra only killed her mother." Kos rubbed at his aching neck. "This is plain old patricide."

"Tempting, too, isn't it?" Bel smiled maliciously at Andre.

"Bel, not now. Please," Kos said. "Look at number five. It's like the one Uta sent, but not identical. Perhaps hers is from a different copy?"

Bel framed the paper with his large hands. "My thoughts exactly."

"So can someone please string this story together for me?" Zoey asked, in her not-really-a-request tone of voice.

Words exploded from Bel as if he'd been waiting for the invitation. "I think it's two tribes mixing. Then a rift of some sort causes them to go to war. Some Hunters are on the side of the vampires. But what happened to the survivors?"

"I think they were enslaved," Pedro said.

"Who?" Andre asked, rare astonishment coloring his speech.

"The Hunters. They were forced by the vampires to give their blood, and that's why they hate us."

"I'm not seeing a lot of coercion here, buddy," Bel argued.

Clearly, they'd already discussed this.

"Look again at the first drawing — the wedding."

Pedro picked it up and studied it, eyes widening. "*Madre de Dios*. Andre, look."

Andre did, only for a second, before he returned his gaze to Pedro. "No."

"Yes," Pedro countered.

"No."

"What?" Zoey tugged at Andre's sleeve.

"Grape vines. They are standing under an arbor of grapevines."

Once more, the group descended into silence, passing the pictures back and forth.

Bel set a drawing down — the one with the child. "Andre, we need to talk."

Andre's jaw went to work, gnashing loudly as they stepped into the cellar for the illusion of privacy. Kos wished it for them, even though he and the other vampires remaining would hear every word.

"Is there something you want to tell me?" Bel asked on the other side of the door.

"Son, nothing has changed. I do not posses the answers you seek."

Kos, Pedro and Zoey exchanged glances. Pretending they couldn't hear each other's every word and action kept vampires sane. Zoey closed her eyes and leaned her head back. Pedro plugged his ears. Kos listened.

"How can you say that?" Bel said. "I'm begging you. Throw me a bone."

"You have been my son for one hundred and eighty years, and still you do not trust me to know what is best."

"Are you listening to yourself? When will you trust that I know what is best for myself?"

His combat boots fell heavily on the stone floor of the cellar as he strode away. Pedro and Zoey looked to Kos again, and he shook his head. No sense pressing Andre. They should let it lie for the time being. Outside, the faint sound of Bel's engine revving told them all he was off to Los Angeles.

His father appeared in the doorway. Bulky muscles filled out his shirt, his face was unlined, even his hair was back to black since they started drinking Blood Vine. But the strain in his eyes, and the set of his jaw, clearly hinted at his two thousand years.

There was only one thing to do — play cards.

"I'll deal," Kos said.

They played all night and into the morning. Pedro was the only one to give Zoey a run for her money. The last hand was a bidding war between the two of them, and when Pedro put his last chips in and called, Zoey showed him her full house.

"*Mierda!*" He slammed his cards on the table. "If we have to flee the estate, let's take Zoey to Vegas."

"Can't." Kos gathered the cards. "Against vampire code to gamble with humans. Speed, hearing, smell. We have every advantage."

"Who enforces vampire code anyway?"

"We all enforce the code when we see it broken. The oldest vampire involved has jurisdiction." Kos shuffled, a singularly enjoyable task.

"So I just need Andre's permission?"

"I wouldn't risk it," he said. "What if a vampire older than me owned the casino? He could decide to throw you into the Nevada desert at high noon."

"Oh."

Memories of Mason rolled through Kos's mind as he dealt the next hand — Mason's too charming smiles, women surrounding him, a predatory look when he thought Kos wasn't watching. *Krist*, that vampire could consume women insatiably. But he was honorable, and she would be fine. She even seemed to like him...

The sinking feeling in his gut was just jealousy. Had to be.

All night, no one mentioned her. Surely it had cost his family of smartasses to skip the ribbing, a small comfort for his aching heart.

He opened the door to his room, and the smell of sex assaulted him. Honey and musk made his mouth water, and he was powerless to resist. He lay down and replayed every moment — her golden hair falling over his face, her legs cradling him, her soft breasts against his chest, and their glorious coming together.

It was quite possible he would never get out of the bed.

The memory of making love to Lena pulled him deeper and deeper into that ecstasy, that place of perfect union with her and the whole world. And then, they were outside Mason's house, arguing. And then, she stood in the place of every woman in Kos's memories of Mason. Her face was on every flight attendant, she'd passed out on Mason's divan, she danced with him in a sleek Audrey Hepburn dress at some night club they used to haunt, she was under Mason, rocking with his thrusts, mouth open in ecstasy.

It was wrong. Those women weren't her. She couldn't be one of them. It wouldn't make her happy.

Then there was the blood, pouring from an open bite in her neck. That should never happen. A vampire never spilled his prey's blood. It was precious, to be lovingly consumed and licked clean, flesh knit back together with care.

He was incapable of sleep; the torrent of images weren't a dream. Was it a flight of fancy? A hallucination induced by her smell? An omen?

Had he been crazy to trust Mason?

Maybe.

One thing was certain—he had to get her. Enough of letting her have her way, letting her find her own destiny. He would bring her back to Kaštel and lock her in that damn cell with Lucas and Leo until she came to her senses and agreed to a human life. Where some human man became her husband, gave her children.

Kos hated the idea, but not nearly as much as he hated her being Mason's toy. And that was all she could ever be to him.

Kos peeled back his eyelids, and the brightness of the room stung. Forcing his body to stir was a battle. Ten a.m. His rescue mission would have to wait until sunset, but he had to get her a message. Only, she wouldn't take his calls. Stubborn thing—she'd probably turned off her phone, or chucked it out the window.

Was she walking along Union Street? Having brunch in one of the cafés? Shopping for clothes too fashionable to wear at Kaštel? Browsing in The Archives Bookshop? He smiled to remember that gem of a bookstore. Every time he walked in, Mattie would shove her horn-rimmed glasses up on her forehead and smile. Those glasses had been fashionable when he'd met her, and now showed her age—seventy something and still cute as a button, but no longer his type.

Mattie would help.

"The Archives. This is Matilda. How can I help you?"

"Mattie, it's Kos."

"Hey there, lover. What's shakin'?" There was a smile in her voice, and it warmed him.

"I need your help—an odd favor." He hated to ask, even though he trusted she'd agree.

"I'm always happy to help. I must owe you a hundred favors."

"I'm not keeping score, but I'd sure appreciate your help with this one."

"Shoot."

"Do you still have that portable CD player behind the counter?"

"Yep."

"How about Ella Fitzgerald? The album where she sings 'Our Love is Here to Stay.'"

"Hmm." The sound of shuffling plastic CD cases came through the line. "I have her singing it as a duet with Louis Armstrong. Will that do?"

"It will have to."

"Is this about a girl, Kos?" Her gently scolding tone said she knew him too well, but Lena wasn't just any girl.

Still, he said, "Of course."

"Please tell me I'm not going to stand somewhere with this boom box and blast Ella Fitzgerald, like John Cusack."

"Seen that movie, have you?"

"My kids were teenagers when it came out. We had it on VHS. I've got that album here too—Peter Gabriel. Want that one instead?"

It had to be a sign. "Mattie, you're a saint."

Her chuckle cut short. "Oh, Kos, I'm sorry. This case is empty."

"Fine. Ella it is."

"Where?"

"Mason's house."

"Mason's got your girl?" The smile in her voice was gone.

"You think I'm right to be worried?"

"I never liked him, Kos."

Lena took a bite of cereal. She had no appetite. But Mason had fed from her, and she needed to replenish. The kitchen window opened onto the garden, and a breeze rustled the dishtowel. She hadn't tried, but she was certain the windows facing the street wouldn't open—only this one, leading out into the high-walled garden.

A familiar melody blew in on the breeze. Lena hummed along before she recognized Ella Fitzgerald crooning "Our Love Is Here To Stay." It triggered memories, of Zoey dancing with Andre, and Susan with Ally, their laughter mixing with the lyrics.

Lena finished her cereal.

The song played again. She missed Kaštel, missed her friends.

She rinsed out the coffee pot, put her bowl and spoon into the dishwasher, wiped off the counter.

The song played again. She missed Kos.

A tear splashed in the sink.

The song played again.

Where on earth was it coming from? Inexplicably tense, she dashed out to the garden and scanned the neighboring houses, but all the windows were closed. The sounded wafted over the rooftops from the street.

In Mason's front room, she pulled back the curtains to see an old woman with a boom box on the sidewalk. She was adorable, in an old-fashioned emerald skirt-suit, and horn-rimmed glasses. When she saw Lena, she set down the boom box, and used her hands to form a heart over her own. Then she made the American Sign Language letter K.

Lena put her palm on the window, tears falling again.

She mouthed the words, *Thank you.*

The woman's smile was sad. She nodded, turned off the music, and hefting the boom box up, shuffled down the street.

Was he coming for her? Please God, let him come soon.

CHAPTER 24

Gracias a Dios, that was the last of it. If Pedro had to spend another minute with Andre and that damn bottling machine, he was going to open the garage door to the last rays of sunset and nuke them both.

The labels were all crooked with Pedro in charge of the roller. Straight lines were definitely Kos's expertise.

Andre closed up the case and loaded it onto the truck. "Are you certain you are able to drive this thing?"

"It's a truck."

"It has many gears."

Pedro just shook his head. You never knew when Andre would prove himself a Neanderthal—at two thousand years old, he practically was one.

Kos strode in, abuzz with anxious energy. It was amazing steam wasn't coming out of his ears, too. "I don't see why you can't do this without me."

Andre slammed the truck's door closed. "It is only the most precious cargo imaginable, Kos. I would expect you of all people to understand. If anything goes wrong…"

Kos did that shoulder scrunching thing he always did when he was thinking about Lena. *Mierda*, women were a pain in the ass—way more trouble than men. Aside from Lucas, who was turning out to be the biggest pain of all.

Kos squeezed his eyes shut and rubbed them with his thumb and forefinger. "You're right. I just…I have a bad feeling about Lena."

Andre frowned. "Take your car. Follow us to the warehouse. Then you can go straight to her."

"Is Matthew meeting us at the warehouse?" Pedro jostled the keys impatiently.

"No." Andre shook his head. "He has obligations—family dinner every Sunday. He gave me the combination to some sort of key pad."

Pedro didn't catch his snort fast enough that time. "Don't worry, boss. I can drive those too."

Andre raised his middle finger in Pedro's direction. The gesture was one modern innovation the ancient vampire had adopted easily.

"Look. It is dark enough." Andre activated the garage door, and Pedro climbed into the cab.

The sky bled into purple over the vineyard, nearly matching the blue-black hue of the fruit, still ripening on the vines. The breeze blew the grapes' sweet scent into his nostrils, promising a good harvest, and soon.

Andre stepped into the seat next to him, while Pedro flipped on the radio.

Andre flipped it off.

Pedro's gut knotted. No music, no cards, no bottles to fill. Andre would want to talk, and about the last thing Pedro wanted to talk about.

"Did you feed from Lucas today?"

Pedro pushed the gas and let out the clutch fast. The truck jerked forward. "No. I'm not hungry." It was the truth. He itched where Andre's gaze traveled over him, but he wouldn't see any signs of hunger.

"Do you think he knows more than he has told us?"

"I honestly don't know. I didn't think he knew this much."

Andre's fingers spread then flexed on his thighs. "It is impressive that he is able to keep his own counsel with your fangs in him. But we cannot tolerate deception, especially from a Hunter."

"For once, Andre, I completely agree."

Pedro turned right onto the highway, heading north toward the distributor's warehouse. Cool air blew through the cab, and he zipped up his sweatshirt.

Andre rolled up his window. "Son, I wish I could have spared you all this. Sent you away before they got hold of you."

"I appreciate that. But, as completely fucked up as my life is right now, I think I belong with you losers."

Andre laughed. "Indeed. I agree." His big hand patted Pedro's knee.

It felt kind of good, that reassuring pat. Like maybe the whole world wouldn't go to shit after all.

With all of that out of the way, the silent drive wasn't as lousy as he'd feared. A light was on inside the office of River, Inc., Wine Distributors.

"You think Matthew's here after all?" Pedro asked.

Andre sniffed, then rolled down his window and sniffed some more.

The familiar odor wafted to Pedro — Hunter.

He locked eyes with Andre and turned off the truck's headlights. Kos was already at the passenger door, his index finger against his nose. Andre nodded, and slid out of the cab like a panther, prowling toward the office. Pedro and Kos followed.

At the door, Andre whispered to Pedro. "I believe the universe is offering vengeance to you this evening."

Pedro's blood came alive, throbbing in his veins, burning to pay this Hunter back for every slice of pain Ethan had carved into him.

Andre put a hand on his shoulder. "Easy. One step a time. Capture him. Unload the wine. Then we go home and interrogate. You will take some time to consider what will satisfy your rage."

He was right. *Poco a poco.* What was the saying — revenge was best served cold? And Ethan Bennett was really the one he owed.

"Apparently the universe likes you better than me." Kos glowered, doing his shoulder thing some more. "You get vengeance, and I get a wrench in my plans."

Andre rolled his eyes and then kicked in the door. It fell with a splintering crash. Pedro lifted the Hunter by the scruff of the neck — he'd always wanted to do that. Kos began to look around the office, and Andre found an orange extension cord and wrapped it around the Hunter, tight, like a boa constrictor. Cool trick. Probably one of Andre's throwbacks from his days as a Roman Centurion. Apparently he could also drive a chariot — not that they ever tried that at Kaštel.

"Derek?" a quiet, crackly voice asked.

Where was it coming from? It sounded familiar.

"Captured," the Hunter grunted.

"Ah. I'm sorry to hear that. Is my friend Marasović with you?" It was Ethan, somewhere on a telephone.

Pedro growled, his phantom wounds pricking at the sound of his tormentor. *Jesu Cristo*, he hated that *hijo de puta*.

"Yes Marasović, and his son, and the new one," Derek replied. Andre gagged him with the end of the extension cord before he could speak again.

"Greetings, Kosjenic. And Pedro, please give Lucas my love. I promise we'll all be seeing each other very soon."

The line went quiet, but the screen of the Hunter's cell phone still glowed under the desk. Pedro picked it up and slipped it into his pocket. On the computer monitor, a spreadsheet showed all the outlets that had ordered shipments of Blood Vine from the distributor.

Kos scrolled down screen. "They're trying to track the sales."

"*Davo.* We will have to prevent that. Maybe provide Matthew with some security."

Pedro babysat the Hunter in the office while Kos and Andre unloaded the wine. Eventually the warehouse door slammed. They were finished. Pedro threw the orange bundle of human over his shoulder and met them outside.

Andre craned his neck to speak over his shoulder as he shut the trailer door. "Will you go to Lena now? Or return with us to interrogate the prisoner?"

Kos reached back and rubbed his neck. His head tilted from side to side, as if he were weighing his duties. Of all the males Pedro knew, human or vampire, Kos was the most honorable. His face turned red, his normally full mouth a thin line in his fine face. Even Pedro could feel the painful pull between the two obligations.

Finally, Kos's hand dropped to his side where his fingers curled helplessly. "Lena will be okay. Hopefully, she got my message and knows I'm coming soon."

Pedro drove back to Kaštel with Hunter prisoner number three locked in the truck's trailer. As they drove through the rolling hills of wine country, his torture replayed, step by step, to the sound of Ethan's words. *We'll all be seeing each other very soon.*

No one bothered to turn on a light inside the cavernous work-room. Pedro shoved the Hunter into the closet and slammed the door.

Kos appeared, and anxious energy rolled off him in waves. The anxiety reverberated inside Pedro, setting his own nerves to thrum and his skin to burn. The twitch of the other vampire's fingers flexing in the darkness made Pedro jump.

The desperation to go to Lena was all over Kos's face. "Did you call Bel?"

Andre's lips pressed together and he shook his head. "I thought it best to wait on you."

"Why do we need Bel?" Pedro backed against the closet door for support and pressed his palms into the wood, hard.

Kos's chest rose with a breath. "He's the only one any good at interrogating Hunters. Didn't you notice with Lucas?"

Too bad Bel had gone back to Los Angeles in a huff, pissed off at his father over old family secrets.

"Zoey's waiting in my office." Andre led the way, Pedro and Kos following mutely.

Zoey sat with her knees drawn up to her chest. Vania and Omar paced in interlocking circles. Good. Everyone was there for the pow-wow. Pedro took a spot in the corner, out of the frenetic movement.

Kos dialed and turned on the speaker phone.

"This is Bel. What's up?" He sounded like he was at the end of a long tunnel.

"We need you here," Andre said.

"What happened?" the distant voice asked.

Kos recounted the events at the warehouse, his posture slackening as he spoke. Jealousy tickled Pedro's gut, and he wished he was the one distracted by telling the story. Instead, images gripped him—of himself taped to a table, of Ethan's nasty sharp tools arrayed next to his head where he had a perfect view. His stomach twisted and he swallowed back bile.

"So, we need you to interrogate him," Andre said.

"No way. You're on your own, big daddy."

Vania snickered behind her hand. Normally, Pedro would have enjoyed their bickering too, but he was too damn wound up.

"I'm out of practice," Andre replied.

"Wimp," Bel said. "Then who's going to do it?"

Zoey flicked her hand up at the wrist. "I have an idea. What about Vania?"

"What about her?" Vania straightened.

"Can't you get his Hunter blood boiling with your special super fire power?"

Oh Jesus. Zoey'd said it. They were going to hurt him...

Pedro doubled over, palm flat against the brick wall to keep his balance as the room spun. No one seemed to notice.

"I don't use my fire to torture. I draw the line at death and destruction."

Bel laughed over the speakerphone—the only one who did. Pedro sucked down a refreshing gulp of oxygen, and the room righted itself. He stood, digging his fingers into mortar.

Kos frowned at him, as if he'd just noticed Pedro's state. He shook his head and mouthed the words, *I'm fine.*

After a moment, Kos went on. "Let's just try good cop, bad cop." Kos see-sawed his head from side to side, his tension apparently returning. Pedro rubbed his own shoulders in sympathy.

Bel spoke from his end of the tunnel. "While I admire your kind souls, none of you is a convincing bad cop."

Looking around the room, Kos's gaze settled on the African vampire. "How about Omar? He's so big it's easy to miss he's a gentle giant."

The huge vampire made a rude gesture at Kos. Okay, maybe not so gentle.

"Omar's bad cop to your good cop?" Bel asked, still sounding a million miles away. "That's worth a try."

When Pedro opened his mouth, the words flew out like trapped birds. "Duct tape him to a table."

Bel laughed, an eerie, distant sound. "If he was there when Ethan had a go at you, that'll scare the piss out of him."

"Who was on the phone?"

Ethan looked up. Gwen stood in the doorway, her mouth agape. He followed her line of sight to where his gold-handled sun dagger stood. Its sharp tip stuck a full inch into the surface of his mahogany desk. How on earth had that happened? He had to unwrap his fingers from the handle one at a time, they had grown so stiff from his crushing grip.

"It was Derek. He's been captured, which is a disappointment. But, the last domino has fallen. The wine is delivered. It's time to get Mason."

"And rescue the girl. What's her name, anyway?"

Ethan tilted his head. "I've forgotten…"

Gwen frowned.

Then the blood slave's name sprang into his mind like a gift from God, sparing him Gwen's judgment. "Lena. Her name is Lena."

CHAPTER 25

"Fucking traitor. I don't understand how you could do it."

In the darkness of the closet, Lucas was tempted to plug his ears. It was possibly the thousandth time Leo had said it. His hostile verbal assault was annoying, but not intimidating, given that Leo was half his size.

Lucas ignored him. His whole life was a waiting game. It didn't matter if he waited in a dark closet, in a bedroom at Kaštel, or in a motel somewhere. Wherever he was, either Pedro or Ethan would find him eventually.

"I need to take a piss," Leo said. "What time is it?"

Lucas pressed his watch's backlight. "Five."

"Someone will bring dinner soon."

It was dark in the closet and he couldn't see the kid, but he could hear his fingers drumming the wall, his shoes scuffing the floor, the fabric of his pants rubbing together as he crossed and uncrossed his legs. Damn, he was restless.

Ten minutes later, he said it again. "Fucking traitor. I don't understand how you could do it."

Only when he'd heard it one thousand and one times did Lucas understand it for what it was—a question.

"I'll tell you, Leo."

The kid stopped fidgeting instantly, and the closet grew perfectly still.

"It wasn't that hard. My brother is a sociopath and a sadist, traits he inherited from my father. Choosing to do the right thing, to defend a man I like against them — easy call."

"Yeah, and look how he repays you. Locking you in a goddamn closet. I bet he's been fucking you like a dog these last two weeks and now he's tired of you."

"I kept a secret from him. I don't blame him for being angry."

Leo didn't reply. He must have expected Lucas to rail against Pedro.

"Let me ask you a question, kid. Don't you think it's sick, attacking a place like this and killing the whole household — humans, nice ones?"

Leo sat silent again. Had he been wondering the same thing?

Finally, he spoke in a perfectly rational tone. "It's not nice, man, but it's necessary, and you know it. They're the sick ones. They've been brainwashed, fed upon. They're tainted."

"Right. Brainwashed."

Leo didn't reply, and Lucas assumed the irony had been lost on him.

Sometime later, Ally brought two peanut butter and jelly sandwiches down to them. It sure wasn't Lena's awesome cooking, but at least it was better than the cold oatmeal at Hunter headquarters.

Leo and Lucas took turns in the toilet with the big vampire Omar as the heavy outside. Leo didn't take his eyes off Omar the whole time they were out of the cell. Omar stared back until, enraged by the glare, he hissed at Leo. The kid scurried into the closet, although by Lucas's account he'd pretty much won the staring contest.

Ally rested her hand on Lucas's shoulder and squeezed before she closed the door behind him. In the dark, he put his hand on the same shoulder and tried to absorb her kindness into his soul.

"That's the biggest dude I've ever seen." Leo sounded like a kid at the zoo.

True enough — Omar was at least six foot six, big and beautiful. Lucas slid down the wall, same place where he'd parked his ass before. The concrete floor was still warm. He banged his head against the wall and closed his eyes.

"Hey Lucas?"

"Kid, do you ever shut up?"

"Don't call me a kid."

"Fine."

"I have a question."

Why not? What else did he have to do besides listen to an angry, idiotic kid rant in a closet. "Shoot."

"Have you always been gay?"

Never mind. Lucas preferred silence. He wanted to say, *I so do not want to talk about this,* but he resisted. "Yes, Leo. From the day I was born."

"You never fucked a girl?"

"Uh, once. It was awful." Was this going where Lucas thought it was? As much as he wanted to end the conversation, some morbidly curious part of him couldn't resist. "What about you Leo? Ever fucked a girl?"

"No."

Yep, just where he thought. Ugly? No. Shy? No. Only one reason Leo had never fucked a girl. Lucas opted for quiet and hoped Leo would too.

"Would you do it to me?"

So it was *it* now, not a fuck? Poor kid. Growing up a gay Hunter was not fun.

Lucas employed his most authoritative tone. "Absolutely not."

"Why?" Leo replied with a whine.

"Because you're just a…you're too young for me. And you shouldn't have sex for the first time in a prison cell, or a closet."

And, on top of not really being into the annoying kid, maybe he should be honest…

"And, because I'm with Pedro."

Even if he hates me, and we're stuck in blow job limbo.

Seated on the floor with his knees drawn up, Lucas dozed in and out of sleep. He awoke with a jolt when the door to the closet opened again. A man was shoved into the dark space and the door slammed behind him. What now?

"Who's here?" the man asked. His voice wasn't entirely unfamiliar, but Lucas couldn't place him.

"Leo Caroli."

"Lucas Bennett."

"Fuck."

Whoever he was, he knew them, then. "That on your birth certificate or just a nickname?"

"Derek Nichols."

Lucas remembered the competent suck up from the mission against Marasović.

The three Hunters sat in silence until Derek spoke. "Lucas, I wasn't expecting you to be held captive—thought you'd be a vampire hero after the stunt you pulled to save that male blood slave."

Leo drew in a breath, about to speak. Lucas kicked him, or to be more precise, he kicked into the dark and hoped to hit the kid. It landed with just enough impact to shut him up.

"Expected wrong, then, didn't you. How'd they catch you?" Lucas had a feeling Derek hadn't been as stupid as Leo.

"Doing a little project for your brother. Got sniffed out."

"I thought Ethan called everything off," Leo said.

Lucas had to give the kid credit. Not a bad question, actually.

Derek cleared his throat. "Yeah, well, I'm part of the research team."

Surely Derek didn't know about the book. What else would Ethan be researching?

"So why haven't they killed you?" Derek asked.

Nope, he didn't know about the book, or he would know their blood was liquid gold to the vampires.

"Mercy," Leo answered, and Lucas smiled in the dark.

Derek snorted. "Yeah, right. But why? No offense—you two aren't exactly hostages worth bargaining for—kid cowboy and fag traitor."

Perhaps emboldened by his new label, Leo spoke up. "Is this like a metaphor or something? I didn't think Hunters and vampires ever bargained?"

Again, not a bad question. Kid was too smart and too queer for whatever small town he was stuck in. With new respect for Leo, Lucas answered the question. "It's not unprecedented. There are a few cases when a high profile Hunter was captured and exchanged for a head start evacuating the vampire's household. But, Derek here knows he's not that important."

"True, and nobody wants to give Marasović a head start," Derek confirmed. "So, seriously, what's your theory on why you are still alive?"

Leo replied, "It's not a theory, man. They didn't kill me because they say I'm a kid, which I'm not. But apparently they don't kill kids."

"They told you that?" Derek asked.

"Yep."

"I'll tell you why I'm alive if you answer one question for me first," Lucas said. He was beginning to form a plan. Leo would cooperate, but would Derek?

"I'll decide when I hear the question."

"Why do you hate vampires?"

"Because they are—"

"Stop." If the answer came that fast, it wasn't the one Lucas was looking for. He gave him another chance. "Don't repeat what you've always been told. Look inside. Why do you hate them?"

Derek was quiet for a long time, far longer than he would need to answer what Lucas had asked.

"Not going to share?"

"Still thinking about it."

"Take your time." There was no hurry, but there was a limit. When they reached the limit, Derek would cooperate or Lucas would have to kill him barehanded in the cell. Not impossible, but it would upset Leo, for sure.

Lucas balled up his sweater and used it as a pillow. Time passed in silence, and he drifted in and out of sleep.

The door opened suddenly, and light flooded in, blinding him.

"Get out here, Nichols," Kos said.

The door slammed behind him. Lucas checked his watch—four a.m.

Outside in the workroom, Derek cursed the vampires with the same old Hunter drivel. A terrible ripping sound began, so loud Lucas's scalp crawled until he recognized it—duct tape being pulled off the roll.

They were probably taping Derek to the table, the same way Ethan had Pedro—nice turnabout move. That could have only been Pedro's idea.

They wouldn't come close to the kind of torture Ethan had inflicted, but Derek didn't know that, which is what would make it effective.

"I wonder if he knows about the girl?" Leo said.

"What girl?" Lucas asked.

"The blonde cook."

"What about her?"

Cold sweat beaded on Pedro's forehead and dribbled down his temples.

"You could just talk, you know. Put an end to all of this." Kos sounded even and calm, like his always-reasonable self.

"Fuck you, filthy parasite." The Hunter spat. He did not sound so reasonable.

They had matching sets of goddamn golden peepers, he and the Hunter. Derek's yellow eyes seemed sharp even though his drivel of hate revealed he was dumber than he looked.

Vertical, he was about Pedro's height, a few inches shy of six feet. But he lay horizontal. Omar held him down, as Andre taped wrists, ankles, hips. It had been Pedro's own damn idea, but it triggered some nasty stress of the post-traumatic variety. He was right there in the shed on Ethan's operating table all over again.

Kos clapped a hand on Pedro's shoulder. "You okay? You're sweating bullets."

Derek's eyes flashed wide. What do you know? His freak-out played right into their plan. Good cop, bad cop, totally fucked in the head cop.

"I'm just happy somebody else is on the table this go round." He tried to sound gleeful, vengeful. He just felt sick.

Kos caught on fast. "Yeah, you were in bad shape when Lucas brought you back. How are your toes now?"

Derek's heart hammered loudly, a steady beat all the vampires could hear.

"My toenails are growing back. The scars are gone around my ankles too. Vampire healing is cool shit. Too bad you won't have that going for you, Hunter." He patted the man's shin.

Derek struggled uselessly under the tape. "Fuck off. You're evil, disgusting—unnatural!"

Was that what Hunters really thought? Because that wasn't how Lucas treated him.

Kos untied the Hunter's shoes. "Bennett took off most of the skin up to your knee, right Pedro?"

"Hey, I don't really want to talk about it." *Truth.* "Let's get down to business. I hear Omar's a real professional when it comes to this sick shit. I'm looking forward to it."

Pedro studied the Hunter. Acrid sweat and a pounding heart gave away his fear, though he looked calm enough. The faster they triggered his panic, the faster they could stop the charade. And Pedro would like to get as far as he could from memory lane.

"You're the enemy of humans and you have to be exterminated! All of you. Evil, parasites. Fuck you."

The hate was his mantra. Derek shouted out anything and everything he had ever been told about vampires, or at least that was how it sounded — like a checklist.

Shit, exterminated?

Somehow Pedro knew that when Lucas kissed him, held him, sucked him, he wasn't thinking about extermination. Derek's hate put Lucas into sharp relief, and made his betrayal with the drawings feel small-time.

Andre stood off to the side, concentrating on the scene with a grave glare.

Kos stood next to Pedro, looking back and forth between him and the Hunter. "Yeah, Omar's the real deal. But I hope it doesn't go that far. Why don't you just talk, Hunter? Save us all this ugliness."

Pedro jostled Kos's shoulder. "Shut the hell up. I don't wanna be spared the ugliness. You saw what Bennett did to me, right Omar?"

"Yeah, man, I saw it. But I don't mess around with extremities. That tape is perfect Andre, just high enough to leave access to what a man values most."

Derek's pupils dilated and his lips were a white line. "You sick fucks! Nasty, dirty, blood suckers!"

Pedro's job was to be fucked-in-the-head cop, so he tried to make his torture sound like foreplay. "Seems like a shame — it's over so fast that way. Ethan really knew how to draw it out."

Kos arranged tools on a tray like an OCD nurse preparing for surgery — perfectly aligned butter knives and garden shears, not the pliers and blades Ethan had used on him…he sucked in a lungful of air, and a bit of tension melted away.

Something about this ridiculous role-play was changing the memory. The shed receded further in his mind.

"Oh, I can make it last for him." Omar's grin cut a huge white crescent in his handsome onyx face. Pedro very nearly smiled back.

Kos sucked his teeth and shook his. "Last chance, man."

Omar smacked him. "Kos, you softie, shut up and cut his pants off."

"Listen," Derek suddenly spat, "I really don't know anything."

"That's what they all say." Omar crossed his long arms over his chest.

"They do." Now Kos was nodding agreeably with that same pitying expression. "You'll have to start with what you *do* know."

Again, Pedro wanted to laugh, but Derek's shout came first. "Seriously, nothing!"

Omar began to cut up the leg of his rumpled khaki pants. Only the sound of the scissors snipping broke the silence. "Okay. Okay. We know about the wine. That it makes you strong."

Pedro snorted. That much was a no-brainer, since they'd tried to burn the vineyards down.

"What else?" Kos whispered, all gentle, good-cop coaxing.

Omar kept shearing the pants open.

"That's it!" Tears ran down the Hunters face, spilling from his widened eyes.

"What's Ethan up to?"

Derek gasped and sobbed as Omar's scissors neared his groin. "I don't know! Oh fuck, stop, please stop."

Omar paused mid-snip. "You think that's all he knows, Kos?"

Kos leaned over and peered into the Hunter's face, sniffing. Finally, he ran his palm up his forehead and grabbed hold of his hair. "Yep. Useless. You really do know nothing."

A loud guffaw filled the workroom, barreling out of Andre, who'd been silent during the entire interrogation. He slapped his thighs. "I don't mess around with extremities! That was a good one, Omar!" He covered his mouth with his big paw. Dude had been stifling his giggles the whole time.

The laughter was contagious, spreading to Kos and Omar.

"No no, the best line was 'Ethan knew how to draw it out.'" Kos doubled over. "Pedro, I don't know how you could turn your own torture session into a dirty joke. You are one sick fuck—the Hunter's right about that." His eyes were watering.

As they laughed, a weight lifted from Pedro. He felt better, a lot better. Free, even.

Still taped to the table, the Hunter's brow creased in utter confusion. "I don't understand."

Pedro met his gaze. "We faked you out, man. We don't do torture. Aren't you glad you don't know shit? You would have felt really stupid if you spilled your guts."

Suddenly, Pedro's limbs tingled, and there were way too many people sharing his oxygen. "I need some air. Gonna walk outside for a while."

Kos got between him and the door. "Hey, you okay? That couldn't have been easy."

"I'm good, actually. It kind of helped. Just need some space."

With one more good-cop nod, Kos sidestepped out of the way.

When Pedro was almost to the door, Andre called out. "Surviving is one thing. It takes a bigger man to face his demons."

It felt good to be outside. The air was cool and sweet. His breaths came easy, easier than they had in weeks. What were his demons, anyway? His lingering trauma? That didn't seem so bad anymore. His feelings about Lucas? He didn't seem like the enemy anymore either.

CHAPTER 26

Kos clasped the Hunter's wrist with one hand, not that he was putting up a fight. Clammy, pasty, reeking of fear — the guy was the epitome of wrecked.

"Feeling a little topsy-turvy?" Kos slid a box cutter along the edge of the table, slicing through tape and freeing the Hunter.

"Go to hell."

"Hmm." Kos didn't look at him, just balled up the tape and tossed it in a trashcan. "That's where Hunters go, I expect."

Without any force, he tugged the Hunter off the table and toward the cell, where Kos nudged him inside.

"Kos?" It was Lucas.

"Not now."

"You need to hear this," Lucas insisted. "It's Lena."

Kos's legs went limp, and he grabbed the doorframe to steady himself. What could Lucas know about Lena?

A slice of light illuminated Leo, sitting cross-legged against the wall. He drew his knees up. "I saw an email about her from some other vampire who wanted to hire her. Sent it to Ethan right before you captured me."

No. That couldn't be true. Lena was safe from Hunters at Mason's. Ethan couldn't know where she was.

"There was no address on that email. He couldn't find Mason's house. And no one followed us."

"What's going on?" Andre stepped up, a pillar of support behind Kos.

Lucas raised his voice as if volume would penetrate the fog in Kos's mind. "Ethan knows about Lena. He'll use her against you if he can."

The only time Kos had seen Ethan had been on the hill above the charred vineyard. Lena had rushed into Kos's arms, and the Hunter's golden eyes had honed in on them. He would know Lena mattered to Kos.

"*Krist.*"

Lucas stood, but made no move toward the door. "Derek. What do you know about this?"

Derek rubbed his eyes, then looked from face to face. Finally, he shrugged. "He thinks he has some kind of secret weapon."

Kos went cold, couldn't feel his hands or feet—only his heart, squeezing, racing. An animal cry burst from his throat, bypassing his brain altogether.

Andre's hand came to rest on his shoulder. "Don't panic. Call her."

"She won't take my calls."

"Shit." Lucas covered his eyes with his palm. "You vampires should have your own soap opera."

Kos tried to push past Andre out the door. "I'm going to find her."

Andre didn't budge. "It's dawn."

Where had the night gone?

"We'll send Vania," Andre said.

Kos pushed again. "I can make it now, if I fly."

"No, Kos. Think. She needs you alive, strong." Without stepping from the doorway, Andre flipped a light switch outside the closet, filling the small space with bluish light. His stare settled on Leo. "Why are you telling us this?"

It was Lucas who answered. "Because Leo is coming around."

"Around?" Kos's brain wasn't working.

"He's starting to see things my way. Becoming another vampire sympathizer."

"You must be joking." Andre leaned into the doorframe. "There is no such thing as a sympathizer among Hunters."

"Why else do you think I'm here?" Lucas asked.

Kos clenched his fists. Damn it, he wanted to punch something—Lucas, Andre…he settled for the wall. A fist sized dent appeared in the plaster, chalk dust filling the small space.

In the silence that followed, he said, "While you all negotiate peace between our races, I'm going to organize a rescue mission."

At Vania's door, quiet snores vibrated through the hardwood. Kos burst in.

"Wake up."

She bounded to her feet in seconds, fully dressed and alert, fine soldier that she was. "What's happened?"

"Ethan knows about Lena. Is planning to use her against us somehow. It's dawn. I need you to find her."

She pulled on a holster, a shiny black leather jacket, combat boots. "I'll start at Mason's."

"Vania. I need you to find her."

"I'll do my best. Not for you, the idiot who let her go. But because I like her, and she makes the best damn scones I've ever tasted. And most importantly, because I hate those mother fucking Hunters."

She slammed her fist into his gut, hard. Enough time around vampires had taught her not to pull those punches.

"Learn anything from Derek?" she asked.

"No."

"Go back. See if he knows where Bennett would take her."

Lena was dreaming again. She knew it was a dream because even after Kos's message, he hadn't shown up to rescue her. And making love with him was too good to be true.

His big hands lifted and stroked her breasts, teasing her nipples. His fingers slid down her belly, over her hips, and parted her legs. A corner of her mind remained firmly planted at Mason's house. But, she gave herself over to the pleasure of the dream as his tongue swept up her core.

The sensations were so real.

Too real.

She forced her eyes to open. Mason's face was between her legs, rubbing stubble on the inside of her thighs.

"Miss me?" His breath tickled her sensitive flesh.

"No."

He laughed, and he wasn't the only one. At the sound of another voice, Lena sat up. A man and a woman watched from across the room. Not again. Lena sighed, exasperation outweighing her fear.

The woman was human, but the man was definitely a vampire—he was too flawless and ageless to be anything else. She rubbed her eyes and saw that the clock next to her bed said quarter to seven in the morning.

"Jarred and I were having such a great time, Lena, that we decided to bring the party home to you. This is Shannon."

The woman was pretty in a faded around the edges way, like someone who partied a little too much for her age.

"Make room for me behind you." Mason's tone was steel, making Lena's jaw clench and her spine go rigid.

Stiffly, she inched forward on the bed and he slid in behind her. He was already hard—a bad sign. Without any ceremony, he bit her and grabbed both her breasts, squeezing. Each finger pressed sharp pain in her tender flesh.

Shannon's eyes widened. Poor girl. She hadn't known her dates weren't human. She pivoted to the vampire named Jarred. Instantly, his fangs were out and he growled, turning himself entirely into a predator. Shannon screamed. He ripped off her dress. She kept screaming. He sprang his erection from his pants, obviously excited by her fear.

At Lena's neck, Mason pulled blood greedily from her vein. She'd never felt it draining from her so fast. Her eyes were fixed to the frightened woman.

Jarred had stripped her, forcing her against the wall, and then he struck. Shannon squirmed and punched uselessly, kicking up with her knees, but he lifted her off the ground and fed. His grunts and swallows were those of a ravenous animal. Shannon succumbed to the arousing bite, fighting less and less. She exhaled a sigh of pleasure, but her eyes were dark with fear. He lifted her and speared her with his penis. She whimpered—a terrible mixture of pleasure and horror.

Mason growled into Lena's neck, and pain exploded at her throat. Pain? A bite had never hurt before. He was ripping her open, draining her dry.

There was no desire, either. She wasn't responding to his bite or to the scene he'd staged to frighten her.

He noticed too. He dug his fingers into her breast harder, then pinched her nipples with vampire strength.

Her eyes burned with tears, but she remained still and silent, refusing to give the son of a bitch what he wanted.

He broke the suction. "What the hell?"

Warm liquid poured down her neck, pooling in her collarbone before it trickled over her breasts. It smelled like a rusty wagon. She'd never smelled her own blood like that—so much of it—

Mason jerked her to face him. "Why aren't you begging for me?"

Shaky, she stood up. He leaned forward, his eyes strangely wide.

The light of dawn broke in around the edges of the curtains. She grabbed her robe and dashed out of the room. No one chased her. A mostly unconscious Shannon slumped over the other vampire, who still fed and thrust into her.

Lena arrived at the garden door and slipped out into the gray morning. The sun wasn't bright, but it didn't need to be. She would have a good dozen hours of safety out there. Barefoot, and only wearing the robe would make it a cold day, but she'd be safe.

Warm blood still trickled from her neck. She touched it, and her fingers came away wet and crimson. It wasn't that much, surely not enough to be dangerous. She pressed her palm to the wound, hoping to form a clot. A shiver wracked her body, and some instinct brought her eyes to the door. Mason stood at the window, and his stare dropped her temperature by another degree.

There he was—her destiny.

Compared to this, her misery at Kaštel had been so childish.

He turned suddenly, and disappeared. Lena found a patch of sun on the brick patio and wrapped her robe around her knees, settling in for a long day.

Only, seconds later, shouts sounded inside the house. Then the door opened and a petite brunette stepped out. She looked like she'd been in a bar fight, with a black-eye, and bruised jaw. How many women had Mason picked up last night?

Lena hopped up to go to her.

"Poor you. Mason—"

"Oh my God, did Mason—?"

At the sound of his name in the other woman's mouth, Lena froze. "Who are you?"

"My name is Gwen Evans, and I'm here to rescue you."

She had a sweet accent, not quite Irish, but melodic.

"But how did you—?"

"I knew Mason a long time ago. I don't want him to hurt you the way he hurt me. Come inside. We're getting you out of here."

Lena's stomach flip-flopped. Was Kos with her, here to save her?

She followed Gwen down the hall to find a group of strange men, heavily armed, dressed in jeans and flannel shirts and work clothes, like a ragtag state militia. Except, these men had golden eyes—so not really men at all. Hunters were the lowest of humans.

Lena's gaze fell like a domino as she glanced from Gwen to Mason and they both looked to another man. When Lena saw him, all her hope fizzled out. Ethan Bennett.

She'd grown used to those eyes in Pedro, and even Lucas. But Ethan's were different. He looked at her like he knew everything about her. She shrunk back, feeling even more naked than she was in the bloodstained silk nightie and robe.

A strange numbness crept from her scalp to toes. Her destiny, her dreams—it was all over. So much false hope, so many expectations, wiped away with his icy gaze. When she saw her father in whatever life came after this, she would tell him he'd been right all along.

She turned to the battered woman and planted her hands on her hips. "He tricked you. He's not here to rescue me. I'm tainted. They'll kill me once they're done with Mason…and with whatever else they decide to do to me, first." And if they knew Gwen had been with Mason, they'd do the same to her. But Lena would keep her secret.

Ethan tsked. "Ms. Isaakson, you could not be more wrong."

Her mouth opened, and a laugh escaped. She expected it to sound hysterical, but it was deep and low. "Oh really? You're going to save me from Mason and send me on my merry way. Why don't I believe you?"

Bennett cocked his head, smiling without showing any teeth. "You haven't broken her yet, Kearney."

"It's more fun to go slow." Mason stood straighter, but his voice rose high and thin with fear.

"I wish I had time to learn your technique, but we must be going."

Gwen shuddered, her little body trembling like a frightened bunny. Lena didn't want to know what they meant, but she sure wanted to comfort the woman. She took a step toward her.

"How do I know you'll keep your end of the bargain?" Mason asked. "I could just kill you all now, and go on my way at sunset."

Bargain? Lena's feet turned to lead.

"If we're not outside in — " Ethan looked at his watch " — five minutes. The house will explode, with us in it. My men are waiting outside with all their favorite incendiary devices."

"So you're on a suicide mission?"

"Hardly. I'm simply certain you'll look after your own skin by giving us the blood slave, and then leaving town."

"Maybe I'd rather go out in your blaze of glory than live with the wasting disease."

"I seriously doubt it." Ethan drummed his fingers on a sleek table near the door, his other hand twisting something in his pocket.

"How do I know that you won't blow up my house once you're outside?"

"You don't, of course, and I wouldn't hesitate to lie to you. But, I do assume that you have a fire shelter of some sort in your basement. Don't all modern vampires take that precaution?"

God he was awful. Hatred churned Lena's gut. When she exhaled, it stung her throat. She flexed her fingers, no longer numb, which sucked, because now she was scared — paralyzed, unable to breathe, pee-your-pants scared.

Her pulse raced and the wound on her neck gushed hot blood. "What do you want with me?"

"Ethan, what's going on?" Gwen stepped forward, still shaking. She wasn't a bunny, she was a Chihuahua with tremors, and Mason had probably made her that way.

That decided it. Lena preferred the Hunters — at least they killed you when they were finished.

"Why are you letting him go?" The little woman's voice rang with surprising steel.

Ethan blinked rapidly, and creases showed around his eyes. For a second, he looked human. Then he turned toward the door and spoke over his shoulder, already leading the way out.

"We must, Gwen, for the greater good. When we trade Lena for Marasović's vineyards, the exiled vampires will continue to die. We eliminate hundreds or thousands of them, by letting Mason go."

Gwen took a step toward him. "But he's—"

Ethan spun on his heel and barked. "Enough."

Lena's head was full of cotton. She must have lost more blood than she thought. "Trade?" Her voice came out as a croak.

"That's right. A trade—Marasović dismantles the shield, and he gets you back safely."

Oh God. If only Mason had insisted on the blaze of glory, it would all be over. No terrible decision for Andre and Kos. And surely Bennett would never let her go anyway.

Hot, rough hands closed around Lena's arms, pulling her elbows back, then shoving her toward the door.

"You've got one problem, Bennett," Lena said. "Andre Maras hates me, and he'll never trade me for the vines."

Ethan ignored her, but she offered up a silent prayer that her words were true.

CHAPTER 27

Kos opened the door to his room and inhaled past the tightness in his chest. Not a trace of Lena's scent. He sniffed the pillow, the seam between the headboard and the mattress, the bathroom towels, the laundry hamper. Nothing. Some vampire—probably Zoey—had done an excessively thorough cleaning job, thinking she was doing him a favor.

He needed Lena safe. The tension in his shoulders had spread, turning all his muscles to stone. Inside the hard shell, his pulse hammered, and he could barely breathe. He'd put her in danger, and he could not let anything happen to her. But he was stuck, useless until twilight.

Deep in the cellar voices murmured—Andre, Zoey, Pedro, Lucas. They were thinking, planning. Thank God someone could. Fear buzzed in his brain like a swarm of bees, stealing all logic, demanding her.

If he could just catch a whiff of her sweet scent, maybe his body and mind would calm, and he could think about how to help.

Her room on the south wing was a wasteland. No personal items remained, and her lingering honeyed scent had turned bitter.

The pantry. Surely he could find her scent there.

He stepped into the kitchen, and the smell hit him like a wave. Was she here? He followed it to a drawer, the odor was so strong he could believe she'd folded herself into the tiny space under the coffee pot. He opened the drawer and jumped back at what he saw—his copy of *New and Selected Poems*, tattered and redolent of Lena.

All her hopes and dreams, shoved into a drawer full of rubber bands and twist ties. He could have made her happy, at least for a time, maybe even given her a child. And instead, he'd unknowingly sent her to Ethan Bennett.

Krist, why hadn't Vania called yet? Surely she'd arrived at Mason's house by now. The first rays of sunlight were peeking over the hilltops, streaking the sky with gray.

A car screeched to a stop in the drive. Who the hell was that?

Moments later someone rattled the front door. It could only be—

The rattles escalated to pounding. A woman's voice shouted in Croatian, calling the door the useless dick of a sheep.

Uta. Typical of her to arrive just as the sun breached the horizon.

His skin tingled in sympathy—she'd cut it too close. He reached the door in seconds and pulled her inside, slamming it shut as the rays singed his hands and face.

She hadn't burned, old as she was, and she looked the same as always, only in modern clothes. Nearly as tall as him barefoot, her tall black heels would put her eye-to-eye with Andre and Bel, which was surely the point. Her auburn waves swept off her high forehead.

She tilted her head, eyes sweeping up and down the length of him. "What matter with you?" Her accent was funny—vaguely Eurotrash, but not simply a Croatian immigrant speaking poor English. A tongue tangled by knowing too many languages.

Awash with fear for Lena, his hatred for Uta didn't find much traction. Still, he was not about to tell her anything.

"So, are you giving your aunt hug?"

"No." He crossed his arms tight across his chest. She knew full well he held a grudge. That was her way.

"Where Bel?"

"Los Angeles."

She let out a breath, smoothing her perfectly smooth hair. Frown lines on her forehead smoothed out too. At least she understood Bel would not be pleased to see her.

"And Andre?"

"I am here." Andre swung open the cellar door with Zoey at his side.

Uta dropped her purse, flashing to his side and seriously invading Zoey's personal space. "You are bonding again?"

Uta's question broke through Andre's scowl, and he replied on a laugh. "I did. Can you believe it?"

"Ne." Her nostrils flared, and she sniffed Zoey from hip to head.

Kos wanted to tell Uta to go back to wherever she'd come. She had the worst timing in the world. Always had.

"She much better than Mila. I can tell."

Krist, Kos hated her.

Andre elbowed in between Uta and Zoey. "What are you doing here?"

"I here representing Yousiticia."

Zoey peered around Andre. "What's Yousticia?"

"The Justicia. It is the council of the oldest vampires." Andre angled himself to form a semi circle with the two females. Kos purposely remained too far removed to complete the shape.

"Andre, you are guessing when I send picture?"

"I suspected, but I hoped it was not the case."

Zoey inched toward Andre. "Guessed what?"

"Bhat Kahn is dying three weeks past—wasting disease. You next in line."

Andre's teeth slid and crunched in his usual grind. "Just what I need."

"How many are on this Justicia?" Zoey took his hand.

Kos already knew.

"Ten," Uta replied.

Hard to believe. Andre was old, but a century ago there were at least one hundred vampires older than him. "What's happened to the rest of them?"

She shrugged. "Wasting, Hunting, sun walking."

What—vampire suicide? Kos rattled his head, trying to clear out the distraction of the puzzling news. Lena was all that mattered.

Uta shrugged out of her jacket. "You are accepting?"

"Do I have a choice?"

"You are knowing choice. They send me because they hope you are not refusing. I am not wanting to kill you."

Andre grasped Zoey's hand. "I do not risk my life unnecessarily. Though, for the record I could easily defeat you."

Uta's fangs were out in a flash, but she was laughing. It gave Kos goose bumps. She was the only vampire he knew who could do that, and it was eerily beautiful.

"Too bad we are not knowing for certain. Give me hand."

Andre obeyed, and Uta pulled out a ceramic vial. She nicked his thumb with her fang and dripped a few drops of his blood into the vial before his wound closed.

"It done." She held up the vial.

Every vampire who had ever been on the Justicia must have bled into it — potent little object.

"Pretend you are happy!" Uta commanded.

No one did.

She pressed the back of her hand to her forehead and let out a soap-opera worthy sigh. "You are bonding. You have miracle wine. But you three are looking like it first day of exile. Why?"

"We fear a former member of my household has been targeted by Hunters…" Andre was at Kos's side in a blink, his hand an extra burden on Kos's shoulder. "Kos loves her."

Everyone's eyes were on him, waiting for him to deny it. He didn't.

"Why she leave?"

The muscles in his throat had seized. He couldn't speak.

Andre's fingers pressed gently into the flesh at the front of his arm. "Mila and I set a poor example for Kos. He fears the bond."

"He is having good reason." Uta's gaze settled on Kos, and her eyes were surprisingly soft. "She is going to another household, and Hunters find her?"

Zoey grimaced. "We think so."

Hearing the words sent him over the edge. The foyer spun. He gripped the banister.

Uta cracked her knuckles. "What vampire?"

He focused on the voices to find his balance.

"Kos's old friend, Mason Kearney." Andre's voice sounded far off, and Kos opened his eyes, hoping the room had stilled. It had.

"Kearney?" Uta's forehead wrinkled as her brows rose.

Kos managed to croak. "You know him?"

"Yes I am knowing that sick twit."

Sick? Kos's phone rang. Please let Vania have good news.

"Is she safe?"

"I don't know. I can't get anyone to answer the door, but I can see Kearney blurring around upstairs. I'm going in through a window."

"Who is this on phone?" Uta asked.

Kost covered the mouthpiece. "She works for Bel. Her name is Vania."

"Yes, yes. Give me phone." Uta reached her hand out.

Kos retreated, taking the phone with him.

"Fine. You are using speaker, so Vania hear me."

Why not? He turned it on.

"Shout to Kearney. Tell him you work for me—Uta Illirye."

Vania's defiance came through the phone loud and clear. "Who the hell—"

"Vania," Andre commanded, "please do what Uta says."

Vania's yells came through the phone. Then there was silence. Finally she spoke. "The door is opening. I'm going in."

"You are giving him phone," Uta said.

Seconds later, Mason's voice came over the line, high and frightened. "Uta? What a pleasure. How can I help you?" Kos had never heard him sound so puny.

Uta rolled her eyes. "Where is girl?"

"Girl?"

"Mason, are you forgetting I am very old friend of Andre Marasović. Where is girl?"

"I didn't hurt her, Uta, I promise."

"My patiences are running out, Mason."

"Hunters came for her."

Kos's heart stopped. If she was dead, he could not live with himself. He would walk into the sun.

Andre shouted. "*Davo.* It is your duty to protect your household."

"I traded her in exchange for my life. That is not against vampire code, Uta. I've done nothing wrong."

Krist, was that true? Vampire code permitted humans to be sacrificed to Hunters? Mason's betrayal slid over Kos in an oily slick of anger and fear.

Uta brooked no argument. "If the girl lives, I am asking her myself if you are breaking code."

Mason was silent. Kos wanted to break every bone in his body before snapping him in half.

"You are not leaving your home, Mason," Uta repeated. Her long fingers drummed on her equally long thighs, belying the steadiness of her voice. Along with her forceful protection, that minute display of nerves sparked some kinship in him, a sentiment for his Auntie he'd thought long lost.

"But—"

"With my power as member of the Yousticia, you are not leaving home under penalty of sun. I will arrive at twilight."

"Yes, Uta."

"Where did they take her?" Kos shouted.

"I don't know. But they want to bargain. Kos, old buddy, you should expect a call."

"Mason. We are not buddies. Code or no code, I'm going to rip you apart with my fangs—"

Uta grabbed the phone and ended the call. "I afraid you are not knowing half. Kearney is dangerous vampire with appetites...*sjeban*."

Zoey drew near to Kos, and her concern practically reached out and touched him. "*Sjeban?*"

"Fucked up," Andre replied, stepping to her side.

Kos went cold, and Mason's wolfish look flashed in his mind.

"What do you mean?" Zoey whispered.

Andre pinched the bridge of his nose and closed his eyes. "Some vampires abuse their bite. They force humans to do things they would not normally want to do."

"I should have known," Kos hissed through clenched teeth. He sank to the floor, his anger at Mason a drop in the ocean of his fury with himself.

Uta kicked him. "Get up. Your girl still alive. Hunters use her to bargain. What they want?"

"My vines," Andre said.

Kos slowly pulled the dead weight of his own body up off the ground, unable to look at his elders for all his shame. *Krist*, what a disaster he'd created.

"So, it true? The Blood Vine is cure?"

"Yes. And Bennett knows it."

"So for this human girl, you destroy a cure for all vampires in exile?" Uta asked.

Kos dragged his gaze to Andre, who glared back, his molars grinding. Zoey sagged against him, resting a hand over his heart. No doubt she could feel whatever turmoil was raging inside him.

"You love her?" his father asked.

Kos couldn't speak, only stare at Andre.

Blood seeped from the corners of Andre's eyes, and pooled in the dip of lids. Blood tears—like he'd shed for Mila. The tears overflowed, and Andre wiped them with the back of his hand.

"I do not know what to do." He bent to embrace Zoey, and his body heaved with sobs.

Kos knew exactly what he had to do. He couldn't let anything happen to Lena, and he couldn't let Andre destroy the vines. He would trade himself for the safety of both.

With a rush of blood, his paralyzed muscles softened—time to take care of business.

Love for his father overwhelmed him. Zoey would take care of Andre now. He looked away from the pair, saying a silent goodbye.

Curled in his hand was the book of poems. He tucked it under his arm, preparing to stand. But from where he sat on the floor, Uta's dark gaze drew his. When he met her eye, she nodded. She knew exactly what he was planning.

Hands cuffed and ankles tied, Lena sat next to Ethan in the backseat. Her neck no longer bled, but she hadn't eaten anything and her brain felt fuzzy. Marin County zoomed by, fancy strip malls with Spanish tile roofs, an A&W, all nestled amidst golden hills spotted with black-green oaks. Life went on for the wealthy suburbanites as Lena's world unraveled, a pawn in a silent war that none of them knew about.

Gwen hunched over the steering wheel, occasionally glancing back at Ethan. She clearly had questions, and Lena waited for her to ask them. Perhaps she could learn something useful from the disagreement between the two…what? Were they lovers? Yuck. What had Zoey ever seen in this creep? He was even worse than Mason, far more icy and controlled.

He exhaled a long-suffering sigh. "Gwen, you best spit it out. You're liable to drive us off the freeway if you get any more agitated."

Lena shifted her weight and listened up.

"You let Mason go." Gwen's tone matched Ethan's chill. "And now you're going to give her back to those monsters."

"Both of those statements are true." His voice was taught and prickly, but he softened it rapidly. "As I've said, in the grand scheme of things, this plan is the most effective. The maximum number of vampires will die."

Gwen faced forward, not turning to speak. "You're using her."

"Perhaps, but for the greater good, and not the parasitic way Mason was."

"But you're returning her to the same fate."

Lena closed her eyes and imagined her well-equipped kitchen at Kaštel, or Andre's brusque feedings, or a chat with Kos over coffee. Hardly the same fate as what Mason had planned for her. She opened her eyes to find Gwen watching her in the rearview mirror.

"Do you want to go back to the estate?"

More than anything, but the cost was too high. So many vampires needed that cure. Lena should care about them, and she did, a little, though Kos mattered so much more. He needed that wine to stay healthy and alive.

"No." She shook her head. "They hate me there. They think I'm stupid and useless and ugly. Andre wouldn't even have sex with me. You're crazy if you think they'll bargain for me."

"Did they ever hurt you?" Gwen asked.

Lena shivered, and found arctic golden eyes pinning her. She couldn't break the stare.

"Answer the question, Ms. Isaakson."

It was impossible to lie to him. "No. They never hurt me."

Gwen exhaled a sigh. "That's good."

Lena changed tactics, trying to stir up the conflict between them again.

"They aren't all bad, you know. Mason is the exception. Most vampires are noble and good."

Ethan glanced toward Gwen, and Lena followed his gaze. She met the woman's eyes in the mirror again. The corners of Gwen's were tilted down, turning into half moons. "You poor thing. They've brainwashed you. I know how that works all too well."

Brainwashing? That was just a crazy Hunter myth. Mason may have controlled Gwen's body with his bite, used it to twist her, even, but he never controlled her mind.

Lena straightened her spine, and the handcuffs bit into her wrists. "I'll tell you this. Andre and Kos Maras are both arrogant, cowardly, and sometimes stupid, but no more so than human men. They haven't brainwashed me. I see their flaws clear as day."

Gwen's eyes remained sad. She really thought Lena was under some kind of mind control. The pity in them made Lena furious. She shouted, spit flying from her mouth. "What about you? You let this asshole pummel you for fun? You're the one who's been brainwashed and used."

Gwen's reply was all quiet calm. "I'm sure it seems that way to you, but the truth is, Ethan just gives me what I need. And my needs make me…" She looked away, until she found her words. "Our arrangement is mutually beneficial."

Ethan's eyes were feverish, sparking with something cruel and frightening.

"Mutually fucked up, maybe," Lena muttered.

Gwen's mouth hardened. Oops, burned that bridge.

Ethan's phone rang. "Is it finished?"

An unintelligible answer rumbled from his phone.

"Good. We'll be there soon. Leave the device on the counter."

Lena shuddered. *The device* sounded scary.

In Petaluma, Ethan said, "Exit here, and take this road to the coast."

If they weren't taking her to Kaštel, where were they headed? Silence returned to the car, and she was no closer to a plan. She had to make sure Ethan could not bargain with her life, even if that meant sacrificing herself.

CHAPTER 28

The vampires huddled behind him as Pedro sprang Lucas from the cell. He smelled good enough to eat, although he was a little ripe. Hadn't had a shower since — Pedro counted back two days on his hand — Saturday. Still, he would take Lucas as-is.

Kos pulled the Hunter out by the collar of his shirt. "Where will Ethan take Lena?"

"Ugh. I am puking." Uta flailed her long arms like a windmill. "Three Hunters here? How do you stand smell?"

Pedro couldn't decide if he liked her. She was a hard-core bitch, but that didn't make her a bad vampire, *per se*.

"I am wanting to kill them all, faster, and then burn up their rancid blood so I am not smelling it anymore."

Pedro growled. "He is mine."

She didn't back down, crossing several steps toward Pedro. With her finger and thumb, she pulled his eye open wider. "*Tako bizarno.* I am thinking I never will see this."

Pedro wanted to shove her away, but his blood held him back, some instinct warning that she was a bazillion times stronger than him. Yeah, that totally made her a *bad* bitchy vampire.

Lucas hopped onto the worktable, legs dangling.

"If he plans to bargain with her for the vines, he will force you to lower the shield, and at the same time lure you somewhere else to retrieve her. But Kos, understand, he doesn't intend to give her to you. His goal is the loyalty of his men so he can control them. He wants to get the vines, and then give Lena to them as a reward."

"Fuck." Kos's face pulled into a mask of raw pain, and Pedro ached for his vampire bro.

Uta stamped her foot. "I am hating Hunters."

Pedro's jaw dropped. She sounded like a whiney seven year old. "No shit, lady."

"No matter how many I am killing, more and more. It is never ending."

"You kill them?" Pedro stepped closer to Lucas.

"This is my job for the Yousticia. Hunters are aggressing, attacking, besieging, I go. I kill them all, and next day, I do it again. Every day for more than century. I sick of it."

"What's the Yousticia?" Pedro asked.

Kos sighed, impatient at the need to repeat. "The Justicia is the vampire council. Ten oldest vampires. Now, can we focus on Lena?"

Mierda. Uta was one of the ten oldest vampires?

Lucas jumped off the table and went to stand next to Kos. "He'll lure you somewhere else, so that when Lena is not delivered to you, you will be unable to stop the destruction of the vineyards."

"But how will that work? Even if I'm elsewhere, I wouldn't give the go ahead unless I had her safe."

Lucas shrugged his lean, powerful shoulders. "I don't know. He's brilliant, wily, and without conscience. He'll think of something."

"Uta, will you come with me, and help ensure her safety?"

Her hands came up in front of her, two loose fists. She wiggled them, working her fingers, as if she were…knitting? She was one weird chick—it must increase with age.

"I am needing to take Kearney prisoner." She made more imaginary stitches. "But there is a way. Bel's crew?"

How did she know about Bel's crew? Kos said they hadn't seen her in more than a hundred and fifty years.

"Yes. They're here," Kos replied, his eyebrows drawn together.

"Bel is still employing the vampire Omar?"

"Yes."

"He is taking Kearney into custody. I am going with you. In case you getting any crazy ideas." She pointed her pantomimed needle at Kos. "Where Omar?"

"He usually hangs out in the dining room, feeding the witch," Pedro replied.

Uta cackled, and then she and Kos were gone.

Finally alone, Pedro turned to Lucas, who watched him intently, his golden peepers staring right through Pedro. Windows to the soul and all that crap.

"You were getting awfully protective of me just now." Lucas tilted his head forward, and prowled back to Pedro.

Pedro drank in his long legs, his rumpled shirt stretched over lean muscle.

"What changed?" Lucas asked.

Pedro raked his fingers through his hair. "Derek. Ethan. You helping Kos. I guess I get it now."

Lucas stopped a scant few inches away. "I just couldn't tell you about the blood. I'm sorry." He leaned in and kissed Pedro.

The kiss was the real apology, and it tasted like a promise. Lucas's hungry tongue demanded, sweeping deep into Pedro's mouth and then across all his teeth. That brought Pedro's fangs out, and one sharp tooth nicked Lucas's tongue. He groaned in pleasure, and Pedro sucked, drawing down the drops of blood before the wound sealed itself.

Lucas pulled back and looked at Pedro with half-lidded eyes.

Madre de Dios! Now he saw what Lucas was promising under those dark lashes.

"Let's go," Pedro said, dragging his man toward his room. Halfway through the cellar he thought of Kos and Lena, and his footsteps faltered. "Lucas. I feel lousy. Shouldn't we be — "

"There's nothing more we can do for them right now." Lucas pinned Pedro to the wall and kissed him again. Fangs grazed flesh, bodies rubbed almost painful friction between them. "Please, Pedro, your room."

The begging made him tingle, made his cock fill, but didn't stir anything darker inside him. Good sign. If this was going to happen, it couldn't be about domination.

Pedro stepped back, hoping his eyes said what he was feeling. Because he wasn't ready for the words and wasn't sure he ever would be.

"Come on," he said, and they ran together, holding hands. In his room, he had them both naked vampire-fast and he laid Lucas down on the bed. He curved his body into Lucas's back and reached around for the long cock he loved to taste. "Are you sure about this?" He hoped his strokes would ensure the answer he wanted.

"I trust you." It was an answer, if not an unequivocal yes.

He breathed onto Lucas's neck. "My bite will make the first time easy."

"I was thinking the same thing. So get on with it."

Pedro didn't need to be asked twice. One long lick up Lucas's carotid. Fangs in, and his man was rolling hard. Groaning, thrusting in Pedro's hand, skin raised up in goose bumps, nipples hard.

Pedro would wait for the deep relaxation, when Lucas had melted under the bite. Until then, Pedro nestled his own erection against Lucas, letting him get used to the hard shaft behind him. His lover pushed back, and Pedro knew he wasn't just surrendering, he was wanting. What the hell had happened to make Lucas feel this way? He would ask later.

Where his head rested on Pedro's upper arm, Lucas was sucking on his bicep. His arousal had triggered skin, and mouth. Any second now, Lucas would go molten with the deep pleasure of the bite and it would be easy for him to open up for Pedro. At least he hoped so. Pedro wanted this to be good for Lucas, and not just because he wanted it to happen again, and again.

Then, he could sense Lucas was ready. Hard to say how, but he could. Still latched on to his shoulder, Pedro reached for a bottle of lube and spread it on his cock. With his slick fingers he dipped between Lucas's cheeks.

He wanted to ask if Lucas was all right. But it was more important to keep drawing on Lucas's blood, to keep all that bliss in his veins. One downside of super hot bitey sex was no talking. From his sounds and thrusts, Lucas was better than okay, and he relaxed, letting Pedro inside him with ease.

Lucas's voice came out husky with need. "I'm ready. I'm yours."

Mine? Well damn, nobody had ever said that to Pedro before. Suddenly, he was desperate to make it true. Slowly, so slowly it was painful, he eased himself inside Lucas and kept on pulling blood. Lucas groaned with unmistakable pleasure.

Fuck yeah, that was a nice sound.

He was all the way in, deep, and the pleasure of it sent electric jolts from the tip of his cock up his spine, where they exploded in his brain.

Madre de Dios—Lucas had given him pretty much everything.

He broke the bite, licking Lucas's wounds closed, and said, "Thank you…"

…for saving my life, for being mine, for giving me this.

He couldn't say all that. So instead, to the best of his ability, he fucked the man he'd fallen so hard for. Fuck was probably not the right word—he'd think about that later.

He reached around for Lucas's cock and worked it in time with his thrusts. It only took a minute for all the new sensations to over-whelm Lucas, and then he contracted as he came, squeezing Pedro's orgasm out and milking him for all he was worth.

Pedro held him tightly, their chests rising and falling together as they caught their breaths.

"Holy shit," Lucas said.

Pedro chuckled. "Yeah. Me too."

"I didn't expect to like it that much."

That earned a full-blown laugh. "What, like you're different than every other dude in the world?"

"I don't know. When I thought it about it, being on that end didn't feel like me. But as soon as we were naked, it wasn't really about who I am as much as it was about being with you."

Pedro was pretty sure those words were way better than the three most people wanted to hear after sex. His fingers played in the dark hair on Lucas's chest. "What made you ready?"

Lucas hooked his ankle around Pedro's, entangling their legs. "Don't underestimate sitting in the dark with your fantasies for two days. I had some time to get over my qualms."

"Yeah?"

"Yeah. But there's something else too—Leo."

Pedro's eyes blurred, his hand fisted in Lucas's chest hair. Was he jealous? That wasn't normally his thing. "Do I want to hear this?"

Lucas rolled over to face him, grinning like he knew what Pedro felt. "I think you do. Talking to the kid made me realize that I don't mind this blood thing between us. I would if it were anybody else, but it's you, so it's hot."

Rolling onto his back, he considered Lucas's confession—he had one to make of his own. Resting his head in his palms, he stared at the ceiling. "There's something about my addiction to your blood that you need to know."

His grave tone must have put Lucas on edge. He sat up fast. "Go on."

"You know how Zoey and Andre are a thing?"

"Some kind of vampire bond, right?"

"Yeah. It starts when a vampire develops a hunger for a particular person's blood. Andre falls in love with her, starts jonesing for her blood, and then, when he actually bites her—something happens. It's like…biochemical. He tastes her blood and then in some bizarro vampire way, their blood is connected together—they feel each other, they only want each other. It's like what happens when I bite you, but it's a permanent thing—apparently, you're inside each other's head, heart, even."

"Sounds hot. It goes the same way when she bites him?"

"Yeah. But with his first wife, a human, it was only one way. Then, when she died, it nearly killed him."

Lucas stilled, like he was holding his breath or something. Yep, he was getting the idea. He scratched his scalp. "So, that could happen to you—you're already only hungry for my blood."

"Pretty much." Pedro licked his lips.

"And then you're double fucked because you need me to be human to feed and you need me to be a vampire to bond with you, or else eventually I die."

Pedro squeezed his eyes shut and nodded.

"Well, there is one solution. Do you think you could feed from another Hunter?"

"Leo?"

Lucas lay down again at Pedro's side. "I actually meant that asshole Derek. He needs a little fang."

It was Pedro's turn to sit up. "I don't get it."

"I'm working on a plan." Lucas's long fingers splayed on his flat belly.

Fuck, he was beautiful, and there was no time to think about that. "*Mierda*, Lucas, spit it out already."

"After a few days in the cell with me, Leo's Hunter programming collapsed like a house of cards. He's gay, and he was alienated like me. Then you all showed him mercy—he'd join your ranks in an instant."

"Seriously?"

"Yeah. Derek's tougher, though. He belongs, he has Ethan's approval. But a bite is very persuasive, and if you push him, he knows there's no reason for all the hate."

Pedro couldn't believe it. "He's straighter than a country road."

"Also true. So maybe Zoey should bite him."

"Not gonna happen. Andre's very jealous. Maybe Uta. But what are we going to do with a couple of sympathetic Hunters, anyway?"

"Turn them into vampires and start a civil war."

CHAPTER 29

Of all the places to bring Lena, Ethan had chosen the cruelest — Kos's house at the coast. Once it had been her sanctuary from Andre, a place where she found herself again after he'd humiliated her.

The fog hung low in the salty, kelp-scented air. When the cabin came into view through the windshield, she finally spilled the tears she'd held the entire car ride.

With its soft, cloud-filtered light and its walls crammed full of bookshelves, walking into the cozy house was like stepping into Kos's arms. The breath rushed from her body, and her vision went black. She grabbed onto a coat rack, steadying herself and breathing deeply. It wasn't over yet, and she had to be brave. She needed to focus.

Maybe she could leave him a message, something for him to find when she was gone. She longed to write the words they both knew were true — she loved him. And he would need to know that she didn't blame him, too. He was still a stupid coward, but no need to write that part down.

Ethan's heartless voice filled the room. "Hello, Kosjenic."

Oh God. This was it. The ransom demand. Her lungs locked up around a chestful of air.

"Yes, she's here. Perfectly safe. A little nibbled on by your friend Kearney. Have you found out about his proclivities yet? That was an ill conceived plan you made."

She could easily imagine Kos stiffening at the charge.

Yes, Ethan was a sadist through and through. "Lena, tell him you're well."

She lunged for the phone, but Ethan held her at arms distance. So she shouted. "Don't bargain with him. He'll double cross you. Don't give up the vines. There's no way to win this."

Ethan chuckled. "She's feisty, but you can hear she is fit and fine." Then he listened to Kos's response.

Her tears returned. She shouted again, sobbing. "I'm not worth it. Don't risk it. Andre will never forgive you."

"Silence, Lena, or I will gag you." Ethan wagged a finger at her like she was a naughty child.

Creep. But she'd said her piece. She curled up on the low couch where she'd once napped blissfully, pulled up a soft woven blanket, and tried to breathe in Kos's scent. Gwen sat in a rocker opposite the couch, staring at Lena with a blank expression.

With hollow politeness, Ethan delivered his instructions. "At precisely one hour after sunset, you may retrieve Lena from your house at the coast. When she is in your custody, you will call your father, and he will do whatever it takes to lower that blasted shield."

Ethan had something in his hand, squeezing his fist so tightly a drop of blood splashed onto the hardwood floor. It was a surprising display of passion. Lena almost smiled to herself. She knew how the shield worked and he didn't, a small pleasure, like turning her back on him in the burned up vineyard.

"Fly here. Alone. We are watching the estate. No one leaves but you."

She tried one last time. "Stay away Kos!"

Ethan crossed to her in three quick steps and backhanded her across the face. Pain bloomed along her cheekbone, and the iron tang of her own blood filled her mouth. She tried to sink further into the couch.

"And finally, Kosjenic, Lena will only have safe passage from this house if the shield is down. All of my snipers will be in position." After a pause, Ethan laughed. "That is wise. I don't trust you either. I suppose it comes down to who can outsmart whom."

He ended the call, slid his phone into his pocket, and went to the kitchen area. At the sink, he unclenched his fist, running it under the faucet. He set something down next to the sink and dried his hands.

Lena squinted, trying to bring the object into focus. Was that one of those plastic toy soldiers? What a nut job — he was like a little boy, trying to play at war, trying to control everyone, a big cruel bully.

Gwen rose. "Lena, would you like to freshen up? You're covered in blood. Perhaps there is something warm and clean for you to wear."

Gwen glanced at Ethan, tucking her chin slightly. The look that passed between them told Lena the woman wouldn't defy him. She might have had a conscience once, but he was her right and wrong now.

And Lena was on her own.

Maybe there were razor blades in Kos's bathroom.

CHAPTER 30

"Can you fly?" Kos asked Uta.

She snorted. "Of course." Leaning forward, she peered at one of the oil paintings on the wall of Andre's office. "This all wrong. The pier here much shorter. And are you not remembering? Tom's house yellow, not white."

Andre handed her a glass of Blood Vine. "Did you hear about Tom's death?"

"I am there." She blinked. "We honor him well. I sing his favorite songs." She sipped the wine, and her eyes rolled back in her head. Her expression was so raw Kos looked away, burning with embarrassment. He did not need to see that look on his Auntie Uta's face.

Andre passed a glass of wine to Kos. "Are you thinking of the tunnel?"

"Yes. If Uta leaves from there, no one will see."

"I am not liking this plan. Your house is trap. They are using explosives."

Zoey set her glass of wine on the coffee table. "Call him back and demand Lena is outside."

Uta shrugged. "He will not be agreeing. Only option is I am finding him before he detonate."

"Of course Lena's safety is most important. But is it impossible to save the vines?" Zoey placed Andre's hand on her shoulder, covering it with her own. She knew him so well—he would think he was comforting her, when really she was holding him up. Another sign that maybe Kos had been wrong about love, and a coward, after all.

Andre shifted his weight. "I do not want to give up hope, but I will do what must be done to save Lena."

And Kos would do whatever he could to make sure that did not happen. He needed to get Uta alone, make sure they were on the same page — he would face down the Hunters, and she would rescue Lena, it was as simple as that.

He had the perfect pretense. "Auntie Uta, I want you to tell me how Bel was conceived."

Andre threw his glass of wine, shattering it, and picked Kos up by his collar. "No."

"Why are you wanting this?" Uta examined her fingernails intently, oblivious to Andre's reaction, or studiously ignoring it.

Zoey rested her hand on his forearm. "Lena wants a child."

"I see. Andre, you are leaving us. Kos and I are speaking of this."

"No." He didn't set Kos down.

His green eyes blazed with…anger? No, it was fear. What was he afraid of?

"Your son is man. He make his own decisions. He having right to know."

"Andre, if we save her, this may be the only way she will stay with me."

The fear still blazed in his father's eyes, but slowly, Andre lowered Kos to the ground. Everyone stared at him, waiting.

He pouted. "*Davo*, this is my office."

Uta shooed him with the hand she'd finished examining. Zoey dragged Andre out before he could explode.

When the door closed behind them, Kos whispered as quietly as possible. "I will need to know about Bel, if she lives. But first, I need to know something else."

She dropped into one of the overstuffed armchairs and put her very high heels up on the coffee table. "I am knowing the answers to many of your questions, I suspect."

"Why did Andre bond with Mila?" He closed his eyes, rolled his shoulders, and hoped for an answer that would free him to love Lena — forever.

"Hmm. Of course you are wondering this. Normally a blood bond does not go so wrong."

His eyes popped open. "Really?"

"It is only because Mila is refusing the bond."

"But if she loved him, why did she do that?" Kos lowered himself onto the sturdy coffee table and leaned closer, resting his elbows on his knees. Uta smelled like the island of Šolta, which was impossible.

A cascade of auburn hair rippled when she shook her head. "Mila is loving idea of Andre, not real Andre."

"But didn't he see through that? He's not easily fooled."

She narrowed her eyes, pinning him. "I'll tell you truth, but you must not blame yourself."

What could that possibly mean? He opened his palms to her. "Okay."

"He love you, want you for son so much he not question Mila enough."

"Me?"

"You are little angel, little version of Andre, following him around vineyard, asking every question. And you have no father, you love him. He choose you, he take Mila too."

That simply couldn't be true. He'd always assumed gruff Andre was a reluctant father, even if a damn good one. "But I remember that he loved her. I remember the way he touched her, spoke to her."

"The bond make him love her. But it bad match."

Andre had done it for him. Kos wasn't the baggage, he was the prize. Warmth rushed through him, the most amazing feeling, thawing places he hadn't known were frozen. Was this how Lena felt, when she finally realized he wanted her? And then he took it away, because he was a coward and a fool.

"All this time, I thought—"

"Maybe, you are waiting for her. You good match? She love you?"

He didn't hesitate. "Yes."

"Good. Now we go save her."

He'd been so wrong, had made a terrible mess. He would make it right, and he wouldn't let Lena, Andre, or the rest of the vampires pay for it.

"Uta."

At the sound of her name, she focused her ancient eyes on him.

He mouthed his words so that no one in the house could hear. "Me. Not her, not the vines."

Her bottom lip swallowed the top one, pulling her mouth into a thin line. Her eyes glistened, and she nodded. For a second, she looked like she cared—his old Auntie Uta, before she stabbed Bel in the back.

The quietest whisper of words floated to his ears, and her lips moved. *Krist*—that was serious old-time vampire power—almost telepathy. "Your father will kill me, but I am understanding this kind of love, and this kind of burden. You do what you must, I save girl."

She stood, and Kos followed her from Andre's office. His father stood mere feet from the door. Sneaky son of a bitch. Good thing they'd been careful.

"Is it true about Mother?"

"Yes." Andre pulled him into a rare hug, resting his face on Kos's shoulder, and gripping the back of his head. They stood locked that way for a long time, and the depth of his father's love made what Kos had to do far worse.

Toes tapped on the stone floor of the cellar, and Uta said, "Yes. Yes. Enough. I hungry. Who can I eat?"

Kos was hungry too. But minutes later, when Susan and Ally stood in the foyer, dark circles under both their eyes, he decided to drink Blood Vine instead. With Lena out of the rotation, and Zoey feeding her young hunger, the two women were tapped.

Uta flung her fingers at the women. "I taking one of prisoners. Your household stretched thin."

"You want to feed from a Hunter? You said their smell made you puke."

There was her damn shrug again. "You are seeing picture I sent, of vampires under sunshine. Maybe it turn me into super vampire."

He rubbed his chin. "You pretty much already are a super vampire."

"True. But, I not walking in sun."

They backtracked through the cellar to the workroom, and Kos opened the door to the makeshift cell. Uta stepped inside. "I am taking grown up."

"Hell no. No parasite is taking my blood. Fuck off."

"Oooh. He is fighter. How fun." She had Nichols on the floor with a hand covering his mouth in a second, muffling his hateful drivel.

That left the kid for Kos. Or more Blood Vine. He needed to be strong for Lena, so the kid it was.

"Leo, right? You're with me."

The kid actually smiled, ear to ear. How had little mister rogue Hunter become a vampire groupie so fast?

Kos sat him on a stool. "Put your hands out and grip the worktable. You might swoon."

"From blood loss?"

"No." There was no sense explaining—he'd figure it out soon enough.

Kos licked his neck and shuddered. Licking men was really not his thing, but blood was blood. Fangs out and into Leo's neck. When his blood hit the roof of Kos's mouth, pleasure exploded through him. *Krist*, that was no ordinary blood.

He was an infant at his mother's breast. He walked hand in hand with a very tall Andre through the vineyards on Šolta. He unwrapped a toy train. He was at a table spread with roast meats and baklava. He was inside Lena's sweet heat. He swallowed, and his veins buzzed with power, an energy far greater than the Blood Vine bestowed.

He was home. Everything was right with the world. He could stop Ethan Bennett. Lena would be fine. They could live happily ever after.

His skin heated with that burning pleasure that could only be—the sun.

He sighed. Could he really be in the light of day? Opening his eyes, the workroom at Kaštel materialized. The Hunter kid rested in his arms, slumped over the worktable.

Leo groaned, stroking himself through his pants.

Kos squeezed his eyes shut, but he couldn't blame the kid. He hadn't given him any warning. He licked the punctures on Leo's neck closed, and steadied him under his arms. Leo found purchase on his stool, gripping the table.

Slowly, he turned to face Kos, his eyes huge. "Oh."

Kos couldn't help but laugh. "That's the part they never tell you."

A door slammed behind him, and he turned to see Uta standing outside the closet. Her hair stood away from her head like she'd had an electric shock. She twisted her pants on her hips, straightening them. Then she smoothed the sleeves of her jacket.

Her eyes locked onto Kos's. Melodic Croatian flew out of her mouth in a rhythm so different from her broken English. *"Jebi me u sve rupe, to je najbolja stvar koju sam ikad okusila."*

Kos laughed again. His auntie was as over-the-top as ever.

Leo stood on alert. "What did she say?"

"She said, 'Fuck me in every hole, that was the best thing I've ever tasted.'"

"Derek's blood?"

"Yeah," Kos replied matter-of-factly.

The kid scratched his head. "That means something, doesn't it?"

Kos took a deep breath, pondering his answer. "Yes it does, Leo. But I sure as hell don't know what."

Finally, Uta finished her wardrobe adjustments. "Kos, I very strong now. We are going to get your girl."

Lena ran her finger over the neatly shelved CD cases. Thankfully, Kos hadn't put them all on his iPod yet. She found it—Ella sings Gershwin. Lena turned the volume to almost silent, queued up "Our Love is Here to Stay," and set it on repeat. She couldn't hear it, but Kos would, even from far, far above in the sky.

Good old George Gershwin was surely right—true love would out last passing fads. Maybe it would even hold up to the biggest mountain ranges. In his long, long life, Kos would not forget her, even if she wished it for him. Hopefully he would at least find the courage to love again sometime.

Gwen perused Kos's bookshelves, but always kept one eye on Lena. Eventually the petite woman settled into a big chair with a dusty leather volume.

Lena said silent prayers and thanksgivings. All things considered, she had a lot to be thankful for—a loving home, friends, one amazing night with Kos. From glass doors in the living room, she watched the sky darken over the ocean. The doors opened onto the deck, built right over the sea cliff, where waves thundered, crashing below.

"Lena, come here." Ethan stood by the front door, and he opened it as she approached. He pointed to the shrubs and alder trees lining Kos's property. "Do you see the snipers?"

"Yes."

"Gwen and I will join them momentarily, you will remain here and wait for Kosjenic."

She hugged herself, staring out into the gloomy twilight. "You're going to blow us up."

"Why would I do something like that?"

She spun to face him. "He knows it's a trap."

"But he will come anyway."

Ethan was right.

Apparently, Gwen couldn't stand for that particular book to be incinerated. She wrapped her arm around it and followed Ethan into the trees.

The clock said Kos was due in ten minutes. She couldn't cut it too close—he was always early, and she had to finish it before he arrived.

She turned up the volume on the stereo, took a deep breath, and strode toward the door.

When she was five or six feet from the exit, a dozen red dots streaked across the doorframe and over her arms, marking her torso with their terrifying glow—the snipers had taken aim. All she had to do was jog those last few steps, and it would be all over.

But suddenly, she didn't want to give them the satisfaction. She lunged back from the door, and ran across the room, yanking open the sliding glass to the deck. Climbing onto the rail, she shouted, "I love you," to the night sky. Then she dove off the deck into the churning, rocky ocean.

CHAPTER 31

Kos had only flown three times in his life, but it was enough to know that Hunter blood was rocket fuel. Energy pumped through his veins so efficiently his breath came in long, steady draws.

Away from prying vampire ears, he had more questions for Uta, and he needed answers before he faced Lena. Instinctively, he shouted over the loud wind rushing past his ears, although Uta was so old she would have heard a whisper.

"Tell me how it works, with the baby."

"Now?"

"If she lives, I must have this to offer her." Kos corkscrewed in the air to glimpse Uta. Somehow, the dramatic setting for this talk seemed appropriate for the airing of family secrets.

She swallowed, her white throat tensing. Then she nodded, and the words rushed out of her. "It is taking blood."

"Blood?"

"Vampire is not having any...*govna*, what is word?"

"Sperm." Kos hadn't known that fact for sure, but it made sense.

"Yes. You are having none of those. But your blood very potent. So, when woman fertile, you pierce your finger and put your blood inside her, with your heritage, your denes?"

"Genes."

"Yes, genes, in your blood. It go inside egg and she makes baby."

Bleeding inside a woman was too easy. Not part of what he normally got up to, but it wasn't so bad, and surely Lena could handle it. "That's it?"

She exhaled, letting him know he was the most infuriating moron on the planet. "No, that not it. If you do only that, your blood is killing egg, eating it."

The skin of his face was dry from the cold air, and it creased painfully when he cringed. "It devours the egg."

"Da. Egg must be stronger, *cijepljena*…"

"*Cijepljena?*" His mind searched for a translation. "Inoculated… like a vaccine? With what?"

"Vampire blood."

"How?"

Uta flew ahead of him and hovered, upright, one knee bent. Her auburn hair blew in the wind. Her gray suit shone like the moon in the night sky—she was a ghostly apparition. Floating there, she made a bottoms-up gesture, as if drinking from a glass.

"Mother drank blood?"

Uta darted up into blackness, then reappeared at his side. "Yes. Every day, so egg is growing strong before it fertil…vhatever."

"Similar to organ transplant, the patient's immune system is suppressed so her body doesn't reject the organ."

"*Da*, exactly."

"So, whose blood did mother drink before she conceived Bel?"

Uta flew alongside him in silence, as if building up dramatic tension before she named the vampire. Only she didn't.

And suddenly the answer was obvious. *Krist.* "You?"

"Yes. And it working, but it having cost."

Kos's stomach descended all the way to ground, hundreds of feet below. What on earth could that mean? Bel was fine—healthy and immortal, with none of the pesky downsides of vampire-hood.

"What cost?"

"*Shash.* You are hearing that?"

They'd reached his house too early, leaving plenty of time for her to explain. But the most important thing was Lena's safety, so he listened. The briny wind whistled past his head, and the ocean waves were a constant roar below, but Kos opened his ears for another sound. The musical notes reached him, and he lost his concentration, free falling who knew how far. Uta grabbed him, dragging him behind her until he found his lift again and flew alongside her.

"This music mean something?"

Unable to manage a reply, he nodded. Lena had sent him a message. Was it a promise, or a goodbye?

They cut wide circles around the property, seeing the position of all the snipers.

She sniffed loudly. "You are smelling C4?"

"Is that what it is?" He'd barely registered the unfamiliar plastic smell.

"Hunters are loving it. They are buying special product, no safety odor added. Are thinking we not smell. Fools."

At that moment, Ethan Bennett and some tiny woman came through the front door. She was carrying Kos's first edition of Tennyson's *Poems, Cheifly Lyrical.* The bitch.

"Woman at Hunt?" Uta said. "Unusual."

The plan could work. He would come up behind Ethan, while Uta landed on the deck and grabbed Lena. The snipers wore night vision goggles, but Uta was fast. They would see one blur of heat in and out of the house without knowing it wasn't Kos. And Kos could tie up Bennett's trigger hand in the meantime; surely he would be the one to push the button. He was the power hungry maniac.

"Kos, look."

The snipers moved as one, training the guns on the front door. Lena stood in its shadows, speckled with their laser sights. *Krist,* she wouldn't. She vanished deeper into the house, and he exhaled with relief.

The backdoor rolled open and she was on the deck rail.

"I love you."

No!

She jumped.

He dove down, even as he heard Uta say, "Go. I get Bennett."

Pedro pushed the tips of his fingers into the white wall of the dining room. He felt like climbing it. Maybe he actually could, now that he was a vampire. But no claws extended, no sticky spidey webs shot out. He would have to do another lap around the table instead.

Zoey hung a new IV bag for the gaunt Trys then zeroed in on the phone, lying on the table. Lucas and Andre's eyes were glued to it too. Pedro joined the party, sitting next to the witch and drumming his fingers on the table.

Andre growled at him, and Trys pressed his fingers flat and still.

The phone rang.

Andre reached for it with a shaking hand. Zoey took it, pressing the green button and the speakerphone.

"Kos?" Andre croaked.

"I have her. She's safe. Do it."

"But…"

A long pause followed, and then Kos replied, "It's the only way, Father."

Tears of blood pooled in Andre's eyes. Trys watched him, waiting for the go ahead. Zoey stood close, propping him up. Lucas stared at the phone, his eyebrows drawn together.

Kos spoke again. "Andre, now. Please. If they blow this place, I might survive, but she won't."

Andre gave Trys the nod.

She opened her mouth in a wide yawn and inhaled. As she filled with breath, color returned to her face. Tendrils of feathery magic retracted into her, caressing Pedro's skin like silk as they floated by. Zoey rubbed her arms, she must have sensed it too. Andre collapsed into a chair. Lucas still frowned at the phone.

Trys looked up. "It's done."

"Thank you." Kos hung up.

Everyone turned to the window, except Andre, who bent forward and buried his face in his arm. No sound came from him, but his back rose and fell in the rhythm of sobs. Zoey rubbed up and down his spine as the night sky began to glow.

Hijo de puta. How many of them were out there? Perhaps a hundred flame throwers appeared on the horizon. It would all be ash in minutes.

Something wet trickled down Pedro's face. He wiped it with the back of his hand, and saw blood. For Andre, and for their vines, and for all the vampires, he cried.

CHAPTER 32

Where was she?
She hadn't surfaced. She wasn't on the rocks.

Kos dove under the water, swimming against the powerful push and pull of the waves. How long had she been under?

It was so hard to see through the forest of kelp and the froth of churned up water. If she'd been dragged out past where the waves were breaking, the current would have pulled her south.

His eyes burned from the salt water. He dove again, swimming out of the inlet, and scanned the shoreline.

There, at the tip of the outcropping—she was tangled in ropes of kelp. Her head was under, but the swell passed, and she surfaced for a moment.

Was she breathing?

He swam as hard as he could. His clothes dragged him; the undertow pulled him. It was much harder than flying.

Finally, he reached her, working to free her from the seaweed. She didn't stir, didn't breathe. Underwater, he kicked his feet as fast as he could, building power, and then launched them into the air.

His house became a fireball, a tsunami of heat barreling toward them. He covered her, diving underwater again.

Above the ocean, the sky went bright, then dark. He kicked toward the surface again, where the water had been heated by the blast. Then he was in the air. He landed on a stretch of sand, and lay her down.

Blood flowed from some place on her scalp, but oxygen was the most important thing. He tried to push the water from her lungs, but he didn't really know how. He compressed her belly, her chest. Nothing happened. He opened her mouth, and blew in, but her lungs didn't expand, they were so full of seawater. He closed his mouth over hers, and sucked with all his might. His mouth filled with brine. He swallowed it, and did it again.

She coughed. He rolled her over, and she coughed and vomited, coughed and vomited. Then she passed out.

He tried to rouse her. *Please God, let her live.*

He held her, trying to warm her. He kissed her, like a fairy tale.

Nothing.

From above the cliffs somewhere, Uta shouted. "Sing. Oh wait, you are lousy singer. Just hum."

He cleared his throat of salt water and did his best with the melody. It had been her farewell. Would it bring her back?

Her eyes fluttered open, and she croaked. "You're really tone deaf."

"Oh thank, God." He wanted to grab her, squeeze her, but she looked so frail.

A hand went to her scalp, where she had a deep gash. She winced. "What happened?"

"You jumped." He seized her other hand. It was freezing.

"I know that. What about at Kaštel?"

"I didn't call. Should be fine." His phone was still in his pocket, soaked.

"Thank God. Kos, I couldn't live with myself if—"

He couldn't wait any longer. He picked her up and cradled her, rocking. "Shh. Brave girl. Don't worry."

She burrowed into him, shivering. He needed to get her warm. Could she make it all the way back to Kaštel, wet and freezing? He was just as wet, and not providing much warmth.

"Kosjenic Marasović, *pieka ti se zgadila.* Fly skinny ass up here and help me."

"Who is that?" Lena asked, mumbling into his chest.

He smoothed her wet-hair, probably mostly to soothe himself. "My Auntie Uta. We're your rescue team."

Lena craned her head to look at him. "What did she say?"

"Old Croatian curse."

Her golden brows arched. "What does it mean?"

"May you find pussy repulsive."

Those eyebrows scrunched adorably.

He grinned. "Don't worry. Unlikely to happen."

She giggled, filling his heart with the best sound he'd ever heard. Better even than after they'd made love.

"Lena, I'm so sorry I let all this—"

"Shh. It's okay. It's over. We're safe. Go help her."

"Will you be okay? I'll just be a minute." He hated leaving her. But he already knew the answer—she was tougher than most of the vampires he knew. She'd jumped off his deck—pretty much a suicide mission. His gut twisted all over again.

"Yeah. I'll be okay."

It was a wasteland on top of the cliff. His house had been leveled. Several of the snipers were dead, bleeding from their mouths and ears—the blast wave had gotten them. Overeager sons of bitches must have used too much C4.

"Kos. You are getting over here."

He followed Uta's voice.

Ouch. She was impaled on a fencepost, flailing her arms like a belly-up cockroach, a dead Hunter skewered on top of her like a shish kabob. Her blood ran down the post, slick and glossy-black in the moonlight.

He pulled the Hunter off. Lucky for her, the post went right through her abdomen, above her pelvis and below her ribs. Re-growing bone took a whole day, and hurt like hell. Her soft tissue would heal in minutes.

"You okay? How much blood did you lose?"

"I not bad. Hunter bleeding his magic right into me."

"What happened?"

"I grab Bennett, but he not have remote control thing. The woman. She have it in book. I am recognizing her. She one of Mason's..." Uta faltered, glancing toward the ruins of the house.

One of...*Krist*. What had Lena suffered?

"She is knowing me too. She is saying she sorry, then push button. I am still holding Ethan. Grab this other Hunter too, for shielding blast." Uta kicked him with her designer heels. Their leather was blistered and the stilettos were warped from the heat. Still, she stood perfectly straight.

"Ethan thrown far. Me and asshole stuck here." She stepped on his hand, and lots of bones popped.

"Is Bennett dead?"

Uta brushed her palms together. "No. He is driving off with woman."

"Damn it."

"Lena okay?" Uta reached for his arm.

"Yeah."

"Get her. I am looking around."

Back at the beach, Lena leaned against a smooth boulder, shivering. She hugged herself tightly, eyes closed, breathing steadily. He knelt next to her, and brushed sand off her face.

"Almost ready. Come up top with me. Then we'll fly home."

"Home."

The word sounded hollow, and he didn't know what to make of her tone. They had a lot of talking to do. He cradled her in his arms, which made flying awkward. But it was just a hop up the cliff.

"Oh, Kos," she gasped. "Your house. I'm sorry."

He set her on her feet, holding her elbow just in case. "All that matters is you're safe."

She surveyed the rubble, not looking at him.

"Kos. You are needing to see this." Uta stood with one foot in a black van that had been knocked over in the blast.

Not wanting to leave Lena, he tugged her along to investigate. Inside the van a Hunter lay dead, his face flattened against electrical equipment.

"What is this?" Kos's shoulders bunched instinctively.

"He looks like Leo." Lena reached for Kos's hand.

He did — fatter and older — probably his father. Uta took a picture of him with her phone. Good idea, the kid might need to see.

"Listen." Uta pushed a button.

His own voice came from a speaker. "I have her. She's safe. Do it."

No. It couldn't be.

She pushed another button, and again Kos heard his own voice. "It's the only way, Father."

Lena yanked her hand away, covering her ears and shaking her head. "No!"

Kos grabbed her before she could pull away, afraid of what she might do.

One more button, his voice pleading. "Andre, now. Please. If they blow this place, I might survive, but she won't."

His stomach wrung itself into a knot. He'd failed after all. Uta would have saved Lena. He should have stopped this.

Uta slapped him and he tottered, his ears ringing. She glared. "I am seeing your thoughts. Same storms brewing in your eyes as Mila's. You are stopping now. You too, girl. It is done. Now we pick up pieces. Start over. This what our kind is doing, always."

Kos leaned against the van and slid to the ground, pulling Lena into his lap. She was so cold and damp.

She sniffed. "Andre will hate me."

Kos rested his chin on her head. "No. He'll hate himself."

"Then I am slapping him too. Now, we are going to Kaštel."

Uta took off her blood stained jacket and gave it to Lena. At least it was dry. She didn't even blink before she put on the gory thing. Uta bent her knees and launched herself into the air.

"Hold on." Kos squeezed Lena tight and pushed off with the balls of his feet into the sky.

The night air froze him to the bone. His fingertips stung from the cold until they finally went numb. Lena shivered against him, crying tears that turned to ice by the time they hit his face.

Would she be okay? She had gashes on her head, a nasty bite mark on her neck.

"Oh no," she whispered.

Below, the red and white lights of three fire engines lined the highway in front of Kaštel. Two more had pulled down the narrow gravel roads into the vineyard. The thump of a helicopter vibrated the air around them, carrying water to dump on smoldering vines.

The smell burned his sinuses. Not just soot and ash, but something chemical—concentrated gasoline. Lena coughed, and he hugged her tighter.

"Napalm," Uta shouted. "We are landing there—" she pointed at the former Hunter lookout "—so no strapping firehunks are seeing us."

"Firemen," Lena shouted back.

"Whatever." Uta dismissed her with a wave.

They touched down on the bald rock. Lena's bare feet looked so delicate on the rough stone. He lifted her again and skidded down a steep hill carrying her, with Uta behind.

At the edge of the highway, Uta said, "Lena, give me jacket so you are not explaining blood to firehunks."

As Lena shed the thing, Kos said, "Uta. Later, you must tell me the other secret. About Bel."

Her eyes went to Lena's and back to his. The muscles in her throat rolled down, as if she'd swallowed a golf ball, but she pressed her lips tight together and nodded.

The hair stood up on the back of his neck, and he soldiered on down the hill with Lena in his hands. What else was there to do?

The dotted yellow lines between highway lanes lulled Ethan into a kind of seething hypnosis.

"With the vines destroyed, the vampires will continue to waste away. You scored the greatest victory." Gwen patted his knee.

He took one hand off the wheel to grab hers and squeeze it, hard. She gasped. Her knuckles would bruise from the pressure across their breadth.

She dared to comfort him, to rationalize with him?

"You are out of line. Say you're sorry."

"I'm sorry," she whimpered.

He released her hand. "Who was the female?"

After a steadying breath, she answered with some composure. "She's an authority of some kind. She rescued me from Mason, and placed me in counseling."

An authority? Did vampires have a formal social structure? That made them more sophisticated than Hunters.

"Ethan, may I ask what is next?"

Ah. That tone was much prettier. He eased up his grip.

"You may. Now we start the war."

CHAPTER 33

The fortress-like wooden door of the house loomed before Lena, and her hand refused to press its lever. She'd already spent her last drop of courage, and facing Andre was the scariest thing she'd ever had to do, scarier even than jumping into the surf.

Kos covered her hand and opened the front door. She tap-danced behind him, but he dragged her around.

Just inside, Zoey and Andre were engrossed in a heated conversation with two firemen. Both stood too close to Andre. They were both big men, and surely didn't realize they should be frightened. She knew better.

Andre turned to look at the new arrivals. When his gaze landed on her, he smiled, his whole face becoming genuinely kind.

Her knees went soft.

He reached out to her. "I am so very glad to see you."

She stared at his hand before she worked up the nerve to take it. Once he had a firm grip on her fingers, he pulled her into a bear hug. With her cheek pressed against his chest, she looked at Zoey.

The vampire's mouth spread into a huge, unexpected smile. "Welcome to the family. I'll go get you a blanket."

Lena stepped back, and Andre released her. Puzzled, she turned to Kos for an explanation.

He took her hand again — he'd hardly let go since they took off from his house. "We have a lot to talk about." His eyes were a cloudy color somewhere in between the telltale shades of blue or gray that made him so transparent to her.

One of the firemen coughed. "Listen. I don't know what kind of circus your little winery is, but the motive for this fire is very suspicious, and nobody in the Sacramento or San Francisco FBI offices knows anything about anti-Croatian hate groups. I'm calling homeland security."

"Ralph?" Lena stepped forward to read his badge.

"Lena?"

"You're a fireman? I thought you owned an ice cream shop."

"Arson investigator by day, ice cream maker by night." He raised one shoulder in a shrug, a boyish gesture on such a bulky man.

"Oh."

"Are you okay?"

Glancing at her bare feet and filthy clothes, she tried to think of an explanation for the gashes on her head and her neck—nothing. "Yeah, I'm okay."

"You live here?"

"Sure do. We love your ice cream. Andre here is the biggest fan. Eats most of it himself." She waggled her eyebrows at Andre.

"It is true, Captain. I like the…um, chocolate?"

Lena forced an amused laugh, patting Andre's forearm. "He means the Deep Dark Chocolate Secret. And Kos here likes the peppermint, or the lavender, when it's in season."

"I'm partial to the lavender myself." The captain took a step away from Andre. "So Lena, do you know anything about this alleged anti-Croatian hate group."

"Yes, sir." Her chin bobbed in a rapid nod.

"Just Ralph is fine."

"Okay, Ralph. They've been giving us a lot of trouble. Started off with pranks, then threats—"

"Phone calls?"

"No, too smart for that, I think. Those can be traced."

He scribbled in a little notebook. "True, true. Why didn't you call the police?"

"Oh, well." She stepped close to him and stood on her tiptoes. "These Croatian guys are kind of macho. They want to take care of things themselves."

He grunted. "Typical. Well, I'm afraid you boys will have to turn this over to the professionals."

Kos extended his hand. "Yes, Captain. I'm Kosjenic Maras, Andre's son, and I can assure you we have every intention of doing so. Clearly, we're in over our heads."

Ralph looked Kos up and down, then did the same to Andre.

"Yes. About that. I am very sorry. I guess you've lost your life's work."

Andre's jaw bulged, and he rubbed his eyes with the heels of both hands, nodding in agreement.

"I can't imagine how I'd feel if I lost the ice-cream shop."

Good Lord, did he just say that? And it had been going so well. Lena patted his elbow. "Yes, that would be a tragedy too, Ralph. So, if you're finished with your questions, I think the family needs some time to grieve."

"Oh, of course. Here's my number, if you think of anything else." Ralph pressed a business card into Kos's hand.

He closed the door behind them. "Lena, that was amazing. Some of the best obfuscating I've ever seen."

What the heck did obfuscating mean? Maybe it didn't matter. It sounded like a compliment. She smiled. "Thanks."

Zoey appeared with a thick robe—Kos's—and wrapped it around Lena. Andre reached one long arm toward her and patted her on the shoulder just like her father used to, and suddenly everything fell into place.

"I'm so sorry. I wish you hadn't done that for me." Tears fell down her face. Andre's eyes filled with bloody tears too, and without thinking, she reached up to wipe them away.

He managed a forlorn smile. "I do not think Kos could have lived with himself, or with me, if I had not."

Pedro and Lucas came out of the dining room hand in hand. Lucas's eyes homed in on Kos, and Lena's stomach flopped—he knew. Kos lunged for him, growling.

Pedro cut him off, stepping between then. "It's true then?"

"What?" Andre asked.

Pedro's face twisted. "We need to talk. Let's go into the dining room."

Lena scanned the faces. "Where's Uta?"

"I here." She practically floated out of the cellar door, dangling Leo from his ankle. His hair brushed the floor, but his head cleared it by inches. Until then, Lena hadn't really noticed how tall she was.

Pedro pushed Lucas into the dining room ahead of him, shielding him from Kos, who tugged Lena through the door. Uta followed, sweeping the floor with Leo's curly mop. Andre sagged on Zoey, who braced him with her shoulder. Lena expected him to be angry or suspicious, but he just looked defeated. Everyone filed around the table, taking places, but no one sat. Finally, Lena pulled out her chair and everyone did the same.

A window stood open, and an acrid breeze blew in, chilling her. She shivered.

Kos pulled her chair closer to his, and rested his warm hand on her thigh. "You need a hot bath."

Hell yes, she did. But it could wait. "I'm fine. We need to be here."

He nodded, then his eyes went gray and he leaned across the table. "Did you know, Lucas?"

"I don't know anything." His eyes flicked to Andre and back. "But something felt wrong about the phone call."

Kos stood, his chair toppling over backward. "Why the hell didn't you say so —"

"And risk being wrong? Risk Lena? I wasn't certain."

Oh God. They'd all sacrificed so much for her. She couldn't look at any of them. She slid to her knees on the floor and righted Kos's chair. He brushed her face with his palm, his touch and his eyes promising she was worth all their costs. Warmth seeped into her from his hand.

Then he turned back to Lucas and tucked his chin, the barest hint of a bow.

"I'm sorry." Lucas clenched his fists on the table. "I'm so sorry. I thought…"

Lena pitied him. But when he saw it in her eyes, he shook his head, and she swallowed the humiliating emotion. He didn't deserve it any more than she ever had.

Pedro clasped one of Lucas's balled hands between his own. "What happened?"

Kos took a deep breath. "Lena dove off my deck into the ocean so we wouldn't sacrifice the vines."

"Oh, no." Zoey covered her hand with her mouth.

Lena's body flushed. They didn't wish she'd succeeded at all—didn't think her life was less important than what they'd lost.

Kos went on. "Uta went after Bennett, but she got skewered when my house exploded."

She snorted. "Fuck you."

"It's true. Ethan got away. Afterwards we realized that a Hunter, we guessed he was Leo's father, had my voice on tape." Kost took a deep breath, and Lena willed him courage. "I never called Andre. They tricked us."

Leo squeaked, his head still dangling above the floor.

But where was Andre's bellow? His fist pounding into the table? His cursing? He stared at the wall, his jaw slack for once, his eyes glassy.

Zoey sniffed. Her words came out as sobs. "All for nothing?"

"No." Lucas spoke with the definitiveness of a leader, capturing Lena's attention. "You cannot do this to yourselves. You didn't know. This is how Ethan wins. He gets inside you. Eats at you. Don't. Let. Him. Win."

Kos was riveted to Lucas, too, and nodded in agreement. "He's right."

"Why do you think it was Leo's father?" Lucas asked.

Uta lowered Leo's head to rest on the floor, and then released his ankle. He landed on his back with a thud, grunting.

She yanked him to sitting, took out her phone and showed him the screen. "This your father?"

Leo crawled up to sitting, caught his lower lip with his teeth and nodded. "Is he dead?"

Lena's heart grew heavy for his grief. How was that possible, given how many times it had already been burdened and broken in one day?

Uta sheathed her phone in the pocket of her jacket. "The explosion is killing him."

"*Krist.* You did it." Kos jumped up, lunging at Leo. "*You* tapped my phone, just like my email. You set the whole thing up."

Uta blocked him.

"No. I—" Leo crumpled to the floor. "I'm sorry. I suggested it, during the operation. We got all of your numbers. But that was the last I heard. If I'd known, I would have told you…"

Kos gasped, rubbing his sternum.

The gesture panicked Lena. "What is it?"

He stared at Leo, palm over palm pressed against his chest, frowning.

"Kos?" She prodded him with her elbow.

"He's telling the truth. I can feel it. I fed from him, and I can feel his emotions."

Zoey groaned. "You fed from him?"

"Really, Zoey?" Kos lashed out in a rare display of anger. "Ms. I-Used-To-Fuck-Ethan-Bennett."

The table split in half with a loud crack, collapsing along the fault line. Andre's fist hung over it, in mid air.

Lena slumped in her chair. Oh thank God. Pissed-off Andre was so much better than paralyzed-with-grief Andre.

"I have had enough. I do not blame any of you, even you, boy. But I cannot listen to another word. I am going to lock myself in my room with my Zoey, and it will be a long, long time before we come out."

He moved in a blur to the door, holding Zoey around the waist like she was a football.

CHAPTER 34

With Kos's hand on the small of Lena's back, he guided her from the dining room. His oversized clothes hung from her, stiff and crusted with salt. Her hair had dried into a wind-blown sweep of gold waves, and somehow, bedraggled as she was, he'd never seen anything more beautiful. When they reached the foot of the broad stairwell in the foyer, he tried to pick her up.

She retreated. "I want to walk."

Okay. It was probably a good sign that she was still stubborn as hell.

She clung to the handrail and paused at every step. At the landing, she halted in front of the old painting, the one of the house on Šolta, with a young Kos playing in the foreground. Perched behind her, he couldn't see her face. Her pulse, her breathing remained steady. But, her posture was unreadable, which left too much room for his dread. After everything, would she leave him? He couldn't let her.

At the top of the stairs, she veered left, toward her old room.

"Lena." He pulled her to the right.

"Really, I can stay in my room, there's no nee—"

He held his ground. "We're past this."

She didn't look at him.

"We have a lot to talk about, but first you need a hot bath, and there is no way I'm letting you go back there to take it."

Wordlessly, she let him pull her along.

Once she'd settled into the tub, he knocked on the door. "I'm going to shower in a guest room. Take as long as you need."

She took forever.

He brought her a tray of food — fruit, a ham sandwich, cocoa, baklava leftover from the party.

Clean, warm, dressed, he waited for her in his armchair, unable to read a word of Tolstoy or Dostoevsky. He even tried Agatha Christie…

Would she still want him, after everything she'd been through?

The door knob clicked, and, wrapped in a towel, she emerged, pink from head to toe.

"Better?"

"Much." She sat on the end of the bed, facing him with her knees together. Good thing it was a big towel, it covered most of her tempting skin from armpit to kneecap.

He sucked his thumb into his mouth and leaned forward to trace his saliva over the wounds on her neck. The flesh repaired itself instantly, becoming the lovely ivory of her healthy complexion.

"Eat." He pointed at the tray. "I'm sorry the cocoa's cold."

She swallowed it in one gulp and started on the sandwich.

"I need to tell you I didn't know about Mason. I should have, but I never connected the dots."

She took her time chewing. "I know. You never would have let me go there. I hope he wastes away in a tiny hot hut in the Mexican desert."

"Wastes? No, he'll have a worse fate than that, once Uta gets her hands on him."

"Good." She stared over his shoulder at a blank patch of wall.

"One day, when you're ready, I hope you will tell me what happened."

She tilted her head, and fixed him with her bottomless eyes. Would he ever look at them again without imagining the sea he'd nearly lost her to?

She curled her hands around the edge of the mattress, sheets and blankets rasping under her weight. "You'll imagine worse if I don't tell you now."

He let out a breath he hadn't known he was holding.

"He wanted to push me. To scare me."

Kos's stomach clenched, but he kept his face impassive. "Go on."

"He bit me, while another woman…touched me."

His clenching gut contorted into a full-fledged knot. To have your body tricked into wanting what you did not want—it was sick. "*Krist*—"

She let go of the mattress to drape a comforting hand over his knee. "Actually, it wasn't so bad. Not my thing, but at least now I know. Susan always told me I should try it at least once." Her slight smile turned all the way into a chuckle.

Damn, she was either braver than a special ops unit, or completely hysterical.

"Did he force…" His tongue got stuck against the top of his mouth.

"Another woman. But, no. Not me. We didn't even…"

When he grasped her meaning, tension melted from Kos's muscles. His shoulders dropped to their natural, relaxed position for the first time in days. He drew in a full breath. "Thank God."

"I'm sure it would have come to that, and worse. But Ethan arrived. Who'd have thought I'd be grateful to him?"

"Can you eat some more, or have I stolen your appetite?"

"I can eat."

She finished the sandwich, an apple, the baklava. Watching her tongue dart out to catch stray flakes of pastry stirred his desire, reminding him of their honey-hunting expedition in the pantry. But she treated the dessert no differently than the rest of her food. She only left a banana on the tray. He didn't blame her. He'd never tasted one, but it did not smell at all enticing.

He knelt down—the obligatory position for what he had to say. "Lena. I've made so many mistakes with you. I don't know where to start the apologies. But—"

She wrapped her hands around his forearms, trying to pull him to standing. "You don't have to—"

"Let me finish. I was afraid. But now I know I was wrong."

"Wrong?" She let go of him.

"About my mother and father. Their love didn't fail. It was never strong to begin with. Ours is."

"Oh."

Silence.

What? Had he thought she'd jump up and down for joy? Maybe she'd already moved on, put him behind her. He couldn't let her go again.

"Lena. I've cared for many women. But I've never loved one before. It scared me to death, that I would fail, and destroy you."

More silence. His shoulders bunched again. She was not making this easy.

"But I love you."

"I know. Your friend with the boom box told me." The slightest smile ghosted across her lips. "And then Andre was so kind. Like I was the daughter he never had, even after he lost everything." She wiped at her eye with the back of her hand.

He laid his palms on her knees. "Lena, will you have me?"

"Of course." She draped her hand over his like a cool damp cloth—a passionless resignation—not what he wanted at all. She went on looking at the wall. "I fell for you the moment you brought me to your room and read to me. If you're sure you want me, there's no way I can say no."

This was not how it should have been. If he'd admitted it earlier, this declaration would have thrilled her, and he could have witnessed her exultation. But this bland acquiescence was all he deserved, even if it tasted like ash in his mouth.

"I do. I will, forever."

"Good. Then it's a deal." She nodded, sounding matter of fact, like she'd just taken a perfectly cooked turkey out of the oven.

A deal—great. He sat back on his heels.

There, on the floor near the nightstand, was his answer—*New and Selected Poems.*

How could he have forgotten? "Uta told me something."

"What's that?"

At least he'd captured her attention enough to finally merit eye-contact. "How to make a baby."

"A baby?" Her red-rimmed eyes widened, and her voice was barely a squeak.

His lips twitched at her hopeful response. "Or two, or three. A family."

"But you said—"

"I was wrong." Although it had some mysterious cost that hadn't entirely escaped his worry.

Her mouth spread into a brilliant smile. "I've dreamed of him."

"What?"

"For my entire life, I've dreamed of a little boy, and he has your eyes."

She'd been carrying around that astonishing detail and never told him, let him walk away? He ached for her, one more heartbreak he hadn't even known about. Then her meaning sunk in. A child. He'd never wanted a family. It was an impossibility, like walking in daylight. But she had seen their son—he was going to be a father.

If only he could be half as good at it as Andre.

He clutched her hands. "A boy?"

"His name is Mirko."

He laughed, shaking his head with astonishment. "You dreamt a good Croatian name."

"Is it? I didn't know." Her lips spread into the most beautiful smile he'd ever seen. A woman who knew she was loved, and would have her heart's desire.

It was too good to be true. The hair on his neck stood up again. What would it take to conceive this son? Would he look as much like Kos as Bel did Andre? Was the dreaded cost Uta had warned him about the same reason Andre had hidden the truth from Bel?

"Kos. Where did you go?"

"What?"

"Your eyes just went gray. You went somewhere else."

"I'm sorry. I'm back."

She was safe, and she loved him, and they would have a son. He couldn't wait anymore. He picked her up, cradling her to his chest, drinking in her honeyed scent, the warm pink silk of her skin. He buried his face in the silk of her hair and sat her in his lap.

"Forever, Lena. I will love you forever. I can do it. I won't hurt you."

She laughed, reaching to cup his chin. "Of course you won't."

Somehow, after all his mistakes, she still trusted him. It was the greatest gift. His cock thought so too—it went rigid as she nestled closer to him.

She noticed, too, and wriggled. "Mmmmm. I missed that."

He loosened his grip on her. "I'm sorry. I'm sure you'll need time. I don't expect you…"

She hopped up. "Kos. You need to be naked."

Opening her towel, she revealed all her perfection. Her ample breasts were still rosy from the shower, and her nipples tightened as he studied at them. Her chest rose and fell, faster and faster. His eyes swept down her soft belly to the golden curls of her sex, and back up to her teasing smile. As their eyes locked, her lips parted lightly and her eyelids dipped over her navy blue irises.

"Naked. Yes, ma'am." He pulled his sweater over his head, unbuttoned his slacks, and dropped them with his boxers in one motion. His cock bobbed proudly, and he wanted to climb all the way inside her.

"Do you ever wear jeans?" she asked. "I mean, if there was ever time a to be casual—"

"You want me to wear jeans. I'll wear jeans. You want me to wear fishnets, fine. Right now, I'm naked, and so are you. I'm going to kiss you."

She wrapped her arms around his neck, standing on her toes to reach his mouth. Hers opened, warm and sweet. He swept his tongue in, gently stroking hers. His hands brushed her buttocks, her hips, her shoulder blades. Where should he put them?

"Kos, I won't break."

With his palms hovering inches over her lower back, he went still, brooding over everything that had happened with Mason. "I don't want to hurt you."

"Maybe I'm in shock. You know what's a good treatment? A solid pounding with one of these." She took hold of him, squeezing him in her small, soft palm. She felt so right, he practically came in her hand. But no, he could control himself better than that—vampire erections were one of his favorite super powers.

He caught the honeyed scent of her arousal and groaned. "I'm at your beck and call." He slid one teasing finger down her arm, across her hip, to where her legs joined, dipping inside her.

She batted his arm away. "Wait, Kos. No foreplay. Just get inside me, like the first time."

"I thought that was just a ruse?"

"I want to remember you're the only man to make love to me." Her cheeks blazed, and her lips curled into a shy smile.

He picked her up and carried her to the bed, laying her down carefully.

She parted her legs for him, tempting him with glistening moisture. But, he didn't rush. He slid into her slowly, letting her adjust. She was just as soft and warm and tight as the first time.

Words rushed out of his mouth. "I love you."

Between her quickening breaths, she said, "I know."

Why did that feel even better than *I love you too?*

He slid in her to the hilt, and bent to suckle her shoulder where it met her neck. When his fangs pierced the vein, her blood hit his mouth, tingling through him like an electric shock. Not that homey bliss of Leo's Hunter blood. Hers was electric, was passion itself, heating him to the boiling point. Down his throat, into his belly, all the way to his limbs, every cell in his body took her in, electrified, on fire.

Krist— this was something new—

She gasped and began moving against him. Her pleasure pulsed through him, wave after wave. He'd never felt anything like it. He reached for her breasts, teasing the nipples. His tightened too. His fingers trailed to where they were joined, and he stroked her. Sparks of pleasure flew from the tip of his cock to his scalp. Low in his pelvis, new sensations built— her need inside him. She clenched around him, and he throbbed, his testicles drawing up. He thrust, she moaned, the fire built, higher and higher, his every nerve sharpened by her. What was happening to him?

In his confusion, he held himself over her and gazed on her flushed face. His fear must have shown in his eyes. She pressed her index finger to his lips. "It's going to be okay."

His heart flashed with a flood of emotion — love returned, longing satisfied. Her feelings in his body—

The bond.

His orgasm came as suddenly as the realization. She rocked her hips to meet his unexpected thrusts, crying out her pleasure. Then he collapsed on top of her.

"Kos, what happened? Are you okay?"

He panted. "Bonded…"

"Oh." Her voice rang hollow.

He rolled off her and pulled her with him. She scrambled to sit up, his softening cock still inside her. "Lena, stay with me. It's okay."

"Aren't you afraid? Until I have the baby, the bond will be one sided, like with your mom and Andre."

Kos rolled off her and took her face in both his hands. "No, sweetheart, I'm not afraid. I trust you with my forever."

He kissed her, knowing the taste of her blood lingered in his mouth. She made a little moan in the back of her throat. "Now, I'm going to take my time with you." He brushed his lips over the mound of her breast.

"Later." She threw her leg over him and began to rock against his hips, building his need again impossibly fast. With her head thrown back, her body arched before him — finally, her exultation was his to see.

A completely new joy filled him, and he knew that with her at his side, he would be in for a wild ride for the rest of his immortal life.

CHAPTER 35

A knock sounded on the door, waking Lena from the most restful sleep she could remember. Kos jerked too, and he carefully extricated himself from her arms. He rolled out of bed. Yawning, she admired his muscled backside as he stepped into a pair of pajama bottoms.

Toes tapped in the hallway loud enough for Lena to hear — Uta. Kos opened the door only a few inches, so Lena could make out the vampire's words, but not see her.

"I am needing you in dining room. Bring Andre."

Kos pointed his chin at her. "Lena needs to sleep."

"If two are wanting to make baby, you are coming now."

Lena stretched her arms overhead. "It's okay, Kos. I'm awake, and I need to know."

"You are bringing Andre and Zoey. We meet in dining room momentously."

"Momentarily," Kos corrected.

She waved away his offered word. "That what I say."

Lena dressed quickly while Kos did the same. He pecked at her kiss-tender lips, and then darted down the hall toward the door.

Still three-quarters asleep and dazed, she pulled her hair into an elastic band as she padded down to the dining room and took a seat next to Uta, whose wagon-red fingernails tapped so fast they vibrated, rather than drummed the table.

"You are feeling all right?"

"Much better, thank you. But what about you?" Lena tilted her head to the flying fingertips. "Vampire style jitters?"

"I fine."

Someone had wrapped a length of thick jute rope around the girth of the cracked table. The polished oak plank sagged along its new fault line, but it held. Still, Lena didn't dare touch it. She leaned back, and the view out the window seized up her lungs. The ash-covered hills of the vineyards rolled all the way to the horizon like folds of black velvet. Skeletal vines reached for the sky. All that nearly ripe fruit, vaporized.

Andre and Zoey filed into the room, distracting Lena from the heartrending scene. They walked hand in hand, clean pressed and dressed for business. They'd clearly been expecting Uta's summons. Andre's stony face could have looked worse. He crossed the room and placed his palm against the window, surveying his wasted kingdom. Everyone waited, even Uta stopped her thrumming fingernails. Kos slid into the seat next to Lena and took her hand. With a slant of her head, she suggested he go to his father, but he mouthed the word, *no*.

Finally, Andre pivoted, scrubbed his face, and narrowed his glare at Kos. "Son, this magic Uta offers — it always has a price. Vampires are not meant to have babies. The secret is best left buried."

"Lena has dreamed of our son." Kos's chest swelled, as if he held the child already. His pride delighted her, made her long for his joy as much as her own.

"*Davo*, Kos, this is dangerous."

He stiffened, squeezing Lena's hand.

Zoey swooped into the space beside Andre. "Baby, they're adults. They need to know. Then they can decide for themselves."

Andre forced an exhalation through clenched teeth. "Fine. Tell them, Uta. *Everything*."

Lena leaned toward the vampire, so anxious for information that she forgot about the precarious table. It shifted, stretching and creaking against its bonds. With all the family tension in the room, she felt as taut as the rope. "Uta, please. I need to know."

No answer.

A car door slammed out front.

Uta stared at some space in front of her nose. Her fair skin had gone ghost-white, her lips had all but disappeared. Her elbow was bent at an odd angle, jutting off to the side. Lena tilted to get a glimpse of the vampire's entire arm. Holy cow. She'd dug her fingernails through her slacks and into her thigh. Blood seeped through her already ruined pants.

"Uta?"

No one paid any attention. They all stared at the door, where Bel had appeared. He held up a clear plastic vial.

Whoa. He was as pasty as Uta, sweating and breathing hard. And, *oh*—she glanced away from the erection tenting his pants. That impressive trait must run in the family.

Uta stared at him, her eyes dilated and glassy, her breathing shallow, her fangs out.

One Mississippi, two Mississippi—their intense eye-lock stretched out for several long and awkward seconds. Lena's still sleepy brain tried to make sense of the weirdness passing between them. Bel. Uta. Whatever it was, it made dread creep up her legs like the stinging-cold water of an icy mountain stream.

Andre went to kneel by Bel. "*Davo.* Son, I'm sorry. I didn't know this would happen, but Mila insisted, and I wanted to try for her. I have always been thankful for you—"

"Father, stop rambling." Kos came to stand behind Lena, sounding perfectly calm. But his fingers betrayed him by digging into her shoulders.

She let him press on her tender skin—the hint of pain provided a place to focus. Because whatever was brewing between Bel and Uta probably meant Mirko could not be real after all.

Uta waved her arm at the distance between her and Bel. "This is the price."

Bel collapsed into a chair, trembling. He took a deep breath. "I don't understand. Price of what?"

Kos stopped squeezing her shoulder, and ran his palms over her arms more gently. "Auntie Uta was explaining to us how Lena and I could have a baby."

His hands shook against her collarbone, and she tried to steady them by crossing her arms and covering them with her own.

For a little while, she'd had it all. But it was too good to be true. At least she had Kos—she would never let him go. She squeezed his hands tighter.

Bel pressed the heels of his hands into his eyes before he rubbed over the top of his shaggy black hair.

Zoey stood and paced a small circle in the corner of the room. "This is because of your blood, Uta?"

"*Da*," she croaked, her voice ravaged by whatever was happening to her.

Like a dentist, Andre examined Bel's mouth.

Zoey's next question was a whisper. "Are you bonded?"

Bonded? Lena inhaled. That wasn't so bad. It seemed like they were dying, or turning into zombies or something.

"Yes," Uta groaned, as if she thought it was a fate worse than the apocalypse.

Zoey whistled. "Bel too?"

He stood, his face now crimson. "What the fuck are you talking about?"

Across the table, Uta stood too, hissing.

Booming from beside Bel, Andre shouted. "Sit down, both of you. I do not have the patience for you to act like children right now."

Why were they so angry? Being bonded wasn't that bad…but they hadn't chosen, had no free will, obviously didn't even like each other. Her hope drained away again. Mason had tried to take away her choices. She couldn't do that to a child.

"Start from the beginning." Bel lowered himself back into his chair.

Kos followed suit, sitting and angling his chair toward his brother. "Lena and I want to —"

"That's not the beginning." Andre took the chair next to Bel. "When your mother wanted to conceive a child, she asked for Uta's help." Andre glanced at the female vampire and the muscles in his jaw bulged.

"What did they do?" Spittle flew from Bel's mouth.

"Mother drank Uta's blood. To make her eggs stronger. And then, her vampire-charged ovum was fertilized with Andre's blood."

"Blood?" Bel whispered. "So I have exactly half of your genes? I'm half an Andre clone?" He looked like he'd just swallowed a mouthful of spoiled milk. Poor guy. She wouldn't like to learn she was half somebody else either, although a son that was half Kos didn't sound so bad.

Bel leveled his gaze at Uta. "So how do we break this connection?"

Could they?

Andre whistled, the unhelpful sound of someone looking onto a trainwreck from a distance.

"We do not." Uta crossed her arms and her legs. "To break, one of us must die."

"I vote you," he said. No one laughed. Bel interlaced his fingers and leaned back, resting his head in his hands. His casual pose didn't fool Lena. And no one laughed, either.

She dragged her knees up to her chest, tucking her forehead into them. Kos kept his warm, dry palm against her neck, letting her know she wasn't alone.

For a long time, silence blanketed the room. Lena looked up from her kneecaps to find Bel staring at the ceiling, inhaling so slowly he had to be pacing his breaths. What did it feel like in his skin, to see this female he'd hated his whole life only to find out she was his bonded vampire mate?

When he finally looked at Uta, his eyes were green orbs with flecks of amber blazing in them—Andre's eyes, but his had never looked so fiery. "How long have you known?" Bel whispered.

"Since you were born." Watery red tears had formed in Uta's eyes but she managed not to spill them.

So long? Lena's heart thudded in her chest. Her eyes filled too, with tears for Uta and for Mirko, who could never be—

"Since he was born? *Davo*," Andre roared. "Did you know it would happen? What the hell were you thinking?"

"I am not knowing," she said. "My sire is telling me about this magic from time when vampires are living with Hunters. Only after Bel is born, am I remembering his stories—the godmother is always having mate. If I am having mate when Mila drank my blood, Bel is free."

"Really?" Lena slipped out of Kos's hold to lean closer to Uta.

Zoey halted her pacing. "So, if Lena drank *my* blood, the baby would not ever feel the way you and Bel feel right now."

Uta nodded, blinking her pink-rimmed eyes.

"You would be insane to consider it." Andre closed his mouth to begin his incessant grinding.

Kos spoke on a sigh. "Lena?"

She turned, and whatever he saw on her face made him close his mouth, cup her chin, and nod yes. She still had a million questions for Uta, for Bel, for Kos, but relief poured over her. She hadn't lost Mirko after all.

Andre was not convinced, and his tone yanked her from Kos's comforting gaze. "It is too risky. I wish you—" His thick black brows drew together. Something had caught his eye. He took hold of Bel's hand, and pried his fingers open, holding up a narrow glass tube. "Bel, is this…?"

Bel nodded absently.

"The gold compound? *Davo*, son, I am so proud of you. A synthetic Blood Vine! Now the fire doesn't matter." He stood, holding the vial up to the light of the window.

Lena's heart flew up into her throat. Could it really be? Could everything be okay?

"It is not working," Uta said.

Bel leaned forward, fists clenching. "Why not?"

"Some things are mystery." She shrugged.

Andre ignored her, addressing his question to his son. "Have you tested it?"

"Not yet, but the serum is chemically identical to what's in Lucas's blood."

"You young ones are thinking you can know everything." Uta huffed and crossed her arms.

"Lexi is making more as we speak. We'll begin clinical trials right away."

"Why you are bothering? I am telling you it not work."

"Why are you talking like that? You sound like a mail order bride someone bought on the Internet."

"Fuck you."

He jumped to his feet. "Tell me why it won't work!"

She spat back her response. "Mystery. Magic. I not know. But I am knowing it not work."

His fingers twitched like he wanted to ring her neck, and Andre pushed him back into the chair.

"Calm down. Don't listen to her. You are the scientist. I trust you."

Bel's head whipped to Andre, his eyes like saucers. His astonishment sent echoes through Lena, of yesterday's surprising welcome from Andre. She went all mushy, eyes brimming with tears again.

Bel rasped out a "thank you," and then he crossed his arms over his chest and put his big combat-booted feet all the way up on the table. It creaked and groaned like an old animal, tipping toward the crack down its center, and he scrambled to get his feet back on the floor.

"Well, great. Sounds like we've got that settled. This has been fun, Uta. Let's do it again in another hundred and seventy years. And in the meantime, have a nice life."

Uta clicked her tongue. "If I am helping it, we are not seeing each other ever again."

The hair on Lena's neck stood up at the same time Bel's eyes flashed wide. Uta blurred to him in that freaky vampire way.

She whispered loud enough to hear. "Ten years since your Lexi is long time. For me, has been since you were born. It get worse now, Bel."

She turned around, her smirk faltering with Bel behind her. "Andre, we speak later about Yousticia. I going home."

Bel pointed his thumb over his shoulder. "You can't leave. It's the middle of the day."

"I am having sun proof car and driver in work room." And then she was gone.

Bel folded nearly in half, slumping in the chair.

Lena imagined which of her various kitchen tools was best suited to slicing air so thick with tension—maybe a serrated knife.

"Ten years?" Kos exploded in a fit of giggles.

Lena cringed at his callousness, but like magic the tension evaporated.

"Indeed, son, that is rather impressive. Even I never made it that long," Andre said, obviously trying to keep a straight face. Friendly ribbing was the Maras way.

Zoey added, "No wonder you think not being able to masturbate is a fate worse than death."

Kos snickered. Lena didn't look at Bel. Best not to let her new brother-in-law see her laughing at his expense.

Ignoring them all, he went to the bar and poured a whole highball of bourbon. He emptied the glass in one swallow.

"I want you to use my blood," Zoey said.

Bel set his glass down with a bang. "No way. Don't make a baby like me. It's not fair. And you can't trust Uta. She could be wrong."

Lena stared at the sagging table. "I trust her."

"Bel," Kos said, "I'm sorry to say it, but I do too. We're going to try."

Bel took his time pouring another glass, and then he squared his shoulders toward his father. "What about you, Andre?"

Andre's face became an apology. "The truth is, I do not always like her, but I trust her unconditionally."

That was all Lena needed to hear. She pushed her chair back and stood, crossing to Zoey. "Thank you. I would be honored to have you as the godmother to our son."

Kos found Zoey and Andre in the kitchen, waiting for sunset so that they could walk through the ruined hillsides. They held hands, leaning their heads in close.

"May I join you, or are you going to the spring, like your first walk in the vineyards?"

"You're welcome to come," Zoey said, blushing at his mention of the time Kos and Bel had found the pair making out like teenagers.

Pedro and Lucas appeared in the kitchen door. "We'll come too," Pedro said, taking hold of Lucas's hand.

Under the rising moon, a steady, cool wind blew, freshening the fuel-scented air with the sweet smell of grapes from neighboring vineyards. The pair moved quickly along the perimeter, Kos and Pedro following close behind. Under Kos's feet, there were no clumps of dried sedge, no leaves blowing, no wildflowers or weeds sprouting on the side of the path—not any more. There was only a layer of ash over gravel and soil.

Andre held his spine straight—he'd put all his hope in Bel's cure. It seemed that show of trust, and perhaps the airing of the great family secret, had done much to repair things between the father and son. Kos hoped it would last.

His father halted and turned his head slowly like a hawk, before darting between the bare trellises.

Kos and Zoey exchanged puzzled looks and then took off after him, while Pedro and Lucas fell in behind. Andre knelt before one gnarled stump, well preserved compared to the rest of the blackened skeletons. He wrapped his hands around it, brushing off the ash. Just one, or two, or three vines like this surviving, and they could rebuild, as they had when they left Šolta. Andre wiggled the stump, and it crumbled — nothing but charcoal.

Kos and Pedro joined the search. They examined every single intact stump. Not one plant remained alive.

"What about the roots?" Zoey asked.

Andre rubbed his hand over his forehead, smudging soot onto his olive skin. "The rootstock is Californian. We spliced the Soltan vines onto it."

"Could we bring more from Croatia?"

"No, my vines were unique, and they were burned to the ground just like this." Andre looked away, pressing his lips into a thin line.

Shoes crunched on gravel, and then Bel and Lena appeared on the crest of the hill. Kos's angel raised her hand, smiling sweetly. In his heart, hope stirred. "Maybe in the spring shoots of the Soltan vines will sprout from the trunks."

Andre attempted a smile, but shook his head.

Bel and Lena reached them, and she tucked herself under Kos's arm where she belonged. He breathed in the smell of her hair — his generic shampoo. She was his, and everything would be okay.

He walked with his family back to the house. Inside the shield, a band of green lawn remained lush. Trys would keep eating her ice cream and keeping them safe until they figured out what to do next.

With one arm around Lena's waist, Kos followed Andre and Zoey, holding hands. Farther up the path, Lucas teased Pedro and Bel. Ancient memories, long locked in their blood, were breaking free, and they promised that everything would be okay.

CHAPTER 36

Slowly, blood filled a crystal cordial glass on the counter. According to Lena's cycle, it was the last one of these little rituals with Zoey. The nightly routine always reminded Lena of the night they had become friends over brandy and grilled cheese sandwiches. The ruby blood looked so beautiful dripping into the glass from Zoey's fingertip, pierced with a little metal shunt that kept her flesh from healing.

The first time Zoey bled for her, she'd said, "I remember when Andre turned Pedro, watching the droplets fall into his mouth. I was mesmerized by it. For the first time I saw that it was life, and not death."

It became Lena's prayer, every time she bottomed up the glass. *I am drinking life. Zoey is sharing her life, so that a new life can grow inside me.*

"Are you nervous?" Zoey spun on her stool to face Lena.

"A little. I know it can take months and months to get pregnant. This is just the first try."

"You can have as much of my blood as it takes," Zoey said, shaking the last drop into the glass and removing the shunt with a wince. Her fingertip healed instantly. Then Zoey reached across the counter top to pat Lena's hand. "Really, as much as you need."

"It's not too late to change your mind, Zoey." Everyone was a little on edge about the risk of an accidental bond like Uta and Bel's.

Zoey waved her hand in Uta-esque dismissal, and Lena laughed.

Then she peered into the glass, half expecting her stomach to revolt. But the regimen of the vampire's blood hadn't bothered her much at all, it was pleasantly salty and metallic and very warm in her gullet. For some reason, when it hit her throat it was much warmer than Zoey's body temperature—like the perfect cup of coffee. Lena swallowed down the blood and licked it off her lips.

Zoey grinned. "Tell me about your boy again, from the dream."

"I've already told you everything—he's got that white-blond hair only babies have. He has Kos's eyes—blue and set a little wide. And his red lips." Lena rounded the counter to rinse out the glass.

"Does he look like you?"

Looking up from the sink, she admitted, "He has my nose, and maybe my chin."

"Adorable—you two will make beautiful babies."

Lena set the delicate glass down carefully on the granite countertop. "Only one. Then I want to turn."

Zoey's smile told Lena she understood all the reasons for that decision.

"I'm not going to change my mind about being the godmother, Lena. I don't know why I'm so certain, but it feels right."

Lena stretched over the counter to take Zoey's hand. "You do know how grateful we both are?"

"I do. Now, go get him." Zoey offered a reassuring squeeze.

When Lena arrived in the room she shared with Kos, her turquoise flannel pajamas with unicorn print were folded neatly on the bed. "Really? That's my baby making attire?"

"You wore those the first night you spent here with me. I remember you coming out of the bathroom, face scrubbed pink, looking so adorable."

She giggled. "I told you my face was pink from your hot water because I didn't want to admit I'd been drinking with Zoey—you were so worried I had a concussion."

"Really? You little liar." He swatted her butt, then whispered in her ear. "When I saw you that night, I wanted to lick you from head to toe."

Between his words and the caress of his breath, her body flushed and her skin heated. "Now's good."

"I have something else first." He took a box from a drawer in his dresser.

One of those small boxes. When he put the small velvet clamshell case in her palm, butterflies fluttered from her stomach to her heart. She snapped it open. The diamond was square cut and surrounded by tiny sapphires in a wide, gold band.

"Beautiful," she rasped.

His eyes swirled gray. "I understand if you don't want it. We can get you a new one."

It was easy to guess at his worry. "Was it your mother's?"

"Yes, but read the inscription."

Inside, it said:

THIS TIME, FOREVER

"Kos, I love it. I love that it was hers, and that we get to make it true."

"Really?" Blue eyes sparkled back at her, the sexiest lopsided dimples creased around his lush lips.

She nodded.

"Good. Now put on those pajamas."

"Then will you lick me all over?"

"Patience, patience."

She took off her jeans and sweatshirt while holding his gaze. There was nothing sexy about the way she undressed, but the air between them conducted electricity. She slipped into the comfy pajamas and climbed onto the bed, sitting in the middle, cross legged.

"Close your eyes."

What was he up to? She dropped her lids, and she was enveloped in darkness, her senses coming alive.

He began to read—a poem about a little boy who could sleep through the mightiest sounds, but who always woke up when his parents finished making love, his footsteps pattering on the floor until he slipped between them in the bed where he'd been made.

By the time he finished, tears streamed down her cheeks. "Kos, can we do it now?"

"So fast? What about the licking?"

"It feels right to do it now."

"It does, doesn't it?" He unbuttoned the pajamas she'd worn for all of three minutes. Distracted, his hands strayed to her breasts and she kept unbuttoning. She pulled her top off and her pants down in an instant.

He released her breasts to pull his T-shirt over his head and unfasten his jeans. There was nothing underneath but that magnificent, always-ready-for-her erection.

Gripping her shoulder, he pushed her back toward the bed. When she bumped it, he nudged her to sitting and dropped between her legs. "I know you're in a hurry, baby, but we need to start with a little licking."

"If you insist." She opened her legs. He caressed every fold with his tongue, and then flicked her most sensitive spot until moisture ran from her core.

He mumbled into her thigh. "I don't know if I like your honey or your blood better."

She laughed. "No need to decide."

He lifted her all the way onto the bed and lay alongside her, propped on his elbow.

"Want to know something else sneaky?" she asked.

"Sure."

"Our first day together, when you were giving me the anatomy lesson, I already knew about my g-spot. I just really liked the hands-on demonstration."

He laughed from some place so deep in his gut that her heart nearly burst.

"I believe it's time for the advanced tutorial then." He slipped two of his fingers into her and found the exact place.

She groaned as he began to stroke her. "How will you…"

"I'll take care of it. Just relax. I'll know when."

He kissed her then, as he built her tension with his fingers inside her and his thumb circling. Her orgasm approached quickly, sending pulses through her core. He withdrew and was back again before she had time to miss him filling her.

The thrust of his fingers was more awkward with the steel shunt in one. But it didn't matter—she could feel his blood filling her, hotter even than when he ejaculated inside her. In spite of the uneven thrusts, the tingling blood brought her an orgasm so deep that she knew her womb would open wide to draw his blood inside. When she grew sensitive and wriggled away from him, he slipped his fingers back out of her and yanked out the shunt to stop his bleeding.

His hand was covered in his blood and her slick moisture.

Some new instinct caught hold of her. "I want to taste your blood." She drew his hand to her mouth.

His blue eyes grew wide, and as she drew his fingers between her lips, he said, "Sweetheart, I need to be inside you, now."

She opened her legs and angled her hips. He slid into her and began rocking them in a perfect beat. His fangs sunk into her neck. Sweet and salt and metal mixed in her mouth. With her eyes closed tightly, she imagined the day she would taste his blood and bond with him. The electric current between them would grow even stronger.

But first there would be Mirko, and now she had found her destiny, and there was love and pleasure beyond what she ever imagined.

Acknowledgments

Sometimes it worries me how utterly dependent I am on others to write a book, but then those others assure me it is supposed to be this way and I feel better. I honestly could not do this without my faithful beta reader Emily Mellott, who reads everything I write first just so I don't make a fool of myself. Secondly, I am deeply grateful for the insights of my writing friends Celia Breslin and Jessica Russell, who always ask just the right questions or suggest just the right tweaks, precisely when I need them.

This book benefitted from the insights of the "Mud Puddle," the online critique group of the Fantasy, Futuristic and Paranormal chapter of Romance Writers of America. I'm so thankful for what I've learned in that group, and especially for the help of Zrinka Jelic, who helped me with Croatian in her native Dalmatian dialect (all mistakes made and liberties taken belong to me alone!) and Ed Hoornaert who kept me laughing as we traded chapters.

I also owe thanks to the Omnific team of editors, designers and publicists who help get this book into readers' hands looking beautiful, and to my mom, who is the best amateur PR person an author could ask for.

And lastly, I owe my husband the greatest thanks of all for the many ways he supports my writing and puts up with my endless obsessing over vampire plot points when we go out to dinner.

ABOUT THE AUTHOR

Amber Belldene grew up on the Florida panhandle, swimming with alligators, climbing oak trees and diving for scallops…when she could pull herself away from a book. As a child, she hid her Nancy Drew novels inside the church bulletin and read mysteries during sermons—an irony that is not lost on her when she preaches these days.

With a B.A. in comparative religion and an M.A. in theology, Amber is a Christian minister and student of religion. She believes stories are the best way to explore human truths. Some people think it is strange for a minister to write romance, but it is perfectly natural to Amber. She believes the human desire for love is at the heart of every romance novel and God made people with that desire.

Amber is addicted to vampire stories, but loves to read all kinds of romance and literature. Her favorite books examine history and cultural origins, like Neal Stephenson's *Baroque Cycle*, Anita Diamant's *The Red Tent*, or Salman Rushdie's *The Satanic Verses*. And, yes, she was named after that Amber, of the classic romance novel *Forever Amber*.

From the wine country of Sonoma County to the foggy neighborhoods of San Francisco, all of Amber's fiction is set in Northern California, where she lives with her husband and two children.

↤╼→Singles↤╾→